SECRET OF THE SANDS

It is 1833 and the British Navy is engaged in surveying the coastline of the Arabian Peninsula. Young and ambitious, Lieutenant James Wellsted is determined that his Navy career will be a path to glory. His plans go awry when two of his shipmates go missing while gathering intelligence and Wellsted must mount a daring rescue. Slavery is still rife throughout Arabia. Zena, a headstrong Abyssinian beauty, torn from her village, is now being offered for sale in the market of Muscat. However, her fortunes change when she finds herself the property of the Lieutenant. She must accompany him on his hazardous mission, little knowing the fate that awaits them. Each will be forced to make a choice — one that will change their lives forever.

Sara Sheridan is an Edinburgh-based historical novelist. She has been nominated for a
Young Achiever Award, received a Scottish
Library Award for her first novel and was
shortlisted for the Saltire Book Prize. An
occasional journalist and blogger, Sara
appears on BBC Radio 4's *From Our Own
Correspondent* and blogs for the *Guardian*
and the *London Review of Books*. She is a
member of the Historical Writers Association
and the Crime Writers Association. Sara also
mentors for the Scottish Book Trust and is a
twitter evangelist and a self-confessed swot.

Website:
www.sarasheridan.com

twitter:
@sarasheridan

Facebook:
http://www.facebook.com/sarasheridanwriter

SARA SHERIDAN

SECRET OF THE SANDS

Complete and Unabridged

CHARNWOOD
Leicester

First published in Great Britain in 2011 by
Avon
A division of HarperCollins*Publishers*
London

First Charnwood Edition
published 2012
by arrangement with
HarperCollins*Publishers*
London

British Library CIP Data

Sheridan, Sara, *1968* –
  Secret of the sands.
  1. Women slaves- -Arabian Peninsula- -Fiction.
  2. Arabian Peninsula- -History- -19th century- -
  Fiction. 3. Love stories. 4. Large type books.
  I. Title
  823.9′2–dc23

  ISBN 978–1–4448–1270–1

Published by
F. A. Thorpe (Publishing)
Anstey, Leicestershire

Set by Words & Graphics Ltd.
Anstey, Leicestershire
Printed and bound in Great Britain by
T. J. International Ltd., Padstow, Cornwall

This book is printed on acid-free paper

Acknowledgements

Thanks are always due to the many on an enterprise such as this because no one can write a book entirely alone. To the archivists who were both kind and patient with me, I extend my sincere gratitude. You are the gatekeepers of our history. David McClay of the John Murray Archive at the National Library of Scotland deserves a particular mention because of his tremendous enthusiasm and support and because he was the person who said, 'Have you heard of James Raymond Wellsted? I think we have some letters from him to John Murray. It could be good material.' There were three and they (and he) started off the whole idea. Dorian Leveque at the British Library was a hub of help and information and Nichola Court at the Royal Society was so enthusiastic that I felt buoyed up for ages after our e-mail exchanges. It is particularly lovely when institutions that could be crusty, fusty bastions of old-fashioned academia turn out to be vibrant, stimulating and very alive. The interest and enthusiasm of those at the Chelsea Physic Garden was very kind — thank you. Alison Halley was a massively well-informed workmate in the genealogical research that went on behind Wellsted's story and deserves a shiny medal! A nod also to all the kind people who guided me through the National Archives, the London Metropolitan archive, the Royal Geographical Society archive — oh, for heaven's sake — there were a lot of archives and societies to get through! Cheers to Ian Gardiner and Dr Livingstone, who helped me by talking about their experiences in Oman — such fantastic, exciting lives you've been leading! Thanks to Peter Upton, author of *The Arab Horse* for his kind help and information about, well, Arab horses! To Carl Phillips for trying to keep me on the track of real history, though I stray on an ongoing basis (novelists being tricky.) Thanks too to Loretta Windsor at the Natural History Museum for giving me a chance to see behind the scenes. Also Anna Taylor, who talked so frankly about her experiences as a black woman in Britain and her background in Ghana — you first got me interested in the issues surrounding slavery and I'm very grateful we got chatting about it.

Gratitude is due to the team at Creative Scotland and, in particular, Aly Barr, for providing much-needed financial support (historical novels take time) and accommodating my poor arithmetical skills.

Then there are those wonderful mainstays — Jenny Brown, my agent (a round of applause, please!), Maxine Hitchcock, the editor who commissioned the book, Kate Bradley who saw it through and the whizzy team at HarperCollins (Caroline, Charlotte, Claire, Kesh and Sammia — alphabetical order, girls!). For these a standing ovation! It is so lovely, in the solitary business of writing, to feel there is a team behind me and, in particular, one that can put up with me being exacting, ambitious and full of ideas that cause work for other people. Thanks for the chats, the reassurance, the swanky party and all the hard work.

To the Greatest Geek, a veritable computer whisperer, who helped me put together www.sarashcridan.com and made that process fun — thanks in English and HTML.

Tx also to all the kind people I have met on Twitter (which I did not expect to enjoy but has been a delight). Such generosity is met rarely in the world.

And, oh, my friends and family last but not least. You deserve the biggest thanks of all for writers are a pain in the arse. They are. They sleep in late, forget to wash their hair, clothes and children, disappear for weeks on end, don't make dinner and, worse, are often more interested in what happened in August 1833 than what is going on at the moment. Much is due to those who supported me in so many ways during the nutjobbery of my crazy, book-writing process. Thank you for taking pride and having faith in what I was doing — the wonderful Sarah Joseph, the Goodwins, the Faulkners, Stephen MacGregor, Gemma Tipton, Lorne Blyth, Frank Hoskins, Lucy Gordon, Liberty McKenzie, Maisie Hennessey, Morag Cormack, Sarah Hughes, Jan Ambrose, Katie Emslie, Annette Matzner and Lee Randall. And then, of course, there is my daughter, Molly (I am so proud!) and my wonderful boyfriend, Alan Ferrier (the most patient man in history — I've researched it).

Author's note about language

I do not speak Arabic and in any case spelling Arabic words with English letters spawns a wide variety of possible combinations that were not standardised until well after Wellsted's day. I copied Arabic words from contemporary manuscripts and hope that the resulting spelling does not prove too confusing for those whose knowledge of the language is greater than mine.

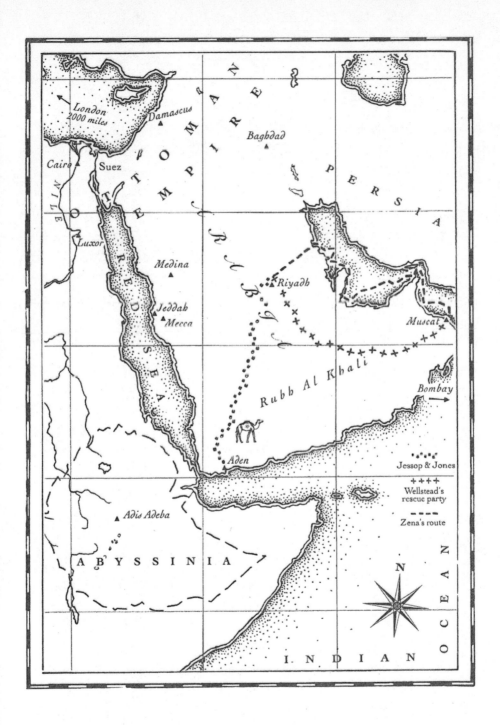

London
2000 miles

Damascus

Cairo   Suez

Luxor

OTTOMAN   EMPIRE

Baghdad

PERSIA

NILE

RED SEA

Medina

Jeddah
Mecca

Riyadh

Muscat

R U B B

Rubb Al Khali

Bombay

Aden

Adis Adeba

ABYSSINIA

INDIAN   OCEAN

N

Jessop & Jones

Wellstead's
rescue party

Zena's route

PART ONE

'Thus in England, where law leaves men comparatively free, they are slaves to a grinding despotism of conventionalities, unknown in the land of tyrannical rule. This explains why many men, accustomed to live under despotic governments, feel fettered and enslaved in the so-called free countries.'

Sir Richard Francis Burton, 1821–1890
Great Arabian Explorer

1

Fifty miles inland from the coast of Abyssinia, Tuesday, 11 June 1833

It is dark when they come, at about an hour before dawn. Far away in London, pretty housemaids in Marylebone are setting the fires while the more dissolute rakes make their way home through deserted streets now devoid of the night's sport. The whores are all abed now as are the Honourable Directors of the East India Company, each to a man concerned that the French, despite being routed, surely have it in mind to capture Bombay, Calcutta and Delhi and unfurl England's grip on its ruby-encrusted prize. In short order, William Wilberforce, hero of The Cause, will rise habitually early despite his failing health, dress in a sober jacket with dark breeches and, discreetly and behind the scenes, preach the rights of these men and women from thousands of miles away. He has been doing so with success, in and out of Parliament, for the best part of fifty years and he will not have too much longer to wait. But here in the village that makes no difference now.

★ ★ ★

In the clearing surrounded by lush foliage, the silence is broken and the sleepy huts made of

3

rushes and daub are already being ransacked. There is little anyone can do and it makes no odds whether the families rise fighting, iron daggers in hand, or wake slowly, sleepily, only half-conscious to the screams of their children. One or two of the quickest slip into the darkness, a jumble of long, flailing limbs and flashing eyes, young men abandoning their mothers and sisters, one child with the instincts of a seer, fleeing on instinct alone blindly into the dark jungle and away from the torches and the sparking embers of last night's fire. A pitcher is knocked over in the panic and douses the rising flames, filling the cool, early morning air with a salty cloud of scorched goat curds that were meant to be breakfast.

It takes only seven minutes to capture almost everyone. The slavers are practised at this. They separate the elderly to one side (hardly worth the trouble to transport even as far as Zanzibar) and beat one old man who shouts so furiously and in such a babble that his own wife cannot fully understand him. There is always one would-be hero. He is usually a grandfather. The slaver known as Kasim consigns him to silence.

The broken body quietens the crowd. The villagers shift uneasily and the raiders turn to the task of sorting through the women. This is the most difficult job for mistakes are easily made with these dusky women in the darkness. Abyssinian slave girls are worth a great deal if they are beautiful. Sultans and emirs have been known to take an ebony slave or two to wive — a rich man's *harim* is a place of no borders and

4

should include every colour of skin, after all. White, of course, is the most enticing. Most men have never so much as seen white skin — all those who have agree it is strange and unearthly, the skin of a fearsome devil, a soul bleached to the colour of dry bones and shocking to the core, like a spectre. But still, on a woman, desirable enough.

In this village the women are as dark as bitter coffee and their young bodies are lithe. Kasim's boyhood friend and business partner, Asaf Ibn Mohammed, eyes the pert titties as if they are liquorice. When he comes to Zena, Ibn Mohammed raises the hem of her winding cloth with the tip of his scimitar and glares at her ripe pudenda. He thinks only of the Marie Theresa dollars that this prize is worth shipped on to Muscat, and how easy she will be to sell. Then, dropping the skirt, he reaches out to check her teeth and nods to his fellow, the one with the ropes.

'This one,' he says in Arabic, his tawny eyes cold, the contours of his face caught in the flickering lamplight so it appears he is composed of nothing but long, thin lines. Paler and taller than Kasim, Ibn Mohammed has an elegant air and looks more like a scholar than a man of action. Today nothing has riled him — the raid is going entirely as he expects, so his temper, which often proves deadly, remains in check. 'Yes, this one will do. Not as skinny as the others and she shows no fear.'

Zena, frozen and so afraid that she is scarcely able to breathe, pretends she cannot understand him. He seems so calm and cold, assured in his right to simply steal her away. Kasim nods silently in agreement though his black eyes sparkle — she can see he is enjoying the process of humiliating the villagers as they are assessed one by one. Something in him feeds off the uneasy atmosphere. The raid isn't merely a living for this man. In the trade he has found his vocation.

I will run, she thinks. *I will run*. But her legs do not move. It is probably a blessing — the slavers do not deal kindly when they catch the ones who try to get away. You escape either very quickly or not at all. This is no time for Zena to show her spirit. As the guards pull her out of the line, she stumbles over the corpse of her uncle, the old man she has just watched Kasim murder with his bare hands. Zena does not look at the body. She tries to ignore the outrage that is rising in her belly. Silently, she lets them bind her along with some of the others and then, with the rising sun before them, the slavers drive their spoils, the pick of the village, away from their homes and families forever.

2

The principal residence of Sir Charles Malcolm, Head of the Bombay Marine, India

The *punkawallah* has been on duty for over twelve hours and the wafting fan has slowed to a soporific movement that is having little effect on the soupy air.

'Feeling better, Pottinger?' Sir Charles enquires as he pours them each a drop of dry, ruby port from the Douro.

'Oh yes, sir. The fever is gone. Had to be done, I expect,' the young man assures his superior brightly, as if he had been serving at the wicket on the village cricket team. For new arrivals, a fever is practically mandatory, though by all accounts Pottinger had a particularly fierce bout and is fortunate to have survived.

'Go on then, have a look,' Sir Charles motions.

The captain crosses eagerly to the mahogany table and pores over the new charts of the Red Sea that arrived at the dock only a few hours before. The papers represent the first step in the Bombay Marine's overall mission in the region, which is twofold. First, to find a way to link Europe to India inside a month by cutting out the African leg of the existing route. If that means developing the market for trade with the Arabs so much the better. Second, to ensure that recent British naval losses on the reefs of the

7

tropical Arabian seas are never repeated. In the scramble for global dominance every scrap of advantage to be had over the French is vital and too many ships have gone down of late due to inadequate maps. For the East India Company these tactics have worked well elsewhere and it is gratifying to Sir Charles that more of the map is coloured pink every year and, in particular, that this victory is in no small measure due to the exploits of his men. It is for this reason that he briefs each of his officers personally at the beginning of their tour of duty. 'Gives me the measure of them,' he says.

Pottinger sees immediately that though the newly arrived drawings are detailed in places, there remain gaps. 'When will our chaps complete it?' he asks.

'Another year, at least. And that is with both ships splitting the work. It's hostile territory and the coastline is complex. We've sent a small exploratory party inland to the west of the Arabian Peninsula from the ship *Palinurus*. Information gathering, that kind of thing. It's a start.' Malcolm is glad that Pottinger is getting to grips with the issues. 'The party comprises a lieutenant and a ship's doctor, Lieutenant Jones and Doctor Jessop. They've gone in south of Mecca with a party of local guides and will travel as far as the camp of a Bedouin emir that we have paid for the privilege. The whole area is desert. The rendezvous is at Aden in four weeks.'

'They sent in a doctor?'

'An officer like any other.' Sir Charles waves his hand blithely. Officers of the Bombay Marine are expected to turn their hand to anything. The corps prides itself on the flexibility of its men — a single officer can make a huge difference, in fact, many of the East India Company's most startling successes have been instigated by a bright spark who has taken the initiative on the Company's behalf. 'Apparently, he was keen,' Sir Charles says.

'So, if we can secure Egypt,' Pottinger muses, 'we will still have to ferry everything across the land at Suez.' He points at the most northerly port on the Red Sea.

In Sir Charles Malcolm's experience, these discussions always come back to the same point on the map but it is good the lad has cottoned on so quickly. The thin strip of land in question lies between his territory and that of his brother, Pultney, who is Commander in Chief of the British Navy in the Mediterranean. Between them, the Malcolm brothers rule most of Britannia's waves and keep an eye on the French for His Majesty. It is acknowledged that Sir Charles has the raw end of the deal. The Gulf is tribal and savage and even if they can oust the French from Egypt, Malcolm is all too aware how difficult it is to move substantial quantities of troops and supplies, to say nothing of trade goods, from one sea to another. There is no obvious place to build a railway to indulge in the relatively new science of steam locomotion. In any case, the land around Suez that is not desert is peppered with saltwater lakes — mixed terrain is, to use Sir Charles' own parlance, the most tricky of all.

The Malcolm brothers, however, act as a team and by hook or by crook they will fix this problem somehow, so that not only will the sun never set on His Majesty's empire, but His Majesty's troops will move as smoothly as possible across it. If Hannibal can cross the Alps, Sir Charles Malcolm will be damned if he can't get British men and goods across what is essentially a thin land bridge, whether he has to employ elephants to do the job or not.

Malcolm marks the chart carefully to show Pottinger what he's hoping for.

'Ooh, the French won't like that,' the youngster smiles.

Malcolm makes a sound like a furious camel and a gesture that clearly demonstrates that he couldn't care less what the French would like. Some of Sir Charles Malcolm's friends and acquaintances have not yet given up on England winning back her influence in French ports despite an almost four-hundred-year gap since the end of the Hundred Years War. Sir Charles Malcolm is no quitter nor are any of his ilk. He takes another sip of port.

Pottinger puts his finger on the dot that marks Suez. 'A canal would be the easiest way . . . But the chart, sir, the chart is everything. We can't go further without it.'

The boy is sharp. He'll do.

At this juncture, Sir Charles notices that the *punkawallah* is lying prone and has dropped the red cord with which he should be operating the fan. The child has fallen fast asleep and, if Sir Charles is not mistaken, is dribbling over the

Memsahib's fancy new carpet.

'Well, really,' the Head of the Bombay Marine bellows, 'no wonder it's like a bally oven in here, and we are trying to think.'

He launches a pencil across the room. It hits its target admirably, striking the boy squarely on the forehead. The child jerks upright, mortified at his dereliction of duty and starts to babble, apologising frantically in Hindi. Then he recalls that it is an absolute rule that the house staff should remain silent at all times. Sir Charles, now somewhat pink in the cheeks, stops in his fury and laughs at the aghast expression on the boy's face.

'Go!' he motions the child. 'Away with you! Fetch another *punkawallah*, for heaven's sake, or we'll broil in here. It's June, for God's sake.'

The boy bows and disappears instantly as Pottinger pours more port into his glass and passes Sir Charles the decanter. 'Thank you for showing me, sir,' he says.

Sir Charles raises his glass. It is unusual for a commanding officer to bother, but Sir Charles always prefers to survey his resources personally. 'Welcome to the Bombay Marine,' he says. 'A toast — to the very good health of His Majesty and, of course, our chaps in the field,' he says as he reminds himself silently that the chaps in the field are getting there. Slow but sure.

3

Rubh Al Khali *on the way* **to the Bedouin encampment**

In the desert it is so hot that it comes as a surprise that a human can breathe at all. At first, when he headed into what the Arabs call the Empty Quarter, with the intention of mapping the unknown, Dr Jessop did not expect to survive, but now lethargy has fallen upon him and he has ceased to worry about what the heat may or may not do. It has become clear, at any rate, both that breathing is possible and that there is no measure in moving from the shade of the acacia tree where the small caravan has halted. It is always hot in the desert, but June is one of the worst months. It is simply the way it has worked out.

'Even in this bloody shade, you could bake a cat,' he comments, dry mouthed.

He is a scientific man and a surgeon; in all probability he is right. Lieutenant Jones, his blonde hair plastered to his head with sweat, can do little more than gesture in agreement. He does not believe that the loose, Arabic outfit for which he swapped his uniform is any help at all with the heat, but he cannot quite form the words to communicate this or to ask if Jessop is of the same opinion. In any case, he has taken off the *kaffiya* headdress with its heavy ropes, for he could not bear them — the damn thing is heavier than a top hat and the cloth gets so hot in the sun that it burns the delicate skin at the back of his neck. Now it is after midday, and when the sun goes down they will start moving again. The Arabs have agreed to travel solely at night to accommodate the white men. They would not do so normally, but the infidels are unaccustomed to the conditions and if they die, the men will not be paid.

In the meantime, one of the bearers, a *Dhofari*, is making coffee. He grinds the beans and adds a fragrant pinch of cardamom to spice it. The *Dhofaris* carry spice pouches; their very bodies seem to secrete frankincense and their robes smell musky like powdered cumin. They bring a hint of Africa, a spice indeed, to the Arabian Peninsula. Amazingly, these men can work in the heat without breaking a sweat. Even now, the man's brother is trying to milk one of the camels that Jessop bought in the market at Sur for the trip, but the beast, bare skin and bone, will not comply. It is a serious business. You cannot carry enough food and water in the desert, and what you can carry either spoils quickly or requires moisture to cook it. Camel's milk is vital. The men have been hungry and thirsty for days and without enough camel's milk to supplement supplies, the skins of water are running dangerously low. The *Dhofari* tethers the beast securely with a thick rope, hobbling the animal's legs in the same fashion they do to stop the camels wandering off when the caravan breaks its journey and the men are sleeping. The beast nonchalantly chews on a sparse plant with tiny leaves growing in a bare patch of sweet grass and euphorbia, while the *Dhofari* guide disappears into his baggage. Jessop strains to see what he is doing. Quite apart from the prospect of fresh milk, which is enticing enough, these Arab customs are important. He is here to find out what is acceptable, how to trade with these people, how to supply British ships and protect them from attack. It is his job to understand this harsh country and to find out if it is possible for Britain to make a profit here. The doctor is looking forward to returning home to Northumberland and diverting society with his stories of the Ancient Sea and her Savages. He already has the title of his book planned, you see. And this is just the kind of thing, he is sure, that will entertain the chaps at home next winter.

* * *

As a vision of Northumberland — a hillside swathed in snow and puddles glassed over with chill sheets of ice — flashes across the doctor's brain like a cool breeze, he reaches automatically for the coffee that is handed to him. 'Thank you,' he says. *Shukran*.

Jones only manages a nod though quickly the bitter taste revives him. He wishes he had not come to the desert. Aboard the *Palinurus* there was at least the prospect of a breeze. They will be back at the coast in perhaps ten days and will rendezvous with the ship a fortnight after that. This seems an interminable period to bear the

14

baking, desiccated hellhole through which they are travelling, though the men surely will endure it — they are determined.

The *Dhofari* squats and sips alongside the white men. 'Tonight we will have milk, *in sh'allah*,' he says.

If Allah wills it.

'We will reach the *Bedu* soon?' Jones checks.

The man bristles. 'Tomorrow, perhaps.'

The Bedouin encampment is the halfway mark — as far as they will venture this trip. Though the arrangement had been made for them and a price agreed, the timescale had been, of necessity, fuzzy. However, now they are embarked, the *Bedu* will be expecting their arrival, for news travels quickly in the desert — far more quickly, the white men are coming to realise, than in London where at least a fellow has a chance of keeping a secret. An adept guide can tell an enormous amount from a few blunt scratches in the sand. These men recognise one camel's tracks from another, how many are in the party and who is injured or ill. The tribesmen have a keen memory for the precise pattern each camel makes on the shifting landscape — the beast's hoof-marks and its individual gait. Out on the sands a mere line out of place tells them there is a foreigner riding a camel. While a desiccated turd robs an entire, long-gone caravan of all its secrets. They are like fortune tellers.

Jones is not interested in the native population and remains unimpressed by their tracking skills. The lieutenant has it in mind to find out more about transporting Arabian horses back to

15

Europe — his own private concern rather than that of the Marine. Thoroughbreds are the only civilised international currency the Peninsula has to offer. Now they cannot send slaves home to London, that is, and it looks likely that the Empire will soon close its doors to human traffic besides and there will be no trade westwards either. Jones had hoped for jewels in Arabia. He had daydreamed of pearls as round as muscat grapes and plentiful as if on the vine, of emeralds big enough to fill a handmaiden's belly button and diamonds bright and copious, like desert stars. His dreams have been quickly shattered. While there are occasional treasures, most of the people on the Peninsula are poor and, like everywhere else in the world, riches are hard to come by. A tenant farmer at home probably owns more in the way of material goods than the average emir. Jones is coming to accept there is little either His Majesty or himself is likely to profit from this expedition. *No wonder the whole damn country is full of beggars. Paupers to a man, the Arabs.* Jones empties his cup and once more curses his misfortune to be sent here of all places after the high society of Bombay where he hobnobbed with senior officers' daughters and gambled copiously in the mess. The cellar in India was much finer than he expected and due to the large amount of Jocks in almost every regiment, the whisky, in particular, was excellent. By contrast, Arabia is an unforgiving country and although some of the officers seem almost to enjoy the hardship, Jones is not one of them. He is merely getting on with what he has to and hoping to get away with as much for himself as he can.

'Good heavens,' Jessop mumbles under his breath, sitting up slightly and staring at the chap with the camel. 'Well, if that doesn't take the biscuit.'

The *Dhofari* finishes his coffee and begins to laugh at the wide, blue eyes of the white men as they realise what his brother is doing. He takes a stick of *araq* from his robe and carefully begins to pick, cleaning his teeth as he studies Jessop and Jones' facial expressions.

'Good Lord,' Jones echoes, his face even pinker than usual. *This country takes everything a step too far*, he thinks. 'Is he actually . . . ?'

'Yes. Yes, old man,' Jessop nods. The doctor is the son of a gentleman farmer and used to livestock but his voice is still incredulous. 'I do believe he is sewing up the animal's arsehole.'

'She give milk soon. Very soon,' the *Dhofari* assures them in a low voice.

This place is completely beyond the pale. Jones shudders. He is thirsty, of course, and hungry too if it comes to that, but he finds himself unsure now if he will be able to drink the camel's milk after all.

4

Zena has never seen the sea before and it takes her by surprise. The Indian Ocean is a startling blue, and the unrelenting African sunshine plays on its surface so that, for all the world, the water could be studded with diamonds or, perhaps, stars. It is the sound that is most striking though — the movement of the waves as they roll onto the sand is like the voice of a great god. The slavers allow the group to stop a moment and the slaves turn towards what Zena calls in her mind, the Giant Blue. She is so stunned by the majesty of it that she is almost glad they have brought her here and stares rapt at the water as goose bumps rise down her arm at the great booming rush of the waves.

It is undeniably beautiful, though some of the others are afraid and one or two let out a scream. The slavers stare openly at the faces of their cargo. This feels like a ritual — something they know to do and the group spends a moment in silence as, after the initial fear, an air of reverent awe descends upon the villagers. These people worship rainclouds and sunshine, they give offerings to the god of thunder, but the phenomenon before them now is so huge that it is almost beyond comprehension. It is as if they have been brought to the very edge of the world. The slavers have stolen the youngest of each tribe and, apart from Zena, who at seventeen

18

summers is one of the older captives, not one child in the party has even heard of the sea.

I had no idea it was so, so . . . The words trail in her mind for she cannot decide which ones to use to describe the shimmering vision before her. As she grasps for an adjective, one of the boys breaks away from the group, free from his bonds since that morning when the slavers clearly decided they had broken enough spirits to simply herd the villagers without having to slow the party by keeping them tied. They watch him whooping with joy as he runs, long-limbed, into the water, falling face down on the bounty for they have been dry-mouthed for days. Water has been in short supply since they left the village. The boy realises, too late, that the sea is salt. Two of the slavers trudge wearily into the surf and pull him out. Laughing, they slap him soundly and he folds on the sand so you'd hardly believe he'd bounced so elegantly into the water.

'It will poison you, you fool.'

Zena is perturbed. The sea is so beautiful it is strange it should be deadly — no one has ever mentioned that before. But then she is learning that in life, away from all she has known, things generally are not what they seem. Not so far.

Kasim and Ibn Mohammed wave the party on. Zena hears Kasim say, 'I always wonder which one will be the brave child.'

Ibn Mohammed only stares. 'The foolish child, surely. That boy will be dead before the trip is done.'

The men agree on this as if it is a simple matter of fact, something they have seen many

19

times before. Zena wonders if curiosity in these circumstances is always fatal? Or is it the boy's propensity for action — the very fact that he tried to help himself that will doom him? She shudders in the sunshine. What on earth are they walking towards? What do these men in dark robes have in mind? Now the ropes are untied, she is not sure what it is that is stopping her from running back into the undergrowth and making for home, where those left behind will surely have buried her uncle, resurrected what was left of the village and, in the sensible way of her family, got on with their lives. She is afraid and yet something here is fascinating — she likes the water. She is enticed by the prospect of seeing the wider world — a place she has already been privileged to hear about but has never visited. Zena glances inland despite herself and then focuses on the movement of her feet. The slavers are watching all the time. They sleep in shifts and can smell dissention, or perhaps courage. You need only pitch in the wrong direction or trip and they will flog you. Kasim's eyes sparkle and Ibn Mohammed, for the most part, maintains his cold outward appearance. She has never met people so removed from those around them. The whole party is cowed and the Arabs need only give an order for everyone to jump to action. The men's authority is impressive.

I will stay, she decides, feeling sick in the pit of her belly. It is important to Zena to pretend she has a choice.

5

To the east, on the ocean, the atmosphere aboard the *Palinurus* has become intolerable on more than one count since the departure of Dr Jessop and First Lieutenant Jones from the complement of officers. *If only the damn malaria had taken Wellsted instead of any of the others*, Captain Haines curses to himself. However much Haines hates losing good men to the fever, even as he is damning his only surviving lieutenant's good health, he feels a wave of shame. He does not admit that the reason he is so angry is because he wanted to achieve what Wellsted has done and write a memoir of their trip so far. Instead, he blusters that the lieutenant is an upstart who has behaved abominably. Still, the captain has to grudgingly allow that perhaps to wish Wellsted dead is too harsh.

The mortalities were unexpected, of course — if Haines had known that a fever was about to break out, he would never have sent Jessop onto the *jabel*. Choosing him for the mission, Haines can't help thinking, was an unfortunate mistake. Had he been aboard, the doctor might have been able to save at least some of the crew from the sickness. But the man was keen and how was Haines to know what was going to happen? Generally, this side of Africa, if a chap survives his first weeks in Bombay, he tends to be fine.

The dead men, of course, wherever their souls may be, probably don't believe that anymore. In only a few days, over half the *Palinurus*' officers and a third of the crew have died. However, despite the losses and the weather, the *Palinurus* is still making progress along the coast, the chart is coming along, the soundings are accurate and the brig has so far not run into a single French vessel. Nonetheless, the captain has a strong sense of duty for his men's welfare, the stricken cadavers buried at sea weigh on his mind and he blames himself. Still, rather than think on it too deeply, he diverts his inner invective towards his only remaining senior officer.

It was only a few days before the malaria outbreak that the captain found by chance the package that contained Wellsted's memoir while he was checking the mail going off the vessel. Damn cheek! Now he wishes he had stopped its dispatch, but at the time he felt so wounded at what the lieutenant had written, so terribly shocked at the man's blatant use of other officers' experiences and discoveries that he went into some kind of shock and simply parcelled up the damn thing again and sent it on its way, for his overwhelming emotion, at first, was that he wanted rid of it.

The book Haines intended to write about the trip would have used, of course, much the same material, but as captain he considers that his right. Haines envisioned reporting to the Royal Society as the head of the expedition and doling out credit where it was due to his talented officers whose dedication, he had decided on wording it, was a credit to both the expedition and the Bombay Marine. He'd have credited Wellsted, of course. However, the lieutenant's manuscript has squarely put paid to any such grandiose dreams and Haines wishes he could recall the parcel, which by now will no doubt have cleared the Red Sea and, safe aboard a company ship, be dispatched westwards to London. What rankles the captain most is that Wellsted did not dedicate the tome to him. In an unheard of lapse of etiquette, the lieutenant barely mentioned any of the other men on board, least of all the illustrious Haines. Worst of all, he is entirely unapologetic, which only makes Haines even more furious. When the hell did the man find the time to write a damn book, anyway?

A knock on the cabin door interrupts Haines' furious train of thought. Three midshipmen hover in the doorway, boys of eleven, twelve and thirteen years of age, dressed in pale breeches and smart, brass-buttoned, navy jackets. Their hair is uniformly the colour of wet sand and they look so alike that they could be brothers, though really they are only brothers in arms. Haines notes to himself that they have been through a great deal, these boys and they are good lads. They have seen, between them, too many cadavers the last few days. As the captain motions them into the room, by far the largest on the ship, the boys seem suddenly taller as if growing into the space. Each of them silently hopes that one day he will be man enough to be called captain.

'Ah. Dinner. Yes,' says Haines.

Jardine, the captain's portly, Scottish steward follows the deputation, closing the door behind him with an unexpectedly deft flick of the ankle. The man's face is like a craggy cliff of pink chalk, fallen away slightly on one side, as if the steward's very person is as old as time and disappearing gradually into the sea. There was, during the time of the fever, no expectation that Jardine might succumb; he is an indestructible kind of fellow. Now in one hand he holds a decanter of brandy and in the other a flagon of red wine, which he lays on the table.

'What is it tonight, Jardine?'

'Mutton, sir. Stewed,' he replies, lopsided in the mouth.

They last resupplied far south of Makkah and bought a flock of small, dark-coated sheep from an unwilling tribe of *Wahabi* for a small fortune. Supplies further along the coast have proved limited. Many of the Musselmen refuse to trade with the English at all although some tribes are easier than others. This coast — to the east of the Red Sea — is proving particularly troublesome. Islam, in this area, appears to be taken to extremes and is most unforgiving in its tenets — quite a contrast to the more laissez-faire *Ibadis* who populate the other side of the Peninsula and to the south. In this neck of the woods the mere sight of white skin often provokes an apoplexy of virulent hatred. The landing parties have been spat upon, screamed at and chased off at knife point by wild-eyed, pale-robed assailants spewing a torrent of abuse,

24

which upon later translation, turned out to mean 'Eat pig, pig-eaters!' and the like. At one port a merchant even pissed into a sack of flour rather than sell it to the infidel ship to be eaten by unbelievers. 'Die empty-bellied, *kafir*,' the man sneered. No amount of money or attempt at goodwill seems to make the long-bearded zealots change their minds. The holy cities are closed to foreigners so it has been mutton for some weeks now, supplemented with thin dates, ship's tack, sheep's milk, coffee, a small amount of cornbread and any decent-sized fish the younger members of the crew can scoop out of the water.

'Well, lads, you did not join up, I trust, in the hope of feasting at the expense of the Bombay Marine?'

Haines pours his officers a glass each.

'A toast, shall we?' he says with largesse.

That very morning the last of the dead was buried at sea — an Irish seadog from Belfast called Johnny Mullins, who fought the malaria like a trouper but lost in the end. All members of the crew who caught the sickness are either dead or cured now. The worst has passed and Haines holds up his glass.

'We survivors, gentlemen. May our poor fellows rest in peace.'

The boys shift uneasily. Protocol demands that they do not start the proceedings of dinner without all the invited officers present. They may be young, but they know the form.

'Come now,' says the captain testily, imposing his authority.

Slowly, the boys concur. Uneasily, they pick up

25

their glasses and down the wine.

'Jardine!' the captain calls for service.

'Yes, sir.'

'Mutton stew is it?'

'Yes, sir. With seaweeds. But . . . '

'If Lieutenant Wellsted cannot be troubled to join us on time, then I see no reason why we should wait on his pleasure.'

Haines turns back to the little group.

'Now,' he says. 'The soundings you took today, young Ormsby. I checked over your work and I was most impressed. Heaving the lead all afternoon like that and collating your measurements with excellent accuracy — why, you are a regular Maudsley man, are you not? We'll have you in charge of this survey yet!'

Ormsby's grin could illuminate London Bridge. 'Thank you, sir,' he says as Jardine shuffles in with a pewter casserole dish, steam emanating from the open lid, and starts to serve the officers their dinner.

6

Jessop and Jones are coming to realise that the *Dhofaris* have a very different sense of time. Or, as the lieutenant puts it, 'You cannot trust a word the buggers say.' It has been another day or two to the emir's camp for almost a week now, and no manner of earnest enquiry elicits any other response from the men, than occasionally, a wry shrug of the shoulders. Jessop restricts Jones from becoming too insistent.

'We are not in such a rush, old man,' he points out.

It is long enough till the men's rendezvous with the *Palinurus* that they have time to lag behind their schedule.

Apart from their inability to keep to a timetable, Jessop finds the *Dhofaris* very pleasant. They are endlessly patient with his attempts to map the route, which is proving extremely difficult. For a start, for most of the day, the brass instruments the doctor brought for the job are far too hot to touch.

'Sort of thing you don't realise in Southampton,' he smiles.

Jones does not find this kind of thing amusing. The tasks are as much his as the doctor's to complete but the lieutenant constantly gives up, the doctor considers, a mite too easily for an English officer who is charged with what is, after all, the fairly routine, if inconvenient, mission of

27

checking the lie of the land. The *Dhofaris* bind their hands in cloth and try their best to assist.

At night, by the panorama of low-slung stars with which the region is blessed, the instruments provide better results. The sand dunes, however, are tricky to render. The wind will move them long before the next British mission comes inland, making that element of the map all but useless. There is no landscape on earth as changeable as the desert, Jessop muses. While the Northumberland hills where he grew up have remained largely the same for thousands of years, the features of the desert landscape might last no more than a few weeks. The doctor does not give up, though. He merely notates all his thoughts and as much detail as he can manage, down to the fact that the thin goats the *Dhofaris* have brought have shorter carcasses than their European cousins and are surprisingly tasty. A chap never knows what might prove a useful piece of information — which shrub will turn out to hold a priceless secret that can be used in British industry, or the understanding of which local custom will endear a later British delegation to an emir or a caliph and secure a lucrative trade agreement. Dr Jessop, unlike Lieutenant Jones, is focussed clearly on what the East India Company requires of him. He notes each twenty-four hours the mileage they have managed to cover and estimates that a thirsty camel can drink twenty gallons in less than three minutes.

As they make camp in the middle of the morning and settle down to sleep for the hottest part of the day under a hastily erected tent that provides shade probably only a degree or two cooler than the baking sand adjacent to it, the doctor dresses a burn on the older *Dhofari*'s hand. The wound was acquired in the service of the British Empire, after all. He daubs lavender ointment across the skin. Kindness, the doctor always thinks, is terribly important to a patient. When he first qualified, many of his patients healed all the quicker, he's sure, for his attention, rather than simply his medical knowledge.

'I don't know why you bother, old chap,' Jones mumbles sleepily to his companion.

'I have the ointment with me, it costs me nothing,' the doctor points out.

Jones turns over. 'Night night,' he murmurs like a child rather than one of His Majesty's finest.

Jessop burrows himself an indent in the sand. *It is really very telling*, he muses. *Jones didn't seem* — he angles for the right word — *so very ungentlemanly when they were aboard ship*. He glances at the blinding orb that is reaching its height. The doctor prefers travelling by the stars. Night in the desert is quite the most extraordinary spectacle.

'Good night,' he returns, rather more formally, and settles down to sleep for a few hours before they get on their way.

7

It feels to Zena as if she has walked into a nightmare. In the low-ceilinged hold of the Arab *dhow* there are eighty prisoners shackled. Seventy-one of them are still alive though the shit swills around their chapped ankles and all still living are so faint from hunger and thirst that they scarcely feel it sting. Most have never before seen so many people as they are now crammed up against and for all it is an abomination not to bury the dead before sundown. They have been eleven days on board the *mashua*. It is this that worries her most. The majority of the slaves are ignorant of the geography both of where they came from and where they might be going, but Zena lived for six years with her grandmother, high in the cool, emerald hills of northern Abyssinia, less than two hundred miles from the cosmopolitan and bustling trading town of Bussaba. The old lady was respected and her house was a prosperous staging post of some renown for travelling caravans and pilgrims. Within its compound, Zena's grandmother's rules were simple and absolute: no weapons, no theft of either person or property.

It was in that place of safety that Zena learnt about faraway lands and the limits of the slave routes. She heard tell of a variety of gods and legends — all of which seemed merely curious to her, for her grandmother believed in nothing except, she always said, the goodness of people as long as you were firm. The travellers talked about where they had been and where they were going to and, though Zena has never seen a map, it is as a result of these many conversations that it is clear to her that eleven days on a ship is further than these men really need to go simply to sell her.

At the port she was separated from everyone she knew and marched aboard another vessel with strangers hand-picked from other slave raids, for it seems, though the slavers clearly prefer the young, the different quality of human cargo merits different destinations. At least that is her best guess, for as far as she can tell, the ships are not sailing together and Zena knows no one aboard. There will be, she has come to realise, no getting away. Simply to survive the crossing will be a feat.

Sitting well-fed beside her grandmother's fire, the names of the foreign climes sounded exotic — Muscat and Sur, Constantinople and Zanzibar, Bombay and Calicut. The strange tone of the men's skin seemed benign, somehow, as they talked wistfully of their homeland or their religious devotions. There were Christians, Hindus, Sikhs, Muslims, Animists and Jews and they came in all shades of brown — Nubian princes, *Wahabi* emirs, minor Persian noblemen, Turkish traders, the dusky emissaries of caliphs and sultans, Semitic merchants, Indian warriors, Somali pirates and Abyssinian bishops. Each and every one of the strangers was tattooed and

31

pierced with the markings of their individual tribe — some shaven and some with long beards, some bareheaded and others with ornate headdresses or brightly coloured turbans. They dressed differently too — in white flowing robes, or embroidered *jubbahs*, or animal-skin capes adorned in ostrich feathers or sometimes simply in a hessian winding cloth. Under her grandmother's watchful eye, Zena served platters of food to all of them — spiced couscous and succulent lamb piled high with melted butter poured on top till it dripped from the edge of the plate. Roasted chicken stuffed with fruit and nuts and gleaming with basting juices. Spicy *wot*, stewed till it almost melted into the hot *injera* bread. Latterly, she danced for the strangers to the beat held by Yari, her grandmother's fat, Anatolian eunuch who played the drums. When they found out she was not a mere servant (one of many) or indeed a slave girl (even more), but a favoured grandchild, many of the visitors paid her attention and left her gifts — a phial of perfume or a length of silk. There are no gifts now.

After the third day aboard, in the darkness of the hold, she can see this new ship is following the coast to the south and, between the intermittent keening of the other women and the praying of the men, silent tears stream down her face. *There can be no going back now*, she mouths. All she can think of is returning to the village, and what might be there if she does. So much loss. A grave. Her mother, always surly. A marriage Zena never sought for herself, now long overdue. *It should not have happened like this,* she thinks. In the darkness, it is safe to mourn so she cries for a long time.

On the sixth day, after silence and exhaustion finally prevail below deck and all surrender themselves to the stifling crush, Zena notices through a tiny strip of light in the bulwark above her head that the land is on the wrong side of the ship and she knows they have turned eastwards. These territories are strange to her — she retains in her memory only some names and meagre scraps of information, but it is enough to realise the scale of the distance she now lies from home and the impossibility of an easy return.

Her grandmother's death sent her back to the village only a few weeks before — back to her parents who had hoped for better for her. The stone compound was inherited by her mother's elder brother who arrived a week after the burial with several camels, a horse or two and a cold-eyed wife in full *burquah*. He took stock of his new home, ordered an ox to be killed and cooked in celebration and banished Zena at the first opportunity.

'Go home and get married, child,' he commanded. 'There is nothing for you here.'

Her presence had always been unorthodox and so, as he was fully entitled, he sent her, with only one servant and one camel, back to the shamble of huts where she was born. She travelled light with just one small wooden box of trinkets and baubles and a few lengths of dark cotton. At the time, she thought the old lady's passing was the saddest thing that would ever happen — Zena loved her grandmother. She had nursed Baba devotedly through her short illness. When death finally came, Zena washed the old woman's naked body and wrapped it in a white linen shroud. The servants buried the corpse and then Zena cried for three days without sleeping. Yari fed her yoghurt and honey though she scarcely tasted it.

Above Zena's head, the hold opens suddenly and those in the way pull back from the bright stream of blinding light that beams down. A bucket of brackish water is lowered on a rope and two more of scraps — rancid fat, raw fish and rock-hard *khubz*. The slaves fall upon it, tearing at each other to secure a cupped handful of water and a mouthful of food. A sound that Zena identifies as laughter floats down from the white square above her head as she eats the mush between her fingers and tries not to retch. Then the light is obliterated.

The following day, a ladder is lowered and two men climb into the darkness. Each has a cloth tied round his mouth and nose, for the stench is foul. Together, they roughly remove the dead, hacking the chains and hoisting the stiff bodies over their backs. When the hatch closes behind them once more, they throw the cadavers into the sea from above, like a fishwife emptying a pan of trash — a shudder runs through the cabin as the survivors hear the splash, though all are relieved the rotting corpses are finally gone.

The night after, the ship arrives in Muscat, rolls up its sail and the slaves are marched onto the deck by the light of the moon to be doused in sea water under the careful, still gaze of Asaf Ibn Mohammed. As the sky lightens and the Muslim call to prayer echoes over the city from minarets dotted along the shoreline of the sapphire bay, Zena catches sight of Kasim in the shadows, feeding scraps to a small guenon monkey he must have captured in the forest — a white-lipped tamarin. The little beast is tethered to him on a string but the animal is cleaner and better cared for than any of the *dhow*'s human cargo. Zena is not sure, but thinks that she can make out that it is eating fruit of some kind. Gently, the man who less than a month ago beat Zena's uncle to death sets the animal to one side with a small, metal cup of water so he can watch the slaves disembarking. He does not move into the light as three huge negroes, six feet tall, bound in muscles, their veins standing out like vines over sculpted stone and their eyes like the eyes of statues, bundle the new shipment ashore into a rickety warehouse. Everyone is so afraid and so glad to be on land again that not one single protest is raised. It would make no matter, in any case, for the handlers are in possession of both whips and the strength of lions. They are deliberately only dressed in indigo loincloths so that every rock-hard muscle is on show. What starving, enfeebled fool is going to try to make his case in the face of such strength? Who would dare even ask a question? These men can slice the weakest of them right down the middle and drink their blood, if they wish it, and no one will say a thing.

Locked inside the warehouse, Zena knows what to expect. She's heard of this. Her skin will be oiled for the marketplace, which is surely close by. She can hear it, smell it. She feels sick with apprehension and hunger as she squats and waits. No one says a word, though two boys, not more than twelve and probably brothers, if Zena guesses correctly, hold hands. Wafting from a distance, they hear the waves of communal prayer that accompany the dawn. The haunting words of the *Salat* sung by a *mullah* with a strong, clear voice: 'You alone we worship. You alone we ask for help.'

I should have run, she berates herself, thinking of the proximity of the undergrowth near the beach. She knows she is confused. One moment one thing, one moment another. But right now running seems as if it would have been easy, certainly easier than the long days on the *dhow*. *I might have made it*, she thinks. *At least I would have tried*.

As the dawn rises, the fiery orange gradually fades from the sky and through the slats of the locked door Zena catches bare glimpses of the harbour, slices of Muscat life in the bright morning light. It is unexpectedly beautiful. She has never seen anything like this place — a huge bay bordered by high, green hills. It is a big city, she realises — larger than any settlement she has ever known. The dock-side is properly paved and the houses and businesses built of a pale mud crammed between the date palms. The newer constructions are whitewashed so they dazzle when the sun hits them, and over time the older ones have muted to a dun brown. Along the dock there is a castle of some kind — a fortification set back from the water's edge, with huge, dark guns pointing out to sea over its battlements.

The dock is already busy — a sure sign of a profitable trading port — with forty ships or more at anchor. Outside, the morning's trade has started — a man with birds in a wicker cage is setting up his stall next to a hawker in a dazzling white *jubbah* with a litter of prayer mats. The men are boiling water over a small fire and are set to brew mint tea with a sliver of cinnamon and some honey which they will sip from delicate, etched-glass cups. Three dirty goats are tethered between the stalls. A toothless beggar with only one leg and one eye struggles past, arrayed in a filthy swathe of rags, his sole possession a *calabash* from which he stops intermittently to drink. One of the traders hastens to beat him away. 'Son of a dog!' the man shouts, waving his arms as if batting off a fly, the tone of his protestation furious. 'Away with you!' *Ibn al-kalb. Imshi. Imshi.*

'They will eat us,' one of the other girls bursts out suddenly as the angry words filter through. Her voice is trembling. 'No one ever comes back when they are taken. They will eat us all.'

She begins to cry, huge sobs wracking her angular, bony frame. The rest of the group remain absolutely silent though a few shoulders round in fear. Zena ignores the hysteric — she

37

knows she will be sold here, not devoured. Besides, seeing Muscat waking up has somehow heartened her. It is not as alien as she might have expected. The city is prosperous, clearly, and if the call to prayer is anything to go by, there are a lot of *mosques* so perhaps it is also devout. She knows it is unlikely she will get away now, for apart from anything else, where can she run to? But this is a large and cosmopolitan place, she knows more about it than anyone else she is locked up with and the worst, surely, is over. She turns her head towards the light and thinks she must, at least, try to remain hopeful. *Someone kind will buy me*, she thinks as she clutches her empty stomach and assures herself that she will eat soon, perhaps within the hour.

8

In a five-storey, palatial townhouse on Albemarle Street, just off Piccadilly, John Murray, London's most prestigious publisher, rises late, the summertime sounds of London finally cutting short his slumbers. Some damn fool is shouting his wares at the top of his voice. Murray has to concentrate for the words to become distinct — he has never woken easily and it always takes him a while to come to full consciousness. After a few seconds it becomes apparent that the costermonger has roused the master of the house over some beets and pears that are available to purchase. Murray groans and reaches over to the other side of the bed. His wife is already gone and he is glad of it. They squabble almost constantly and he tries to avoid her whenever he can — the damn woman is as bad as his mother. She will, like many upper-class ladies, leave town at the end of the month to visit friends in the country, and Murray (unlike many upper-class gentlemen) will remain in the capital, shot of her for a few, satisfying weeks. It is a cheering thought.

He makes use of the chamber pot and stows it back under the bed. Then, rather than calling for his valet, he washes in a desultory fashion, pulling on his wig haphazardly, preoccupied over whether he might have chocolate this morning with his rolls, or coffee. Still debating this, he takes the stairs down at a sharpish trot to the sunny, yellow drawing room on the first floor. He never will get used to the portrait of Lord Byron over the mantel, though, of course, to remove it would cause a scandal were further scandal required. It has been a good ten years since Murray's father famously burned Byron's memoirs to safeguard public morality, and hardly a week passes even now that he is not asked by some starry-eyed matron or other if the old codger had, by chance, ever mentioned to his son the nature of the manuscript's contents. Murray considers the matter both foolish and tiresome. He is a serious man of science and his interests do not stretch to poetry — unless perhaps it is German poetry — or indeed to much in the way of scandal. Byron's musings on sherbet and sodomy might have funded Murray's education, but now, as he has been known to dryly remark, it is time to put aside such childish things. At least in conversation — for Byron's full canon still graces the great publisher's list and sells at least several hundred copies every year. In addition, each week Murray receives by post a number of attempts at Byronic genius, all of which, on principle, he consigns to the fire.

Coffee, Murray decides.

The enticing smell of fresh bread is floating upstairs from the kitchens in the basement and he can almost taste the melting butter and lemon conserve already. A glass of rhenish, some ham perhaps and he will be set.

There is a pile of correspondence on his desk

and, as it is Friday, he might have passed it by for it is his habit to ride on a Friday morning, but there is one packet that catches his eye. Neither the handwriting nor the paper is extraordinary but in the small, nondescript, black wax seal there are embedded some grains of sand. Murray breaks open the packet with a satisfying click and inside lies a manuscript bound in worn card, accompanied by a covering letter dated several weeks before and written in a neat hand.

Dear Sir,
I wish to offer for your consideration an account of my recent exploration and adventures on the island of Socotra where I have been humbly employed as an officer of the Indian Navy during the current survey of the Red Sea by the ship Palinurus. *I hope you might wish to publish my unworthy writings and find them of some small interest.*
Yours, etc.,
James Raymond Wellsted (Lieutenant)

Murray crosses the room and spins the leather globe until he finds the Red Sea. Then he peers short-sightedly to try to identify the islands nearby. He has never heard of this Socotra place but with the help of a magnifying glass he quickly plants a firm finger over the speck of the island, which is far smaller than his nail. It is perched to the east of Abyssinia and to the south of Oman.

41

I must ask George about this, he thinks.

Murray will be dining that evening with the President of the Royal Geographical Society and his beautiful wife, Louisa. The manuscript might make for some interesting dinner conversation over the roast fowl and jellied beets. His wife will not like it, for her interests do not run to anything the least bit sensible, but Murray, like most of London, is eager for news of the Empire's burgeoning territories — the more exotic, the better — and a keen sense for a bestseller is in his blood. If it is written well, an explorer's memoir is generally a sure-fire success. So many people these days are either venturing abroad themselves, or have relations in the far reaches, that there is something of a vogue for travel writing and Murray's view is that he will be publishing more and more of the stuff. After all, it is worthy, educational and occasionally exciting (all of which he approves far more than any damned fiction). There is a market, he fancies, for some kind of guidance for those embarking on life overseas. He must make a note of that, he thinks, and scrambles around for a clean sheet of paper. In any case, the prospect of dinner tonight is especially entertaining and, he is certain, there may even be pear pudding, for that costermonger had been right outside. Cook surely will have availed the household of fresh pears if it is possible, will she not — first of the season this early in July? *Socotra, eh? Sounds fascinating*. Murray hopes George will be able to tell him if the island is Arabian or African, for a start. An interesting conundrum given its position on the map between the two territories.

Murray rings the bell and the butler appears almost instantly.

'Bring me breakfast here, would you?' he asks as he sinks into the high-backed, wooden chair at his desk and pulls a plush, yellow, velvet pillow into the crook of his back. The long windows behind him let in a flood of light — perfect for reading. Many of England's greatest publishing success stories have started their journey at this desk, in this light.

'Coffee, I think. And tell Jack I won't need Belle saddled just yet.'

And with the tiniest speck of sand loosing itself from Wellsted's missive and falling onto the wide, dark boards that span the floor, John Murray begins to read.

9

It is almost midday when Jessop and Jones spot the tents. Nothing moves out on the burning sands, even the scorpions have buried themselves. The first they know that there is any life at all is the eddy of dust that floats into the air as the men come out, tiny specks on the horizon standing at the fringe of the lush oasis, to watch the foreigners and their party arrive from well over a mile away. While Jones' attention is immediately taken up by the Arabian horses tethered in a makeshift corral, Jessop considers the place itself extraordinary. Despite the heat and the difficulty of the journey, the doctor is glad to be here. As the senior officer, he took the decision simply to keep going because, with the instincts of a true traveller, this time when the men said they were close to reaching the destination he believed them.

Now, he is ushered into the emir's tent and makes his *salaams* as he has been shown in Bombay, in preparation for just this kind of occasion — an introduction to someone of some small power who might be of use on His Majesty's business. Jessop gives the emir the payment that has been agreed and then entreats the ruler to allow him to help the children of the camp. The doctor can see the young ones are suffering from an eye infection. Thin and angular as baby storks, they tarry at the tent flaps, blinking through their swollen eyelids, batting off the flies, their feet bare and their arms like sticks. Fresh burn marks pock their little legs — the Omanis treat pain with pain and burn flesh to purify from disease; it is the best they can do.

'I am a doctor,' he explains. 'Let me try my white man's medicine. I will do my best.'

'*Bitsalam yadak*,' the emir replies graciously, which Jessop takes to mean, 'May God keep your hands safe.' A good sign, surely.

In another tent, Jessop inspects the eleven children who seem even more like fragile, strange, featherless birds now they are grouped together. When he asks questions, the women tending them shy away, but one of the men becomes a go-between, attempting the translation. In the main this is achieved by the means of hand movements as much as the Englishman's sparse Arabic vocabulary, which is hindered further by his accent. The upshot is, Jessop concludes, that the infection has been spread by the kohl used on the youngsters' eyelids. Kohl is widely believed to be medicinal in Arabia and is used to keep the eyes moist, but often people do not wash it between applications. When one of the children got a windblown infection, it spread rapidly to the others. Now one or two are even sporting pustules ripe with suppurating mucus.

'Bring me water, please,' he asks his translator, who eyes him with suspicion, but returns quickly with a flask nonetheless.

Calmly, Jessop takes each child in turn and washes away the black powder with precious water. The children squeal for they are used to cleaning themselves only with sand — water is far too scarce to be used for bathing. As the drops slide down their faces, they lap them up with their tongues, unwilling to allow even a teaspoonful to go to waste. Once the infection has been cleaned, the doctor breaks out the contents of his leather bag. This is one of the reasons he joined the service — Jessop likes to help and, big of heart and strong of stomach, he shows no horror or revulsion at whatever he is presented with. He mixes a solution of vinegar and applies it to each child in turn as an eyewash. It stings. The younger children make a fuss, the older ones succumb in silence.

'That should help,' he says. 'We will look at it again tomorrow. *Salaam*,' he says, bowing as he takes his leave.

* * *

Jones has stationed himself by the corral and has been trying to strike up a conversation with the horsemen. The refinement of the breed is most appealing. The finely chiselled bone and the concave profile, the comparatively high level croup and high-carried tail make the Arabians an enticing prospect. They are wonderful, majestic beasts and no mistake and the lieutenant has to admit he is moved when he sees two of the robe-swathed men from the encampment saddling up. They cut a queer kind of dash that stirs excitement in the whole group, and while the doctor faffs about with the barefoot children, everyone else comes out to watch the men set off. Where they are riding to is a mystery — perhaps they are only taking the animals for their daily exercise. The horses are worth a fortune; Jones isn't sure yet where the best of the money is to be made, but he can almost smell that there is money in it somewhere — be it shipping home pure breeds or using an Arab stallion to cover a mare of another breed — there is something for which he knows the fashionable and wealthy around St James's will pay through the nose. Some already are. Napoleon rode an Arabian, of course, but that is no matter for the King himself now has one — a present that arrived last year from the Sultan of Muscat and Oman. To Jones this is as good as receiving direct royal approval for his project. It is the sheer quality of the animals that will attract society and he knows if he can get a shipment or two back to Blighty, he'll make his fortune. No smart family wants to be without the latest breed to take the royal fancy.

Jones pulls out his notebook, his mouth almost watering at the thought of the stud fees and what he might achieve when in receipt of them, given the faded glory of his family's London house. He clears his throat and, with a sense of history, or at least publicity, puts pen to paper, for he will need notes to validate the authenticity of the animals and his experiences in selecting them.

The emir seems glad of our company and has invited us to feast with him. It is no cooler but the water here is very plentiful if slightly sour in taste. Coming in from the

47

desert my camel drank for a full ten minutes. Brave beast, she has served me well and kept us supplied in milk the last days of our journey. There are seventy or eighty people in the encampment — the emir, his family, retainers and slaves. All are respectful and courteous. I envy these men little other than their horses — the horses are beautiful, though, and very fine.

By contrast, it is immediately apparent that the *Bedu* are less impressed by the infidels. Some of them have seen white men before — those who have taken caravans to the coast where if you linger long in any seaport between here and India you are sure to catch sight of a *Nazarene* — strange-looking creatures. Their blue eyes remind the *Bedu* of the sky, seen through the empty eye sockets of a bleached, white skull. They are haughty too, like living phantoms, zombies greedy for the lifeblood of Arabia. When the white men speak they always ask questions and the *Bedu* know what that means.

'You do not have horses in England?' Jones is challenged bluntly when he enquires about the breeding habits of the animals, where they can be bought and for how much. The *Bedu* are close to their livestock — camels, horses or goats — and at least as protective of such property as they are of their wives. Animals are their only measure of wealth and the truth is that they are unlikely to sell any of their horses unless they have to. Itinerant tribesmen rely on their livestock not only for food and transport but to

48

find water — a good camel can save your life in the desert, and water is the only treasure that matters out on the hot, dry sands. Gold and precious jewels cannot save your life like a decent steed. The horse, of course, has the advantage of speed and intelligence over the camel and they are necessary for successfully raiding other encampments or carrying important news.

There is a legend in this tribe that as a child, perhaps thirteen years old, the emir was caught out on the sands with only his horse for company. He survived two days without water and did not succumb to panic (a legendary feat in itself). Then when it could go no further, he used his sabre to slaughter his horse and drank its blood to survive. He made it back to his father's camp on foot the following afternoon with the animal's blood still crusted on his clothes and around his mouth. He had sucked the carcass dry. It is a tale acknowledged as so extraordinary and heroic that still the people of this tribe tell it to their children and will do so for several years after the emir dies. More importantly, the emir's enemies tell the same tale to the children of their own camps — as a warning. The tough young man has grown up into a fierce opponent and he is respected and feared across the entire region.

The emir's men are as hard-nosed as their master, Jones thinks. They continue to bat his questions back to him, revealing nothing in the process. When Jessop strolls out of the family tent he comes to stand by the lieutenant.

'Nice animals,' he says, with a nod. 'I'm glad we arrived today. Several of those children might certainly have gone blind, or died even. If the infection gets into the blood it will poison them. I hope I have been able to avert that.'

Jones is not listening. 'Thing is with these Arabs,' he says nonchalantly, 'they are great traders. They are trying to make me feel like a fool in the hope of gaining a better price.'

10

Zena is running. She is running so fast to get away that she doesn't even feel the ground beneath her feet or the sun on her skin. Her body is almost silent — the way a *dyk dyk* moves through the trees at speed — the flash of a leaf and the movement of a branch. It's like being invisible. Zena has hardly ever had occasion to run before — not since she was a child and she played with the others, hiding in the bushes and splashing in the stream. That was many years ago now, and this kind of running is different. It is a sensation that is both desperate and strange. Her breath comes fluidly and the further she goes the more energy she has. She does not look back. She can take any direction she likes. At least that is how it feels at first. After a little while she realises that she is being followed so she picks up the pace, stretching her limbs further.

I'll never stop, she thinks. *Running is all I want to do now. Running until I get shot of these strange men and this strange place.*

The thought is no sooner formed than a hand claps down heavily onto her shoulder and pulls her to a stop. Forcefully, the palm pushes her onto her knees. Her heart flutters as she tries to stay upright. Her stomach turns. She has a sudden burst of energy and tries to pull away, but he is shaking her whole body, forcing her to the ground.

'Wake up! Stupid female!' the voice says.

Her limbs twitch as she opens her eyes, the lids heavy and her vision bleary with sleep. She bats her hand in front of her as if to move a fly and it is struck sharply.

'Get up!' the voice orders as she rubs the stinging flesh on her fingers.

The darkness of the warehouse is a shock and at first she can't make out where she is. In her dream she was running in the sunshine. Still groggy despite the blow, for it was a much-needed and wonderfully deep sleep, Zena struggles to her feet, feeling confused. The man before her is small and his rounded belly shapes his *jubbah*. He has a purple and green embroidered cap on his balding head and he inspects the girl with the sharp eye of a cold-hearted appraiser.

'Yes, this one will do well, I think. Kasim said she was a worthwhile piece. All in all this has been a very good consignment.'

Zena wonders how long she slept. About half of the people who were stowed in the hut are now gone, and in the doorway there are two old men, black *sidi* slaves, carrying a vat of something that smells rancid. Her appetite sharpened, she feels a rush of hope that she might be able to eat it.

The plump auctioneer moves on, separating twelve of the Abyssinian slaves from the others. Then he takes each in turn, ordering them to circle around, show him the soles of their feet and display the insides of their mouths. When he is satisfied, he waves the *sidis* into action and

52

they move around each person, their dry, old hands smoothing the gloopy oil onto the slaves' parched skin and rubbing it into their hair to make it glisten. They are trying to make it look as if the people who survived the journey from Africa were well cared for during the trip. One or two cannot help licking at the fat on their forearms. They wince at its bitter taste and are slapped for removing the shine from their skin. Then, with a rough brush with wire bristles, the *sidis* comb the hair of the boys, leaving the women be. Most have hair that is still dressed with plaits and beads from their village days, when it was styled by their mothers and sisters. Zena realises that these ordinary hairstyles look enticing, exotic and strange to the eyes of Muscat. Arabic women cover their hair with a veil.

It crosses her mind that for some odd reason she would like to look her best now. She wants them to see that she is no ordinary Abyssinian slave girl like the others. She has been well brought up and loved, adored even. At her grandmother's house she had slaves of her own. Now, her heart sinks as she looks down sadly at her dirty, tattered dress. It is a thin piece of material, originally a green colour, now brown from the dirt of her long journey. She must look pitiful.

She takes a deep breath and runs her hands over the glistening skin of her arms to give at least a little comfort. *I am alone. I am going to be sold*, she thinks incredulously.

The doors of the shed open and let in the

light. It is afternoon now — the sun has moved across the sky. Beyond the barrels piled up near the doorway, a crowd is gathered and Zena catches a glimpse of a podium surrounded by a jostle of people, all craning to get a better view of the proceedings. The auctioneer leads the way with the *sidis* ushering the dozen slaves into a line behind him. The marketplace is crowded to capacity and there is no hope of getting away; her dream of running will remain just that. Besides, in the light, clearing the path, are the handlers who ushered the slaves from the ship to the hut that morning. The men tower over the heads of the crowd as they ensure the short auctioneer can make his way unhindered. Zena smiles at the sight. The top of the man's head comes only as high as their bellies. These men must eat whole chickens to have grown so tall and strong. She pulls her shoulders back and thinks that at least the top of her head will clear the height of their chests and perhaps make it as far as their shoulders.

My name is Zena, she intones to herself and, with a pinch of sadness, she comes to understand that her name is all she has left now as she steps into the heat and the light of the market.

At the auction stand there is a pause so that prospective customers can peruse the goods. Beneath a tatty canopy men peer out of the crowd, strange faces in a strange town with leering, needy expressions, hungry to possess others. Zena lowers her head, but even so she is aware she is arousing interest. A snatch of

54

conversation, a lewd remark. It makes her skin prickle. Under the watchful gaze of the guards, two men prod her in the chest and discuss matters to which her Arabic vocabulary does not extend. She has been protected from all this, she realises. She had no idea of the cruelty and the humiliation that was possible. As the men cackle with laughter she tries not to look at them. She tries not to cry.

'Are you a virgin?' one asks. *Baakira?*

She has heard the word once before when her grandmother refused to allow a neighbouring merchant to take Zena as his wife. Now she pretends not to understand. The man redirects the question to the guard.

'That one can be whatever you want her to be,' the man replies. 'She is beautiful.' He makes the word sound as if it is an insult.

A boy next to her is ordered to open his mouth and another man, who has emerged from the throng, holds the tongue down with a stick so he can check the child's teeth. If there was anything in the boy's stomach he would vomit, but as it is he only makes a dry sound as if he is being strangled. His eyes dart in distress, but no one does anything. As the man moves towards Zena, she keeps her gaze averted. He pulls her head back and stares into her face but he does not use his stick to probe her mouth. He lingers though and she can feel his breath on her skin. Then, slowly, he lets go and walks carefully right around her.

Not him. Zena has never prayed. It was not her grandmother's custom. However, the phrase runs through her head again and again, as if she is pleading with some greater being. *Not him*.

A bell is rung though it can hardly be heard over the throng of voices. The man instantly retreats into the crowd. Zena raises her eyes just long enough to see that there are several finely dressed Arabs now turning away, who have looked but not come forward. Perhaps one of those. It occurs to Zena that her grandmother has endowed her with a sense of optimism. Even here and now, she feels optimistic. *I will be all right*, she tells herself, though she is batting off a cold shadow that is creeping from behind.

'Gentlemen,' the auctioneer begins. 'Today, fresh from Abyssinia, we have a selection of the finest. The absolute finest!'

A scrawny girl is pushed forward into the sun beside the auctioneer's podium. Her dress is badly torn, exposing the top of her legs. Her shoulders are slumped and one of the guards pokes her to make her stand up straight.

'And for this little one!' the auctioneer tries to whip up the crowd. 'She'll brush up well enough. A price beyond rubies perhaps?'

Zena heaves in a breath, only glad that all eyes are now on the auctioneer and that momentarily she is not the focus of attention.

'What am I bid? Twenty, sir? No, surely not? Come now. She is a little thin perhaps but is there not more? I beseech you. Ah, thirty. Thank you . . . '

And the auction has begun.

11

Lieutenant James Raymond Wellsted has not taken dinner at the captain's table, but instead he remains on deck as the shimmering, marmalade sun disappears in a blaze into the vivid, blue sea and the stars rise. He has some dates and tack in his pocket and that will do him fine. The night sky in Arabia is breathtaking and little enough in Wellsted's life has caused him to take in his breath in wonder, so he greatly appreciates the huge, low moon and the clarity of the studded constellations so close to the equator. Especially now, when so many of his fellows have died. Staring at the moon is the closest he allows himself to get to expressing sentiment. The last few days have been grim and Wellsted already misses each victim of the sickness — two of whom he has known for more than ten years for they were midshipmen together. The younger members of the crew have taken to asking his advice of late on matters of navigation and Wellsted has taken his mind and theirs off the death toll by playing the expert and showing them what they need to know to guide the *Palinurus* towards Suez, where the brig is set to rendezvous with Captain Moresby on the *Benares* and make an attempt to sound the very northern limit of the map.

Wellsted wishes he had been stationed aboard Moresby's vessel. Quite apart from the buckets of vomit and the delirium that has reigned of late aboard the *Palinurus*, conditions are cramped and that has made the atmosphere worse now that Haines has made known his objections to Wellsted's manuscript. The captain appears to care more about Wellsted's scribbles than he does about losing half his officers.

Thirsty, the lieutenant makes his way to the galley and orders hot coffee. Aboard ship the coffee is not as good as ashore. He has watched the Arabs carefully as they grind the roasted beans and brew them over the campfire with a witch's pocket of spices, but no matter how exactly he emulates their actions, right down to using a rough mat of palm fibre to strain the liquid of its grains, he never can make his concoction taste as good. Still, James Wellsted prefers even poor ship's coffee to the liberal dose of alcohol the crew imbibe daily. The lieutenant likes his head to be clear. He likes Arabia too. He finds the language comes naturally, the flowing robes give a sense of freedom and the undiscovered nature of the land provides an unspoilt enticement.

Back at the prow, he savours the dryness the coffee leaves in his mouth. Haines' dinner is finishing and he can hear the midshipmen leaving the cabin, laughing and drunk as they make their way below deck to squeeze their tired bodies into closely packed hammocks. They are pleasant enough — gentlemen's sons, all three of them, rich in family money and social advantages. Like Wellsted, they left home very young but unlike him they never saw the hideous poverty of the English streets (for it is easy, passing in a carriage to ignore it). Bombay with its skeletal beggars and stinking slums on open display shocked them, the pitiless harshness of Arabia is worse and the rampaging malaria over the last few days has reduced them to tears privately, though each has done his duty and masked his shock from the men. Still, the youngest, Henry Ormsby, has taken to drinking a good deal. He carries a hip flask of brandy inside his jacket. When he arrived on board he had to be warned about gambling. Pelham, one of the crew, a sardonic ne'er-do-well with few brains and fewer teeth, was caught dicing with the young gentleman and was deemed to have taken advantage of Ormsby's youth and the ready supply of bright shillings from the youngster's family allowance. The man was flogged for the offence. Unfairly, in Wellsted's view. Ormsby had begged to be allowed to play and had gambled his money fair and square. If he had won he would have pocketed the winnings.

Captain Haines, with his moral standard hoisted ever high, was scandalised, of course. Wellsted, however, was brought up in Marylebone with his grandfather, Thomas, at the helm. Thomas clawed his way up from a cottage with a dirt floor. He'd worked hard and taken every opportunity that God had given him, and some that were sent by the devil too. A truculent, unforgiving old man, his life's purpose is to see to it that at least one of his grandchildren rises in society. He pushed his son into the upholstery business and then begged, borrowed and stole to make sure that his workshops were stocked with fabrics so fine that both staunch traditionalists and the avant-garde of the *ton* sent their business to the Wellsteds and paid, more or less, whatever Old Thomas chose to charge.

'Where do you find these wonderful silks?' the ladies breathe. 'I have never seen any fabric so perfect in my whole life.'

The wily old man says nothing — but it is not a complete coincidence that James' younger brother, Edward, is apprenticed to the customs service the same year that James joined the Bombay Marine.

When the Indian naval commission came up, Thomas spent almost the entire family savings on securing the position for James.

'He's bright. He'll go far. He's our best chance,' Thomas insisted.

James' parents were slack jawed. It was a fortune, but they complied. Iron of purpose, Thomas dominated the Wellsted household for years, marshalling the entire family behind his purpose: to rise. To this end he made sure that his grandchildren understood the poverty around them on the streets — the constant threat of sliding backwards, of having nothing at all. He'd show them the hoi polloi as if to say, 'This is what's possible', you can belong in the salons of gentlemen customers, all fine damasks and mahogany finishes, with the fire stoked and the servants scrubbed, well fed and respectful, but you can fall too and fall far. As a result, James has seen ragged gin whores aplenty and a regular freak show of pestilence. In London decay simmers constantly, breaking through the surface if only your eyes are peeled. The whole, crowded city is built on a barely contained plateau of shit — open sewers in the streets. Never far away, the Thames is a stinking, rancid, stagnant strip of thick slime, running through the centre of the city. Nothing can live in it.

In such surroundings, people are cruel and even in the gentrified streets of Marylebone, women, children and animals are beaten till they cower by their husbands, fathers and masters. Worse, James' grandmother died in the front room of number thirteen, of the pox. Blood gushed from her ears and her sphincter lay open permanently for two days as vitality (if you could call it that) seeped from every orifice. In the end, exhausted and ravaged, she begged to die. The boy was a mere eight or nine and, his eyes already open to the world, about to leave for his dearly bought commission.

'Well now, James Raymond,' his grandfather said, standing dry-eyed over his wife's dead body. 'The old lady will not live now to see you make the Wellsted fortune. We can go no higher, your father and I. It's the education, you see. Whereas you, with all your letters, well, you can take us up. By hook or by crook, Jamie boy, whatever you have to do to win the prizes, for there will be prizes and no mistake. Make us proud.'

An ant crawls over the old woman's milky eye. She has been dead less than an hour.

'Swear you'll bring it home, James.' The old

man grips the youngster's wrist and slams the child's hand down on the corpse's stiffening breast. 'Swear to me on your grandma's dead body that you'll shine. You'll make a gentleman no matter what. Steal it, plunder it, swindle it or earn it fair. It doesn't matter to me. Swear on her broken body or go to hell yourself.'

The harshness of Arabia does not shock James Wellsted one bit. He has few scruples about writing his memoirs. He has credited those he believes require credit — Chapman gave Wellsted use of his diaries before he died and he offered help when he was writing about geological specimens. Another officer advised on the Greek translation the lieutenant used. Wellsted will be damned if he'll kiss Haines' arse. He knows that the captain is not generally liked, and his objections to what Wellsted has done are questionable. He'd simply have liked to get his account in first. Well, damn the old man — it's first past the post, the British way and the captain will simply have to lump it.

Against the sound of the lapping waves, Wellsted does not hear Haines approaching in the darkness.

'I could have you up on charges, Lieutenant, for refusing the captain's orders. Dinner in my cabin, I said.'

'I didn't realise it was an order, sir. I thought it more an invitation.'

Haines makes a derisory grunt. His breath is sour. Wellsted can smell it keenly on the thick, evening air.

'I'm so hurt,' the captain mumbles, 'that so

62

many good men, who have now given their lives for the service . . . that you are stealing their credit. It is wickedness, Wellsted, not the act of a gentleman.'

'I found what I found in Socotra,' Wellsted replies evenly. 'I simply noted down what I had done. I have named the others.'

Haines snaps. 'You were my assistant. An assistant, that is all.'

Wellsted does not rise to the bait. They have had this argument before and Wellsted can put his hand on his heart and say that the majority of what he claimed in his memoir is his own work. He'll find his way, by hook or by crook and it will be a better memorial of the men who've died than Haines' interminable snivelling.

The captain, still outraged, waits a few moments but Wellsted only stares silently towards the inky outline of the shore.

'You were right not to come to my cabin tonight, I suppose,' Haines continues in a vicious tone. 'It is a good idea for you to eat alone. It will give you time to think — to consider. Shall we say for the rest of the tour, Lieutenant Wellsted?'

James knows the man is insulting him. For any officer to be banned from the captain's table is a dreadful blow. Certainly, the gossip of such disciplinary action will animate the crew for days and when they make port it will be wondered at all over the service. Captain Haines has the outer appearance of bluff liberality, but those who work with him know well enough that he is dogged in his thinking and takes a dislike often to individual members of the crew with little reason. For James, banishment from Haines' cabin is little skin off his nose, in the long run. The worst the captain can do is work him hard and neglect him a little and he's survived worse than that. Also, as things stand on board, Wellsted is the only senior officer, which puts Haines over a barrel. The midshipmen are green as gooseberries in a lush, English summer and the captain needs the lieutenant to continue the survey. If Haines hoped that Wellsted would baulk at social disgrace, he is disappointed.

'As you wish, sir. I shall dine alone.'

The captain brushes his palms together as if he is cleaning them. 'Well then, carry on, Wellsted. Keep the watch, will you?'

★　★　★

For hours there is nothing on the sound but the endless, penetrating blackness relieved by the low, whirling brightness of the stars. If you stare at them long enough they send your head spinning. The temperature has plummeted so that the night is merely pleasantly warm after the searing intensity of the day's sunshine and Wellsted keeps watch comfortably without his jacket. By the light of a candle that is magnified only slightly by a brass ship's lamp, he writes home to Molyneux Street. Neither his father nor his grandfather can read but he knows his younger siblings, infants when he left, will have learnt, as he did in his time, and will relay the household correspondence to the older generations. 'Once a person can read,' Old Thomas said so solemnly that he could have been quoting from the Bible, 'a person can be employed to hold office, a person can marry above his station, a person can *execute wills*.' All the young Wellsteds are literate, even the girls. James' letters home are relayed, like most Arabian traffic, via Bombay and take weeks to arrive. Still, he writes regularly, never hoping for a single word coming in the other direction, for it is not the Wellsted way.

An hour or so before dawn, he smells the day's cornbread baking in the galley and his appetite is sharpened. He wonders briefly if the last supply of bitter water they managed to obtain further down the strait is responsible for the fact the coffee on board is so substandard. The water is difficult to stomach without mixing it with something, and the men have been taking it with sheep's milk. Perhaps that is the key. His mouth is watering now and his stomach grumbles — he knows there is some cheese left — hard and mostly rind, but he has a yearning for it nonetheless. He is about to make his way to the galley when Ormsby reports to take over Wellsted's duties and allow the lieutenant a few hours of sleep before the day's survey gets properly underway.

'Morning.' The lad stretches and reaches inside his jacket for his flask. He offers it, but James declines. Then, shrugging his shoulders, Ormsby takes a draught and smacks his lips as the liquor hits his bloodstream.

'Will you break your fast with me?' James offers.

65

Ormsby nods. 'Yes, sir,' he says.

'Good. We can fetch it from the galley and eat here. We'll see the sun come up. Then I must sleep, I think.'

'This weather's quite the thing for a picnic. It feels almost fresh this morning,' Ormsby smiles.

'Give it an hour or two!'

Ormsby's eyes fall to the small bottle of dark ink and the roughly made quill his superior officer has been using. His pupils shrink and he feels uncomfortable. Wellsted has been writing again. This is what has caused all the trouble and he is hoping that there will be no more. The captain has been moody for weeks on end and has taken it out on everybody.

'I'm writing home, you idiot,' the lieutenant says fondly. 'My grandfather likes to keep up. He's an invalid these days. I send a letter now and then — to keep the old boy going.'

'Ah,' Ormsby nods, though he can hardly really understand. His grandfather, after all, is a committed Christian, a Conservative and the brother of a duke, who scarcely if ever leaves his well-run and comfortable estate in Gloucestershire and would be horrified had he seen even half of what James took as read during his Marylebone childhood. The most the old man hopes from his grandsons is that they will be *good eggs*.

'Yes. My family likes the odd letter too,' Ormsby says. 'They are awfully fond of news. I should really write to them more.'

He wonders if he might see some interesting fish today — the coral reefs are teeming with brightly coloured, odd-looking marine life and Ormsby has been sketching what he sees. It keeps him amused and he is hoping, if he can learn to swim, that he will be able to make a comprehensive study of the shoals of strange creatures, for as his grandfather says, the Lord's design is in everything.

'Come on,' says Wellsted. 'There is the last of the cheese left. We can toast it on top of the oven.'

12

The very same day that Zena is auctioned off, on the kind of brisk but sunny English summer morning of which men in the desert can only dream, at his cousin's substantial, terraced, stucco mansion on Cadogan Place, William Wilberforce, a man of principle and a social pioneer, receives the news that the Bill for the Abolition of Slavery is set to pass the Commons. He celebrates by catching influenza and three days later he is dead. It is decided to bury the old man's body in Westminster Abbey, close to his venerable friend, William Pitt. He is, after all, one of Britannia's own — a national treasure. The funeral is an enormous event. Both Houses of Parliament suspend their business for the duration as a mark of respect, and most members actually attend the obsequies personally. All over the British Isles toasts to the new, enlightened age are drunk by Whigs and Tories alike and Wilberforce is universally mourned from the public house to the pulpit and back again. His obituary is read aloud at a hundred thousand breakfast tables. In Wilberforce's home town of Hull private subscriptions flood in to erect a monument one hundred feet high to his memory. Ladies across the country pray for the great man's eternal soul, dab handkerchiefs to fresh tears and furiously cross-stitch samplers of the better-known liberal maxims concerning slavery including the famous *Am I Not A Man And Your Brother?* Immediately there is earnest talk of Wilberforce's beatification, despite his personal commitment to the cause of Evangelical Anglicanism and lifelong antagonism to the Papacy. Mild-mannered, staunchly Protestant ladies in the Home Counties are heard to say, 'Still, dear Mr Wilberforce was a saint. He *was*, *wasn't he?*'

All this, however, affects business at the slave market in Muscat not one jot.

★ ★ ★

Zena is pushed into the clear space in front of the auctioneer and he calls for offers. 'Twenty,' he starts. 'Anyone at twenty?'

At first there are several low bids, two from the man who treated her harshly in the slave pen. Zena feels her chest tighten. The bidding, however, is spirited and the offers come fast. When the man drops out at fifty, she allows herself a sliver of a smile. The price continues to rise ten silver dollars at a time. Zena can hardly believe this is really happening. That she will be owned and that she is powerless to stop it. Sadness swills around her empty stomach and the world stands still. It is a curious sensation.

As the price rises above a hundred and fifty, it is between two parties. One is an Abyssinian, like herself. The man sits, still-eyed, in a litter at the side of the bazaar, only raising his black finger slightly to register his interest as the price spirals on. Her stomach surges with some kind of hope.

69

At least he looks familiar.

Yes. Him. Someone from home, she thinks silently as she stands stock-still in the sun.

The auctioneer skilfully bats the opportunity back to the other man still in the game — a blue-robed Arab pulling on a *hookah* pipe beneath an intricately fringed, white parasol.

'Two hundred dollars,' the auctioneer shouts triumphantly. 'Do I have more?'

Zena has to admit, this is a handsome price for an Abyssinian 17-year-old, who may or may not be a virgin. It is certainly more than any of the others have made.

'Have I any advance?'

There is silence. The bidding is still with the Abyssinian, who nonchalantly refuses to look at his opponent. All other eyes turn to the Arab, who considers a moment, tosses his head and refuses to go any higher.

He has got me! she thinks. *One of my own.* She wants to tell him, in her own language, where she comes from and what brought her here. Surely he has bought her because they are from a common background. Surely his house will be the same as her grandmother's, for how else would a wealthy Abyssinian run their home?

Eagerly, she lets them lead her from the podium and tether her to a post beside the clerk. There she overhears the arrangements being made for her payment and realises this man has not bought her for himself. He is a slave, only doing his master's bidding. He counts out his master's dollars.

'My name is Zena,' she says, with a rush of

70

enthusiasm. 'I come from the hills. Near Bussaba.'

The man hisses at her like a spitting snake, affronted by her impertinence. One of his attendants roughly ushers her away. She glances back at the man in slight confusion. He is still counting out her price and making his *salaams* to the auctioneer. She wonders if he was sold here himself. She wonders if he can remember what it felt like. There will be no fellow feeling, she realises sadly as she is tethered again. When the business is concluded, she follows the litter, docile and under guard with two other women, *sidis*. They come from another shipment, seemingly purchased earlier at a far lesser price. As they progress through the cramped, busy streets, Zena's appetite is so sharp and her sense of smell so elevated that the aroma drifting from the street stalls selling thick, sticky pastries hits her like an assault of honeyed sesame sweetness in the warming air while the nutty scent of coffee almost stops her dead in her tracks. She can think of nothing else. The truth is that right now she would thank someone more for a plate of food than for her freedom. The business of the marketplace is so frantic that she is diverted by the constant stream of images. *Just breathe in*, she thinks as the honeyed sweetness wafts towards her. Instinctively, she knows she must not think about what is happening or she will cry.

Not far from the palace on the front, but away from the direction of the *souk* they step through a huge wooden gate studded with dark nails.

Inside is a shady courtyard lined with blue and green tiles and dotted with huge bronze planters sprouting dark, glossy leaves interspersed by an occasional splash of garish brightness — an exotic flower or two. White archways lead away from the entrance over two storeys. Zena could swear she smells orange blossom and cinnamon and just a hint of a chicken boiling in the pot.

The litter is set beneath a date palm and the gold muslin is drawn back as the man swings his plump legs to the ground. He walks past the three women, inspecting his purchases slowly from head to foot. The one to Zena's left whimpers. She smells, Zena suddenly realises, as the other women do, of the oil used to burnish their skin — the odour is acrid, stale and unsavoury. A flicker of emotion crosses the man's face though it is impossible to read. He waves his hand airily and the two other women are led off by a male slave. Zena watches them go. Then the man walks around her again, inspecting her even more slowly.

'Bathe her,' he orders at length.

He speaks Arabic with an accent. Zena drops her head as a mark of respect. She will try to talk to him again. This time in his adopted tongue. She has to.

'Sir,' she says, 'I am very hungry. Please may I eat?'

It is an audacious request from one who has spent the past two weeks up to her ankles in excrement, sleeping only periodically, propped up against a black-tongued corpse. Worse, it is a request from one who is a mere chattel and who has already been berated for even talking. But she cannot stand it any longer.

'You speak Arabic? Ha!' the black man laughs, though what comes out of his mouth sounds more like a dry bark.

He has no heart to laugh with, Zena thinks, but instead she tells him where she learnt the language they are speaking. 'My grandmother taught me. In her house she had guests who were traders and I learnt to talk to them.'

'That is good. Good,' his brown eyes widen, pleased at his luck. 'You speak the tongue — you are a bargain.'

He smells of butter and honey and Zena is so hungry that she would willingly lick his skin.

'Please, sir,' she ventures, emboldened by the conversation, blurting out the question. 'What are my duties here?'

The man stares blankly. 'I was once a stranger too. I came from the marketplace. You will work hard here. Your master is a great man — you will work to please him.'

He does not tell her she can rise in the household as he has done. He is anticipating that he will win his freedom soon, as some slaves do, having proved their worth as family retainers. He will never leave the service of his master, but he will not be owned, or indentured, he will be a free man — a *huss*. He does not mention it. There is no point. After all, this slave is merely a woman and, apart from her beauty, and now the advantage she will have because she speaks Arabic, she has fewer uses than a skilled person like himself. His master has bought her only as a bauble and as she gets older her decorative effect will diminish and her value lessen.

'What work will I do, sir?'

Another dry bark. 'Nursemaid, *habshi*,' the man says.

Zena feels an immense wave of relief wash over her. She has no experience with children, but nonetheless it sounds like an easier job than many who have been bought that morning will face in the afternoon. She smiles.

'Feed her,' the man orders as he turns away. 'Then bathe her.'

★ ★ ★

Four black slave women guide Zena through an archway into the house. Through a series of shady passages their strong arms shepherd her without touching her skin. She smells the roasting meat and the baking bread so keenly that she almost breaks into a run. The slaves speak a mysterious African language that sounds like music — a cacophony of clicks and long vowels that soothes. Zena does not understand but it is clear where she is meant to go. Their chatter heightens the pace. This house is a maze, a labyrinthine warren of passages. It crosses her mind that she will never know what is around the corner here — there is no pattern. The place is vast and sprawling — one long corridor turning the corner into another short one, one room locked and another without a door at all. After two or three minutes of increasingly fragrant and warm corridors they cut into a huge room, lit by high windows. At last — it is the kitchen. For a moment, the group hovers in the doorway.

After being shipbound and starved, the delicious fecundity, the sheer generosity of the provisions on display seem an impossibility to Zena and she is stunned. Hand-hammered, bronze pots hang from the ceiling. On a table as far away as possible from the fire, fruits are laden onto wide, clay ashettes. It is all Zena can do not to rush over and reach for a pomegranate, sink her teeth into the ruby-coloured flesh and let the sweet juice run down her chin as she sucks it dry. A bough of dark, succulent grapes, trailing its leaves, is propped against a clay bowl of oranges with glossy foliage, darker in contrast to the vine. Bunches of fragrant mint fresh from the farm stalls of Muttrah hang above from a shelf of honey jars and preserved nuts that are so close she swears she can almost taste them. Around the oven, two thin boys are baking pitta bread, which they pile onto a huge, bronze sheet. A dead animal is butchered by a fat man with a cleaver. His bare chest is speckled with bone and blood as he flings the pieces of meat into a wooden box of marinade that smells of lemon, garlic and chilli. And overseeing it all, a huge Nubian chef is directing all the work, while kneading a handful of pale pastry with fat fingers that send clouds of flour into the air over his head and dust his figure into a ghost-like apparition.

Zena's knees feel suddenly weak and she thinks she might faint until one of the slaves fetches a bone cup of milk and a small dish of thin gruel with a long-handled spoon and some dry *zahidi* dates. She remembers to thank the man, only just, nodding and clasping her hands in a pantomime of gratitude, before she falls, open-mouthed and ravenous, upon the meagre meal, her stomach retching at the sudden plenty, her throat swallowing at the same time. Tears stream down her cheeks. There has never been a meal more delicious. As she rouses herself from it, the cup drained dry and the plate empty, she notices that they have all just stood there and watched her gorge herself, sucking in the food, almost without chewing. Licking her fingers of the remnants, she feels suddenly ashamed. The other slaves show no emotion. *Perhaps they never felt the same hunger*, Zena thinks as the crockery is taken from her with dead-eyed efficiency and without skipping a beat the party moves on, back through the unnavigable passageways of the house.

She knows they will wash her next.

I wonder what the children will be like? she thinks and she places a hand on her full belly as she follows the party upwards to the tiled bath-house, replete with a brazier for making steam.

The water is tepid. It feels cool in the heat of the day and makes a delicate trickling noise as the old woman scoops it up in a glazed clay jar and then pours it over Zena's hair. Another girl, not much older than herself, mixes oil of lemon with oil of thyme and thickens it with date paste. It is as if she is being basted — prepared for the pot. The efficient hands simply do their work, sponging her, soothing and anointing her skin with oil, combing out her long plaits and resetting her hair into a smooth coil. They are neither gentle nor rough and they say nothing. Zena asks, first in her own language then in Arabic, what they are doing, where she will be taken next, what the family is like.

'Please,' she says, 'tell me about this place.'

But not one of the slaves even acknowledges that they understand what she is saying and she gives up and simply allows them to pummel her clean.

When a slave arrives bearing a diaphanous, aquamarine *kaftan* of fine, silken gauze, Zena does not even wonder. Who can say what is unusual in such a place and what is common? The others are dressed in plain, pale robes of rough cotton, but what does that mean? Surely personal servants of the family merit a more luxurious uniform than common house servants. The hands dry her with white linen and as she slips into the dress they bind up her hair in a golden turban and draw leather sandals onto her feet, instructing each other in the strange musical language that Zena cannot understand. After the *dhow* and the slave market this is heaven — no matter that they are only doing what their superior has bid them. No matter that they do not acknowledge her in any way.

★   ★   ★

Before dusk, Zena is delivered to a room on the first floor that smells faintly of incense. There is a wide bed, a carved screen, an ornate rug with velvet cushions of red and yellow scattered about it, a window covered with a wooden shutter and evenly spaced brass lamps ready to be lit for the evening. Beside the bed there lies a covered flask of water flavoured with mint, a box containing rose jelly and another of honeyed pistachios. Zena inspects everything and then sits on the bed. It does not seem like a child's room. She waits until the *muezzin* has made the call to prayer. She waits until the sun has sunk from the sky and it is absolutely dark. The scent of night flowers wafts in through the window on the perfumed air from tubs far below outside — moonflowers, nicotiana and jasmine. She desperately tries not to doze but her belly is full, her skin is silken and the cushions are tempting. In the end, she succumbs and cannot help but fall fast, fast asleep.

What raises her is a strange noise. A cackle. She jumps up into the pitch darkness, panicked, and it takes her a second or two to realise where she is. She trips over a small table and then recovers her balance. Then in a flash she remembers.

Before her there is a man in the doorway carrying a torch that flickers in the breeze from the window. The bright flame sends strange shadows over his face so that she cannot tell what he really looks like. But he is finely dressed in a long, bright robe. His dark hair flows like a woman's and when he smiles he has the teeth of an animal, white, bared and ready. He cackles again — the sound a hyena might make, or a dog. Zena falls to her knees.

'*Salaam*,' she whispers, drawing her hands together in supplication and raising her eyes only high enough to see that he wears an array of gold rings on his long fingers.

'They sent you?' the man asks.

Zena nods and looks up at him. 'I was bought today. In the marketplace.'

The man laughs and beckons her towards him. Now she can see that he is younger than she first thought — perhaps twenty or so. He motions her to turn around so he can inspect her.

'What did you fetch?'

'Two hundred dollars, I think.'

He casts his eye over her coldly. 'They think this will tempt me,' he says in a derisory tone, but the comment is not directed at Zena — he is talking to himself and has turned away. He puts down the lamp and proceeds to sit on the plump cushions by the window, picking up a sweet from the rosewood box and chewing it as he mulls things over.

'Light, girl!' he calls.

Zena hovers for a moment behind him, and then realising that he means her, she springs into action, taking the lamp from the low table and lighting the others one by one. The room gradually takes on a buttery glow. She can see now that the man's silken *jubbah* is edged with intricate embroidery and that he wears gold earrings in a low loop in addition to his collection of rings. His eyes are pitch black — the darkest she has ever seen. She lays the lamp once more on the low table and steps back to wait for another order. But, before one can be given, the door opens and a slave boy enters. Taken back at the sight of Zena, he retreats slightly.

'Ah, come in, Sam. Come in. Don't worry about her,' the man says, his dark eyes turning from the view across the midnight city and back into the room again.

His gaze, Zena notices, is suddenly bright. The slave boy has skin as black as Zena's own. He crosses to his master and kneels beside him. The man's jewelled hand falls languidly onto the boy's shoulder and then runs down the smooth skin of his strong, well-defined arm, stroking with surprising gentleness.

'A nursemaid,' Zena realises. 'They wanted me because . . .'

The boy raises his eyes towards her. 'Is it your wish for this *habshi* to watch us, Master?' he asks.

The man cackles once more. He leans down and kisses the boy on the lips.

'Go!' he says over his shoulder without even looking at her. 'Leave me!'

Zena bows and leaves the room as gracefully as she can manage but in the hallway she hovers. Her mind is racing. She doesn't know where she ought to go. She cannot remember the direction of the bathhouse or the kitchen. The household is asleep and the maze of hallways is dark and silent. There is no one around so she crouches against the wall and decides to wait. The master, may, after all, call for her when he has finished.

13

Jessop has thoroughly enjoyed his stay at the encampment. He has made notes about the *Bedu* and their way of life, the details of the trading routes of the tribe and their customs of war and has even managed some observations on the way one family interweaves with another. The site is temporary, of course. The *Bedu* are set to graze their animals there till only saltbush remains. The wells fill up once a season and the *Bedu* will stay to drink the water dry and then move on. The tents are comfortable enough though and, like most nomads, the tribe is hospitable to a fault. An Arabic tribesman will go hungry himself in order to feed his guests lavishly. It is well known that if you come across a camp in the desert and are accepted as a guest, you'll always be fed better than the people who actually live there.

By the third and final day, the doctor is gratified to see that there is a marked improvement in all but one little girl who, Jessop now fears, might well lose her sight as the infection progresses. Clearly it had advanced too far by the time he arrived and he knows there is little more he can do for the child but clean the pus and hope her body might rally. The danger is septicaemia, blood poisoning. If the little girl succumbs to it she will almost certainly die. He has tried to transmit this information but fears it loses something in the translation. The devoted mother, meanwhile, has placed a copy of the *Quran* under the girl's sleeping rug and spits into the child's face to clean it (starting Jessop all over again on the painful process of the vinegar eye wash). Now, leaving her daughter in the care of others, the woman has taken to following Jessop, entreating him to save her daughter in the same way he worked his magic on the other children. No amount of explanation or reassuring smiles and hand gestures seems to communicate that he can do no more, and she neglects her domestic duties and hovers in her dark *burquah*, a little behind the white men, occasionally breaking into a keening wail that makes Jones start.

'I do wish she'd stop that!' he says. 'Bloody hullabaloo.'

Jessop fans himself with a flat square made of rushes. He realised early on, even before they left Sur, that his concerns are different from Jones' and he has now become tired of the repeated conversation about breeding strains and fetlocks, shipping livestock via Bombay, how much a chap might need to furnish a Knightsbridge house decently or fix its leaking roof and how Arabia has little to offer civilisation.

Today is their last in the encampment and Jessop wishes he could discuss what he has found with Jones, but the lieutenant will not engage in conversation on any other topic than those most dear to his wallet. Still, it has become clear the more Jessop uncovers about conditions inland, the more difficult supplying any reasonable traffic of British ships seems to be. Both water supplies and tribal territories shift with such alarming regularity that he has come to the conclusion that the business of resupply might need to be assessed almost every time a British ship docks and treaties of alliance would have to be constantly renegotiated. It was hoped matters might prove more stable here than on the coast, but from his enquiries he now understands that if anything they are less so and there is very little out here in the hinterland anyway — it makes no sense even to use the place to ferry supplies. It is simply too dangerous and travelling through the desert has proved painfully slow. He'll be glad to get back to the coast and rendezvous with the *Palinurus* when it comes back down from the inhospitable north.

Preparations are underway for the party's departure. The *Dhofaris* are making sure the camels drink as much as possible before the return journey and both Jessop and Jones are wordlessly steeling themselves for the privations of the trip. There is little enough to pack and, apart from overseeing the animals, the bearers and guides lounge drinking coffee, picking their teeth with *araq* and sharing the last of their supplies of *qat* leaves, which they chew open-mouthed. Stimulated by the effects, they argue over nothing in particular for hours while the *Bedu* avoid them. The tribes are not enemies, nor are they friends, Jessop notes in his diary. At prayer time, the *Dhofaris* and the *Bedu* lay down their mats separately, at meals they skirt around the edges of the other's group. They have not travelled together and so the oath of the caravan where one traveller will fight to the death for another and all are brothers does not apply.

On the last night, Jessop and Jones eat in the big tent, sitting on huge, hard pillows grouped around a central, low table piled high with food so laden with fat that it shines in the dim light from the oil lamps. The *Bedu* carry naphtha, harvested easily from the surface of the infertile plain and distilled into a crude fuel for lamplight, which smells faintly medicinal. 'Arabia,' Jones maintains, 'consists of land either too desiccated for cultivation or too poisonous. It is as well that God has given them *naft* for they could not afford candles.'

The emir and his eldest son sit to one side — the officers are cross-legged on the other. The boy has scarcely started to grow his beard, but he is accepted by the men of the camp as a leader in waiting. He is, after all, the son of a great man and wishes that he could be lost on the sands and make a name for himself, as his father did. The men respect his lineage and his pluck even though, as yet, he has had the opportunity to prove neither. He spends more time now with the adults than the other children and as a result has not succumbed to the eye infection, or at least, has not had kohl applied to his eyes by the solicitous woman who started the spread of the sickness.

'Your people do not pray?' the emir asks Jessop, as if in passing.

So far, the emir has answered the doctor's questions but has shown little interest of his own. This last night, the atmosphere feels stilted and the doctor is glad that the emir has thought

84

to make an enquiry or at least start a conversation.

'Ah. No. We do not pray as you do — five times a day.'

For a long time, the emir does not respond. After the silence has started to drag he turns again to the white men. 'And you eat pig? Drink the grape?'

A grin breaks out on the doctor's face. 'Yes. Yes, all my people do.' He reaches into the bag he always carries with him and helpfully pulls out a picture of King William on the face of a decorative, enamel miniature. The likeness shows His Majesty at his coronation a mere three years before.

'This is our shah,' he explains, 'our caliph. Sultan, perhaps. We call him a king.' Jessop is unaware that carrying this manner of representational likeness is deeply offensive to followers of Islam and tantamount to idolatry. The emir's son glances sideways at his father to see what he might do, but the emir affects scarcely to notice the miniature.

'Your shah is powerful? He has many camels? Many horses?'

'Ah,' Jones cuts in. 'Yes. His Majesty King William loves horses.'

This is, in fact, not strictly true. His Majesty is a sailor rather than a landlubber and his concerns are largely marine. In the main, he becomes enthusiastic about horses only if the animals are racing and he has taken a bet. But the comment at least brings the conversation round to a subject upon which Jones wishes to elaborate and he grasps upon it, becoming suddenly quite animated.

'I am sure His Majesty would be most impressed by an animal of the tenor of your fine beasts. The sultan kindly sent him an Arab horse last year from Muscat and His Majesty by all accounts is completely taken by the creature.'

The emir does not rise to the suggestion. He reaches out and picks at some gleaming couscous that has been piled before him. As he raises it to his lips there is a terrible sound. At first Jessop thinks there has been a stir that has woken the animals but as the ululation starts up in earnest he realises it is the women. They are screaming in chorus. No, not screaming, not really. It is more as if they are *singing* their screams. A slave enters the tent, slips to the emir's side and leans, as discreetly as any footman at Windsor Castle, to whisper in the emir's ear. The couscous stops in midair. The emir's face, if it is possible, becomes stonier. He looks at Jessop and Jones and Jessop thinks fleetingly that being caught in his gaze is like being a butterfly pinned to a board. He has a terrible sinking feeling in his stomach and a sudden longing for his matchlock, which is safely stowed in his saddle bags, with ample ammunition, ready for the journey they will start before dawn. He wishes fervently that it was nearer to hand.

'I say,' says Jones, now outside the tent where he can see the *Dhofaris* scattering like buckshot into the night. 'Whatever is going on?'

Jessop makes to rise but a heavy weight bearing down on his shoulders renders it impossible. Suddenly it is as if darkness closes in on the tent, the polished scimitars, like lightning bolts, the only brightness. It is hard to tell exactly how many men are in the shadows drawing their traditional, curved knives.

'*Ibn al-kalb*,' the emir growls. '*Nazarene ala aeeri. Ya binti. Ya binti.*'

'Your daughter?' Jessop asks, picking out the word. 'Why? What has happened?'

'*Ya binti. Ya binti*,' the emir repeats darkly in his distress as the eyes of his son flash in horror and the hideous sound of the keening women in the background grows ever louder and more frantic.

And after that, it all goes dark.

★ ★ ★

When Jessop and Jones wake again they are bound to each other with a rough cord. Shifting, they each notice that their muscles are stiff and sore and that they are thirsty. The atmosphere in the tent is stifling. Slowly Jessop comes to realise that they are being held on the far side of the settlement and that the tent has been pitched quite deliberately in the full glare of the sun. The *Dhofaris* have gone, their animals are forfeit and it will be hours before they are given water, never mind food.

'I don't understand,' Jones sinks into self-pity with an ease that does not entirely surprise his fellow officer.

'It's the little girl,' Jessop explains. 'I think the little girl died.'

87

14

The *Palinurus* waits for more than a week in the blinding heat for the officers to arrive at Aden. While the crew repair the sun-bleached decks, Haines paces and waits with the single-minded bad temper that is now all too familiar to everyone on board.

'They should have been here at least a week before us,' he keeps repeating, as if a mistake has been made deliberately, only to bait him.

The *Dhofaris* at port evade questioning like petulant teenagers and it is clear that there is no measure in pushing any of that tribe for more information for neither violence, nor courtesy nor bribery has any measure of success.

'I don't know, sir,' they say over and over again, denying all knowledge of the British expedition.

A man on the street, a trader, a beggar, an *imam*, the son of a caliph — it makes no difference who the captain asks or what he offers — they simply smile and wave him off. Frustratingly, there is no way of telling if any of the men at port were part of Jessop and Jones' expedition as they hired their own hands.

'I know they are lying, the bastards,' Haines swears. 'They know. They just won't tell us.'

The general consensus is that he is right. But no one is sure what to do about it. After two days of fruitless enquiries, Wellsted steps up.

'Please, sir,' he petitions the captain on deck. 'May I have permission to head inland?'

Haines blusters. The midshipmen look at each other. The hands simply stare at the captain, their shadows cast long in the midday sun. This is the kind of conversation that should be confined in officers' quarters, but Wellsted is not welcome in the captain's cabin. Haines is about to berate the lieutenant when he realises where that conversation will lead.

'If I can get inland I'll pick up the *Bedu*,' Wellsted continues. 'They'll know what's happened. We must try something else, surely.'

The *Bedu* are the gossips of the desert. Everyone knows that. Haines takes a draw on his pipe and blows the smoke close to Wellsted's face in defiance. He is determined not to lose his temper in front of the entire ship nor, if it comes to that, his dignity.

'Yes, and I'll forfeit you next, Wellsted, and return to port with not one fully trained officer in my crew,' he sneers as if Wellsted is laying a trap for his reputation.

'I won't go far, sir. Just to where the desert meets the coastal territory. It might take two or three days at most. We're stuck here anyway.'

Haines considers. He looks over the tatty rooftops of Aden and up into the hills. He wishes he had sent Wellsted instead of Jessop on what it is now clear has been a doomed mission.

'We owe them that at least, sir. An investigation of a couple of days?'

Haines taps out his pipe. He will have to account in Bombay for the decision he makes here, and Wellsted will be in his rights to make it known that he requested permission to search further and that the captain deemed it unnecessary. That might look shabby. Haines tries to think what Moresby would do.

'Oh very well,' he snaps. 'You'll go alone. No more than two days and the first sign of trouble and you get back here.'

★   ★   ★

At the camp inland, at the crossroads where the trade from the sea meets the trade from the sands, Wellsted makes his *salaams*. A white man is a curiosity here, though unlike further north where they are considered a threat, these travellers are men of the world — they have seen most things before. At the oasis news is swapped easily no matter the colour of your skin. After all, only a fool does not want to know what he is travelling into.

Wellsted drinks the obligatory coffee and eats sweet, lush, *mujhoolah* dates with the other men. The tribesmen laugh at the story of his first attempts to ride a camel and marvel at the length of the journey across the sea from Southampton. Wellsted knows this swapping of tales is an important part of the bond of the campfire. He also knows that the closer in time to an event and closer in geography, the less opportunity there is for hyperbole to take over. So when the men tell him they heard that a party of two infidels, lead by *Dhofari* guides, have offended the emir and are now taken and

90

at his disposal, he believes them.

'Do you know their names? What do they look like? Are they alive?'

The *Bedu* are nonchalant. They sip the coffee slowly and speak without intonation, for noisy or enthusiastic banter is considered low bred. They do not know any names for the *Nazarene* or if the men are still alive. Their news is a fortnight old at least. Who can tell what might have come to pass by now? One of the men has golden hair though, that much is certain. And (here a shrug of the shoulder) the other hurt the emir's daughter.

Wellsted cannot imagine Jessop being stupid enough to dishonour a woman in a camp where he is receiving hospitality. The doctor is a gentleman in every sense of the word. However, he is delighted that on last sighting at least, Jessop and Jones are alive.

* * *

'And what are you expecting us to do now? Hare off across the desert on a wild-goose chase?' Haines is incandescent with rage when Wellsted reports to him. 'The natives are raving. Storytelling round a campfire. And even if it's true, Jessop and Jones are probably dead by now,' he insists. 'Bound to be. I'd say their guides did for them. That's what I reckon. Jessop had instruments worth a fortune.'

The captain prefers the certainty of a blood-and-guts beheading by the savages of the ancient sea. Wellsted realises the man has been overly influenced by the fundamentalism of the *Wahabis* further to the north. Their threatening behaviour, all heavily armed, wild promises of doom, dark beards and flashing eyes are a jumble of aggression that has coloured the captain's view of every Musselman in the Peninsula. Now he does not appear to grasp the difference between the tribes or at least does not apply any such knowledge to his judgements. Still, the idea of a band of renegade *Dhofaris* does not hold water with Wellsted if for no other reason than the guides' bonuses for any trip are always payable on return to the coast.

'The *Dhofaris* are business minded and largely liberal,' he points out.

'You are dismissed, Lieutenant,' the captain snaps.

After a week waiting at Aden to no avail, it is clear that Haines is so ill-disposed towards Wellsted that the lieutenant wonders if he ought to have presented his findings as the result of an enquiry made by one of the midshipmen. He keeps his peace for whatever he says only provokes outrage. Still, the captain clearly does not feel comfortable abandoning the search entirely.

'We will continue to Muscat,' he announces. 'There may be news there.'

It is, for everyone on board, a relief to cast off.

★   ★   ★

After a brief rendezvous with the *Benares* during which Wellsted is forbidden to attend the

92

officers' dinner, the sight of Muscat harbour is welcome to every soul aboard the *Palinurus*, and all for entirely different reasons. The truth is that in the wake of the malaria many of the crew had not anticipated making it back around the Peninsula alive and, having unexpectedly done so, they are only too delighted to be able to avail themselves of the illicit grog shop that trades from the back of one of the old warehouses down on the docks.

Wellsted, however, has not given up on the missing officers and, refusing to discuss the matter with the midshipmen, who have taken to asking him questions they ought to reserve for their commanding officer, the lieutenant obtains leave to go ashore. With the ship safely at anchor and his duties complete, Wellsted strides out from the dock and makes for the office of the Navy's agent in Muscat, hoping that the man might have some contacts that will help in the search. Haines' priority is to dispatch a report on a clipper that is to leave for Bombay directly but that, Wellsted cannot help thinking, is more about covering the captain in his decisions than actually finding out what happened to his men.

As he strides out, he ignores the stares a white man in naval uniform necessarily excites on the crowded streets of the capital. He ignores too the pressing heat of his well-tailored jacket as he passes through the stripes of sunshine and shade. He is not under orders but that matters little to him — he simply wants to know what has happened, not only for Jessop and Jones' sakes, but also because it's important to build up his knowledge of the Peninsula and how things work here. In fact, if he is to make his name, it is vital. By hook or by crook. Whatever it takes.

The agent's office is a modest, whitewashed, two-storey house a little way up the hill and beyond the frantic press of streets that make up the dockside district. The man's name is Ali Ibn Mudar and he has served the interests of the Indian Navy for the best part of twenty years, for which he receives a hefty retainer in addition to the proceeds of the thriving business he runs as a trader in textiles, particularly silks. These two activities dovetail well and Ibn Mudar's ships often obtain preferential treatment when they come into contact with Indian Navy vessels. Ibn Mudar speaks perfect English. He has, it is rumoured, a European wife, captured from a shipwreck some years before and bought at an astronomical price for his *harim*. This lady has never been seen in public and no one knows if the rumours are true, but if it is she who has tutored Ibn Mudar in what can only be assumed is her native tongue, she has done a good job; he speaks English, somewhat comically though, with a heavy Irish accent. For this reason he is known in Bombay, exclusively behind his back, as Mickey Ibn Mudar or Our Dear Mickey. That notwithstanding, the agent is considered well-connected, helpful and courteous, and although Wellsted has never met him before, he has high hopes as he knocks on the sun-bleached front door and waits.

Inside, he is shown into a cool, tiled courtyard by a young slave boy in a robe as yellow as a canary, his eyelashes so long that they could dust the ceilings of their cobwebs. The boy offers Wellsted a copper bowl of cool water and rose petals in which to make his ablutions. He does so noticing how much better he feels only a little way out of the oppressive heat. Then, courteously, the slave ushers him upstairs and Ibn Mudar welcomes the young lieutenant into his office on the first floor. The slatted wooden shutters keep the room shady and warmed by the sun, and also give out a pleasant aroma of sandalwood. Between the slats and cut-out stars there are glimpses of an impressive view over the bay. To one side there is a large, cedarwood desk with scrolls of accounts and ledgers stored behind it on a series of intricately carved, wooden shelves and burr cubby holes. On the other side there is a comfortable seating area with low, embroidered cushions and goatskin throws. This is not the agent's home, however. That is far grander and much higher up the hill. He prefers to keep his working life separate, always has.

As the man smiles and rises to greet his visitor, Wellsted quickly notes that Ibn Mudar's plain *jubbah* is made of very fine cotton — curiously unshowy given that the main part of his income comes from a textile business. The lieutenant considers mentioning his own family's background in the same trade but deems it inappropriate. Instead, he sizes up the Navy's agent silently. Ibn Mudar, with a greying beard, in his mid-fifties, is only slightly overweight and his eyes seem to take in everything and give nothing away. He clears his throat to make his *salaams*, but he does not invoke Allah. The custom in this office is the same as it would be in Liverpool or Southampton so the Navy's representative reaches out to shake Wellsted firmly by the hand and smiles.

'How do you do? I was to send to the ship shortly, you know. Would you partake of a coffee, Lieutenant?'

Wellsted does not laugh, though not to do so is an effort. The man's accent is as thick as treacle. He might as well be from Cork. 'Thank you. I would enjoy a coffee.'

The agent waves a hand and his slave disappears to fetch what is needed as the men sit down together on the pile of cushions on the floor. Wellsted likes him immediately. There is something cut and dried about this man and competent too. Our Dear Mickey feels like an apt moniker.

'You have come for your letter from London, have you?' Mickey says.

Wellsted starts. He has, in his whole time in the service, never received a personal letter. It is an amazement that such an item has found him here.

'From London?' he repeats, the shock showing in his voice.

His heart races with the realisation that this could be a momentous turn of events — is it possible that Murray has already responded to his manuscript? Surely it will take longer than this, but then who knows the ways of the famous publisher? It has, he counts the weeks, probably been long enough. With surprise, he notes that his palm feels suddenly sticky and his stomach flutters nervously.

Mickey reaches into a large, burnished box beside his cushion and passes a folded envelope franked in Mayfair. Wellsted breaks the small, red seal. Inside, the handwriting is haphazard — not what he would expect from a man of Murray's education and renown. Wellsted takes a deep breath, comprehending that this missive is even more momentous than one that might contain John Murray's comments on his account of the Socotra trip. This letter has emanated from his family home in Molyneux Street and is dated in May — two months ago.

Dear Brother,
I regret to inform you that after some months of suffering our grandfather has died. We buried him at the parish church a week past. Apart from this sad news all is well here. Edward has taken the oath to be a customs man at Greenwich. Please when you write now, address yourself to our father.
Most sincerely,
Your brother,
Thomas Wellsted Jnr

James turns the paper over. It seems unnecessarily brief. He remembers young Thomas as an infant only just out of his nappies and rosy-cheeked, learning to climb out of the cot — a child as he had been in the year James

Wellsted left home. For a moment James indulges himself, wondering what the boy looks like now or if, indeed, there might be more infants that followed his departure and he has nameless brothers and sisters growing up in his parents' home. A Charles perhaps. Even an Emily or Elizabeth.

Mickey allows a pause long enough for Wellsted to take in his news, whatever it may be. 'All is well in London, I hope,' the agent says gently.

'News of home, that is all,' Wellsted dismisses the letter briskly, pushing it into his pocket. He has no time for personal matters or at least he never makes any. 'I did not come for the letter,' he admits. 'I am here on another more serious matter. We have two officers gone missing in the interior. They were led across the *jabel* and into the desert by *Dhofari* guides to visit the *Bedu* several weeks ago. Dr Jessop who was our ship's surgeon and First Lieutenant Jones. They missed their rendezvous and have not been heard of since. We docked at every decent-sized port along the coast but have found out very little, though outside Aden I encountered a group of *Bedu*. I heard the men were prisoners of the emir — that they had offended him in some way and were being held in his caravan. The description the *Bedu* gave was consistent with the appearance of the men though the captain — Captain Haines, that is — believes them dead. When we made rendezvous with the *Benares* however, Captain Moresby was of the view that we must be sure.'

Mickey scratches his cheek with a long, carefully manicured finger, which sports a thick ring of yellow gold with a red stone embedded on the face. He takes a sip of his strong coffee.

'Captured by an emir's caravan and held there? Now that's not good. I will make enquiries,' he says. 'Leave it with me, Lieutenant Wellsted, and I will see what I can find out.'

'It is a matter of some urgency, sir.'

Ibn Mudar bows. 'Of course. Immediately.'

With the efficiency of a man who is used to getting a great deal done, Ibn Mudar calls his slave boy.

'Bring me Rashid,' he snaps. The yellow-robed child immediately disappears to find the chief clerk, who is stationed at Mickey's warehouse, a few streets away.

Wellsted's cup is refilled and the agent asks polite questions.

'And your work? How goes the survey?'

'Slow but sure,' Wellsted grins. 'The reefs are all but impossible but the charts are coming along.'

'Any French vessels?'

This is of interest to any trader with ships on the nearby seas.

'Only very close to the Egyptian coastline. Where you would expect, really.'

'It will be good to have maps,' Mickey points out and Wellsted says nothing in reply, only downs the rest of his coffee.

'Do you think they might still be alive?' he asks.

The agent's face does not alter its expression

one iota. 'My brothers would say it is in Allah's hands,' he says. 'Let me see if I can find out what Allah has in mind. I will send Rashid the moment he comes. He is the man for this job. Leave it to me.'

The men shake hands and Mickey sees the lieutenant to the door of his office.

★ ★ ★

While he waits, Mickey strokes his thick, salt-and-pepper beard and retreats back onto the comfortable cushions in the corner of the room to consider matters. The British survey interests him tremendously, for if it is successful there will be a far greater volume of English ships in the Red Sea and he will be contracted to see to their needs. He is determined to do his job well for the English. Mickey is inclined to do everything well — he is careful and fastidious in all his dealings. He will apply this to the search for Jessop and Jones — which potentially, he realises, is one of the most dangerous situations with which he has been asked to help. Men die all the time, but kidnap is a different matter.

Watch out, he says to himself. *God knows what they are up to, the tricky bastards. And now there are two of them missing.*

When Mickey thinks of the English, the voice in his head is always that of his Irish wife, Farida, who maintains that without question the English are untrustworthy. Her tribe, it seems, are perpetually at war with the lily-skinned sailors, though they share the same tongue. Mickey trusts Farida's judgement. He was young when he bought her at auction after she had been captured on a shipwreck. He was a brash, young buck of a merchant of twenty who had made his fortune quickly. He wanted to show the world that he was cosmopolitan and he knew an exotic, white-skinned beauty in his *harim* would make his name as much as any bale of fine silk ever had. There was no question of love. When he met her, however, he realised just how much he had focussed all his attention on his business and how little he knew of the world beyond it. At first he expected she resented being captured and sold, but she told him frankly after only a fortnight, that his house was a hundred times the size of the cottage in Rowgaranne, County Cork, where she was brought up, that she had spent much of her young life there hungry, cold and in want and that she would gladly stay in his beautiful *harim*, especially as his wife.

The land of white men still seems to Mickey like a fairy-tale kingdom. The landscape Farida describes is undoubtedly accurate and yet it is so outlandish. She swears on her life that Cork is so rainy that much of the land is bog, and so cold that sometimes when it rains the drops freeze solid. He finds this particularly difficult to imagine — Mickey, for all that he is a trader, has never left the south of the Arabian Peninsula and the thought of freezing, squelching mud flats is almost incomprehensible to him. That the people who live in such a place should subsist on potatoes and that spice is almost unheard of is bizarre. In fact, he finds the lack of camels and gazelles in the stories his wife tells of her homeland profoundly eerie. And the infidels have such strange names — Macgregor, McLean and O'Donnell.

'Why, you are silly,' Farida laughs, dismissing him with a wave of her elegant, snow-white hand. 'That's only your *Ibn*. Macgregor is the son of Gregor (that is the name of the man who taught me to read — our priest at home) and O'Donnell (which is my name, you know) is Son of Donnell. It's exactly the same as yours — Ibn Mudar — the son of Mudar. Or Ibn Rashid is the son of Rashid. The word Ibn is only O or Mac in English, or rather in the Gaelic. We shan't go into the Fitzes now, my dear. But it's only a way of identifying your family — like all names. Don't you see?'

★　★　★

At first Mickey can't get used to it — European languages simply have too many consonants. He is certain that he'll never become fully accustomed to the sound.

'You Arabian lads,' Farida continues, 'have great swagger and no mistake. We only call our chief soldiers, our boxers and wrestlers The Knife or The Hurricane. Whereas you fellas have legions of names like that — serious fellas can be Al this or Al that. The Dog, The Thief, The Lion. Well, fair play to you, I say. You're warriors one and all. You can be my Ali Ibn Mudar, Ali Al Malik — Ali the King. I am your possession now, after all, and you my master, like royalty.'

Mickey kisses his wife hotly on the lips. She is a wonderful woman. She has taken to his household far more easily than could have ever been hoped and, better still, she is a boon in business. Farida has no qualms about Arabian manners or customs and her open-mindedness rubs off on her husband, who finds himself more and more intrigued by her tales. His world is opening up.

The strangest thing of all though is that in Farida's country, it seems, men only take one wife. Or, as she says with a characteristic giggle, 'One wife at a time'. This shocks Mickey to the core — it seems such a barbaric practice.

'But what happens to the other women the man desires?' he says.

'Exactly, my boy,' Farida grins. 'Now in these parts here you have what I would term a practicable system. I can see this working out very nicely indeed.'

Over the years she has remained indescribably foreign for all her aptitudes and the whole-hearted fashion in which she has adopted her new, Arabian life. While his other brown-eyed beauties scent themselves interminably with exotic oils, coil their hair into glossy ringlets and dote on the nursery of children that they have produced, Farida or Fanny as she originally wished to be called, on her very first day demanded pen and ink to draw pictures of the plants in Mickey's courtyard garden and write reams of descriptive prose and poetry. Within six months of her arrival, the Pearl, as he has come to call her, is speaking Arabic like a master at the university. She reads and memorises long portions of the *Quran* and fashions herself a set of silk garments from the *harim's* stock of materials that prove to be deeply enticing to Mickey O'Mudar.

'Never been without a bodice. Not going to feckin' start now,' she says.

Mickey never can tell what she is going to do next, what she might read or what strange ideas she will voice. The thing he likes about her most, though, is the fact that she is clearly interested in pleasing herself as much as she pleases him — both in bed and out of it. This is an irresistible challenge after years of women bred to compliance. Farida is a matchless pearl indeed and, illuminated by the spark of independence that is so natural to her alongside her fierce intelligence, she stimulates him body and mind. It does not matter to him one jot that in all the years she has not borne him a child. In fact, it adds to her allure, her difference from his other wives. It is also probably the only reason why the other women in the *harim* accept the strange, pale-skinned foreigner. She is not — as far as they are concerned — competition, for she has no son to compete with their own. She is, they think, a mere dalliance to keep Mickey amused.

'Do you mind?' he asks her.

'Well you can't say we haven't given it a good enough shot,' she giggles.

He loves her all the more for being so contented. Farida has the admirable ability of being able to adapt and he'd never be where he is today if it wasn't for her. It was Farida after all who made the navy job possible. He might not have taken it had she not encouraged him.

When he tells her of the opportunity that has presented itself, Farida makes no judgement on his lack of manliness in sharing his concerns — she takes it in her stride as easily as she has taken their habit of discussing literature and art (also, now he comes to think of it, unusual).

'Well now,' she sips a glass of rose-water and pomegranate juice and contemplates Mickey's smooth, chestnut skin as he lies naked beside her on purple, satin sheets that she picked herself from the lavish stock of textiles available to all his women. 'Into bed with the English is it, eh? Well, my advice, dear husband, is to take their money. They have acres of money, the English. Take their money and charge them plenty, treat them fair — true to yourself — but never trust them. Individually they are fine, I'm sure, but as a nation they'll stab you in the back as soon as look at you. My father, God bless him, used to say there are four things you can never trust — a bull's horn, a dog's tooth, a horse's hoof and an Englishman's smile. And a man such as yourself, a fine man with brown skin, is worth even less to them than a penniless Catholic. Remember that, my darling, whatever happens, whatever friends you think you have made — you are a darkie to them and that's all.'

In what can only be described as ongoing training, his pale-skinned wife teaches Mickey a thing or two about matters European and briefs him in British manners and business customs as a matter of course, so that when he agrees to

Allenby's proposition and takes up the post of naval agent, the officers with whom he comes into contact feel instinctively that somehow he understands what the Navy needs. Quickly he is trusted and liked throughout the service.

These days though well into her forties, and displaying with each passing year, were it possible, less interest in his household and domestic matters, it is still Farida who Mickey seeks out most regularly for company and advice. It is she he most desires when it comes time to retire. He has tried asking his other wives for their opinion but the conversations never go beyond what they think he wants them to say. Her delight these days, as always, is her frantic scribbling and reading any Arabic text that comes her way. She quotes poetry, whispering well-constructed if profane lines in her husband's ear as she pulls him on top of her pale flesh. Most surprisingly of all for a woman, she has, as far as he can remember, never been wrong about anything.

There is a clattering sound on the stairway to Mickey's office as Rashid arrives from the warehouse. He has recently put henna in his hair but immediately decided against the resulting shock of colour, so he is wearing a long headdress to cover the luminous orange while it fades. The material sways behind him lending an unaccustomed elegance to his entrance.

'*Salaam aleikhum*,' the boy bows.

He comes from a long line of *Ibadi* herdsmen and he learnt to read purely by chance, when he was taken ill and sent to Muscat to the house of a distant relative. Having discovered indispens-able administrative skills, which have benefited Mickey's business immeasurably, Rashid never returned to the shit-poor caravan where he spent the first ten years of his life. He is, however, a competent horseman and good with a camel. He knows how to survive on the sands.

'I need you to come with me,' Mickey says. 'We will be gone for a few days. There are two *Bedu* I want to find on the *jabel* who can help me. Two white men are missing. We must find them. Though first some enquiries in town, I think.'

Rashid hovers, hopping from foot to foot very lightly in a barely perceptible movement that Mickey completely understands.

'Oh yes, Rashid. There will be bonuses if we find them. For you and for me. If they are still alive.'

15

Six weeks into their captivity and having moved camp twice, Jessop comes to understand that the curse of being a doctor is the knowledge of what a man can survive and what he can't. His is a profession that does not countenance much in the way of hope. He wonders if it is for this reason that Jones has survived more easily than he, for Jones has been able to believe that the treatment they have received in the camp will kill them, that it will end soon. Jessop, however, understands that the emir has a particular talent. He is extremely good at keeping men alive. Just. The heat has exacerbated their decline, and when he thinks of it logically he knows that it really hasn't been that long. For heaven's sake, the *Palinurus* will only recently have abandoned the rendezvous point at Aden. But every day of this has been hell — the heat and the terror of never knowing when they may be hauled from the tent and made to march for miles overnight or, worse, perhaps be beheaded. Jessop is sure he read somewhere that it is beheading that is most likely.

The men have quickly become two ragged piles of skin and bones — the doctor is a good two stones down on what he considers his fighting weight of two hundred pounds, at which he left Bombay all those months before. He has little fight left now. For a while he hoped the abrasions caused by their initial struggle against the ropes might cause blood poisoning or that the sign that the emir had branded agonisingly on the white men's buttocks might become infected to the same effect but neither of these possibilities has transpired to release either him or Jones from their captivity, and he has become resigned simply to waiting, endlessly, and hoping despite himself for food and water. If the meagre rations stopped, at least there would be an end to the whole damn business. In this weakened state, a couple of days of privation would certainly do it.

However, when their stony-eyed jailer arrives and pours some warm, brackish liquid from a goatskin down Jessop's face, he cannot help but lick at it in desperation. The survival instinct, he notes, is stronger than his logical response to the situation and thirst turns any man, even a scientific kind of chap, into a panic-stricken, babbling, begging fool. The doctor has come to realise that a man will sit in his own excrement, wracked by hunger pains, baking in his own skin, and still he will survive despite himself.

'Me too,' Jones begs and receives a dark dribble of lukewarm liquid.

Jones, it has turned out, has no dignity and less goodness. Jessop does not blame him, and it is hardly a surprise. Jessop suspects that when Jones is occasionally taken away by one of the guards that he is gratifying the man sexually for extra food. Firstly, he never mentions what happens when he leaves the tent, which is odd. And then the lieutenant's weight has not dropped as dramatically as the doctor's own. Jessop is not sure what he would do given that opportunity — Jones' blonde hair is clearly of more interest to those so inclined. In any case, he does not like to think about it preferring, when he is not wishing fervently for death, instead to fantasise about either crisp, green apples and a stroll he took shortly before his departure through the winding lanes of his father's estate or, occasionally, the madman's dream of escaping the tent, stealing a camel and somehow outrunning and outfoxing the emir's well-fed warriors on their own territory, to make it back to the coast and safety. Both these dreams seem equally outlandish and unlikely but they occupy him nonetheless. Out on the *jabel* there are *falaj* — stone-lined irrigation systems to carry the water. They were built by the Persians more than a thousand years ago. Jessop dreams of bathing in one. Why won't the man simply let him die?

Most evenings there is thin soup of some kind or other — the watered-down, half-rancid remnants of meals served days ago at the emir's table. The moisture in this mush is as important as the nourishment though Jessop has noticed he is sweating less and as a consequence he cannot cool down. He knows he is in the advanced stages of acute dehydration and thinks it would be good to write to his professor at King's about the phenomenon. The old man would be interested, no doubt, for the human body is always endlessly fascinating to him and he values practical experimentation above all else. Both of the men have lost the ability to grow their beard and the thin, straggly wisps on their chins are matted against the skin. If you think about it too much, it becomes devilishly itchy.

Jessop is jolted out of this reverie by the voice of his companion.

'I don't see it,' Jones says his first coherent words in several weeks that have not been formed to beg for food or water. 'I've no idea how we are ever going to get out of here, old man.'

Jessop laughs more in shock than in amusement. He had assumed that Jones, like him, was wishing for death but that clearly has not been the case.

'Really,' Jones continues, as if it is only just occurring to him, 'at most we could run if we could get through these ropes. But then how would we survive? There's sand everywhere. Sand and baking sun. This whole damn country is just an oven.'

'We're not going to survive,' the doctor says wearily. 'At least, I hope not for much longer. A little more privation and we'll be there, my friend, and that is my considered, medical opinion.'

Apparently, this has not occurred to the lieutenant. Perhaps, Jessop wonders, he thinks this is a tale in some story book and we have to get out because, as white men, we are the heroes. It occurs to him that Jones did not have much of a grasp on reality even before their fortunes changed, and now he does not comprehend that he is filthy, ragged and hovering on the cusp of death.

'But they will send someone when they realise we're missing, won't they? I mean, we're British subjects.'

The lieutenant manages to sound almost outraged. It's actually quite admirable and Jessop can't bring himself to point out that Haines is well-meaning but not always effective and that it will take an extraordinarily effective man to cross the burning sands and come to find them. All this to be done quickly — for in current circumstances, the doctor does not give himself or his companion much more than a few weeks of life. A man given no food can last three months, of course, there's always that — and they are at least receiving some rations. But still, he considers, with the heat, another two months seems an impossibility unless things improve.

In any case, it is not, as far as the doctor can see, in Captain Haines' nature to marshal his men into a search party or to undertake what would surely be an arduous negotiation with the *Bedu*. If the emir were for turning he would surely have done so by now. Their best hope is that he has sued for ransom, though there has been no mention of that, and truly the fellow would have a cheek, given they'd paid for his hospitality already. Jessop feels outraged. He didn't kill the damn girl on purpose. In fact, he cured all the others. There is no accounting for it; the emir is grieving, he is not reasonable. He may never return to reason and that's the truth. It is too exhausting to think about.

'How long do you suppose we have been here?' Jones cuts in on the doctor's rambling thoughts. 'How long do you think it will take them to rally the troops and come for us? It's really not on. Seems to me that we've been tied up for far too long, anyway.'

It's a good question. Jessop tries to work out how long it might have been but the trouble is that one scorching day merges into another. It's impossible to measure time.

It's weeks, he thinks, *not months*. He's sure of it though he is aware that in these conditions he is easily confused. For all he knows they could have been here a year, perhaps, or longer. The imprisonment in the tent is punctuated very occasionally by a sandstorm or a few days of exhausting marching to another oasis where the tent is set up again and the two men are bound again to a stake. Once, they were lucky and the ropes were long enough to allow them to sleep on their stomachs. Sleeping on the stomach, Jessop has come to understand, diminishes the pain of extreme hunger. Today his bonds are far too tight, however, to manage it. They've been bound like this, he thinks, for ages and ages, though how long that actually is escapes him.

'They've certainly held us for several weeks,' is the best he can do.

'Well, I hope the rescue party make it soon,' the lieutenant says testily, as if his carriage is late for the opera or the vicar and his sister have, inexplicably, not turned up to take tea. 'Really I do.'

16

After some weeks, Zena learns that she is all but invisible to everyone in her master's household. The servants come and go, each with a prescribed list of duties that they undertake like clockwork. She need not clean nor cook nor even wash herself — everything simply seems to happen without any effort on her part. A tray of food arrives twice a day. Jugs of scented water are delivered so she can be washed. There are clean clothes and a doe-eyed, tongue-tied negro girl combs and dresses Zena's hair. She is a *sidi* slave who speaks neither Arabic nor her own Abyssinian tongue nor, indeed, any language at all it seems for, she never says a word to anyone, and will not indulge even in sign language, for Zena has tried. It seems to her that the slaves clean the furniture, make the bed, refill the lamps, sweep the floor, leave fresh water and jellies for the master's delight and care for her in the same way that they look after everything else — there is for them, no distinction between their master's inanimate objects and the girl who is confined to his room day after day. It is all very businesslike.

This must be what it feels like to be a pet, Zena thinks, and then she realises that in her experience, even a pet is shown some affection.

Meanwhile, each morning the master rises shortly after sunrise, prays and leaves. In the evenings he returns to the room with one of three or four slave boys, who are his favourites, and occasionally two of them at the same time. Zena spends almost all day at her seat by the window where she finds she can pass the hours simply watching the activities on the street. There are white *jubbahed* hawkers and earnest, serious-faced slaves going about their business, intriguing, covered litters carried by muscle-bound black bearers and keen-eyed messengers, stick thin from running errands and always keen to be on their way. Down the hill she catches glimpses of the azure sea, all the way across the bay and out to the Strait of Hormuz. At night, the stars are fascinating, though none of the shapes they make in the sky are familiar or at least appear in the location she expects them, as seen from the fragrant, lush vantage point of her grandmother's compound where she used to sit and listen to the crickets in the darkness and trace shapes between the specks of bright fire above. In Muscat, Zena loves the sunsets and after the blazing sky settles into darkness she enjoys watching the bustle of so many far-off people moving indoors, eating with their family and feasting with friends as the city closes its shutters and lights its lamps.

When the master arrives back at his room it is always very late. Zena lights the *naft* in anticipation though when he swings briskly through the door he only dismisses her casually as soon as his slave boy arrives — just as he did the first night she met him. Lying in the hallway on the cool earthen tiles that line the floor, she hears a lewd cry or two from behind the thick, cedarwood door and falls asleep after midnight, staring at the low moon and waking only as the *muezzin's* calls start when the first red line of dawn appears on the horizon. *Prayer is better than sleep*, they echo around the bay from minarets all over the city, summoning the men to the *fajir* and lending a rhythm to Zena's day even if she does not pray when they call. As the music fades, the door to the room opens and the master's boys step over her on their way back to their own quarters. Then she waits patiently, hovering outside for perhaps half an hour or more, listening to the household wake up — the sound of far-off doors opening and closing, a child's voice and a woman's laugh — before the master himself leaves and she can take her place, like some kind of ornamental doll, a place holder, on the cushions by the window.

The rhythm of the days numbs her and after the initial relief that she is fed and cared for, it does not take long until Zena is bored to distraction. In such a situation even a small change in routine can come as a shock so she finds herself taken back when one evening the master returns alone and in a fury. He slams the door and, flinging himself onto the cushions like a child in ill-humour, he pokes a smooth finger into the brass-bound box of rose jelly that is replenished daily. Then he takes a deep breath and sighs heavily. It is a dramatic sigh. The master is trying to communicate.

Zena hesitates. Her huge, black eyes flick towards the doorway. The slave boy will be here any minute. The master takes another deep breath and heaves it out again. This is quite the most interesting thing that has happened in the last fortnight. Zena decides to make a move. She crosses the room gracefully, her hips swaying beneath her blue *jilbab*. She presses her hands together in supplication, lowers her eyes modestly and bows down to the ground, prostrate at the master's feet.

The master raises another rose jelly to his mouth, dropping a trail of powdered sugar across the velvet cushions. He stares openly at Zena's long, curled hair splaying across the carpet towards him. He thinks it is like the surf on the shore, reaching towards him on the sands. He is tempted to kick but manages to restrain himself.

'What they sent you for, I don't know,' he says.

Zena looks up and smiles. She is no fool and there is no measure in letting him treat her like one. 'Oh, master, I think they have sent me hoping that I can tempt you. That is what you said yourself, is it not, the first day I arrived?'

'Yes. Yes,' he laughs. 'You are right. That is exactly it.' He makes a dismissive noise and waves his hand to demonstrate how ridiculous this notion is. 'My father thinks because I like Aran and Sam and they are black like you . . . *Galla*. Pshaw! He is a fool! How dare he?'

Zena feels embarrassed. What can she say? That they have spent a fortune on her? That in the past many men have found her attractive? That three years ago her grandmother had an offer of two horses and a white peacock for her hand in marriage, if the Arab trader who made it could be assured that she was a virgin? That an *imam* promised a chest of gold but the old lady did not want to let her go with him for she believed Zena too young. The old lady protected her, she realises now, too much. 'We will find a grand, Ethiopian prince for you, my love,' she promised, 'when the time is right. And you will bear a king for our own country.'

The master does not care about any of that. There is a moment's hesitation and then what Zena finds she can say is this. 'Shall I dance for you? I used to dance at my grandmother's house.'

The master regards her. He stares into the distance, distracted by his fury at the situation that has brought her here. Then he gestures with his hand. 'Dance then,' he says curtly.

There is no music, not even a drum, but that doesn't matter. Zena simply imagines Yari playing for her as he has a hundred times before. She imagines that Baba is still alive and she is dancing for the old lady's guests after a magnificent feast. She raises her arms and starts to gyrate, easily finding a rhythm of her own and, lithe as a *dyk dyk* in the bush, she dances back to Abyssinia in her mind. Her hair falls in a curtain and she tosses it aside to the rhythm, she stamps her feet and sinuously moves her hips, she flutters her eyelashes and flashes her eyes. She is as smooth as a fast-flowing river and she dances, whirling like a dervish, tossing her hips like a girl for hire at the bazaar. She moves frantically as if all her days of inactivity can be kicked away in the rhythm. She dances until she is not even

118

aware of the master anymore, and when the music in her head stops, her skin is flushed with delight and she is panting as she falls on the vivid cushions beside him with a wide smile.

He claps. He laughs.

'If ever I was to . . . ' he starts, moved by the display momentarily before he catches hold of himself and suspends the sentence, hanging in the air. 'You are very beautiful,' he finishes. 'For a woman.'

'Do you think,' Zena asks him, 'that they will take me away if you don't want to . . . ?'

The master shrugs his shoulders. 'I don't know what they are going to do. All my slaves are employed elsewhere tonight so that I will come back to you here and we will be alone. I almost slept downstairs. They want me to marry, but if I do they fear I will disgrace the family. When there are no children a wife can insist on a divorce.'

There is an earnestness in his tone, a crack of emotion too. Zena feels sorry for him.

'I can sleep here tonight,' she says, 'if you would like it. No one will know what has or has not happened.'

The master looks at her as if she is insane and for a moment she thinks she has gone too far. Then he reaches out and pulls her towards him. Zena has never been kissed before. The master's mouth is soft and tastes of sweet rose-water and she finds, to her surprise, that she kisses him back easily. Kissing, she thinks, is like dancing — much better when you lose yourself in it and don't think too much. The sensation is pleasant.

She sighs as she breathes in. His skin smells of the smoke of his *shisha* pipe — aromatic and musky. There is a gentleness in his movements that is surprising and the brush of his small beard on her skin makes her cheek tingle. Zena falls back on the cushions and the master runs a lazy hand down the line of her body.

'It is no use,' he says sadly. 'You are too . . . soft.'

Zena puts her arms around him. She is unsure what more he could want. At least the kiss has broken the monotony. There is a frisson to this seduction business, she thinks — a pleasure. At last something has at least happened. The master, however, looks forlorn. Zena knows to comfort him.

'No one will know,' she promises. 'No one will know. Come on, let me put you to bed and I will sleep next to you. Give me your hand.'

★ ★ ★

The next morning when the slaves arrive to wash her and clean the room, they bring a new *jilbab* made of white gossamer so fine it could be a cobweb. It is cut to reveal an enticing glimpse of her dark cleavage and edged with gold and silver ribbon. With it there is a box containing three thick, gold bracelets and an ankle chain with tiny bells along its length. Two sheer, red scarves for dancing are laid beside the cushions in easy reach. When the silent *sidi* comes she dresses Zena's hair and threads a clinking strip of pretty amber beads through the coils. Then she scents the trailing wisps with orange blossom. After-wards, there is a hot plate of roasted chicken and a sweet, milky pudding with slices of sugared lemon and a swirl of rose syrup.

They are watching, Zena thinks, moving carefully, for now with each gesture she tinkles like a bell. *They know that I danced for him. They know that last night I didn't sleep outside.*

17

The morning that Zena tucks into the first meal she has had in months that consists of more food than she can manage, it is well over twenty years before Sigmund Freud will be born in the Austrian town of Pribor. In fact, Freud's mother is not yet even a twinkle in her own father's blue eyes, and as for Carl Jung, his genius is a good forty years off seeing its first light of day. So it is true to say that nobody — not one single soul — in the whole wide world, has any particular idea why Kasim and Ibn Mohammed, the most renowned slavers in the whole Peninsula, hate it so much when they come back to Muscat. This should be, after all, why they undergo the privations of the long slaving trips — the triumph of making money enough for a luxurious home, endless feasts with their friends, a host of slave girls, a *harim* of submissive wives, a nursery of children and all the material goods a man can desire. Thanks to their dedicated barbarism in the stealing of what, over the years, has been thousands upon thousands of souls, Kasim and Ibn Mohammed are among the richest men in Oman and the regular tributes they pay the *soultan* for the privilege of being his subjects would keep the population of the whole country lavishly in couscous and roasted goat for a year.

Mickey sends a message with Rashid, a couple of hours ahead of his arrival. He wants to announce himself. When he reaches Ibn Mohammed's compound, the boy is waiting outside under the shade of a plain, pale, canvas awning that runs along one side of the house. Rashid, constitutionally unable to make any kind of effort that is not strictly necessary, crouches by the door and rises to his feet only as Mickey is directly before him.

'You delivered my note?'

'Yes.'

'Did he say anything?'

Rashid shakes his head.

Mickey is concerned that the men are too lately arrived and will be too busy to help him, but if anyone can find out what happens beyond the *wadi* and across the *jabel* out on the sands it is Ibn Mohammed and Kasim. Both have a well-earned reputation as hard men who are as unforgiving as the harsh desert itself, and they boast a network of contacts, spies and informants that will make the job of locating Jessop and Jones and negotiating their release considerably easier. The *Bedu* that Mickey is hoping to engage for the job will come on board more easily if Ibn Mohammed and Kasim give their names to the mission. Ever the broker, Mickey is in the habit of seeking as much help as possible for any job he undertakes and when matters are as tricky as this one, he is certainly wise to do so. Finding Jessop and Jones will not be an easy business and freeing them will take real skill.

He is standing at the heavy, studded door and has smoothed his robe and told Rashid to smarten up ready to knock for entry when, unexpectedly, Kasim trots briskly towards the house, alone on an ornately bridled black stallion, his saddle trailing intricate weaving work and long red tassels that look particularly impressive against the animal's black, glossy flanks. In a black robe and a long, dusky *kaffiya*, Kasim is a vision of darkness with a small monkey perched on his shoulder like a familiar. As he reaches the gate he pulls on the reins, raising a cloud of pale dust as the horse's hooves stop dead on the parched ground. Kasim dismounts fluidly next to Mickey with the little monkey still clinging to him. His lavish robe swishes behind, making the whole action rather balletic and, with his chocolate eyes lowered, he bows respectfully.

'*Salaam aleikhum.*'

'*Aleikhum salaam.*'

The men, knowing each other of old, kiss lightly three times on alternate cheeks.

'They sent for me when they received your message,' Kasim explains with a flash of his milky teeth.

'You were at home?' Mickey is all politeness.

Kasim gives only a slight shake of his head. 'I went to the *wadi*,' he says, aware that camping in the valley outside town is hopelessly eccentric when he owns a lush compound of his own and could stay with any number of good friends inside the city's walls.

Kasim does not know why they call Muscat the Jewel of Arabia. He values the open air and excitement of the chase and the city feels like a dungeon to him whenever he returns. He behaves as evenly as he can towards his slaves, servants and wives while he is constrained within Muscat's high, white walls but he longs to be free no sooner than he has greeted his relations and checked his stockpiles of gold. He considers the place hot, dirty and tiresome, the round of hospitality expected of him feels like pressed labour and why most men prefer to stay in the city rather than adventuring on the high seas or the mountain trails, he does not know — a view he expresses publicly from time to time, much to the shock of Muscat society. By contrast, Ibn Mohammed hides his loathing of the capital and does what everyone seems to expect of him on his return though, had Dr Freud been born some years earlier and already embarked on his career, he might have noted that Ibn Moham-med beats his slaves ferociously when in residence in his Muscat compound while on his slaving missions he is known as the more gentle one (this of course, given the nature of the men's business, is a relative term and does not hold true on those occasional moments when Ibn Mohammed loses his temper).

These days, Kasim and Ibn Mohammed do not personally run or capture shipments of day-to-day working slaves — the recent outing in Abyssinia was for *habshis* and they had, in fact, hoped to find more of the unusual or rare in the villages they raided. Like most wealthy and successful slavers, they have several managers, great brutes of men who undertake regular forays into Africa on their masters' behalf and

125

bring out cargoes of negroes to ship all over the region and beyond — for *sidis* make up the majority of the trade even though they are worth only a few dollars each. The advent of the British anti-slavery blockade is a case of mere strategy to both Ibn Mohammed and Kasim who will simply find a way around the new rules to allow them to continue to make money by selling the people they steal. When he heard that the British had banned the trade and their ships would block all traffic, Ibn Mohammed commented drily that the wind blows in both directions. He claims for himself the authority of one to whom Allah has gifted personally the right to sell others if not in one geographical location, at least in another.

Now in their late thirties, the men have been trading together for some years, since they set out on their first travels on a whim fresh from the schoolroom and unsure what they wanted to do with their lives. It was only when, quite by chance, they had the opportunity to raid an encampment that things fell into place. Now they are specialists — epicures and collectors — as much as businessmen. Kasim has already started to plan his next foray into the Heart of Darkness — he has heard tell of *Zigua* eunuchs in the hinterland of Somalia — and he only hopes he can convince Ibn Mohammed to leave the charade of Muscat life soon. Eunuchs, like virgins, are the holy grail of slave trading in the Middle East — a fine, black eunuch most of all — there is a demand for that kind of creature from Turkey all the way to India and they are sure to fetch three hundred and fifty silver dollars each, sometimes more. The *Zigua* are known for their long limbs and fine teeth. Kasim can hardly wait to be off. That very morning, while bathing in a shallow water hole up on the *wadi* he was bitten by a camel fly. The insect's tiny mandibles, like daggers, left a thin trail of blood down his thigh. He squashed the creature between his fingers and felt, he realised, curiously satisfied, for he is a man who does not mind pain in the slightest. Now he is dry again and dressed, he feels the sting on his skin and decides that, failing an early departure by *mashua*, he will camp in the *wadi* for as long as he can without raising the ire of his wives who seem to want to look after him for some reason. He feels uneasy, some might say guilty, about refusing to allow them to do so, but he does not really wonder why. In the meantime, Ibn Mohammed, without the escape valve of the *wadi*, will act so viciously towards his servants, slaves, wives and children that his whole household will breathe a sigh of relief when Kasim finally convinces him they have spent enough time in Muscat and can once more respectably depart for the African coast. Just the thought of it makes Kasim's heart pound. He can't wait to get away.

Kasim pats his horse's neck and surveys Mickey. He cannot help but notice each time he comes home that more and more of his contemporaries have become fat and complacent and this fills him with a horror for which he has no explanation. Now, when they return to

Muscat, normally five or six weeks out of the year, each day feels like a month and he shuns this kind of thing as much as he can. He has only come so he can tell Ibn Mohammed about his plans to return to Africa. Up until now they have considered an exploratory trip to capture some Circassians in the north, but *Zigua* eunuchs, now he thinks upon it, make far more intriguing game and capturing Circassians might only enrage the Turks who are more difficult to deal with than ill-educated tribal chiefs in the hinterland of the Dark Continent.

'Thank you for returning to town so swiftly,' Mickey bows, unaware of just what a trial it is for Kasim to make the short journey from the *wadi*. 'I need your help.'

'For the white men? The infidels?' Kasim knows all of Mickey's interests and is not one for beating around the bush. His tone is dismissive.

'Two went on a foray into the desert some weeks ago and have not returned. There are rumours they are being held by the *Bedu*.'

Kasim shrugs. Mickey, he notes, has greyer hair than the last time they met, over three years ago now. At the side of the cloth trader's face there are strands that are almost completely white.

'You look well, my friend,' he lies nonchalantly, for he can think of nothing else to say — certainly nothing about the subject of Mickey's concern. The white men are nothing to Kasim — you can sell the women but the men make poor slaves and in any case, their capture causes ructions. Europeans demand their male soldiers and sailors back if you steal them fairly in a fight. Besides, if these two missing *Nazarene* have been taken by the *Bedu*, he knows the men must have perpetrated some hideous crime against the emir. The *Bedu* can be mercurial but something must have happened, they would not have taken the white men for no reason at all.

'What did the pale-skinned ones do?' he asks.

'Allah alone knows.'

Without looking, Kasim strikes the door of his friend's house to call the servants. 'Come,' he says.

He is here now and has, after all, nothing better to take up his time. Besides, Mickey has been a good customer over the years and has a fine reputation. The bonds of brotherhood are strong across the Peninsula and influential men help each other as a matter of course. He might as well, he reasons, hear the story before he can get Ibn Mohammed alone and enchant him with the idea of not one *Zigua* eunuch but perhaps a clutch of them with children — yes, very small *Zigua* children, that can be dressed in feathers — to frame the eunuchs when they present them for sale to their private, most wealthy clients.

'Let's go in. We will drink together and share a pipe. I have an appetite. We will see what we will see about your *ajamiyah* friends.'

'Thank you, Kasim,' Mickey bows formally.

The two men enter the shady courtyard, Kasim pulling the reins of his big black stallion behind him as the red tassels bounce lethargically against the animal's shining, black hide and Ibn Mohammed's slaves rush to welcome their master's important guests.

129

18

Farida has never discussed with her husband the proprieties of a good Arabic wife, but then she is not Arabic and she knows that Mickey will forgive her anything. Some time ago, after three long, if largely enjoyable, years of marriage and at the grand old age of twenty-three, she finds that she does miss the world a little. The freedom of it. She has looked down on the street from a distance one time too many from her *bulchur*-scented chamber and now she thinks, *Feck it!*

It does not occur to her that she might ask to go out. Even if she receives permission she will have to venture into the city in a covered litter and most likely will have to think of a damned purpose to setting foot (or gilded wooden frame) over the door. Farida likes her life in Muscat, but still, in County Cork, a young girl is accustomed to being able to walk into town and see what she can see. She rummages to find herself a black *burquah* that will hide everything — her status most of all. Plain black is for poor women or the very, very old and she wants to defy notice.

'Like the bleeding dowager herself,' she smiles as she disguises herself. She finds that her heart is pounding as she pulls the dark veil over her pale hair and stains her hands and her feet with a few drops of walnut oil. It is, she thinks, like obliterating herself. Wiping out her unique, white-skinned beauty and disappearing.

130

Knowing the rhythm of the household, it is easy to slip down the back stairs like a maid meeting her midnight lover or a woman who has been sequestered for three, long years stepping out into the light. It will be brief. She has perhaps an hour before anyone will come to tend her, to bring minted water or scented oil to the bedchamber where normally she reads for most of the day. And so, that first time, her heart racing like she is set to win the Derby and she only a slip of a girl with the frisson upon her, Farida sneaks into the *souk*.

In life there are few things that remain thrilling and even the most profane pleasures pale with repetition, but Farida finds that her heart still thunders to this day when she leaves Mickey Al Mudar's household on the sly. After seventeen years of careful espionage, no one suspects a thing. She is always restored and calm, as if nothing has happened, before anyone can wonder where the master's favourite wife has gone. Farida indulges this guilty pleasure with circumspection, perhaps three or four times a year — but she relishes each outing, drinking in the street scenes like a woman driven mad with the thirst.

She wanders wherever her feet will take her, past a corral of donkeys dusty from their trip to market or two men haggling over the price of anything from a brace of fowl to an ornate, cedarwood screen with inlaid, brass edging. The stalls selling copper and diorite always have an exciting clamour. The sound of life outside the silent rooms of Mickey's mansion is like

131

babbling music to her and the smells fire her up so she feels like dancing, floating almost, a black spectre greedy for more. A woman in a *burquah* does not raise a glance on the city streets, and she finds that when no one can see your eyes, you are free to look where you please and in Muscat there is plenty to command Farida's attention.

The market quarter is one of the biggest in the whole Peninsula, second only to Sur. The confines of Muttrah stretch for a good mile and what you can't find in the maze of its streets and alleyways isn't worth owning. A hub of trade from the east coast of Africa to the west coast of India and north as far as Turkey, you can buy anything from a Nubian slave to a pocketful of diamonds, a bolt of silk to a herd of white goats and the place teems with men of all creeds and colours.

Farida drinks it all in — the exotic dress and the barefoot children, grubby in their poverty, sometimes on their way to classes at the *mosque*, carrying the shoulder blade of a camel in their hand, for that is what they use in this strange place instead of a slate. She wonders at the outlandish reptiles in cages and the cinnamon scent of almost everything baked and drizzled in a gloss of honey. Over time she comes to recognise individual stalls and shops — the familiar scribe who sits, always still, his quill and ink shaded by a tatty, maroon canopy as he waits for his next commission to walk out of the throng — the important business of an amulet to be written to protect a much-loved son, perhaps.

The stall that sells the ornate silver casings is a few steps up the street and the fellow does a brisk trade in portions of the *Quran* to fill them. Then there is the turbaned, Indian ancient with his stall of colourful cotton *jubbahs* and *dishdash* tunics, conducting what always looks like a most convivial tea party with an array of men haggling over the quality of the cloth and the cut of the sleeves as they sip their aromatic, mint tisane and try on *hauza* turbans. There are goats tethered in bells so they cannot escape without raising a clatter and then, oh, then there are the fine Arab horses. The first time Farida sees one she is overcome by a desire to touch it. A bay roan, it is a gorgeous buff pink and led by a *Bedu* who is taking his mount beyond Muttrah, away from the *souk*. For the girl from Rowgaranne it is a jaw-dropping sight. Farida knows her horses. Her father was stableman to a duke and he always swore that Arabs are the prettiest breed. Still, this desert steed makes His Lordship's finest stallion, the pride of her father's stable, look like a carthorse from Yorkshire. She puts out her hand to touch the animal's hide.

'Gorgeous,' she murmurs and she wishes her father could see it.

Once, she follows Rashid when she catches sight of him buying almond fancies. She trails him to the small house that Mickey uses as an office.

Ah, so it's here, she thinks.

Once she has found it, Farida returns again and again. It feels good to walk by and think wickedly, *My Mickey is in there and I am here*

133

outside and off to see some fine horses that are for sale in the souk *this afternoon.*

Farida treasures these outings. She moves like a dark spirit along the thin streets, watching Muscat, raising her eyes to the windows of the upper floor of the houses where, shielded by cotton awnings or wooden shutters she sometimes catches a glimpse, the tantalising shimmer of a woman like herself. The wife of a wealthy man who, unlike Farida, is content to remain sequestered from the world, gilded in *taler* necklaces, pregnant half her life and tinkling wherever she goes.

Three or four times she's seen British officers, their faces pink in Muscat's unholy climate, sweating their way round the *souk*, looking for souvenirs, their shadows long on the sandy ground. This day, this very day, she sees one — the first in over a year. He is a tall man in an immaculate uniform with the braid and buttons of a lieutenant. The paleness of his skin is quite shocking.

From London and no toff, she thinks, catching his accent as she passes him, sprawled leisurely on the cushions of a carpet stall. He has kind eyes though. *Blue like the sea and the sky*, she thinks. *And he is drinking it in.*

What fool wouldn't? Muscat is like a mind-altering drug. A stroll in its streets is like getting drunk for the first time. This fellow has an air of pleasing intelligence and looks as if he's enjoying the to-and-fro nature of the merchant who is offering his goods. The white man has a quiet determination though he remains relaxed.

He's enjoying himself. You could trust him, yes, he is trustworthy. The Pearl considers a moment. She wonders what would happen if she leant over and simply said a few words. It wouldn't take much.

'My name is Fanny O'Donnell. I was shipwrecked, kidnapped and sold many years ago. Send word for me to my sisters and brothers. They'll know them still on His Lordship's estate. And here I am living like a princess, so don't pity me for one second, Lieutenant.'

Surely he would say, 'Madame, you must let me be of assistance.' She sniggers; his voice is so *English*. Still, Farida keeps her silence, loitering by a stall selling tatty scraps of cloth, watching. He seems a strange creature to her now, even if he is one of her own, and of course, she knows full well she'll say nothing, for it would certainly cause a scandal, if not (heaven forbid) a political incident. Dear God, she doesn't want them to take her back. No, far better they all think she is dead, she muses sadly. It is only her sister she misses, in truth. The youngest one: Annmarie. Lord knows where she is now — the little dote.

Farida turns, pretending to examine some fabric on a stall as Wellsted stands to leave. The salesman lights a rock of frankincense and lets the officer perfume his clothes before he steps back into the sunshine. He does not take notice of the lady in her *burquah*, hovering in the shade watching him as he walks away.

Winding back towards the compound, sneaking carefully back to Mickey's very fine, gilded cage, Farida breathes especially deeply. She luxuriates in the uneven paving stones and the dusty kerbside — the array of imperfections that make the world real and the kick of her ankle as she strides in whichever direction she wants. Last of all, she passes the old, blind man, half-naked from sheer need, who sits a few doors up from the *mosque*, begging the charity of his fellows. She always brings him something — a slice of cake, a tiny speck of frankincense or a silk scarf. Farida has no money, she has not had any money for years. Still, she presses the gift into his hands and he blesses her as she hurries on her way back to the shaded elegance of her chamber. It is only like this that she can guard against her life becoming too smooth, too easy. She'll think about it this evening — all of it. She'll think of it for days.

Muscat is the best city on earth, she smiles to herself, the even slope of the steps rising beneath her signalling her homecoming. *I'll never be cold or hungry again.*

19

Zena stations herself by the window for most of the day while the slaves come and go. Outside, the same characters go about their business and she comes to pace herself by their familiar movements. She has never seen the master on the street but he most likely travels in a palanquin. Yes, she can see him in her mind's eye, lying behind sheer curtains, being carried to his appointments and social engagements — the mysterious business of what a man does during the day.

She realises quickly that the house only a block along belongs to one of the slavers. It is odd to watch the men who stole her come and go from a distance. Even though she knows she is obscured by the carved shutter or the curtains, depending on which she chooses to employ, at first she feels that they can see her nonetheless. She endows Kasim and Ibn Mohammed with the all-seeing eyes of godlike beings, and her heart beats a little faster each time she catches a glimpse of them. Beyond the fear, she feels frustration. These are the men who killed her uncle in cold blood and they ride out in Muscat like any other, unpunished for their actions. Slavery is legal — but murder?

The unfairness rankles. Zena has begun to long for her freedom. Even being allowed to walk in the street seems an impossible liberty. It is for this reason that she takes particular interest in the women who pass by her window.

Generally they are wearing the *burquah* but each is still distinguishable if Zena looks closely. A flash of ankle or wrist can be most revealing. Deportment is also important — some walk tall while others, hidden from the world, slouch along. Most have shoes — sandals, in fact — and these are much more individual than the long, black robes that obscure most of the detail of their wearer's appearance.

These women choose their own shoes, Zena thinks.

She takes pleasure in noting that this one is barefoot and therefore very poor, and that another has finely plaited leather shoes with a small heel or wears an elegant silver ankle chain. Once she thinks she catches sight of a flash of milky skin as one lady swings past with a gait that can only be described as musical. It must, Zena considers, be a trick of the light, for the woman's skin seemed almost to glow it was so pale.

One day she is attended by an old *sidi*. The slave has been sent to shape her nails. She crouches over Zena's hands like a fortune-teller, smoothing the edges with a strip of pumice and painting on a dark, thick oil to make the cuticle malleable. They are alone in the room. Zena continues to watch the street over the old woman's head. When the *sidi* speaks it is unexpected.

'You want to go out, my lady?' she rasps. The woman's voice sounds as rough as the pumice, as if she has been sucked dry.

Zena laughs. The comment is an exciting diversion. 'It would be nice to go out,' she admits. 'Do you ever leave the house?'

The woman lifts her head. Her eyes are the colour of butter, the irises like hazelnuts. 'I have not been outside for forty years,' she admits. 'I was brought here when I was your age.'

Zena pauses, trying to form the question as diplomatically as possible. 'You belong to your master, like I do?'

The old woman laughs. 'No. No. I am a *sidi*. And the master here prefers his own women. Your master's father, that is. I have always been a house slave. I think at first they were afraid I might run away, so I was not permitted to go to the market. And then, after a while, it simply became that I did not leave.'

Zena leans in and takes her eyes off the street. She's glad that her position in the household is easily distinguishable from the old lady's. She does not want to end her days bent over a young woman's hand, making the fingers attractive enough for her master's pleasure.

'Forty years,' Zena marvels, considering it. 'Did you never want to run away?'

The woman shakes her head. 'No. No. They behead you for running away and they are bound to catch you. Where is there to go? My brother ran.' The woman's voice falters. 'We were taken together. They caught him. They chopped off his legs at the knee and left him to bleed to death in the marketplace. In front of everyone. They have no pity, the masters, if you disobey. They told me

139

it took him a long time to die.'

Zena feels sick. She has been considering just this matter, though has come to the same conclusion. There is nowhere to run to and she looks so distinctive that she is bound to be caught and returned. It makes sense that the punishment for insubordination is heavy but she had not realised that it was death. She lays her hand on the woman's shoulder in pity.

'I'm sorry,' she says.

The woman's eyes betray her surprise that the pretty *habshi* has sympathy for what happened. No one has had sympathy in all the years she's been here.

★   ★   ★

Later, Zena sits below the sill, her eyes peeking over the rim. The street is less crowded now for the sun is high. It seems unbelievable to her that she might never leave this house again — that this place with all its comfort will become the confines of her world. It does not feel it's possible. She is daydreaming about what it would be like to leave, if only for a few minutes, when a hundred yards down the road a man rounds the corner. Zena sits up. He stands out immediately for he is the strangest creature the girl has ever seen. His skin is pure white, his eyes, she peers in wonder, are blue, and he wears a fitted jacket and trousers with golden buttons and braid embroidery. Unlike the *jubbah*, which mostly masks the shape of the body it clothes, this uniform shows the man's strong limbs and thick torso. He walks with a purpose that is quite impressive, and then stops at the market stall on the corner and inspects the pastries that are on display. He is, Zena thinks, interested in food, for he makes his choices carefully and the stallholder packs up the pastries, bowing and smiling all the while.

Zena finds that her heart is beating fast. Without thinking, she grabs a small, brass-framed mirror from the side table and, like a schoolgirl, deflects a sunbeam across the street, aiming for the fellow's face. At first, she misses but manages to make the buttons on his jacket gleam. Then, slowly, she diverts the beam upwards. As he turns into the light, she makes out the tone of his eyes — can they really be so blue? She has never seen such a thing. She squints to make out his face. He is laughing. She smiles; he knows it is a joke. His eyes are searching for the source of the light but he is not angry, only curious and amused. Zena takes this in before, in a panic, she dives under the ledge, giggling and hugging the mirror to her chest. She waits for a few seconds, counting to ten, and then carefully peers above the sill once more, hoping he will still be there.

The officer has turned and is haggling briefly with the stallholder. Then he pays. The baker bows, making his thanks, and Zena thinks that the white man has most likely paid too much for his pastries. She can tell by the smug expression on the stallholder's face. Then, as the stranger turns in the direction of the dock, the sound of the call to prayer seeps across the city from one minaret to another. When he walks, he looks powerful, she thinks. That's the word. Zena raises the mirror and follows his muscular figure down the hill with a trail of light on his heels. It's the closest she will come to going out and for now it will do.

I mustn't be childish and ungrateful, she thinks. The master's house, after all, is comfortable and she is well treated and safe. She shudders at the thought of the poor *sidi's* brother. Things, she realises could be far, far worse.

20

After three days docked in Muscat, the midships of the *Palinurus* smell like a hops house and Ormsby, with too little to do, has entered a cycle of drinking himself to a stupor, playing cards with his fellows and passing out in his tiny hammock, day after day. The other midshipmen have made a half-hearted attempt at surveying the twin forts of Al Jalali and Al Mirani as well as drawing maps of the walled city and its three fine gates. This is solely for the practice of it, for Muscat, unlike the interior of Oman, is freely open to Europeans, or as open as an Arab city can possibly be, and all salient points of its defence system and architecture are already in the hands of the Navy's high command. Still, Haincs oversees the boys' efforts and suggests improvements, for one day, who knows, they may be called upon to provide maps of somewhere that no white man has ever been before. Preparation for such an eventuality is everything — an Englishman is always at the ready.

The crew, meanwhile, are fully employed; the carpenters have planed down the rough edges and hammered everything back into place and now the unskilled men are painting the new wood. The deck is swabbed so clean you could eat off it. Most importantly, the craggy steward, Jardine, has bought enough spices (ostensibly for the captain's table) so that if he ever again has to eat mutton for three months straight he can, at the very least, marinade the filthy stuff and make a curry. He has a wide repertoire of recipes suitable for this eventuality, gleaned from the sweet-faced, dark-skinned little *bibi* with whom he has an arrangement back in Bombay at the port on the island of Colaba — he only wishes he had had his spice box with him when they hit the supply problems at Makkah. He won't let that happen again.

At three in the afternoon, his papers in order, Haines bursts tight-lipped onto the deck and makes an inspection of the rigging and the repairs. In particularly poor humour, he picks at details and orders several perfectly satisfactory jobs to be attempted again, for he has been presented with a quandary this afternoon — a summons from the palace delivered by a blue-robed messenger bearing the royal seal. The *soultan* wishes the pleasure of his company that evening, and the company of his senior officers. For choice Haines would take the midshipmen, but of course he has to take Wellsted if he takes anyone, and he does not want to attend the palace alone. In the shady recesses of his mind, just beyond his reach, the captain knows he is being mean-spirited but the truth is that once he is launched upon a certain course he finds it difficult to veer from it and the fire in his belly about Wellsted's behaviour over the manuscript is burning as brightly as ever.

'This rope,' the captain comments, kicking a

144

carefully tidied coil on deck, 'is a disgrace. Do it again.'

The men fall to it in the heat and Haines stands watching them. He feels no better. As Wellsted marches along the dock towards the *Palinurus*, the captain easily spots him from a distance. When he comes up the gangplank smartly, Haines is waiting at the top.

'Been ashore then, Wellsted?'

'Yes, sir.'

'Well, I will be requiring you this evening, Lieutenant. The senior officers of this vessel are to present themselves in the service of the sultan, when the sun goes down. Dress uniform, of course.'

'Yes, sir,' Wellsted salutes.

'Where the devil did you get to, anyway?'

'I went to the *souk*, sir,' Wellsted says.

He likes the market in Muscat. It's cosmopolitan. The *soultan* is liberal — come one, come all, if you've something to sell — the streets of Muttrah welcome everyone. Wellsted is unaware he has this very day been spotted by both Farida and Zena. He has spent most of the afternoon smoking a *shisha* pipe with a rug merchant from Constantinople. The fellow has taken an ornate old Portuguese house up from the waterfront and plies his wares there in some style. They discussed the habit of Muslim rug makers in making sure there is always one thread out of place in their work, for perfection is the province of Allah alone and to do otherwise is blasphemy. More importantly, the man swears blind that he saw French ships off the Somali coast not two months before — far further south than the British might like.

'The *souk*?' Haines' tone is derisory. 'A spot of shopping, is it?'

'No, sir.'

'If you're thinking you might use your allocated space on this trip, it is out of the question.'

Officers are entitled to request hold space for their personal profit. It is one of the perks of an Indian Navy commission — though Wellsted has never used his. He has his eye on a far greater prize than a few guineas. He is after respectability. After all, trade is the very thing he wants to get away from.

'No, sir. Not that.'

'Well?'

'I just went to see it, sir. I find it interesting. While I was there, I heard the French were nearby a couple of months ago. Three ships headed westwards and then south down the African coastline off Mogadishu. I thought you should know.'

Haines thinks he must mention this in his dispatches. The directors of the East India Company naturally spend a good deal of their time anticipating what the French may or may not do. Haines wouldn't like to say why the French might be off the coast of Somalia — their territories in Africa are predominantly to the north and west and even going to the Seychelles or Reunion, the French Navy usually follows the line of their protectorates and head around the Cape rather than sailing south from Egypt. The most likely explanation is that the buggers have been slaving. One way or another, he'll be damned if he is going to congratulate Wellsted on procuring this information — the chap is only doing his duty after all. He dismisses his lieutenant haughtily as if he is an errant midshipman who has been up to no good.

'I see. Well, off with you, then. Come for me when the *muezzins* are making their song this evening. Be ready.'

'Yes, sir.'

★ ★ ★

Below decks in his cramped cabin, Wellsted opens his trunk and pulls out his dress uniform. He has not worn it since Bombay but it is clean and only needs an airing or at least as good an airing as he can manage. The cabin is baking and, coming in from outside, he notices the long-seasoned wood still smells fresh from the forest when it gets hot and the pine resin's musky aroma is roused. He hangs the blue jacket with its gold brocade alongside his dress breeches on the back of the door. Then he decides to get one of the boys to polish his boots. First though, he picks one of the pastries he bought and savours the almond paste and honey stuffing. The Arabs bake well, he thinks. Then, licking his fingers clean, he shaves in the bucket of cold saltwater. The brine stings his skin. When he is done with the cutthroat he stows it carefully and passes a brush through his hair. It will be interesting to see inside the palace though the truth is that the lieutenant invariably feels out of place in fine surroundings. He comes far more into his own in the dockside taverns or striking up a conversation with a man who has something to sell. He heartily prefers life in a caravan, camping under the stars, to the brief periods he has spent in ambassadors' residences and at the disposal of the aristocracy even if, ultimately, that is where the plan he is set upon is heading.

'Polish these will you, Hughes?' he pokes his head into the hallway and catches the ship's boy as he is passing. 'I am off to the palace tonight.'

The boy's eyes light up as he grasps the officer's footwear. 'Yes, sir,' he says, and hovers a moment.

Wellsted nods to give the boy permission to speak.

'Will there be dancing girls, sir? At the palace.'

'Dancing girls?'

'Yes. I saw some in the bazaar. Darkies. Dancing on chains, sir. Mr Ormsby calls them belly dancers. Half-naked they were, sir, begging your pardon.'

The boy begins to hum a tune and raises his arms to demonstrate the way the slave girls move, then he giggles.

'Ladies' man, eh?' Wellsted teases him. 'Well, I suppose there might be dancing girls tonight. Couldn't say. But hopefully dinner will at least be better than we've had on board of late.'

Banned from the captain's table and hence also Jardine's culinary ingenuity, Wellsted has been subsisting on the same food as the men

148

— of a far lower quality even at port than he would like. His body, always lithe, has become quite wiry.

'Still, keeps body and soul together. A high shine on those boots, Hughes, if you please,' he says breezily and disappears, closing the door behind him.

★   ★   ★

At six o'clock, the sun sinks into the sea, its brazen colours bleeding over the horizon, and Haines, on deck with old-fashioned captain's feathers in his dress cap, fixed in place with a gold cockade, marches down the gangplank with Wellsted behind him. The men each carry a brass lantern on their way along the dark waterfront and the light picks up the glint of the embroidered brocade on their jackets and the brass buttons, polished till they almost glow. The relief after the heat of the day is palpable, although even at night Muscat is still hotter than the midday of an English July. The smell of fully fired bread ovens and roasting meat wafts out on the evening air and the glow of *naft* lamps oozes yellow light like syrup between the slats of the shutters all the way up the hillside. The night flowers are open and the streets, usually as full of animals as people, are deserted apart from here and there where luminous figures in bright, white *jubbahs* float like spectres along the dock-side, the stragglers heading home from the *mosque* after evening prayers. They disappear up one side street or another shadowed by a black slave or two dodging out of the way of the free men between the palms. The officers enter the palace courtyard, the gates swinging open before them, and are greeted by a slave, one of many waiting at the disposal of the sultan's visitors.

'Captain Haines. Lieutenant Wellsted,' Haines announces, as if the two men could be anyone else — there are few naval men in Muscat at any one time and the *Palinurus* is currently the only European ship at anchor.

The man motions for them to follow him.

Inside, the rooms are a riot of detail and colour. Every surface is ornately decorated with bright tiles or carvings of a detailed geometric nature. A series of courtyards open to the stars and lit by burning pools pepper the matrix that the slave navigates easily. The air smells of burning *naft* and *luban* with the occasional whiff of frankincense, as shadows dance across the broad, glossy leaves of exotic oasis plants and up the carved, pale stone of the palace walls. There is music; the haunting sound of an *oud* and a *khallool* — the Arabian lute and flute — and the chiming of the *sajat* bells. The exotic melody slips smoothly down the hallways like a snake. As they come to the court, the slave steps out of their way and they enter, both officers making their *salaams* amid the clatter of the bells and the hum of conversation. There are no women in the room, one would not expect them. Instead, there are groups of Muscat's well-dressed merchants and retainers, *imams, mullahs* and minor aristocracy, arrayed in a kaleidoscope of colourful silks, gold and precious jewels that would put a Mayfair dinner party to shame. Most of the men crouch on pillows, smoking and laughing. The room feels like a rarefied version of the *souk* and Wellsted finds himself relaxing at the welcome familiarity of it. To one side there is the orchestra and beside that there are three young dancing boys, clean-shaven, with their eyes heavily outlined in kohl. Their dress is effeminate to a white man's eye. Draped in lurid silks, their smooth skin glows in the lamplight, patterned with brown henna and thin strips of gold tied around their bodies. Jaunty hats, like bright bowls, sit upturned on their dark hair. Raphael himself could not array them more finely.

At the head, all eyes respectful of him, the ruler of Muscat, Oman and Zanzibar, Said Ibn Sultan, father of many children, husband of many wives, smiles graciously at the two foreigners. Resplendent in a red *jubbah* with a thick, purple silk sash and a magnificent turban wound around his head, he is comfortably seated on a huge leather cushion with gold ribbon at the edges. The sultan strokes his trimmed, greying beard and his eyes are bright with interest. Ibn Sultan is perpetually intrigued by pale skin and European clothes and is particularly gratified to note that the younger of the two men before him has not picked up even a hint of a tan on his travels, which sets his skin in particularly high contrast to his vivid blue eyes, and that the older one is wearing some rather striking feathers and a sufficiency of gold brocade. Immediately, it is the younger man that interests him most — his eyes are the eyes of a strange animal and Ibn Sultan is fascinated by all things foreign and strange. His jaded palate craves novelty and he always finds himself slightly afraid of white men, though he would never admit it and in any case, he thinks of the emotion as thrilling. He motions Wellsted forward.

'You will sit near me,' he commands.

Haines stiffens. He is the senior officer but he can hardly argue with a sultan over precedence.

Wellsted lowers himself onto the cushions at Said Ibn Sultan's knee. He is careful to display the soles of his feet to no one for that would be the height of bad manners. There is, it seems to him, no position where it is possible to be comfortable for long without displaying the soles of his feet, and the lieutenant always ends up with pins and needles after an Arabian meal; however, he does the best he can and then accepts the small cup of spiced coffee that appears instantly at his hand.

'*Shukran,*' he says.

Haines, further along, takes his place next to an emir. To Ibn Sultan's disappointment, the captain removes the hat with the feathers and places it out of sight. Then he takes a long, slow draw on a *shisha* pipe.

'They drink coffee in London?' the sultan enquires.

'Yes,' Wellsted nods. 'Though not as strong and never spiced. We drink ours often with cow's milk or cream. I like it the Arabian way, the taste of cinnamon, cardamom and cloves.'

'You drink rotten grapes also,' the sultan comments.

Wellsted laughs. 'Sometimes. I think I prefer coffee. It keeps the head clear. Have you ever tasted rotten grapes, sir?'

The sultan shakes his head. 'Allah forbids it,' he says simply.

'*Allah yahfutha*,' Wellsted answers immediately. May Allah keep you.

Gradually, the food starts to arrive. There is a whole, roasted sheep, the skull smashed to release its meat, the eyeballs blackened, the ears roasted to a crisp leather and the swollen tongue succulent, pink and fragrant — a slippery meat much prized, as Wellsted knows from his brief forays inland. The custom is, as far as he can tell, to leave that to the end of the meal. There are platters of butter-basted chicken stuffed with apricots and fish baked whole and decorated with cucumber and pomegranate. Gleaming piles of steamed couscous and rice and branches strung with dates and grapes are borne by slaves who will not meet the eye of those they are serving. At the same time, dainty pastries of honey and almonds, piles of sugar-encrusted jellies and pink, coconut fancies are placed on the low tables, sending a waft of sweetness towards the lounging men on the cushions. It is more than even a large gathering such as this can possibly eat and the grin on Wellsted's face is entirely genuine. The sultan immediately warms to him. It is his experience that men always want something and are at best guarded in his presence, at worst downright deceitful. To

153

witness another's delight is unusual and for it to be simply on account of a meal at court, where all are well-fed, is almost unheard of.

'You are hungry?' he asks the officer.

'Yes, sir. On the water our supplies are meagre and at port it has been very busy.'

'And your people usually eat with knives, as I understand it. A strange custom to us — your race must be very warlike, Lieutenant, to bring naked blades to the table, where you feast with friends.'

The sultan pulls off a piece of lamb from the shattered cheekbones — it is said to be the most delicate and delicious meat. He motions Wellsted to do the same.

'We do, sir. Cutlery we call it. The Arab way is more direct.'

The sultan notices that the other English officer is not talking to his dining companions and that he is having some difficulty with the custom of eating only with his right hand. The meat is slippery and balling the couscous into manageable mouthfuls is a skill that the captain has evidently not yet acquired. The floor around him is already scattered with failed attempts and ferrying even a small amount of the food that he takes from the plate as far as his mouth appears to require the man's full concentration and will take, in his absence of aptitude, several tries. A lump of chicken falls and rolls down his dress jacket, marking it badly with a slick of grease. Wellsted, by comparison, is deft and quite relaxed and yet he is the junior of the two.

'There are only two officers on your vessel?'

154

the *soultan* enquires.

'Myself and Captain Haines,' Wellsted says. 'And three midshipmen — boys, really. We lost the rest to fever.'

The sultan nods and then goes in for the kill. He likes to see what he can stir up when he has the opportunity to talk to white men about their tribal factions and has found that he can affect ignorance if necessary to deflect any offence. It is merely sport — the fun of provoking a genuine response. Here, as in all palaces, the truth is rare.

'You British fear the French, do you not?'

Wellsted is not fazed. 'We beat the French, sir. Though they are strong in Morocco and in Egypt. I fancy they might fear us more.'

'I have had the French at my table,' the sultan says vaguely. What he means is that the English have beaten the French away and made the slave trade westwards all but impossible. It is, in his view, ridiculous. His revenues from slavery are down. However, the English are making up for it — financially, at least. The recent treaty that he concluded with His Majesty in response to the British antipathy to slaving has given the sultan a most gratifying lump sum and he is replacing his revenue from the human traffic by selling cloves to Europe, which is proving a money-spinner of unexpected proportions.

It is the *soultan's* belief that the survey the white men are undertaking is on account of their longstanding feud with the French. He is right, though he has not taken this line of thinking to its logical conclusion. However arrogant Said Ibn Sultan might be, it would never occur to him that he might connect two seas by digging out large portions of the desert as the British are considering and the French will in due course effect. In any case, he wants to make it clear that he is happy to take British money.

'I do not miss the French,' he nods.

Wellsted accepts this information gracefully, while deftly popping thin strips of meat into his mouth. When he speaks, the lieutenant's tone is completely open, his appetite is piqued and all he can think of, at this moment, is dinner.

'They are culinary masters, the French, sir. Their rotten grapes, well, I shouldn't say it, but French rotten grape is the best in the world. On board we drink wine from the German states and it is fine enough. But a good red burgundy is a wonderful thing. I am sure the French enjoyed your hospitality. Your kitchens must be magnificent.'

The sultan laughs. He has never been to his kitchens and has no notion of how all this food is prepared. But he is enjoying this new white man — it is most diverting to hear the fellow talk and the sultan is mesmerised by Wellsted's movements. *The Nazarene are such outlandish beasts,* Ibn Sultan thinks. *They are so alien. Ajamiyah is the word. Like rare animals, they are otherworldly — yes, that is it. White devils, white ghosts. Djinns from the north.*

'Out on the *wadi,*' Wellsted continues, oblivious to the sultan's particular fascination, but his blue eyes shining nonetheless, 'we shot birds. Odd creatures — sand grouse, I think — but they were delicious roasted over the fire.

And we had wonderful oranges fresh from the trees. My hands smelled of fruit the whole day.'

'You like the *wadi*?' the sultan asks, intrigued at the very idea. There has, of course, been poetry written about the nobility of *Bedu* encampments. The beauty and freedom of a nomad's life. But the *soultan* has always lived in a palace of one kind or another and camps very rarely — only if he has to travel — and then in some considerable style.

'Oh yes, sir. I like the *wadi* very much. In my country, the stars and moon do not hang so low. On the *wadi* and up on the *jabel* I fancied I could catch them in my hand. It is a wonder, sir, a true wonder in your land. I climbed the *jabel* one night to see how close I could get to it. The *jabel*, sir, is rough country. My shoes came to pieces afterwards — they were navy-issue and very sturdy. I wonder how your subjects manage — so many go barefoot in those conditions. Your people must be very strong.'

The sultan finds his mind wandering. What must it be like to camp, alone, outside Muscat, and shoot your own food out of the sky. To be so excited by the stars that you will climb a hill to try to catch one. Travelling as he usually does, with an entire entourage, is not as direct. It has aroused in him no particular affection for the harsh interior away from the prosperous trading ports.

'Have you been to Zanzibar, Lieutenant?' he enquires.

The island is his favourite possession — the sea is never so blue as off its coast and the coralline rock is easily carved so the buildings are magnificent in their ornamental splendour. Though Muscat is cosmopolitan, there is no doubt, the island's position to the south makes Zanzibar Oman's most prosperous trading post with all the attendant splendours that go with the accumulation of large sums of money on a pivotal point between many cultures. The truth is, though, that it is not the trade that entices the *soultan* but the buildings, which are magnificent. The great man feels more at home there than anywhere else in his territories. He spends a good deal of time on the island and he often thinks that although Muscat, of course, is the capital, it's Zanzibar that truly deserves to be his first city.

'No, sir. I have never been to Zanzibar, though we mapped the island of Socotra, which was of tremendous interest. It is beautiful — the desert roses and the dragon's blood trees. There is a wonderful morning mist that renders the scenery of the hills particularly lovely.'

The sultan waves his hand as if to bat off this inferior geographical location. 'But you have been inland here?' he asks. 'On the mainland? In the desert?'

If he considers this a trick question, Wellsted does not show it, he merely shakes his head. 'No, sir, not without your permission. Only at Aden a few miles, as is permitted.'

The sultan's political sensibilities are twitching. The western end of the Peninsula, particularly to the north is often the subject of territorial wranglings — the fringes of the country are fluid

158

and subject to frequent change. There are several oases where his men regularly clash with the *Wahabi* and come off sometimes worse, sometimes better. At Aden there have been difficulties because of its proximity to Africa. Anywhere you can set up a slave market is bound to be profitable and therefore worthwhile fighting over.

'At Aden you say?' he enquires. 'Why there?'

'I was in search of two fellow officers, Dr Jessop and Lieutenant Jones, who have gone missing.'

Wellsted hesitates but the sultan smiles.

'It was at Aden, sir, that I heard a rumour of them.'

'That they offended the *Bedu*?'

'Yes, sir. Yes. Did you hear that too?'

The sultan laughs. He has found the nub of it at last, he thinks. 'If you have something to ask of me, then you must merely say so, Lieutenant.'

Wellsted smiles. 'Yes. Sorry, sir. We would like to find them. Our naval agent, Ali Ibn Mudar, is making enquiries and if there is anything you could do to help in this matter, His Majesty King William would be most grateful.'

'But you would like to find them yourself, I think? You are that kind of man.'

Wellsted nods.

'You cannot travel far inland of Muscat, Lieutenant. It is dangerous country and you are a *Nazarene*. As soon as you get into *Wahabi* territory they will tear you to pieces whether you are under my protection or not. Your fellows went in from the *Dhofari* side and only travelled a few days. To find them, you will have to roam

159

further. The *Bedu*, as you know, do not stay in one place for long. They set up camp all over the desert — they trade as they go and follow the water. To find them will be difficult and they are as likely in *Wahabi* territory as in my own. If I give you permission, I am only granting you leave to die.'

The sultan pulls the wing from a succulent chicken as if to demonstrate the technique.

'Even with royal approval it is too dangerous. You,' he points out, 'have blue eyes. You might as well be a woman travelling alone.'

'Yes,' Wellsted says sadly. 'That is probably a disadvantage. I see what you mean.'

'The interior is for the *Bedu* and for slavers, of course. They travel heavily armed and remain, for the most part, unmolested.'

'Slavers,' Wellsted wonders out loud. 'Do you think that our officers might have been taken into slavery?'

The sultan inclines his head and shrugs his shoulders very slightly. 'Who knows, Lieutenant Wellsted. White men make poor slaves.'

'I see. Quite,' Wellsted beams, entirely unoffended by this shortcoming in his race.

'I will think upon it,' the sultan promises.

The orchestra changes rhythm to a slow and haunting melody and, having found out what was wanted of him, the sultan loses interest. He abruptly turns away from the lieutenant and starts to talk to the fellow on the other side. Wellsted pops a piece of moist chicken into his mouth and savours it slowly. The young dancers are gyrating in the corner to the lyrical sound of the *oud* and he wonders what the ship's boy, Hughes, might make of them — they are almost the same age after all.

'Queer lot,' he imagines the boy saying in his sing-song Welsh accent. 'Not like them hoochy-coochy girls at the bazaar. There's pretty.'

Wellsted smiles at the memory of the boy dancing his imitation of the slave girls in the passageway. This feast feels familiar and he is more at ease here than he has been in weeks, he realises. It is good to eat his fill again and to be in company. He looks around. There are so many fascinating sights among the richly robed hoi polloi of Muscat. On the other side of the assembly he notices a small monkey sitting on a cushion next to its master. The animal is eating a banana. Both these items catch the lieutenant's attention for they are unusual and quite rare. Bananas must be imported — this feast is amazingly luxurious, he thinks and picks off some more meat, slipping it into his mouth as the monkey carefully finishes off his dinner and looks around at the assembled company with such elegant composure that Wellsted bursts into laughter.

'He is a fine little fellow, is he not?' a voice next to him says.

The man sits down. He is tall and dark with an authoritative air. His skin smells of leather. From nowhere, the slaves run to put a cup of coffee into his hand. He knocks back his drink in one, smacking his lips.

'My friend caught that monkey in Africa. He is very fond of it.'

Wellsted smiles. 'I can imagine,' he says. 'He is a cheery little chap.'

Asaf Ibn Mohammed hesitates a moment — nothing about Kasim could ever truly be deemed cheery, not even his pretty pet. When he first captured the monkey it chattered almost all the time but after a fortnight Ibn Mohammed's childhood friend had so tamed the little creature that he did not even require a tether to stay at his master's side. He has never raised his hand to the little beast. He has never had to. Kasim is a natural queller of independent instincts — a true enslaver.

'So, as I understand it, you have lost two men,' Ibn Mohammed says evenly. 'Ali Ibn Mudar has told me of it. He asked for my help.'

Wellsted pushes his hair back from his face. There is something in this man's tone that makes his muscles tighten, as if he ought to get ready to run.

'You must be a powerful man if Ibn Mudar believes you can help them,' he says.

Ibn Mohammed laughs. 'They teach you in Bombay to flatter the Arabs, do they not? They teach you to eat like a man, even how to sit down. Well, I do not need you to tell me whether I am powerful or not. And please do not go on to mention honour and respect — really, you white men must think we are fools.'

'Please accept my apologies.' Wellsted sees no measure in angering this strange man any further.

'You have talked to Said Ibn Sultan of this matter?' the slaver asks.

162

'I have.'

'They say that your captain wishes you dead, Lieutenant. What is it you have done that displeases him?'

Wellsted casts a glance over at Haines who has given up trying to eat and is sitting with the detritus of his meal around him. This man is well informed about life aboard the *Palinurus* and as far as Wellsted is concerned that is a good thing, however disconcerting. A well-informed man is exactly what he needs — Mickey has clearly done well to consult him. With the subject broached, the lieutenant is determined that he will not be distracted — not even by insults.

'You chose to come to me, not to Captain Haines. And the matter in hand surely is the missing men. Are Jessop and Jones alive?'

Ibn Mohammed stares straight into Wellsted's eyes and the lieutenant has to steel himself in order not to shudder. Those eyes are like long, blank tunnels that pull him into a cold place from which there is no escape.

'My information is three weeks old, or perhaps slightly older. They were alive then,' Ibn Mohammed says flatly.

Wellsted does not let the relief he feels show on his face.

'Can you have them released?'

'Ah,' the Arab says. 'Someone will have to go and get them. There will be money involved, naturally. And a negotiation. As they have no doubt told you in your Bombay, negotiations and good manners are terribly important to we Arabs.'

'Fairness,' Wellsted says plainly, 'is important to all men, though few benefit from it, in my experience — in London or here.'

'They say your Lieutenant Jones squeals like a pig,' Ibn Mohammed continues evenly. *Khawal.* He almost spits the word. 'Not really a man at all, Lieutenant.'

'How much money will it take to get them back?' Wellsted asks. 'And what must we do?'

Ibn Mohammed is about to answer. He has a natural sense of drama and is set to make the white man wait for the information that he so desires. He leans in slightly and takes a breath, but before he can speak the *soultan* notices that he has arrived at the table and slaps him on the back heartily, removing all sense of mystery, for the great man himself now wants to know.

'What of these two men missing in the desert, Ibn Mohammed?' The monarch sounds bluff. 'They have offended the *Bedu*. A difficult business. If anyone can help our British friends here, then surely it must be you. As I understand it there is not an oasis between here and Riyadh that does not send its news to you and Kasim.'

'We were only just talking of it, Your Highness,' Wellsted bows. 'And this man — Ibn Mohammed, is it? — says that the men are, to his knowledge, alive.'

'Alive?' Haines voice booms over from the other side of the room. 'Are you sure?'

Ibn Mohammed does not give the captain the courtesy of an answer (for who cannot see the man is a fool?). Instead, the slaver bows low to his *soultan*.

'Lieutenant Wellsted wants to fetch them himself,' the sultan says eagerly. The notion clearly amuses him

'Ah,' Ibn Mohammed's smile tightens like a vice.

'I told him — the *Wahabi* will kill him. But if you were to offer him your protection. If you were to shelter him, to go personally, Ibn Mohammed, to see to these men . . . ' The sultan trails off.

Ibn Mohammed's smile is fixed now. He nods courteously. No man argues at court with his ruler. 'As you wish, Said Ibn Sultan.'

In a moment, Kasim is at his partner's side and the sultan continues.

'Yes. Yes. Kasim too,' he nods. 'With both of you, he will be safe, surely. And whatever these white men have done, well, you will dispatch the business in the most honourable way. Bring them back.'

'The Indian Navy cannot wait at port for Wellsted to trail off into the back of beyond,' Haines starts. 'His Majesty's orders for the ship *Palinurus* . . . '

The sultan dismisses the captain with a wave of his hand. 'He has my permission. I insist on giving the lieutenant my permission,' he states baldly.

Wellsted bows. 'Thank you, sir,' he says. 'I will be honoured.'

'The first white man to cross the desert,' the sultan muses, thinking how interesting it will be to see what happens. 'Perhaps it is time one of you tried.'

21

When, over breakfast, Mickey hears of what has taken place at the palace the night before, he bursts out laughing, spilling thick, creamy *labneh* onto his lap. The juxtaposition of Wellsted being taken into the interior by Muscat's richest slave traders seems hopelessly comic at first. The Englishman is pale as milk and, as far as Mickey can tell, despite a couple of forays up a mountainside in Socotra and the day's trek to the oasis at the edge of the desert where he picked up the information about his fellows, the lieutenant is absolutely inexperienced in the hardship of travelling across desert terrain.

The Empty Quarter, or *Rubh Al Khali*, is one of the most formidable deserts on the planet and hardly the place for a white man to start to learn about survival on the sands. Mickey is enjoying the image that has appeared in his mind of the look on the man's face when he realises that his jolly jaunt will prove to be the most dangerous journey of his life. Then it strikes him, suddenly, that it may not be comic at all and that Lieutenant Wellsted is in fact, in grave danger. Neither Kasim nor Ibn Mohammed can be pleased they have been sent on this mission (which truly is beneath them). Worse, that they will have to undertake it in the company of a pink-faced novitiate will come as much of a slap in the face as having to go at all. The slavers are, without dispute, hard and difficult men — the hardest and most difficult. Kasim told Mickey the afternoon before, as he carefully ate his way through a plate of cheese curds, coriander and cucumber at Ibn Mohammed's compound, that he was planning his next trip to Somalia. When Mickey mentioned the notorious pirates off the coastline, Kasim shrugged his shoulders at the dangers.

'The *Zigua* tribe are elegant,' he said, by which Mickey understood that the tribe were marketable and worth the risk. If anything, Mickey had the sense that Kasim would relish the opportunity to kill a pirate or two. To be sent into the desert instead of sailing to the profitable and exciting shores of eastern Africa will rankle the men horribly, he is sure — and neither Kasim or Ibn Mohammed are men that you could possibly wish to rankle. They are far too ruthless for that.

'Now I must amend my plan,' Mickey mumbles.

He had intended to head north himself that afternoon in order to contract a family of *Bedu* that Kasim recommended as middle men. Given the insular world of the desert tribes, Mickey reasoned that if desert *Bedu* dealt with desert *Bedu* it would keep tribal tensions and inter-racial hatred to a minimum and the trade would go off as smoothly as possible. Now the sultan has ignored those sensitivities, for he is sending not only the slave traders but another white man as well, and in the process has probably raised the ransom price quite considerably.

167

'Feck it!' Mickey says under his breath. 'Feck it!'

He scoops up the spilled *labneh* and downs the last of his painfully strong coffee, then Mickey Ibn Mudar leaves the house and makes directly for the dock to try to improve matters on the Indian Navy's behalf.

★　★　★

The *Palinurus* is quiet. The deck is newly washed and is still drying in the sun but the captain has not yet emerged and the crew are passing the time dicing and drinking under the shade of a tarpaulin that has been set up for the purpose. The midshipmen are nowhere to be seen; they have left early for an outing to inspect the city walls. Mickey walks on board unchallenged and makes his way past the first of the carefully furled square sails before Wellsted gets to him.

'Morning, sir,' the lieutenant smiles. 'You have found us at rest.'

Mickey shakes his hand warmly. 'You are off to the desert I hear, Lieutenant.'

'Yes,' Wellsted beams.

'With Kasim and Ibn Mohammed.'

The smile fades.

'I am glad to see that this worries you as much as it worries me.'

'The sultan ordered them to look after our interests,' Wellsted says evenly.

'I rather think that may be my job,' Mickey replies, his tone ominous. 'And for a start, we cannot send you into the wilderness as a Nazarene.'

'My eyes are blue,' Wellsted echoes the *soultan* the night before. He isn't sure what else to say — he can't help his colour.

There is a crack as the low door to the captain's cabin opens and Haines emerges onto the deck, putting on his hat as he steps into the sunlight.

'Ah, Mr Al Mudar!' he hails Mickey. 'Well met! What can we do, sir, about this nonsense? Wellsted going to the interior on a damn wild-goose chase? Jessop and Jones are dead by now. Do you not agree?'

'Oh no, Captain.' Mickey makes a little bow. 'We have good information that the men are being held alive, though how long they might survive I cannot say. I think, sir, it would be foolish not to try to rescue them.'

'And this is the man for the job, is it?' Haines indicates the lieutenant. 'My last fully trained officer,' he sneers.

Mickey casts his eyes skywards. It is not what he'd have chosen, there is no denying it. 'Yes, sir. The sultan has spoken.'

'The bally sultan, is it?' Haines booms.

Mickey looks round nervously. This is not the manner in which the citizens of Muscat speak about their ruler and down on the docks there are enough English speakers for the insult to be understood.

'Please, Captain,' he says. 'His Majesty recognises the sultan and I fear . . . ' his voice tails off to a whisper, 'We must accommodate his

169

wishes. It is sport to him, I expect, and if Lieutenant Wellsted does not now fall in with the wishes of our illustrious ruler, then no mission may be sent to rescue the men at all.'

Haines considers this momentarily. Not sending a mission is, of course, his preferred option, but he knows he cannot really take it. For a start, a group of the men have stopped their dicing on the deck and are congregated, hands behind their backs, listening to every word. The captain knows that he cannot refuse to send a rescue mission for two of his crew when it has just been stated the men are alive, and he certainly does not feel he can do so in front of men he is expecting to fight and perhaps die on his orders. He's been grappling with this all morning in his cabin and he finally gives up the tussle. To be honest, it is a relief to do so, the midshipmen are competent enough for the short voyage back to Bombay and it will be a damn sight more pleasant on board without the lieutenant anyway.

'Oh, very well,' he dismisses Wellsted with a wave of his hand. 'You will return to Muscat, Wellsted, on completion and report back to Mr Al Mudar here, who will be well aware of the Marine's movements and which ships can return you to Bombay. He will provision you, will you not, Mr Al Mudar? Be as quick as you can on His Majesty's time, Wellsted, for God's sake. We're not paying you to sightsee and buy souvenirs.'

Wellsted tries not to smile too widely for he is aware that this will only bait the captain, but

Mickey smirks — there are no souvenirs in the desert; the English treat everything as if it is merely the opportunity for a picnic. It perpetually surprises him that they are so effective.

Wellsted salutes. 'Thank you, sir,' he says.

Mickey takes the lieutenant's arm and nods at the captain.

'Safe voyage, Captain Haines. I will look after Lieutenant Wellsted to the best of my ability,' he says and then, turning to Wellsted, he leads him away along the deck. 'So you must be Turkish, I think. Come,' the agent insists, 'we will go to a shop I know of and dress you in Turkish clothes. It will also account for your accent. You must speak Arabic now at all times, Lieutenant Wellsted. You need the practice. We have not got long. When the *soultan* commands, all obey. Come with me.'

* * *

The men walk down the gangplank and Wellsted feels butterflies stirring in his stomach. This will be an adventure if ever there was one. Mickey cuts along the dock and up an alleyway towards the heart of Muttrah, past stalls selling strange-looking birds in wooden cages, calabashes strung onto long poles and long-haired goatskin water flasks. A group of *Bedu* loiter in the shady interiors, smoking among piles of basketware, leather boxes and tapestry bags. Both Mickey and Wellsted know that any conversation they indulge in on the street can be overheard so they remain silent as they climb the cobblestone incline, weaving through the crowd. They pass purposefully through the jewellery quarter, where beads of malachite, amber and turquoise lie on display and cheap, brass bangles and shoals of rings in basketware containers are pushed to the front of the stalls. Dancing jewels — bell-strewn, thin chains of different lengths and shimmering silver earrings and headdresses adorn the interiors and deep inside, in the dark to the rear, there is the occasional glimmer of a well-cut stone changing hands. In one stall there is a donkey, in another two goats tied to a rock.

After a few minutes, Mickey veers to the left and knocks on the door of a flat-fronted house up a poor side street. The child who opens it has bare feet and a thin cloth, greying with dirt, draped around his bony frame. Mickey snaps something in Arabic and the men are admitted. They clatter upwards on a dusty, stone staircase directly in front of the door. Upstairs, as they enter, two women run from the small room, their black robes flying in their haste, and all that is left behind them is a fat man who, Wellsted realises, he has been able to smell since they entered the house. The odour is a mixture of garlic, grease and stale sweat. The fat man offers them a copper shaker containing a liquid that smells very faintly of rose-water to freshen themselves while he claps his hands and shouts for refreshments. Despite the show of hospitality, he eyes the lieutenant carefully. The same child who opened the door appears with a tray of mint tea. His nails are ragged and crusted with dirt.

He carefully deposits the tea at the fat man's side and scurries from the room.

The house is cramped and the sound of its inhabitants moving around, the clatter of plates and odd snatches of muffled conversation, penetrate its thin walls. Wooden boxes lie on the floor, spilling their contents haphazardly. It is difficult to tell if this place is a shop or a home or both and what purpose the room may be put to, for in one corner there is what looks like a pile of old bedding while on a table to one side there is a collection of grimy lamps of all sizes — the kind of array by which Aladdin would be fascinated and on account of which he would immediately fall, no doubt, into an adventure. The smell of cooking emanates from downstairs though the aroma of baking *khubz* is obliterated as the fat man gesticulates in welcome. Wellsted and Mickey crouch on cushions and each accept a grubby glass cup of mint tea with a thin film of oil on top.

'I have brought my friend,' Mickey explains. 'He needs a disguise. Used clothes, not too fine, in the manner of the Turks, a goatskin for water — something worn but serviceable — and a weapon — no, two weapons — *khandjar* knives.'

The fat man peers at Wellsted and it is all that the lieutenant can do not to veer away from the stench. 'Yes, yes,' he mumbles.

From those two words alone it is apparent that the merchant has some kind of strange speech impediment; Wellsted can understand what he says though he has to concentrate. The man's voice is singsong and his manner far more formal than the surroundings warrant.

'He is to be Turkish, you say. But he is very pale, is he not?'

Mickey nods but dismisses the comment with a wave of his hand indicating that his headdress will have to provide cover. Wellsted will simply tie his *kaffiya* across his face and make a mask — a *litham*. It is not an uncommon manner of dress, particularly in the desert.

'You wish him to appear an Anatolian warrior?'

'No. Not a man of war. Definitely not. A trader,' Mickey decides. 'Comfortable, understated, not too wealthy but neither a pauper. Inconspicuous. The Turks are dangerous, Lieutenant, or their military men are. Ten years ago they razed Riyadh to the ground — a dispute over sovereignty. It is still held badly in some quarters. We will make you Turkish on account of your colouring, but it must be clear always that you are a Turkish trader not a soldier, do you see?'

Wellsted nods. He is well aware that the Ottoman Empire is a well-built bully of a state which is outgrowing its borders like a muscle man bulges out of his clothes. The Turks' territories extend to the Balkans in the west and well into Tunisia in northern Africa. Even though they have been booted northwards by the desert Arabs, they are bound to try their luck in the desert again and attempt to move the line of the border southwards and dominate the Peninsula once more, if they can.

'I understand,' he nods.

The fat man's cheeks gleam with sweat but he does not speak, only thinks for a moment about what Mickey has said and the white man's response. He has been privy to a conversation about which he feels uncomfortable, as if the two men have been discussing matters of the *harim* or personal financial arrangements. He discards the information with a grunt and then heaves himself off the cushions and leaves the room. Mickey regards the tea glass before him and places it carefully back on the tray.

'He is right,' he says, 'about your skin. You are very pale.'

Wellsted shrugs. There is little he can do about his inability to pick up a tan. He has spent most of the last ten years on sailing ships, and if that hasn't done the trick, nothing will. Instead, he turns his attention to the issues with which he will have to deal.

'Do you believe, sir, that my life will be in danger from Kasim and Ibn Mohammed?'

Mickey looks around as if Wellsted has made this comment in a crowded room and he is expecting it to draw attention. He leans in conspiratorially.

'They won't kill you. But they would let you die, I imagine.'

'The oath of the caravan — ' Wellsted starts.

Mickey stares at him with eyes so wide that the lieutenant stops mid-sentence. 'The oath of the caravan applies, perhaps, to poor *Bedu*, or an oath between Muslim brothers, shall we say? Kasim and Ibn Mohammed owe you little. Less than that. Please, do not be naïve. They are only

175

taking you on the sultan's orders and it will be no shame to them if you die as long as they do not brandish the sword that kills you. Kasim and Ibn Mohammed have their uses but this is not how I would have chosen to rescue Dr Jessop and Lieutenant Jones. Please, make no mistake, Lieutenant, you mean as little to those men as a poor Catholic means to King William.'

The lieutenant's eyes narrow. 'What?' he says. 'Whatever makes you say that?'

'It is an expression one of my wives uses.' Mickey almost blushes. 'Is it not colloquial?'

'No. Is your wife . . . ?'

'She is a white woman. British.'

'I see.'

'And not a believer as it happens,' Mickey continues. 'In my religion or her own.'

Before Mickey can say any more, the fat man returns with a bundle of clothes and insists on Wellsted stripping to try them on. He motions his instructions and peers short-sightedly without reservation at the lieutenant's legs, which are so white that he judges them almost blue. One robe after another is discarded until they come to a plain blue *jubbah*, which is slipped over a pair of loose, red trousers. Then Mickey demonstrates the correct manner to drape a white *kaffiya* and shows Wellsted how to holster his *khandjar*, which is visible to all and a Turkish knife, a small, razor-sharp, one-sided dagger, which is hidden within easy reach. The *khandjar*, however, is pure Arab. The curved blade is sheathed in an ornate casing as is the fashion, with silver filigree over the moulded leather.

'It is beautiful.' Wellsted handles the weapon.

'You must learn to use it,' Mickey shrugs.

His own *khandjar* is so encrusted in decoration that it is difficult to believe it can be used for killing, though in Mickey's comfortable Muscat life there is little need for violence and his knife is, in truth, entirely ceremonial. By contrast, Wellsted's weapon is quite restrained in design. Mickey says nothing about it though he feels vaguely paternal as he buckles it over the lieutenant's belly, for it is a father's duty to give his son his first *khandjar*. Then he carefully demonstrates where to fasten the two worn leather belts that the fat man hands to him, smooth as His Lordship's valet.

'This way you can carry a skin of water easily,' he explains.

Last of all, the fat man brings thin, leather shoes and helps Wellsted to step into them. Mickey is delighted, moving a stray fold of fabric to one side as he peers at the details.

'Like this,' he insists. 'Like this. It is foreign but not too foreign. Good. I think perhaps you might even be a noble Turkish man. An *effendi*. We shall call you Kalil Aga Effendi. You will have to grow a beard, of course,' he muses, surveying the result carefully as the fat man pulls Wellsted's naval uniform into an untidy pile and hands it over, swapping the uniform with Mickey for payment — a small goatskin pouch with its hair completely worn away. The sound of clinking metal demonstrates that the purse contains coins but, it seems to Wellsted, unusual for an Arabian deal, that the amount has not been discussed.

'Kalil Aga Effendi,' Wellsted repeats.

'Yes. Looking like this you will pass,' Mickey pronounces, slipping a thin band of tarnished gold onto Wellsted's index finger as a finishing touch. 'You look like a Turk, from a distance at least.'

Wellsted gazes down at his robes. 'The man who owned these . . . ?' he wonders out loud.

The fat man shrugs his shoulders. 'Dead,' he pronounces. 'He died of the fever last week and his slaves sold everything.'

'I see.' Wellsted does not feel uneasy.

'You can ride a camel already?' Mickey checks.

'Yes. The first time I rode a camel,' Wellsted starts good-humouredly on his campfire story which has stood him in good stead, but Mickey stops him short, waving off the fat man's offer of the customary parting frankincense as he makes for the door.

'That is fine,' he commands. 'Come now, Lieutenant.'

He bows curtly to the fat man, who looks relieved not to have to endure the ritual of perfuming his guests before their departure. Then Mickey leads the way back down the staircase.

As they wind through the dusty, cobblestone alleyways back towards his office, Mickey picks up his pace. 'Come,' he says. 'They will be provisioning themselves — but it will not be long before they summon you. We must hasten to my office. Come. Come.'

'Rashid,' he calls as they enter the doorway. 'Bring me Rashid! Climb the stairs, Lieutenant

178

Wellsted. We are running out of precious moments. It is my duty to make you ready — to give you the very best chance of survival. Rashid! My assistant will show you the most important thing.'

Wellsted brightens. 'And what is that?' he enquires curiously.

Mickey looks at him askance and then reaches into one of the cubby holes behind his desk. He tosses a small rug in the lieutenant's direction. Wellsted sees it is of a Turkish design — red with a traditional, intricate gold and black pattern. Mickey motions for him to lay the carpet on the ground.

'Why, you must learn how to pray, sir. You must be part of the brotherhood. You will perform *wudu*, you will understand the direction of Makkah. This prayer mat will be your own *mosque* in the desert. How could you be one of us, how could you be Turkish or a nobleman without it? You must learn immediately how to pray.'

22

Zena watches the fuss from her window and she is glad the slavers are leaving town. At Ibn Mohammed's compound more than a dozen thoroughbred camels are gathered, some for riding and some which will serve as pack animals. The riding camels are tethered in the shade while the supplies are loaded onto their cousins. The doors to the courtyard are open and the expedition's activities spill onto the street.

Ibn Mohammed inspects what the men are doing. He kicks one of the bearers hard, then he hits the man in the face for some mistake. The slave falls to the ground but does not fight the rain of punches and Ibn Mohammed gets bored and walks away. Watching from the shade, insouciant, Kasim loiters, while another slave grooms his horse. The little monkey climbs the litter that will be hoisted onto one of the baggage camels, jumps to the ground and then starts climbing again. Kasim orders the animal be taken away — the monkey will not be going on the trip.

Three *Bedu* wait silently nearby with a still and endless patience that draws Zena's eyes to them, while Ibn Mohammed moves quickly, checking ropes and inspecting the goatskins, two wicker cages of chickens, an over-stuffed sack of flour and two huge boughs of dates that will keep the party supplied between oases. All the while,

Ibn Mohammed causes ructions in his wake, the bearers each nervous he will target them next, keeping their heads down and refusing to meet his eye.

Zena thinks that the weeks have worked some kind of magic. She is not afraid of these men any more. Now she merely loathes them and everything they stand for. She watches the compound carefully though she isn't sure why. There is, she keeps telling herself, nothing she can do. She licks the final smears from the plate of pudding she has eaten for breakfast and settles down on the cushions. It is good to feel her body filling out again. This morning there is a little roll of fat around her hips. She leans back and kicks her legs in the air so she can feel it wobble. Then she laughs. She is no longer the terrified child who arrived, half-starved, jumpy and desperate.

Every evening, she dances and laughs with the master. Whether he brings back one of his slave boys or not, he still lingers at her side, orders her to perform and talks a little of his day which, it turns out, comprises of an endless round of social calls interspersed with some shopping and a game or two of *shesh besh* of which he is clearly fond. In contrast to her daytimes, the evenings are frantic. Two days ago the master ordered drums for his room, which one of the slave boys plays with great skill. The way he pounds the rhythm reminds Zena of the drums of celebration in her village. Now and again, the master rises to dance to the cadence, though he has no natural elegance. Still, he grabs one of the silk scarves and whirls it over his head, trying to

181

copy the sinuous movements of her hips, though he cannot. At least it makes him laugh. When he has done, he watches her dancing alone and then sometimes they kiss but it never goes any further. Kissing Zena makes the master down-hearted so she cheers him with stories of the hills near Bussaba and the cosmopolitan traders she met when she lived there. He likes her descriptions of the men's clothes and asks about their individual tastes — some will not eat pig and some will not eat any animal. Each god makes myriad demands of its believers and Zena and her grandmother always complied with the travellers' requests, or rather those of their individual deities. The master is fascinated.

'So the men who wear ostrich feathers — what do they believe?' he asks. 'And the ones with orange turbans — will they never cut their hair?'

Zena tries to explain the tenets of Animism or the Sikh refusal to shave. Her knowledge, in truth, is sketchy and she makes things up where she has to, but it keeps him amused between the drums and the dancing. Sometimes she rubs his feet with thick, scented oil, which appeared one day in a brass phial on one of the low tables. They think of everything.

If he desires one of his boys, he dismisses Zena and she sleeps on the cool tiles outside his door, but if the master is alone she lies next to him on the bed. It is more comfortable, of course, but difficult to settle. He drapes his arm around her and passes out immediately, snoring so loudly that Zena only dozes in and out of consciousness beside him. There is, of course, plenty of time for sleeping during the day and on the days after she spends the night in his bed the food that is sent from the kitchen is better. She thinks to herself that it is difficult now to imagine what it feels like to be hungry when her belly is full. The slaves bring everything she needs before she has to think of it for herself. Still, she'd give a day's food to be free to venture out and explore the city she can see from her window. Or, the thought occurs to her, a week's food to choose for herself who she would like to kiss.

She shifts on the low, wooden divan, distracted by this notion. She tries not to dwell on it, despite herself. Daydreaming of how things could be better only means feeling more discontented with the way things are. Zena does not jump up when the door opens. The *sidis* come and go throughout the day and she scarcely notices them now. She turns comfortably onto her side and closes her eyes. There is a pause of absolute silence and then the slave girl's repose is disturbed by the loud crack of clapping. Zena opens her eyes and peers over the back of the padded bench where she is horrified to see the Abyssinian who bought her all those weeks ago. He has his hands on his hips and a stern expression on his face. The man has never visited the room in all the time Zena has been in residence. Something has clearly come to pass and immediately she jumps up to make her *salaams*.

'Ah!' he says with a sneer. 'So I have caught your attention at last.'

The Abyssinian motions her to turn so he can

183

inspect her, taking his time to do so. His eyes move across her skin carefully as if he is checking her for damage.

'Take off the jewellery,' he orders.

'Why?' Zena asks.

It is an innocent question but the man only claps his hands in fury and points at her as if he might have her beaten for her insolence.

'Do it, girl! Who do you think you are?'

Slowly, Zena removes the bangles, the ankle chain with its tiny bells and a ring. With some difficulty she pulls free the string of beads that have been woven into her hair and the seed pearls that fall from her earlobes like tiny raindrops. She carefully deposits the tangle of finery on the colourful cushions where she has been sitting and no longer meets his eyes. The Abyssinian is not fond of her like the master is, and she realises that she has behaved inappropriately. The slave master inspects her once more until, seemingly satisfied, he turns to leave the room.

'Come,' he orders, motioning with his finger.

Zena does not ask where they are going.

Outside the room, two house slaves are waiting — both male. They fall into line and wordlessly follow the Abyssinian through the shady hallways. As her bare feet slap against the smooth tiles, she wonders if she is going to be bathed or if the master has decided to move rooms or perhaps even give her a small room with a bed of her own. During her sojourn in the master's quarters she has never explored any further than the tiles outside his door. The house is as labyrinthine as she remembers it and it occurs to her that it is odd she has never ventured down these corridors for herself. Like a tame bird, she has stayed where she was put despite the door of her cage being left open, and all her dreams of escaping the household. Now, from behind one closed door she hears two women laughing and behind another the sound of a string instrument played poorly, as if by a child. Three *sidis* pass, carrying trays of food decorated with gemlike green grapes and slivers of orange. Zena can no longer smell a meal before she sees it but she does wonder whose breakfast the lavish achettes contain.

The master never talks of his relations, other than to sneer at his father's marital intentions for him. Now Zena realises that there must be fifty people living in this vast house and that is not counting the slaves. It's a large family — wives and children, all in separate rooms around the compound. She wonders suddenly what the other women are like and if, unlike her, they move freely, even visit each other during the day. Each household has its own rules on such matters. *I might explore later*, she thinks as she anxiously turns her head, trying to take it all in — and to memorise the path back to the only place she belongs now — her master's chamber.

At last, they descend the stairs and come into the courtyard where she first entered the house several weeks ago. A thin Nubian in a vivid green *jubbah* and a red embroidered cap, stands in the shade of a palm, sipping a glass cup of coffee. The Abyssinian bows.

'Here she is,' he says.

Zena feels suddenly uneasy. What is this man doing here? The hairs on the back of her neck prickle, her fingers are numb and her heart is pounding. She senses something is wrong and pulls away as one of the slaves tethers her smoothly with a rope. Her stomach is turning over and her hands are shaking and sweating at once.

'What is happening? What have I done?' she pleads quietly, her eyes wide as she whispers to the slaves, her breath sweet and milky.

No one answers, no one will meet her gaze or even pay her the least attention as the rope is tied tightly around her wrist and a veil of sheer silk to cover her for modesty's sake, is placed over her head. It is as if she is as inconsequential as she is invisible — everyone else here seems to know what to do and none of them say a word.

'He has spoiled this one, she is very indulged,' the Abyssinian says to the Nubian, 'but she is beautiful and her Arabic is excellent. I am sure she will fall into line with some proper handling.'

'She dances?' the Nubian enquires as he surveys her carefully, bending down to get a proper look and pulling the veil aside.

'I believe so.'

The Nubian nods, as if striking a bargain. 'You are right about her beauty. My master has instructed me to say that your master honours him. In settling his debt so generously, he settles it with honour. *Subhan Allah*.' Glorious is Allah.

'My master's father has instructed me to offer you gold instead of this worthless girl,' the

186

Abyssinian says graciously. 'He will pay the two hundred dollars he bought her for — a greater sum surely than the debt your master is due.'

The Nubian bows. 'Thank you,' he replies. 'The *habshi* will suffice for she was the bargain that was made.'

Zena feels sick as the Nubian takes the rope in his hand. She is trembling. She does not want to leave. 'But my master,' she stutters, 'he will be home when the sun sets and he will be expecting me . . . he cannot want me to go.'

A flicker of a smile crosses the Nubian's face. 'Your master has given you to mine, girl. You will dance for someone new tonight.'

'They offered you gold,' she says desperately. 'They offered you gold instead.'

The Nubian ignores her and turns to go. Zena stares in the direction of the Abyssinian, pleading silently with him to say something more, but he is only bowing. She does not know it but he is wondering how much longer the young master's disgraceful habits will be tolerated in his father's household. The boys and the gambling are both illegal and his indulgence in such pursuits shame his honourable father, while losing this girl over a game of *shesh besh* is simply a waste. Though he thinks the young master should be beaten for his wickedness, the wise old retainer says nothing, of course, and he does not meet the pretty little *habshi*'s eye. Instead, he bows to the leaving guest.

Zena's heart pounds as the slaves rush to open the heavy door and she is taken away. Her mind floods with blind panic. This is not what she had in mind when she made a wish to leave the household. No one helps her. No one comes to stop him from taking her away and she is pulled, though she gives no real resistance, her heart racing harder even than when she was taken from her village. *It makes no sense,* she thinks. *He likes me, I know he does. And I like it here. I feel safe. Why would he send me away?* Desperately, she fumbles for an explanation that no one has any interest in supplying. But still she tries to find the words, frantically hoping someone will do something to help. Zena gulps in the hot air as, terrified and panting, with no choices presenting themselves, she steps out into the relentless sunshine of the busy Muscat street and the thick doors of the courtyard close behind her, cutting her off from everything that has become familiar.

Halfway up the street at the corner, pulling her like a tethered goat, the Nubian loses patience with the girl's reluctance. She is dawdling, staring around and pulling back heavily. She is acting as if she is stunned and, for the man, it is far too much effort to guide her. He jerks the rope.

'Have you not learnt yet that it is useless to resist?' he spits.

Zena's temper flashes suddenly and she stamps her foot onto the hot stones. The Nubian raises his hand as if to strike her. No one in the street even notices as she pulls back, cowering. The Nubian sighs and then desists, not wanting to mark the girl before his master can inspect his property. He jerks his head to indicate that she is to follow and when he pulls the rope again she is tame once more and they turn the corner past the preparations for Ibn Mohammed's caravan on which she looked down so loftily only a few minutes before.

Outside the compound the Nubian greets one or two of the men — retainers in Ibn Mohammed's household who shake his hand and clap him on the back. All ignore Zena completely as they stop to exchange pleasantries. Zena peers inside the courtyard around the edge of her veil. From his vantage point under the tree, Kasim regards her plainly and she is unsure if he even recognises her. Next to him there is a plump, older man in a light cotton *jubbah* and a pale-skinned Turk who looks somehow familiar. Her mind is racing too fast to place him. These men are newly arrived, drinking coffee and talking quietly. When the Turk notices her she feels half-naked in her sheer *jilbab* and see-through veil, realising that many of the women in the doorways are in full *burquah*. Her stomach lurches at his gaze and suddenly she feels as if everyone is staring at her and whispering. *Look*, she thinks, *look at him eyeing me*. She feels furious and ashamed all at once. Still, she cannot help noticing that the Turk's eyes are a piercing blue. He points her out to his companions while still keeping his eyes upon her and the plainly dressed, grey-haired man walks over.

'Aziz?' he addresses the Nubian.

'Master,' the man bows with a serious air.

'This is the girl?'

He walks around her. 'Well, Farida will be pleased, no doubt.' Ibn Mudar, having won this girl in a bet, has no real use for her other than to gift her to his favourite wife. Slowly Zena realises that his eyes are not searching — the old man does not desire her. It is a relief. He seems scholarly and detached. He is, in fact, wondering what poetry his wife will employ to describe this creature. *As black as night*, he can hear her lilting voice saying. *The girl is a veritable dancing shadow. She's a flicker is she not?* Mickey often wonders what his wife might think of things.

'And she dances?' he checks.

'Yes. He assured me. And her Arabic is excellent. She has been educated.'

'You can read?' the old man asks Zena.

Zena nods. 'Only a little,' she says quietly.

'Yes, yes,' Mickey pronounces. 'That will be fine.'

The Nubian is about to move off when Kasim and the Turk stroll out of the compound and into the street with their coffee cups still in hand.

'A new wife for your *harim*?' Kasim enquires.

'No. A present for my wife,' Mickey says.

'We will not be trading this trip,' Kasim comments flatly. 'There will be no business in it.'

'We will trade in white men's souls,' Wellsted chimes in, finding it odd that dressed this way it is so easy to separate himself from being English.

Kasim shrugs. White men's souls are nothing to him. 'A girl like this, in Riyadh,' he says, 'is worth a hundred dollars more than in Muscat.'

'Really?' Wellsted is fascinated.

However much she's worth, he finds he cannot

190

take his eyes off her. There is something delicate and yet strong in her demeanour — something almost otherworldly. He wonders if it is simply too long since he has seen a woman or at least one who isn't shrouded in what amounts to a tent's worth of thick fabric.

'Why is she worth more in Riyadh?'

'Because she is so dark,' Kasim explains. 'The further from Africa you go the more the pretty ones fetch at auction. I recognise her, actually. She came from our last shipment. They have dressed her hair and fed her, but it's the same girl. She made two hundred Marie Theresa dollars. The rest of the village where we found her were not worth that much all together.'

Zena's eyes remain glued to the dusty stones at her feet.

'There is some profit in it, then,' Wellsted says.

Mickey smiles. 'But you do not approve, Lieutenant. I can hear it in your voice.'

'No, sir,' he admits to the agent. 'I cannot approve of one man owning another. It does not give the second man a sporting chance.'

Mickey bursts out laughing. 'What chance do you think this girl would have? If I free her now what can she possibly do?'

Wellsted considers. 'Why she can read — can she not teach? Marry and have a family?' He looks at Zena. 'Where are you from?' he asks, his gaze still steady.

Her heart is pounding so fast that she thinks she might be sick. Still, she looks composed, like an elegant statue or a scene from a painting. Mickey has drawn back the veil and he notices that her eyes are wide yet still and she stands as if she is held back a little from the scene around her — as if she is not really part of what is going on.

Zena thinks she is going to vomit sweet, milky slop all over this strange, pale foreigner whose clothes smell unwashed. This is a dangerous conversation and she knows it. If Ibn Mohammed strikes one of his men for packing a chicken incorrectly what will he do if he overhears a conversation such as this? Kasim, who she has seen with her own eyes murder any who resist him, has recognised her. They know she is nothing — only a stolen woman.

'Africa. Near Bussaba,' she manages to say, her mouth suddenly dry. *His eyes are extraordinary,* she thinks. *Blue like the sea.*

'You have family there?'

Zena nods. She thinks she has family, but of course, there is no way to tell what happened after she left.

'You expected to marry before you were brought to Muscat?'

She nods again, but does not explain she was unwilling.

'There,' Wellsted beams.

Mickey strokes his beard. 'Very well, Lieutenant, very well.' He considers for a moment or two. 'I will give you this girl as a parting gift, my *effendi*. She may prove useful on your trip for barter. But you must do with her what you will.'

Kasim's eyes brighten with anticipation at this development. There is little he likes so much as a bluff being called. 'You will sell her,' he says, 'you'll see. When we get to Riyadh, you will sell her for three hundred Marie Theresa silver dollars and you will pocket the profit and swallow your moral objections.'

'We cannot take her into the desert.' Wellsted is shocked.

'Why not?' Kasim is mocking him. 'If you set her free now she'll starve without your help and protection.'

'It's dangerous. She is no use in the desert. Think of the temperatures.'

'You have no use for a beautiful slave girl?' Kasim bursts out laughing. 'She is from Africa and you think it will be too hot for her! It does not surprise me, my friend, that your fellows find themselves caught by the *Bedu* and need to be rescued. It does not surprise me at all.'

Wellsted draws himself up. If he leaves her here, he reasons, the girl will never be free. If she comes he can see to the matter at the end of the trip.

'All right then,' he says. 'Thank you, Ibn Mudar. I accept your gift. We will take her in our caravan, under my protection, and when we have secured Jessop and Jones' freedom she shall also have hers. I will find a position for her as a free woman when we return. I swear.'

Shaded again by the sheer veil, a tear slopes down Zena's cheek but none of them see it.

'Now, for a start,' Wellsted says, 'we need to get her some travelling clothes, do we not?'

Mickey Ibn Mudar smiles. 'Yes, the responsibility of a master is upon you. And this boudoir outfit is not suitable for anywhere other than the *harim*. Let me assist. Aziz,' he addresses the Nubian, 'fetch a *burquah* for the lieutenant's *habshi*.'

The brightly dressed Nubian drops the rope immediately.

It is then Zena recognises the Turk. It is something about his body, the way he moves as he turns. He is the white man she half-blinded with the master's mirror. Why, she wonders, is he dressed that way? She has the sudden urge to tell him, 'I made you laugh. You squinted. That was me. I have seen you before.' But, of course, she says nothing, only thinks that close up, his pale, long hands are eerie, as if they are the hands of the dead. The blue of his irises looks savage. That this strange creature is her new master both fascinates and revolts her. He is confusing on every level. Unknown and intriguing, a new danger that cannot be second-guessed. Even in her grandmother's house, where she thought she had seen every kind of man, there was no one who looked so alien. It is eerie. When she was kidnapped from her village, at least Zena understood the direction, the motivation of the men who took her. This man could want anything no matter what he says about giving back her freedom. His Arabic is heavily accented and his vocabulary is strange and off-kilter. Zena knows she is good at sizing people up but she cannot read this strange creature at all. As she walks inside to change into the *burquah* he has provided, she turns to look at him.

'I don't want to go to the desert with you,' she whispers under her breath.

194

'What?' Aziz asks, his voice tetchy, as if he is dealing with a difficult child. This slave girl is clearly troublesome and he is glad he is not going to be responsible for her in his master's house.

'Nothing,' Zena replies. 'Nothing.' And she follows him inside to change.

★ ★ ★

It is an hour or two before midday by the time the caravan sets out. Mickey clutches each of the free men to him, kissing them three times as is the custom, and then he waves them off, smiling and nodding at the gates of Ibn Mohammed's courtyard. Leaving Muscat is a slow business, for the streets are not designed to easily accommodate bulky groups of men and beasts and in this entourage there are over twenty men. Each leads his camel carefully so as not to overturn the tables and the mounds of wares outside Muttrah's stalls. Some riding camels are followed by a pack beast tethered on a short rope that brings up the rear. Because she has never ridden a camel before (a fact that causes hilarity among the other slaves), Zena is given a single beast to manage.

'This one,' the head slave thrusts the bridle into her hands. 'Take it. This one is easy. It's a stupid camel. It will follow even a woman.'

Zena does not retort. She watches as the streets become more residential and the houses smaller and wonders how she managed, once more, to come into the care of Kasim and Ibn

Mohammed. It is clear after only an hour that the white man is not really in charge. A mixture of hate and fear swills this way and that as Zena considers her options. Leaving the city feels even more like leaving home than the last time they took her. She wonders, momentarily, if she can drop hold of the camel's bridle and slip unseen down a side street. The caravan is busy and the men might not notice, but before she can decide, the slave next to her suddenly starts up a conversation.

'Leave the girl alone,' Kasim snaps at the boy. 'I have my eyes on you.'

And the moment is lost, for she knows Kasim's dark gaze is relentless and that if she has caught his attention there is no way she will be able to escape. *I should have been quicker*, she curses silently, grinding her teeth.

As they reach the very top of the hill and the houses become less frequent, they mount the camels properly and Wellsted takes one last look at the ship in the sparkling bay. On deck he can just make out two of the midshipmen, back from their excursions, dapper in their uniforms and overseeing some work that is underway at the mast head. They will set sail for Bombay in a day or two. He waves but receives no response from the tiny figures and then he turns onto the *wadi*. *In disguise, they are not able to recognise me*, he thinks. *Still, they know I am leaving. Perhaps the distance is simply too far to make me out.*

On the *wadi*, the ground is mostly mixed shingle and it takes concentration to ride across it on the camel's splayed hooves. This is, Wellsted thinks, the right place for him to be. Conditions aboard ship the past weeks have been intolerable and even though Ibn Mohammed and Kasim clearly despise him, their throwaway comments are not a patch on Captain Haines' incessant tirade. Besides that personal consideration, he has been given the *soultan's* permission to roam freely in his territories — an honour never before bestowed upon a foreigner. If he is to make his name, this will be his best chance, he thinks, never mind that his mission has the more noble purpose of a rescue. The Navy loves its pioneers. The societies in Bombay and London, of interest to all important men, thrive on the accounts of Britain's soldiers, sailors and empire builders lucky enough to be able to make excursions such as these. Not only might there be rewards but he is discovering the world on behalf of his country — on behalf of his family, it occurs to him. He suddenly feels Old Thomas' presence and spins around in his saddle, half-expecting the old man's ghost to be seated to the rear. Instead, behind him, the girl, completely covered in a dark *burquah*, is riding in tandem with one of Ibn Mohammed's slaves. All he can see of her is a pair of dark hands clinging onto the camel's worn, embroidered saddle on either side and a glimpse of her eyes. She seems steady enough with Kasim right behind her.

'What is your name?' he asks.

'Zena.' She looks startled.

'Zena,' Wellsted repeats. 'Zena.' It rolls easily off his tongue.

Ibn Mohammed brings his camel alongside at

a sharpish trot. The idea of asking a slave for her name amuses him. He does not know the name of his own house slaves and if he wanted to call them something, he would decide on a name on their behalf. The white man clearly has no idea.

'They are as hopeless as these stupid beasts,' he motions towards Zena. 'A camel without a master will not last more than a year, you know. They need to be tended. We give them a purpose and when they run away they are lucky if they last even the twelve months. Slaves likewise.'

Wellsted thinks he sees the whites of Zena's eyes flash from the thin strip open across her face and he approves. It is a sign that she has spirit.

'Well, sir, we shall see,' he says. 'Perhaps my *habshi* will surprise you.'

Ibn Mohammed laughs. There is nothing left in the world to surprise him. He has seen it all. 'Come,' he motions, 'we can go faster.'

He gallops to the rear of the camel train. Then he rounds on the final animal, poking the she-camel's tail with his long riding crop and making a loud, high shriek in imitation of an excited male. The group laugh as the terrified camel shoots ahead, convinced there is a male in the party, trying to mount her out of season. The slave perched on the high saddle clings on for dear life and in his wake everyone picks up their pace. The slavers seem, Wellsted notes, quite jolly now they have left Muscat. It is as if, in passing beyond the city's limits, they have been given a purpose.

'Keep up!' Ibn Mohammed shouts as he passes Wellsted.

They are hoping to make forty miles this first day, northwards over the *wadi*, as far as they can towards the rocky hills of the *jabel* beyond. It is an ambitious undertaking and one for which the Arabs have not procured a map. Still, they seem to know what they are doing and it feels good to be off the ship and out in the open. He clicks his tongue to encourage the camel.

'Gee up. Come on,' he says. And then catching himself, he changes the exclamation to '*Seent*' for he is Turkish now — Arabic is his second language and he must speak it at all times. With this exclamation, he lets out a cry that mimics the others around him to egg on his camel even faster and he speeds up thinking that, for all the fuss the Arabs make about the desert, it seems natural to be here. It is easier than one might expect, he decides, in this alien landscape, among these alien people, for a chap to feel completely at home.

PART TWO

'For this cruel land can cast a spell which no temperate clime can match.'

Wilfred Thesiger, 1910–2003
British explorer, soldier, travel writer
and expert on the desert

23

Mickey comes back to his office early that afternoon having seen off the party for the hills. It has been a busy couple of days and while he has been seeing to all the Wellsted business two or three ships have arrived at port whose cargo he must oversee. He discusses the papers with Rashid, brusquely leaves orders about a consignment of wool, supposedly finest Kashmir, that is not up to scratch, and arranges to deliver to the palace a bale of golden twine and tassels that has at long last arrived from the specialist workshops at Jaipur. The shipment is on order for the *soultan's* bedchamber and has been designed to mirror the intricate fretwork already in place about His Majesty's walls. For this last there will be no charge and the delivery is dispatched immediately to the royal palace with a flowery letter to commend the gift.

With these details seen to by the middle of the afternoon, Mickey leaves Rashid in charge of the warehouse and eagerly heads for home where he plans to bathe, feast and relax. Many men of Mickey's station in life insist on being transported by litter. Some of the more macho, while eschewing bearers, keep a horse in place at all times and pick their way through the city's streets mounted, carrying a large parasol with ornate fringing. Mickey prefers to walk — it helps him to think. As he winds up the hill, his appetite builds, for in the rush he has eaten little today and the piles of almond fancies for sale on the pavement stalls and the mounds of fresh spices and herbs that are sold by endless country tribesmen in cheap *jubbahs* smell wonderful. Before the streets lapse into the area of solely residential compounds, Mickey finds himself diverted by the pretty baubles on display and enjoys being greeted, as he is often, for Mickey is a well-known and well-loved figure in the city of Muscat.

A few minutes later and a pang of regret twinges in his stomach as he steps through the heavy double doors of his compound; he had wanted to give that *habshi* to Farida and now he has arrived home empty-handed. The girl would have been a wonderful present — she can read, after all, and he is sure that she is bright. However, he decides, perhaps it was best to send her away. A vision passes across Mickey's brain of the hot-blooded young fool who owned her, shouting he was invincible with the dice, in a coffee house near the palace the afternoon before. Of course, the boy should have been sent back to his father to be disciplined, not taken on at the backgammon table. If Mickey didn't know better he would say the kid was drunk. Unlike most of his fellows, Ibn Mudar knows all too well how drunk men carry on for he has seen such behaviour often among his employers. However, he now concludes that for the youngster the procuring of a skinful of beer or a flagon of wine was, if not impossible, highly unlikely. After all, how many misdemeanours can a young buck manage in one afternoon? Gambling and alcohol on top of the rumours that circulated about the boy's sexual preferences? It is too much depravity to be imaginable. In any case, though he beat the boy and won Zena fair and square, he should not have been gambling at all and he remains uncomfortable about his victory (Mickey wonders about the role of Allah in such circumstances). Perhaps it is all for the better that he has given the girl to Wellsted. The lieutenant might need the collateral of a valuable slave later in his journey — and for this purpose a good *habshi* is better than gold for she becomes more valuable the further the caravan treks northwards. Besides, now he can probably charge the Indian Navy two hundred dollars for supplying her; though slavery has been banned, the British are pragmatic about the need for proper disguises for their men when working in the field.

Mickey washes his hands in the cool, copper bowl scented with lime flowers that is proffered towards him, as his head serving man, the Nubian in the green *jubbah* who fetched Zena from her master's house, claps to announce his arrival. At the signal, half the household's slaves appear to do their master's bidding. Mickey, meanwhile, pours himself a cup of coffee from the pot that has appeared at his elbow. He eats half a dozen of his favourite dates, the sweet *khadrawy* variety that Aziz orders for him from an oasis inland.

'I will bathe,' he commands, and his personal slaves peel off silently to make everything ready.

There is the burnished copper bath to fill and the linen drying cloths to fetch and warm on the brazier. The men (for long ago Mickey decided he did not wish to be served by female slaves in his personal toilet) disperse like a troop of crack marines to undertake their duties. The rest continue to wait wordlessly to see what he will command.

The courtyard is tiled in a pattern of glossy blue and the loitering masses are colourful in their household livery of green and yellow set off with the occasional splash of red either in the exotic foliage or as a felted hat for the more senior members of staff. Mickey tarries only a moment before he surrenders to his true desire. Putting the glass back on the tray and throwing the pits of the dates to one side, he dismisses them all and strides out wordlessly for Farida's quarters.

When he enters it is clear that, unlike the rest of the household, his wife has not been apprised of his arrival home or at least has ignored it. Farida is contorted in her position but perfectly relaxed, arched like a cat on the comfortable, low divan; she is reading a book, which is almost upside down, so that her long hair trails on the floor as she follows its story. She has taken to washing henna into her glossy locks for recently she has found that her mousey curls are greying. The rich red only highlights the milky paleness of her skin, though not much of that is on show today. She is wearing a long, purple robe and her thin feet, which Mickey cannot help but picture stretched in climactic satisfaction, bear an intricate painted design of coffee-coloured swirls and dots. This, he knows, takes some hours to effect and involves a ritual that Farida finds tiresome but to which his other wives occasionally convince her to succumb. The room smells, as always, of burning incense. Farida's favourite is a costly cinnamon and frankincense blend, and there are vases of elegant flowers — upon which she insists — changed every couple of days and placed at intervals on low, brass side tables between the piles of books. The green boughs curl like dancing snakes through the pillars of bound paper. Between the white jasmine and golden geophyte, Farida looks up.

'Ah there you are,' she says, as if her husband is somehow at her pleasure rather than the other way around.

Mickey falls on his knees beside her and flings his arms around her shoulders, planting a long, salacious kiss on her plump lips. Then he leans over to inspect the poetry book she is reading in Arabic. Handwritten, it is so old that the pages are made of stiff parchment and it is bound in dark, embossed leather as thick as his hand.

> May the rain pour in benevolence, when it
>   falls,
> O, the time of our union in Andalusia.
> Your union was but a dream,
> In slumber, or a stealing by sleight of hand.

'Union,' he murmurs approvingly. 'Slumber.'

Farida strokes his face as if she is sinking into a featherbed of pleasure. As they lie together there is, unaccountably, a rapping on the *harim* door. Mickey sits up and Farida stares. At such an instance she should, of course, run off in shame, rather than let an unknown visitor see her, but instead she looks rather eager at this unprecedented turn of events, and Mickey does not have the heart to banish her.

'Come in,' he calls. *Ta'aal.*

The Nubian enters with his eyes averted. He is carrying a letter with a heavy red, wax seal. The dark writing on the front is in English.

'Rashid received this, master,' he says, his deep voice as smooth as creamy pudding — *Kishk al Fuara* served with tea-engorged raisins, Farida thinks. Still somehow, despite his timbre, he manages to sound apologetic at this intrusion. 'Rashid wants to know what to do. He said he could send the letter on to the person to whom it is addressed, if you feel it is important to do so, but to catch them up, the messenger will have to leave immediately. He asks your bidding?'

Mickey lifts the faded paper that envelopes the missive. The black ink blazes the legend: *Lieutenant James Raymond Wellsted, The Ship Palinurus, Indian Navy, via Bombay.* On the reverse, the large wax seal bears the crown, shield and stars that make up the coat of arms of the Murray clan and a return address in Albemarle Street, Piccadilly, London, England.

'Ah,' Mickey says out loud, 'he is well connected then, at least.'

He thinks for a moment, weighing the options.

'No,' he decides. 'This can wait. Wellsted will be almost at the *jabel* by now. What possible good can this news do him in the desert?'

He waves the Nubian away and places the letter on a side table.

'Now what was that about?' Farida asks as the door clicks closed. 'Did I see mention there of a publisher in London?'

Mickey laughs. She misses nothing, the wonderful woman. 'Very well, I shall tell you the story, my darling,' he says, pulling her closer and stroking her hair.

Farida squirms until she is comfortable and sucks contentedly on one of Mickey's fingers. Her interest is, of course, piqued by the missive. A lieutenant, it said on the paper — like the man she saw in the *souk* only the day before. Lieutenant Wellsted. Nothing lights up Farida like a spot of intrigue. Mickey starts the story as if he is telling it to a child.

'There are two white men, naval officers, who have gone missing in the desert. Doctor Jessop and First Lieutenant Jones of the Indian Navy's ship *Palinurus*. They were taken by the *Bedu* while on a mission in the interior. The British are exploring the Peninsula. Anyway, these men have been taken further inland, I think, than any white man has been taken before and they are held captive by the *Bedu*. Today, another officer, the recipient of this letter, has gone to find them at the instigation of our *soultan*.'

'What? A white man?' Farida's eyes are alight. 'This lieutenant?' She motions towards the letter. 'Wellsted?'

He had looked determined as he sipped his coffee, but hell, this is a lot for a white man to take on and he seemed so young somehow.

'Yes,' Mickey laughs. 'A white man, as white as you, I think, and his black slave girl and two of the most fearsome slave traders you ever did see as his guides. I myself disguised the poor man to give him some protection. I dressed him as a Turk — a trader. But they are an unholy party and the slavers are furious at being sent like lackeys. It is at the *soultan's* behest however. His Majesty is adamant so off they go.'

'And will he rescue these men — Jessop and Jones?'

A shadow of uncertainty crosses her husband's face.

'Ah, poor souls,' she says. 'Touch and go. And this fine man with his publisher friend may never get his letter either, I suppose. He's blue-eyed, is he? Tall? Very pale, but with a pleasant manner. I can see him now, in me mind's eye.'

'I'll keep the letter for him,' says Mickey, thinking that she is so perceptive it's quite amazing. 'Yes, he's a blue-eyed boy. And you're right — I liked him. He seemed younger than he must be, to be honest, but he'll come back, I hope. God willing. *In sh'allah.*'

Farida considers a moment. Surely they aren't done with the matter yet. 'My dear,' she says, 'there must be more to the story than that. If these white men are kidnapped, well now, there's a whole tale there and I want to hear it. So, my husband,' Farida sits up and runs the tip of her little, pink tongue down the side of his face, 'if I were to pleasure you, my darling, would you tell me everything, for I am parched to my bleachers

210

for a decent tale. All this poetry,' she waves her hand dismissively at the thick and expensive book she has been reading, and then places her palm seductively on her husband's crotch, which responds very satisfactorily to her caresses, 'the thing is that it's boring me arse off and I could do with a decent yarn. Lord, I'd do practically *anything* for a spot of amusement.'

As she envelopes him in her flesh, breathing Ibn Al Hajjaj's words of love, Mickey decides that even if he does not know exactly how Dr Jessop and Lieutenant Jones raised the ire of the emir, he can always make up a suitable explanation for Farida's pleasure — one worthy of the illustrious Mr Murray himself and surely better than any story Sir Walter Scott has written, if it comes to that. Yes, when they're done he'll summon her a fine explanation and perhaps even a decent account of fixing up Wellsted as a Turk, to boot. She'll like that. *But later*, he thinks, *I'll do it later*, his mind disappearing, as he slips gently inside her.

24

Into Rubh Al Khali: *the Empty Quarter, August 1833*

After days hiking up the *wadi* to take them as far north as possible before having to cross the *jabel* and enter the desert, the slavers' party camps just before sunset, where the land begins to rise. They have followed the line of the mountains for days now and tomorrow the intention is to climb upwards and tackle the higher ground. The men, Lieutenant Wellsted included, pray together, the small mats laid carefully in a line, wild hawks wheeling in the distance. No tents are raised though the *Bedu* busy themselves setting a fire and one man kills the last four of the chickens with a chilling efficiency and pulls the feathers so they can be roasted. Another prepares copious amounts of *khubz* for it is the custom not to measure supplies too carefully and to feast whenever you have enough to do so, even if it means starving later. All Arabian culture is extreme — gorging or starving is only natural here where there are harsh, burning deserts and violent sandstorms, where the law can lop off your limbs as a penalty and where for medicine, more often than not, the patient's skin is burnt to a crisp. Death is perpetually too close not simply to enjoy what you have and damn the prospect of tomorrow.

Zena is given the task of replenishing the goatskins from a shallow well at the base of the mountain path while two of the *Bedu* water the camels, for there is a good, clean spring here. Later they will have fresh water only intermittently and most of it *sorhan*, that is water which is opaque and does not travel well. It becomes foul the longer it is held, but they will still have to drink it.

Wellsted gulps his coffee greedily. He is a man with an avid appetite. The mountain air is clear and from the higher ground the view back over the *wadi* is breathtaking.

'Where you come from, does it look like this?' he asks Zena as she pours his coffee.

She pauses for a moment and then shakes her head. She feels shy speaking to him, especially when everyone is listening. 'It is greener, more lush.' She turns away to pour for Kasim and Ibn Mohammed.

Wellsted does not ask anything further and instead sets down his cup and enthusiastically sets off for a high ledge two hundred yards above. 'I won't be long,' he promises. 'I want to see the view.'

Ibn Mohammed sighs. He has promised the *soultan* he will protect this foreigner, and if the man dies this close to the *wadi* and less than a week from Muscat, it will be a great disgrace. Wordlessly meeting Kasim's eyes and agreeing that he will do the duty, Ibn Mohammed follows the white man up the side of the mountain to see from a distance the path they have already trodden.

'Don't come if you don't want to,' Wellsted insists.

The slaver does not reply for there is no point in arguing — of course he does not want to come. Of course he has to. At the top of the slope, with his surveyor's training kicking in, Wellsted jots a rough map into his notebook. The sun will disappear in half an hour. Below them the slaves are setting up a cooking pot. Ibn Mohammed peers over Wellsted's shoulder. He thinks the man a mere tourist, though he has to admit the lieutenant has certainly been paying more attention than he appeared to. The map is very accurate. By the time it is finished, the sky has faded into twilight and they can smell the chicken.

'Hungry?' Wellsted asks cheerily as they set off down the hill, their descent slower for the lack of visibility.

But hunger for Ibn Mohammed is only a weakness and he will never admit to that. 'It is time to eat,' is as much as he will concede.

The saddles are placed in a rough circle for the men to lean against, with felt rugs in a rainbow of dusty colours thrown over them for comfort. Zena hovers at Wellsted's elbow. Though she has not become accustomed to his appearance, she still cannot rip her gaze from his strange features and his sky-blue eyes. It is his movements that are most intriguing. He is very even as he walks and rides. She finds herself transfixed as he carries his saddle or arranges his *jubbah* before sitting down. His gestures are elegant — the way he moves his hands or raises

214

his eyebrows when he talks. It moves her and she realises it is fortunate that her interest is shielded by the veil, and she is free to gawp.

When the food is finally ready, the free men eat first. Kasim, Ibn Mohammed and Wellsted choose what they want, eat their fill and then stand to one side, washing their hands and sipping coffee as the servants and slaves take their turn. The scraps of chicken are picked until the bones are dry and can be eaten with a decisive crack, leaving an eerie kind of skeleton beyond any recognition or cdibility. Like locusts, the men consume the bread and gulp from horn cups of camel's milk.

With the meal over, no one speaks as the canopy of stars opens above them and the thin moon begins its ascent. When it is time to sleep, all lie stiff-limbed with the saddles forming a loose circle of protection against the open space. Since they set off, Zena has not been able to sleep in company with the men; she feels too self-conscious. The ground is stony and the star-strewn sky is too bright. Tonight, she continues to watch Wellsted's pale face, luminescent in the moonlight. At peace, asleep, he looks like a corpse. It is his white skin that makes the illusion so convincing, she thinks, for corpses lose their colour, though of course, her grandmother was as black as liquorice and in death her skin only lost its lustre rather than its tone. After a while, the girl gets up silently and pokes the embers of the fire as she has done every night so far. There, she sleeps fitfully on her haunches, dozing but warm, never settling to

215

a proper repose. From time to time she watches her master, like a child fond of a pet and conscious of its every movement.

★ ★ ★

Wellsted wakes before the camp rises at dawn. He lies enjoying the relative coolness of the air and checks to see if the girl is in position as usual, wakened and tending the fire, ready for the coffee to be heated. Sleepily, he registers that she is not in place. As he rolls over he catches sight of her figure — a vague shadow in the half-light, a little way off, beside the shallow well. He freezes. Zena is washing herself. She has removed the *burquah* and is pouring a thin trickle of water down her skin. That is a plucky decision, he thinks. With water so scarce and modesty so vital it might even be an act of rebellion. The lieutenant is mesmerised. With the sky still dark, Zena looks like the silhouette of a water nymph — some kind of magical creature from another world. The lieutenant has never seen anything so beautiful. He swallows, transfixed as, naked, she stretches lazily, brushes the water off with her palm, and then carefully coils her hair into place before pulling her *burquah* over her head. His breathing seems too loud — he is terrified that she will notice him and yet he cannot look away. *No wonder they stole you*, he thinks. No wonder some man paid two hundred dollars to possess such beauty. Wellsted will remember this moment for his whole life — it is the first time he desires

216

something for himself that is not dedicated to his own advancement. It is the moment he falls in love. The girl drinks a long draught of water and turns back towards the fire. As she approaches, he closes his eyes and takes a deep breath as if he has been asleep all along. Zena prods the fire and sets a pot of water to boil. It is almost sunrise. He could swear he hears her sigh and within five minutes the spell is broken, slavers stir and the aroma of coffee scents the air.

★   ★   ★

The men pray again, the *Bedu* murmuring something about prayer being better than sleep as if they miss the *muezzin* and his haunting music — the first call of the day. After a breakfast of coffee and more camel's milk during which Wellsted manages to rip his gaze from Zena by pure force of will, they saddle up and lead their animals along the stony path to the higher ground. This is where they must quit the safety of the *wadi* and continue into the mountain range. The *jabel* is a rough wall of rock between the valley and the desert, in many places only navigable by foot, if at all.

'This is the slowest part of the journey, my friend,' Ibn Mohammed tells Wellsted as if he is speaking to a fool. The slavers are only tolerating their travelling companion, that much is clear, but the lieutenant takes it in good part. He shows no sign that he minds being the idiot pupil, the man who has no idea.

'And so we will not ride here?'

'If the men mount the camels there surely will be losses, so we lead them.'

It is a long, hot day and hard going. This is, after all, the hottest part of the year. The men banter as they make their way slowly up the rocky path. Kasim tutors the infidel in pronunciation and teaches him vocabulary.

'And so, the word for 'sun'?' Wellsted enquires, the shingle splaying from his camel's hooves as the sun shines down relentlessly.

A sliver of a sly smile plays around Kasim's full lips. It amuses him how little the white man knows. 'In the *Quran* the word is *shams*. But it is also referred to as *siraaj*, which means a torch or as *wahhaaj* which means a blazing lamp.'

'Thank you. In my language we have only one word for it,' Wellsted admits.

What he does not add is that England is a good deal less sunny than anywhere he has been in Arabia and in London there are many more words for rain than an Arab need ever employ. He is keen to learn, not to prove how clever he is and he submits to the role of pupil willingly.

'*Siraaj*,' he practises. '*Wahhaaj*.'

*　*　*

By nightfall, they have reached safer ground. With the food finished and the final prayers said, Zena, thoroughly exhausted, decides to make her bed outside the circle of saddles. She hopes that she will feel able to sleep soundly if only she is away from the men. As she settles, Kasim shouts to attract her attention. Then, when she does not

218

jump at his command, he abandons his position by the fire and stands over her.

'Move,' he orders, pointing her back towards the group, herding the girl like a mule or an errant sheep that must be bullied. 'Over there.'

Chastened and afraid of his hectoring tone, Zena sits up and pulls the rug towards her body, gazing towards Wellsted for confirmation of what action she should take. He is her master, after all, and it is his orders she will follow. Such insubordination takes guts for in the normal run of things everyone jumps at the slaver's command. Kasim laughs.

'Order your *habshi* inwards,' he insists. 'If you want her to last the night, that is.'

Wellsted flicks his hand to indicate Zena should do as she is told. 'Here,' he says, 'next to me.'

Ibn Mohammed snorts lewdly, Kasim returns to his position by the fire and the group settles quickly.

'Goodnight,' Wellsted whispers and turns respectfully away from his charge. His instinct is that he must not take advantage of the girl in any way. She is so vulnerable and he wants to protect her. The truth is that he is in awe. He falls asleep thinking of her washing in the half-light of the early morning, a smile on his face.

Even though she is tired and her belly is full, Zena still finds it difficult to drift off. She can feel the white man lying beside her, and the other men too, all around. She occupies herself considering Wellsted's country. By sheer logic, given the questions the man has asked, it must be a place where there are no rocky mountains and men do not own each other. When she tries to comprehend it, she sees an eerie crowd of white-skinned *djinns* in her mind's eye, peering at her, reaching out long, spindly fingers at the end of elongated, bone-white arms. She hopes Wellsted will not take her to his homeland almost as much as she hopes he will not fulfil his promise and set her free, for so far from her Abyssinian home, whatever will she do without a household in which to live? Zena does not relish the thought of making her own way in the world now she has seen more of what the world is like — she wants to be free, but does not see how that can be possible. She wishes her grand-mother had seen her married and that the old lady had been able to let her go. Heavens, even marriage to a cowherd would be better than this. Her nerves are on edge.

Just before midnight, she senses a movement in the blackness beyond the circle and her body stiffens. During daylight hours, she is aware that the slaves constantly eye her, as if under the dark *burquah* her body is a secret prize. God knows who else is out here, on the high mountain path, watching and waiting. Her ears burn as the movement beyond the fire repeats itself. The noise is coming nearer. Zena freezes, scarcely able to breathe. Her eyes are wide open, searching the ebony pitch. Someone is there. Something. She can hear it edging towards her, closer and closer, from behind.

She gulps a mouthful of air and automatically her hand closes around a large stone. When she can bear the tension no longer, she jumps up, ready to kill if she has to, ready to fight for her life.

'Help,' she gasps, but her mouth is dry and the word comes in a whisper.

As she peers towards the sound, the darkness is unaccountably empty. She looks closer but no one is there. Turning sharply, she checks her travelling companions to see if any of them are missing but the figures slumped around the dying fire are in place and no one has stirred. For a moment, Zena wonders if there is a phantom, if out on the *jabel* ghosts lie in wait for human flesh and the *djinns* she should fear are here in the mountains rather than in some far-off, alien place peopled by white men. A cold terror creeps across her skin and in temper she throws the rock away. Whatever it hits, moves. The sound is further off this time and she makes out a long, dark snake — a python perhaps or a horned viper, a cobra, or a puff adder — it is too dark to tell. Whatever it is, it is sliding away into the stony hinterland, like a venomous spirit, low into the night. In fright she lets out a sharp, high-pitched squeal and recoils, tripping backwards over her master, scrabbling to find another stone.

In a second, Wellsted is awake with his knife in his hand. He jumps up and grabs her arm, pulling her out of the way. He checks the others but the rest of the party only turn over and slumber through the disturbance or perhaps merely ignore it.

'What happened?' he asks. 'What is it?'

221

Zena's voice breaks. She starts to cry. 'A snake,' she explains. 'It was a big one. I threw a rock and frightened it off.'

Wellsted pulls her down, out of the line of sight. 'I heard they will sleep near men for warmth,' he whispers kindly. 'That is all. Don't worry.'

Zena's wide, frightened eyes are all he can see of her. 'It was a snake,' she repeats pointing into the darkness. 'It might have been a constrictor.'

Wellsted lifts the thin carpet on which she has been lying and moves it to the inside tier of the sleeping circle, putting himself between Zena and his saddle.

'That girl is too jumpy,' Kasim growls, without rising.

Almost immediately the most feared slaver in Muscat is breathing deeply again. Zena feels a sting of outrage. The snake might have attacked, had it not been for her vigilance.

'It's all right,' Wellsted comforts his charge. 'It's gone now. You did well to make it out at all in this pitch. Come — sleep closer to the fire. It's safer.'

He hands her over as if she is lady and he is her protector, for how else might an officer of the Indian Navy behave? She feels herself relax as she pulls the blanket into place over her frame.

When dawn comes, Zena wakens from her first deep sleep since she left the city, and the coffee is already brewed. There is a fuss among the livestock — a slave is basting a camel's skin in butter for the beast has developed the mange. Still sleepy, she rises and drinks some milk, sweet and so fresh that it is warmed by the animal's body rather than the sun. Wellsted smiles at her from the other side of the fire, saddling his camel ready to go. She smiles back.

'Come,' Ibn Mohammed wrangles the men. 'All of you! The sun is rising ahead of us! Today we can ride!'

Zena nods at one of the slaves. The man has only half his teeth left in his head and a strange tattoo on his cheek that forms a dark cicatrice — a spiral. He spits as he holds the camel while she hoists herself onto the high saddle and gees the beast into the caravan that has formed, waiting to be off.

The snakes will not come now it is light, she thinks as Ibn Mohammed continues to curse the laziness of the men who are not yet in line, and Wellsted, at the head as if he is born to it, leads the party into the mountains. Zena sees Kasim notice him. *The white man,* she thinks, *is surprising them, but then that is not necessarily a good thing.*

As the men move higher, the way is stonier and more difficult until, at last, almost a fortnight after the caravan left the streets of the capital, the stones turn into shingle and within two hours they thin to a fine sand, at first of different colours — with black and green mixed copiously with the white. Then the spectrum of colour fades completely until it disappears into a haze of white heat and sand. Any words for sun, or heat, or sand seem somehow an understatement. When the desert appears, it is breathtaking. As the boulders disappear and the trees and bushes evaporate, the undulating dunes stretch for miles only punctuated by a stray boulder or the bleached-out, skeletal remains of what was once an olive tree.

There has been no rain for months. Anything that lives in these conditions must bear an impossible torment of burning, baking, parching and scorching. The scorpions are hiding below the dunes, the vultures circle, looking for any oryx that have strayed this far, hoping at the very least for a square meal of dead snake or lizard. The flies have disappeared for the air is a furnace. To the lieutenant, the landscape seems larger than anywhere on earth he's been — an immense void in the business of the world. In a heartbeat, he understands why religions are born on the sands — there is nothing here for a man but his own mind. He will enter this place only with what he can carry with him and will leave the same way.

'It's like a cathedral,' the lieutenant mouths in a whisper. It is not for nothing that the Arabs call *Rubh Al Khali* the Empty Quarter.

Turning, the lieutenant senses a change in Ibn Mohammed. He catches a genuine smile on the man's face for the first time since they met. This wilderness is his home, he thinks — the less life the better. The pride of Muscat belongs here and not among the social niceties of city society.

'You cannot map this in your little book,' the slaver sneers, proud that his homeland cannot be tamed and measured by the infidel. 'The sands move,' he says sternly. 'You cannot write them down. It is too large. The desert runs from here

224

till Cairo. Sand and wind all the way.' Both Ibn Mohammed and Kasim are from *Bedu* stock. Their families have travelled in this way for many generations. They are born to it. If it disconcerts the white man so much the better.

Wellsted is suitably daunted. He wonders how — and if — Jessop and Jones have survived. The Arabian customs of hospitality and the quaint oath of the caravan make sense now he truly comprehends the scale of the desolation. In an environment such as this, these customs are not courtesies — they are the only way to stay alive. Only a fool would enter this place of emptiness without knowing with some degree of certainty that his fellows will do anything to save him. It's different from what he saw at Aden — there he only hovered on the fringes and could not see the scope of the void. Just like Mickey showed him in Muscat, he pulls his headdress into place across his face, mask-like as a *litham*. If he does not cover his skin now he realises he will burn the already pink flesh so badly that it will flake away entirely in the searing heat. Behind him, the *habshi* sits absolutely straight in the saddle.

'How far away are we from Jessop and Jones now? When do you think we will get to them?' the lieutenant asks the slavers.

Ibn Mohammed's tawny eyes narrow to a slant. Time is meaningless here. No man can rush in this heat for long. If you push yourself hard you will simply die quicker. Experienced travellers take their pace from the camels.

Kasim is more accommodating. He considers the lieutenant's question slowly. He does not

225

know exactly where the emir has camped but their destination certainly is a long way to the north. They will meet *Bedu* en route and ask for directions and in the meantime they must simply check their position at night by the stars, and in the daytime by the direction of the wind, when there is any. If they are lucky they will travel perhaps 40 miles in a day and they are making for Riyadh, which is a long way off — 750 miles or so. That is a journey of twenty days (though time in the desert disappears and the slavers have known caravans make less than 15 miles in a whole day if the sand is very soft). In any case, from Riyadh they will have to make a new plan — depending on the news of where the emir has pitched. Like many things on the Peninsula, the target is moving.

'Within a week, I hope,' he says slowly, knowing this is hopelessly optimistic. 'Perhaps two weeks. Three. *In sh'allah.* Though of course, it may be more.'

Ibn Mohammed turns his face into the sun.

'Of course. Of course,' Wellsted agrees. Look at the place. As he gestures at the landscape, Zena slopes directly across his view sending the now-familiar sting of protective feeling through his frame. 'A week. A fortnight. A month. How could anyone know? *In sh'allah.* Indeed.'

25

It has been over two months since their capture, not that Jessop and Jones are aware of that, and for a brief period Jones has been removed from the tent. It is the fourth time this has happened.

'Well,' he says under his breath, 'this is a turn-up. I wonder what in the hell they want now?'

He is unsure what he is supposed to say as none of his officer's training or indeed the first-rate education in the schoolroom in his family's shabby house on one of Knightsbridge's smarter streets has prepared him for this. A gentleman is never naked, at least not in public, and Lieutenant Jones is of the view that the emir's tent is certainly a public place. In London he knows that the gentlemen of the Whatley Club recently inspected an Indian prince who was put up to the job over dinner. When an autopsy is performed on a black man or a Chinaman, the Medical School is packed to capacity. All society has a natural interest in anything or anyone different from itself. Still, he is uncomfortable. It's not the same for a white man. A nigger is a savage and lives naked in the wild. A white fellow, in particular Lieutenant Jones, certainly does not. Having to wear the *jubbah* is bad enough.

The emir peers at Jones' golden pubic hair and tuts loudly. One of the other men laughs hysterically — not an action designed to make a chap stand proud. They have not inspected Dr Jessop like this, for the doctor has not left the prison tent at all, except when they have marched with the caravan. They are most likely more interested in him, Jones muses, because Jessop is older and is not blonde. Besides, it is Jessop who killed the emir's daughter so, he thinks, to the emir and his men, he, Harry Jones Esq., is the superior specimen — far more interesting than Jessop's mud-coloured hair, which is clearly not diverting in the least. The attention is an honour, he flatters himself, and perhaps there will be an advantage to it. A fellow never knows what such savage men may do. But they have picked him and that is surely a good thing.

'I can sing,' he says, hoping to please the assembled tribesmen. 'Sing,' he says again loudly over the rush of conversation as they try to understand what he has said. He takes a deep breath, recalls his days in the church choir at St Luke's and decides to simply show them.

'God Save our Dear Great King
Long Live our Noble King
God Save the King
Send Him Victorious
Happy and Glorious
Long to Reign Over Us
God Save the King.'

Jones is felled with a brutal blow to the stomach before he can stir himself to the second verse.

The emir clearly does not appreciate an anthem. He might be an old fellow, but he can move quickly if he wants to. Apart from feeding himself, it is the only time Jones has seen the ruler take any kind of action. Normally, his minions do everything. The emir retakes his seat and Jones watches, curled up, from ground level. There is an enticing scent on the air of jasmine oil, which he vaguely remembers as the scent used to perfume the emir's robes. While it transports Jones to a lately unvisited place of fresh, clean linen, two of the tribesmen pull the stinking lieutenant to his feet and this time he stands silently, trying not to tremble.

When a man approaches with a knife in his hand, Jones wonders fleetingly if it is worth fighting the grinning hyena that wants to cut him, though it quickly becomes apparent that the intention is to lop a lock of blonde hair from the lieutenant's matted head. Once that is done, the emir considers his investigations completed. He waves away the white man and Jones is thrown his tattered old *jubbah*, given a drink of water and a handful of dates and walked back to the stifling furnace of the tatty, grey tent where Jessop remains tied to the stake. On the way, the guard pushes him roughly, his hand groping Jones' genitals. This action, slyly repeated at any opportunity, has ceased to surprise the lieutenant and he only motions to be given a few more dates, with which the guard generally complies before laying his hand firmly on Jones' arse. He never seems to want anything more and there is, Jones tells himself, no harm in it. Or at least, no more harm than in anything else to which Jones is being subjected.

Best not to say anything, the lieutenant thinks, the soles of his feet burning on the scorching sand. The whole inspection scenario is bizarre and the guard's actions afterwards even more so. Jones always makes the same decision — just to keep schtum. Otherwise, he would have to share the dates with Jessop, quite apart from bear the humiliation of admitting he's been inspected like a farm animal and manhandled like a whore. He wonders for a second what the emir wants. Perhaps, Jones thinks somewhat optimistically, he will be forced to mate with one of the emir's dusky women. He remembers reading somewhere about the propensity in tribes of welcoming strangers in this way. He saw a book one time in Bombay, with engravings. It was an illicit night fuelled by whisky and the sheer boredom of the officers' mess when he and his friend Lieutenant Whitelock took to the slums in a *tanga* and bought what Whitelock referred to later as 'a charming time'. Charming. It cost, if he recalls correctly, a mere handful of Indian rupees — not even a proper, English coin. Now what did that book say? Something about healthy breeding strains, if he remembers rightly, though everyone here seems a relatively uniform pale coffee colour, bar one or two of the slaves. And since Jessop healed the children (well, almost all of them) Jones hasn't once on his (admittedly limited) excursions seen any evidence of illness. Still, he could be just the shot of fresh blood that the emir wants for his people. It would certainly explain the damn fellow's interest in his naked flesh. Yes, he thinks, indulging the schoolboy fantasy and blocking out the humiliation he has just endured with the humiliation he doled out in happier times to the shy 15-year-old whose father sold her first to Jones and then to Whitclock. Yes — breeding strains — that's probably it.

The jailer pushes Jones roughly as they enter the tent. He falls easily into place, next to his confederate.

'You all right, old chap?' Doctor Jessop grunts.

Jessop is concerned for Jones' welfare. After all, he is the man's doctor. The Navy has solid, scientific information about how long a man can go without much food and Jessop is fully appraised of the details though the statistics don't account for the heat or the fetid conditions. Such squalor, Jessop feels, can only add to the pressure on the body to succumb. Still, Jones looks quite perky and, the doctor thinks vaguely, the fellow smells different from when he left. There is a sweet aroma from his breath. Can it be possible? Jessop wonders what they gave him. The thought of something that tastes sweet is most diverting. He finds himself fantasising about Turkish delight as the lieutenant shrugs and submits himself willingly to being tied up by the guard. Why not?

'God Save the King,' he mumbles.

'And our good men in the field,' Jessop replies automatically.

It is, after all, a standard military toast.

231

26

Farida has been patient for weeks now but she can't stop thinking about it. Mickey leaves the letter addressed to Lieutenant Wellsted on the low side table. The next day, she transfers the missive to the shelf of books by the window and there it sits ever since. She does not know if her husband has left the lieutenant's correspondence in her care deliberately (for surely it belongs in his office) or if he has simply forgotten that the letter has arrived. What Farida does know is that it is his expectation that Wellsted will not return alive to Muscat and perhaps for that reason he has been careless with the fellow's mail. Whatever his thinking, Farida is drawn to the sealed paper on a daily basis. She passes it through her fingers as if it is of the finest silk and turns it over again and again to read the enticing address of the sender. Albemarle Street, Piccadilly, London. The wax seal is slightly uneven when she runs her finger over its face and the edge of the paper beside it sports a small, tattered edge, which, most likely, has worsened with her repeated handling. Farida sniffs it tentatively and then slips the letter back onto the shelf again between two volumes that Mickey is unlikely to take down. *It is*, she thinks, as she slinks back across the cool, tiled floor, *like being sent a daydream*.

Farida has never been to London. When she

left Cork it was for Dublin and then the port of Liverpool. From there, she worked her way down the west coast of England and into Wales, coming to Bath, she remembers, on her nineteenth birthday. There, she and her friend Maria worked a particularly efficacious scam, posing as ladies. Dressed to the nines and apparently guileless they agreed, upon much coaxing, to ride in the carriage of one gentleman or another (the gentlemen being always married, of course, and invariably the worse for drink). The story was that they were sisters from the North of England and happened to be out in the park without a chaperone. Both Maria and Fanny were dab hands at making themselves sound like they were born and bred in Yorkshire rather than Galway and Rowgarrane respectively and that they were respectable, if somewhat naïve. Generally what ensued in the carriage, of course, was most improper. The next day, a ne'er-do-well called Edward Brand would call on the gentleman and make an unholy fuss about what the fellow had done with his sisters, taking the poor, innocent girls off like that and compromising them cruelly as if they were strumpets and harlots, by God, instead of good, clean English ladies too innocent for their own good and now ruined forever. Such is the traffic of gentlemen in Bath that it was clear that if they didn't milk it dry, it was entirely possible for this glorious scam to work for months on end, if not years.

'You've picked the wrong family, sir,' Edward

would spit, 'and I can promise you, your wife will hear of what you have done, and her family too. Yes indeed. It is a disgrace, sir, a disgrace, and no compensation is possible. Our family may be poor but our silence cannot be bought.'

This last statement was, of course, untrue. Mr Brand wrought compensation every time for no man wishes to be unmasked to his parents-in-law and his wife.

'It's a doozy,' Maria laughed. 'Works every time.'

It worked almost every time, that is, until the last, when poor Edward got carried away in his role and foolishly duelled for his sisters' honour. The gentleman who killed him had some title or other. Farida has forgotten his name now. After the funeral, the ladies moved to the south coast and it was there that Fanny bought a passage to India with the remainder of her monies. Leaving England was an easy decision.

'And why not?' she loses her temper when Maria said she wouldn't want to go to any of them nasty, foreign places. 'Is Portsmouth so lovely?' Fanny gestures around the shabby room the women have taken for a tanner a week. 'I'd as soon see the world as stay in this stinking hole.'

'But, Fanny, we can go to London,' Maria intones it like a Hail Mary. London is her holy grail.

'London! London is the same as all the rest! And me getting no younger and you neither. London will eat us up, my girl. I'm for some adventure, Maria, and some heat on my bones.

Won't you come with me and try something different?'

Maria declines.

I wonder what happened to her? Farida smiles. It has worked out very nicely indeed, in all possible manners. She never in her life thought she'd actually fall in love and with such a good man. Mickey is a treasure. 'So,' she wonders out loud, catching sight of the letter, 'am I homesick or just a nosey old woman? What's drawing me to you, like a postmistress with an undeliverable?'

It is a testament to Farida's ability to defer pleasure that the letter lasts as long as it does — well over a month. In the end, she makes it till the air cools very slightly and the late summer sun does not rise quite so early or set quite so late. One Monday morning, she steams the wax seal carefully and flicks it open with tremendous satisfaction. The top of the paper is dated in June and Farida thinks it is a shame that Mr Murray had not roused himself to write earlier, for the letter missed the lieutenant by only a matter of hours. What seems nothing in London can make all the difference in the dominions.

'Ah well,' she sighs as she folds open the stiff paper and settles down with relish to read the letter on the leather seat by the window.

Dear Lieutenant Wellsted,
I am writing to thank you for sending to me your account of the trip you made to the island of Socotra. It is a well-constructed and informative piece of writing and I will

235

be *honoured to prepare it for publication
and will arrange to forward you two guineas
in return.
Yours, etc.,
John Murray III*

Guineas, eh? Farida ponders. A guinea is a
gentleman's coin. Out of habit, she turns over
the paper, as if to check that the money is not
somehow attached. Still and all, two guineas is
hardly overgenerous, she thinks, for a fellow who
has written an entire book by hand and risked
his life, most likely, in the process. She sniffs at
the paper to see if she can catch a whiff of
London town from the pages on the inside but
there is nothing. Then she reads it again. He's an
interesting fellow this Lieutenant James Raymond Wellsted. He's not bad-looking, clearly
very brave and a writer too. Farida laughs at
herself for being such an old con woman. Even
now, she can't help looking for an angle when
something unexpected falls in her lap. She
reseals the letter very carefully, with a tiny stick
of burning wood, and places it in clear view so
that Mickey will come across it when he next
visits her. He'll probably take it away, of course,
but that's only fair.

*I'd say a fellow like that will make it through
the desert,* Farida ponders. *And if he does . . .*
The notion trails. She has been thinking for the
last while about writing a letter home — just to
let her family know what happened.

They think I'm dead, she says to herself with
finality.

For a moment she considers the words she'd use in the letter — how to encapsulate everything into a few sentences that wouldn't sound crass or crazy. Farida cannot quite form the words.

Feck it, she dismisses the notion. *I'll worry about it if Lieutenant James Raymond Wellsted makes it back to Muscat, poor soul.*

And Mickey Al Mudar's favourite wife turns her attention to the climactic *kharja* of a poem she has been studying. It is written in Arabic but is clearly Spanish in its derivation. The interplay of the Semitic and European is of interest to Farida for obvious reasons and it will, she thinks, take up most of her afternoon. Some of these Arabic verses are very racy, she murmurs with satisfaction as she draws close to the window and settles down for the afternoon.

27

At home the weather eases in September, but the same cannot be said for the desert. It is a very long journey, Wellsted has come to understand, not simply on account of the time it takes as on account of the effort. The caravan slowly follows the emir's trail across the baking wilderness from one oasis to the next for a month. It surprises Wellsted to find the traffic of men and animals so constant. The chance encounters with groups of *Bedu* following the trade routes slow progress but there is no question of not succumbing to the custom of brewing coffee with the strangers, for they can tell the party what is up ahead.

Wellsted takes notes. It seems that families and sometimes whole villages of nomads trail across the wilderness along the criss-cross of unmarked and unseen paths that from custom or sheer expediency are the routes all travellers follow. These family caravans are engaged on simple enough business. They are asserting their rights to the *falaj* — the water courses — or driving their camels and goats to market, wherever they believe they can make the best trade. Many are simply looking for some grazing — a scrap of land with small-leaved bushes or patches of sweet grass — somewhere they can settle for a few days. They are like cawing birds, wheeling seagulls that land to eat and swap their news before they carry on across the sands, a flash of

238

white, crying their news as they go.

At first, whenever they meet another party, Wellsted's appearance attracts attention. The leather-skinned *Bedu* eye the thin Turk and his straggly beard with curiosity. It is only natural, for in this environment, when presented with anything that is not sheer sand and sky a man will become fascinated by it. The first time they reach a thin oasis of a few, scattered palm trees, Wellsted thinks he has never seen anything like it. Still, the truth is that as soon as the *Bedu* hear the names of Kasim and Ibn Mohammed they are more interested in the slavers than the *effendi* and their faces split into wide grins. This action displays more often than not, a startling paucity of teeth and a range of expressions so interesting that the lieutenant wishes he had better skills as an artist than a cartographer.

Kasim finds it amusing that though he is known as a slaver the men they meet do not ask if he is here about his business. They have no fear that their wives and daughters will be borne away. In fact, there is a charming simplicity in the manner they express delight to have come across such distinguished company with whom to drink their coffee and swap news. Perhaps the customs of the desert are so ingrained here it is simply impossible for a *Bedu* to imagine anyone breaking faith.

After the third week, Wellsted senses that he is finally accepted. He settles into the persona he has been given and adopts the ways of his fellows as if they are second nature. Now, whatever caravan they meet, the *Bedu* no longer stare at

239

the Turk to assess him. His accented Arabic is more easily understood and the second-hand clothes are as if his own. He is certain he has acquired a swagger, though without seeing himself in a glass (there is no reflective surface for hundreds of miles in any direction) he cannot decide whether his Arabic gait has arisen from prolonged periods of riding his camel or simply the more general change that has come over him, living on the sands. Whatever has made the difference, he is no longer acting a part when he bows, clasps his hand to his heart and says *salaam aleikhum* before introducing himself.

Keen for company, he keeps a weather eye to the horizon. Most of the caravans tell more or less the same tales and the main news is that of a wild sandstorm, a *simoom*, which hit the desert six months before. It raged to the south, near Niswa, the ancient capital — a deadly, wind-driven wall of sand almost a mile high as it moved across the Empty Quarter like a force of God.

'You could not breathe, nor see the hand before your face,' they swear.

Several families have not been seen since and the tribes are still taking stock, trying to clarify who survived as whole dunes shifted, smothering those caught in the direct path of the storm. If you were not lucky enough to find shelter, it is unlikely you came through.

'We had only a few minutes,' one old man shakes his head. He has the kind of face that makes it difficult to believe that he hasn't seen everything in his time, but he swears the sandstorm took him completely by surprise. 'There was hardly any warning at all, when we saw it coming towards us. We were lucky and were in a place we could hide, though my son's eyes were damaged — a rip in the cloth he had used to cover his face. It pleases Allah now that he can only see with one eye. My brother, though, we have not seen my brother since the day before the storm hit. Do you know Hanif Ibn Mussaf? Have you seen him?'

It is a hopeless quest, of course, but you have to have sympathy with the asking. Many of the strangers are on the lookout for lost children or slaves who have gone astray either in the *simoom* or simply in the more general course of their travels. These people are abandoned with a stoic nonchalance that is curious to a naval man. Wellsted is reminded of how a cry of 'Man overboard' marshals an entire crew in the Navy and no one asks if the man in question is the cabin boy or the captain before they respond. Here, rank is more important to the prospects of rescue (for who would retrace their steps miles across the burning terrain for a mere slave boy?). In the main, it seems those who fall by the wayside are left to fend for themselves, especially if they are expendable and defenceless (poor, enslaved or simply very young). How anyone could survive alone without at least a camel to provide milk and find the way to a watering hole, Wellsted cannot see. But still, they ask about their lost ones. This is not because they believe that the lost souls are alive (though curiously, there are stories, myth-like in their lack of likelihood, of survival against the odds), but rather because they are hoping you have taken a passing interest in any tattered *jubbah* or pile of bleached bones that might have caught your eye. 'His *jubbah* was blue,' they insist. 'Have you seen a blue *jubbah*?' Or, 'The child was only seven. The bones will be very small.'

These sombre enquiries naturally come first, after the serving of the coffee. With that out of the way, the conversation continues. Like the later pages of the *London Illustrated News*, the news that transpires after the headlines is more frivolous. There is, for example, the sheer tabloid scandal of the youngest son of one caliph, 'A good boy, until now, but he has a fire in his blood and could not cool it when he argued with his father,' all this explained with flashing of eyes and large hand gestures to signify the scale of the conflict. 'So the boy took off with only his camel.' A pause here for effect, for to leave by yourself and take only your camel is a feat of either legendary bravery or extreme foolishness, the judgement of which in this case, is as yet undecided. 'Even as we speak,' the old men (they are always old, for some reason) assure the rapt listeners, 'he is travelling towards one of the seaports ruled by a rival family, where it is rumoured there is money to be made diving for pearls in the waters off Bahrain. Allah be with him.' Here Allah is always invoked for the *Bedu* find this fact the most scandalous of all. 'He will work for someone else,' they breathe to make the boy's intention absolutely plain. It transpires the

Bedu, despite their poverty, are fiercely independent.

'You cannot trust the pearl merchants,' they tut, as if the life the boy has set off towards can possibly be harder than a nomadic existence fuelled by camel's milk and coffee.

'As if the earth would ever yield up her bounty so freely for the benefit of man,' one old sage sighs at the foolish impossible expectations of youth. 'Why would Allah be so kind?'

He is unaware, of course, (as are they all) that beneath his feet lies one of the world's greatest oil reserves and that in time, every one of his great, great, great grandchildren will be millionaires. The only use the *Bedu* have for the *naft* is to harvest it where it rises to the surface and use the sticky fuel for their lamplight. In any case, even in the great metropolises of Western Europe there are, as yet, no machines that can make use of the Peninsula's natural resources. Steam is the emerging power of the decade and that is fuelled by coal. For the time being, nature is holding her irony in reserve and the *Bedu*, like the sons of Al Saud, mostly go barefoot and, if not intimately acquainted with cold, they certainly know hunger very well.

Having listened to the gossip and added a few choice snippets of Muscat extravagance to spice the conversation, the slavers ask for directions.

'North,' the *Bedu* always gesture, the sleeves of their white and blue *jubbahs* swaying with the force of the movement, as if to demonstrate that the emir's camp is not only northwards, but that

243

it is also still a very long way off. 'A day off Riyadh.'

Riyadh is practically the only town in the interior in this region and most directions are navigated by its location. From what Wellsted can gather, it is a small place of only a few thousand souls, living on a precarious supply of water that is only just sufficient to keep its population alive. The soil is good and there are both date palms and fruit orchards. In the desert that is miracle enough.

During such exchanges, with the men introduced to each other and the pecking order established, Zena sometimes arouses a little interest. Even obscured by her *burquah* it seems the men are transfixed by her shapely wrists and ankles, both of which are periodically on show as she goes about her chores.

'A prize investment,' Wellsted hears one say wistfully.

Several times, visitors try to barter the dark girl dressed in black for a camel or two though none of them formally ask who owns her, they simply seek to swap with whoever they think looks the easiest touch. Ibn Mohammed sees all and his stony gaze silences all negotiations. He does not care, of course, about Zena, but a pair of camels (even of good pedigree) are not worth a pretty Abyssinian female. Ibn Mohammed has never made a poor trade in his life and will not bring dishonour on his caravan by allowing anyone else to do so. As the would-be purchasers shrink, Ibn Mohammed nods to Wellsted as if to say, she is yours, do you want to barter her? He

244

does not. As he has come to know the girl better, the idea horrifies him more and more.

Zena, for her part, ignores such exchanges and adopts a dignified air as she continues to serve coffee or prepare food while the men talk about her as if she is not there. If anyone were to look closely, they would see her stiffen slightly and her eyes land upon Wellsted at the next opportunity, to check he is not tempted by the offer. It has happened so many times now that she no longer feels her stomach turn at the prospect, for she is coming to trust that her new, pale master will not barter her, whatever he ultimately intends (this has not yet been settled with any clarity and she does not feel she can ask him).

Once, when she is serving, a *Bedu* lays his hand lazily on her foot. Obscured by the crowded sitting mats, no one can see as he strokes her skin slowly, running one hand upwards past the ankle as he proffers his cup with the other. Zena lowers the scalding coffee pot as if to pour but instead she burns him quickly on the skin of his shoulder. The man jumps, but he says nothing, only pulls his hand away. If Wellsted did not watch her so closely, he'd never know.

Good girl, he thinks, smiling. *I knew she had spirit*. Her tiny rebellions intrigue him as much as her beauty.

⋆　⋆　⋆

That night, Wellsted settles Zena to sleep beside him. The camp is settled and the desert is silent,

245

except for the camels grunting. It is the only time of day they can talk without everyone else hearing and they have made a custom of whispering a while before going to sleep.

'It rains almost every day in London,' he says.

Zena cannot imagine that is true. His eyes are like sapphires, she decides, sheer, glassy blue. The fascination of watching him talk, move or sleep has not dissipated nor has the thunderclap that accompanies his occasional touch.

'When we leave, I shall tell them about it here,' he decides. 'I shall talk at the Royal Society — I know it.'

That must be a good place to talk, she thinks. Wellsted has mentioned the African Association and the Geographical Society many times. She imagines these places must be something akin to a gathering of men in the *souk*. Zena enjoys his stories though of course there are questions, which she has not as yet had the nerve to ask. For a start, if it is perpetually raining do they pitch tents in this London simply to keep dry? Are the streets canopied and does everyone wear turbans to keep off the weather? She thinks how lovely it must be for the strange, pale Londoners not to know thirst and, if the stories are true, she can see no downside to the master's mythical home town. Wellsted has not properly explained to her that the rain is often accompanied by a biting coldness that in living memory has frozen the great river Thames to an icy, polluted standstill or that many of the capital's citizens are starving to death, ravaged by disease and abandoned by their fellows. The idea of being

246

frozen to death, a real danger in the winter months for many of the poor in Wellsted's home parish, is beyond her. In Zena's vocabulary, in either her own dialect or in Arabic, she knows no word that means 'frozen'. She has never seen snow or ice or, indeed, heard of them. In any case, it is not something that Zena, for all her education, finds possible to envisage. All her life winter has been a more pleasant season than the summer. Thirst is her greatest enemy and she has only ever felt cold when once, as a child, she caught a fever and though her skin burned she felt chilled to the bone.

Wellsted takes a breath. He has decided to bring up the matter. 'You burnt our guest today,' he says.

'I'm sorry, but he . . . ' She is not sure how to explain the liberty the man took. The thought of it still makes her furious, though there is no point in expressing her anger and instead she steels herself for the master's rebuke. It does not come.

'Well done,' he says. 'I don't know how you bear it — the brute. I am sorry, Zena. I wish I could look after you better.'

For a moment, she thinks she might cry. It seems a long time ago that Zena had servants and slaves. She misses being cared for and, if she allows herself to think of it, which she does seldom, she feels a dull pang of love for her grandmother. The thought saddens her despite the fact that the desert is proving intriguing, and this man most of all. She pulls herself up on her elbows. All she can see of him is his face, a pale

247

blue orb, glowing in the pitch.

'You did well,' he assures her.

'Thank you.' There is a lump in her throat, but she controls it.

They have reached a line that neither feels ready to cross.

'Well then,' he says, turning away, 'Good night.'

Zena, for all her travels, is unworldly, and she has no words for the sparks she feels shoot through her. That he would say such a thing — an act of kindness — is astonishing. That he would then turn away and expect nothing for it has unexpected power. She wishes her grandmother had not been so protective, and that she understood better what passes between a man and woman. As it is, she simply enjoys the feelings and wonders if they are what lightning is made of, for everything in the world comes back to the weather. Tears like rain. Smiles like the sun. Hair as dry as sand and fear like the dark ocean.

'London,' she mouths silently. 'Marylebone.' The strange names roll around her tongue as she attempts the pronunciation. Dreamlike as lullabies they send her to sleep.

28

'I can't imagine what the hell you were thinking, man!' Sir Charles blusters at Haines, as he whacks the captain's report onto his desk. The monsoons are past now and the heat is building up slowly again which is more than can be said for Sir Charles' temper about which there is nothing leisurely. It is excellent, of course, that Haines has captured a French vessel on the journey back to Bombay, but the cargo! It doesn't bear thinking about. 'What in the name of the Almighty are we supposed to do with them all?' the Head of the Bombay Marine explodes.

The captain looks sheepish though he harbours a twinge of annoyance at his lordship's reaction. He should, he is sure, be treated like a damn hero.

Malcolm strides to the window and looks down on the French ship. It is a fine piece of booty. But still. 'Did you lose any men?' he thinks to enquire at last.

'Not one.' Haines leans forward. The captain can't help sounding smug. Why the hell shouldn't he? 'And you have proof now, sir, that the French are still slaving. That surely is a good thing.'

Malcolm wipes his face with a handkerchief. His skin is slick with sweat. You'd think he'd acclimatise, but in his view Bombay's weather is simply getting more unpleasant. If it's not the bally, baking sun, it's the humidity of the monsoon driving everyone to distraction. He takes a swig of Madeira from an intricately engraved glass, without offering any to Haines. He's too taken up with the problem in hand to think of anyone else's comfort. The captain sits back in the mahogany seat on the other side of the desk and swelters.

'They didn't see us coming,' he says with the air of a boy relating a triumph at the school sports day. 'It was very late and we had no lamps up, you see. We knew immediately what they were up to and I had my midshipmen blast them. The Frenchies didn't know a thing about it. They hardly stood a chance. The boys were admirable, sir. Ormsby certainly deserves a commendation. It's a pity the lad is too young to promote. The Frenchies will have to be returned, I suppose? Still, the crew are delighted — there's nothing like the prospect of prize money to encourage the men.'

Sir Charles nods. 'It's not the bloody Frenchies I'm concerned with, Haines. But I suppose it is well enough done, Captain.'

Haines beams. At last Sir Charles appears to have realised what he has achieved. 'You don't have to worry about the cargo, sir,' he assures his superior.

Sir Charles grimaces. It's the cargo that is the nub of course. There is no protocol for what to do with captured slaves (who, by the letter of the law, aren't slaves of course, for slaving is illegal and simply does not exist any longer). Shipping the forty youngsters back to Africa is inconvenient in the extreme — a complete waste of resources and, besides, there is no way to know exactly where the blighters actually come from. They cannot be kept in Bombay (or at least not easily, for they are ill-educated bush children with no skills and every one of them darker than an Untouchable. Whoever would employ them? Certainly not the Bombay Marine). Worse, Lady Malcolm is an ardent abolitionist and if Sir Charles does something that she deems to be wrong, he'll never hear the end of it.

'I don't suppose,' Haines suggests, 'we have any ships leaving for Ceylon?'

Malcolm pauses. Now that is a very enterprising idea — for years the captain has brought nothing but problems to the table. Now, at last, here he is offering a small solution. Lagging behind London and tardy in its responsibilities, slavery is still legal in British Ceylon, in fact, the plantations are crying out for extra hands. The slaves, or as Sir Charles prefers to think of them, the cargo, cannot be dispatched, of course, on a navy vessel. The Bombay Marine does not run slaves — its mission and duty is to liberate them. No, no, that would never do. But he is sure he can have one of the men discreetly find a private clipper bound in the right direction. Pottinger might be the man for that job, — the young Englishman is proving tenacious and effective in every way. Lady Malcolm need never know and this will be far easier to keep from her than trying to place the skilless, hapless cargo anywhere in Bombay

251

where they are worse than useless. Yes, Ceylon will do very well.

'Good,' Sir Charles smiles slowly. He motions towards the bottle of Madeira and Haines nods curtly and pours himself a glug. The men click glasses and the thick, amber liquid raises a syrupy splash on the rim. 'Yes. That will sort things out. Good. Now, tell me, you are sure Doctor Jessop is dead, are you? Lieutenant Jones as well?'

'Oh yes, sir. I wouldn't have let Wellsted go on the damn, wild-goose chase, but he is hopeless as an officer, my last choice for any task. Besides, the sultan, for God knows what reason, absolutely insisted on it,' the captain fumes, unable to contain himself. 'Lieutenant Wellsted is untrustworthy in the extreme. He has terrible Arabic and poor seamanship skills. The man is fine as an assistant, nothing more.'

Sir Charles nods, taking this in. The captain's assessment doesn't tie up with his own, albeit brief experience of the lieutenant, when he was stationed in Bombay. Nor is it consistent with what he's been hearing lately from London, where, it seems, Wellsted has written some kind of interesting account of his experiences in the region. Though Haines has first-hand experience of the young officer at close quarters and under pressure, his lordship is inclined to take the view of John Murray more into consideration. From memory, the lad's demeanour is good and he has passable manners. In any case, Malcolm hopes Wellsted will make it out of the desert alive and that Haines is wrong (not for the first time) and the lieutenant brings Jones and Jessop with him. So many of these young chaps die that it's difficult to keep up with the ones that are left, and to decide what best to do with them. When there are such heavy losses be they due to malaria or battle, he sometimes feels as if he is watching an investment being flushed down the river. Malcolm has always felt that the service is founded on the expertise of its officers and that those officers are its best public face. He hates to waste them.

'I hope he's taking decent notes,' he says. 'At least then we might get something out of it.'

Haines shrugs his shoulders as if to say that he couldn't tell what Wellsted may or may not do and, in any case, he certainly isn't responsible for it.

'Right,' says Sir Charles. 'Lunch, I think. Must be getting back.'

He can dispatch this news later. London will be interested in the French activity and, all things considered, the captain has done well. Malcolm only wishes that the man didn't *moan* all the time. He's had a problem with every crew he's ever led. It is most tiresome.

Haines stands to attention and salutes.

'You must come to dinner,' His Lordship says as an afterthought, though it is telling that he does not set a date for this. He's thinking that he'll ask the chap on short notice one night when they are down a fellow — sometime when he needs an extra body for bridge or billiards rather than conversation. 'Billeted all right at the mess are you?'

'Oh yes, sir,' Haines beams. The captain does not understand the slight and is looking forward to some decent cooking, the opportunity to catch up on his reading and perhaps even to making a start on the book he has been meaning to write for the last five years. Now, of course, he will have to direct himself to some other area of interest than the Socotra trip, but he is sure he will think of something. The marine life of the Red Sea perhaps. Young Ormsby has spotted an interesting fish or two.

'The mess in Bombay is fine for me. It's good to be back, sir.' He shakes Sir Charles' hand warmly, and salutes before he leaves the room.

29

As they travel further north, the party enters *Wahabi* territory. The strangers they now encounter have the long beards of their sect and their dark eyes are serious. Prayer times, until the change of jurisdiction, are a gentle and pleasant affair but now they take on an air of fundamentalism. Instead of family groups and a ramshackle collection of servants that make up the *Bedu* caravans, the *Wahabi* travel without women and are accompanied mostly by uniformly thin and faceless slaves. As a result, the conversations over coffee take on a less familial air and the news is of politics and power struggles. Once more, Wellsted's Turkish disguise lays him open to suspicion.

'Why do you travel with a Turk?' one man asks Ibn Mohammed contemptuously. 'They stole our cities. We took them back.'

The power struggle in the northern territories is ongoing.

'The *effendi* is an investor,' Ibn Mohammed assures the man. 'He has the blessing of the Sultan of Oman to travel with us.'

But none of the men accept that. The boundaries of the sultan's territories are long passed. His Highness is a foreign ruler here and, worse, one who is maligned.

'No. No,' they insist, bitterly, a rush of bad feeling overtaking the coffee ritual, 'this man is a

Turk.' They spit the word. 'You should cast him out.'

They are equally as shocked at the notion of a woman travelling with the party and eye Zena with contempt as she goes quietly about her chores.

'I wonder which one of us they think is worse?' Wellsted whispers to her.

Zena only stares. He is a fool if he does not know a woman is the lowest of the low and a female slave lower still.

That night the *Wahabi* refuse to sleep in a settlement where there is a Turk and after dinner they take their leave. 'We will make our camp an hour or two further,' they say. 'None of us will sleep with such a man in the party — we might as well make our way.'

'We have travelled for weeks with him and, truth be told, I spar with him. The man could have killed me several times,' Kasim informs them, just as coldly. It's true, the men have taken to sparring on the sands before dinner — Kasim tutoring the lieutenant in the use of his *khandjar*. After the featureless days, if they have no company it at least provides a little sport. The *Wahabi* shrug. The fact the Turk has not killed his travelling companions makes no matter.

'It is better we leave,' they say. 'He is a Turk.'

The rudeness makes Wellsted blush though the Arabs are unaffected. Amid almost ceremonial politeness in most matters, each man on the sands must make his own decisions and say what he feels.

'I'm glad they've gone,' he says to Kasim when

the men have disappeared into the darkness.

The slaver only shrugs and the camp settles for the evening.

Much later, past midnight, Kasim is jerked awake in the darkness. He never wakes unless there is good reason and in this case, his instincts arc not to be faulted. Ibn Mohammed's eyes are already open. Someone is approaching the settlement. The slavers have not got where they are without an almost psychic ability to second-guess who their enemies arc and what they will do. While Zena blundering into the darkness after a snake does not merit more than a grumble and a short interlude between bouts of deep sleep, the mere movement of a robe out of place and a scimitar or *khandjar* being drawn carefully from its scabbard, raises them immediately.

Ibn Mohammed lies prone for all of three seconds. A flicker of regret passes across his face as realisation dawns. He can hear four of them — it can only be the *Wahabi* who left the camp a few hours before. Experienced raiders, they are all but silent as they cross the sands in the near blackness afforded by the thin moon and sneak towards the oasis, no doubt imagining it defenceless. Who else can it be? He signals Kasim who nods curtly in agreement. No one can be allowed to attack, even if all the men have come for, most likely, is to slit Wellsted's throat. In all honesty, if the *Wahabi* knew the truth of his identity, it might well be worse. On the long list of those deserving of contempt, the northern tribes hate the infidel more than they hate the

Turks, but that is by the by.

The slavers can take the four men easily, of course, but Kasim decides to wake the lieutenant. It only seems right. He slips to his feet and lays one strong hand on Wellsted's wrist and another over his mouth. Kasim's eyes jerk to the higher ground. 'Your chance to fight for real, my friend,' he whispers.

Ibn Mohammed, a solid black shadow with his dark *kaffiya* draped over his face, rolls away, draws his weapon and sneaks behind the line of attack so stealthily he is almost invisible. He is born to this. Deftly, like a ghost, he kills two of the intruders before they realise the camp is alert to their plan. Their throats slit, the bodies fall to the ground quicker than the blood can slide down their skin. They do not even reach the first slave, still dozing, dribbling in sleep on the fringes of the sleeping circle. The two raiders who are left reach the prone figures before they comprehend they have been seen and their kinsmen are dead. They do not retreat but push ahead to complete the mission. One looks for the Turk, ready to cut out his heart. The other easily captures Zena, who does not scream as she wakes, only sinks her teeth into the man's arm as he tries to pull her up the hill.

It is his voice that cries out into the still, desert night, the first sound that really breaks the silence. In a raid like this the girl is fair game. Moving swiftly, Wellsted easily avoids the other fellow and falls on the kidnapper, ripping Zena free of his grasp. The lieutenant does not even bother to draw the *khandjar* or the long-bladed *khattirah* he has been learning to use. Instead, in sheer fury and without thinking, he reaches straight for the kidnapper's throat and he strangles the raider with his bare hands, such venom in his heart that he can think of nothing else as he squeezes the man's life away. As the body falls, Kasim, with his blood high, uses his *khandjar* to slit the man's gullet just to be sure. The lieutenant, it turns out, is as good in a fight as when they practised. Kasim moves off to trail the last assassin.

'Are you all right?' Wellsted checks Zena. His heart is pounding at the thought of her being taken. He's known for a while that he cares about her, but this murderous fury has surprised him. How dare these men?

Zena nods and then circles, peering into the darkness, terror pulsing through her as she scans the dunes for signs of a further onslaught. God knows who else is out there. She lays a hand on Wellsted's arm in gratitude and squeezes. When their eyes meet it is like a moment that is stolen from everyone else.

'Shall I run?' she whispers.

'No. Stay here.'

Her breath is quick in panic and he can hear her panting. She steps back a little and Wellsted lays his hand on her shoulder as he checks to see where Ibn Mohammed and Kasim are focussing their attention.

'Stay behind me,' he tells her and she falls gratefully into his wake.

The slaves are rising now, woken by the sound of violence. The sleeping men jump to their feet, calling to their friends and ready to fight for their lives in the lacquer-black darkness. Ibn Mohammed is furious for the final assassin is lost in the panic.

'Quiet,' he shouts down the dune, but it is too late to follow the sound of the man's robes moving away and the *Wahabi* is gone.

Kasim makes a sign that shows the attack is over. Of the four, three are dead.

Zena reaches out. There is a shape on the sand. It is Wellsted's notebook.

'Here, you dropped this,' she says. Her hand is shaking as she gives it to him.

'Come,' Wellsted gestures, as elegantly as if he is a *Bedu*. 'Sit near the fire. You are shaken.'

There is something so fragile about her. When she looks up at him, he has a vague sense of guilt, for there should be no real bond between them, he is sure of it, only courtesies, and yet he has just killed a man for trying to steal her, and the killing was not for courtesy's sake. He has never felt such hatred in all his life. The passion surprises him and, unlike Zena, he is not too young to misunderstand it. He thinks of the moment after, when their eyes locked and the empty desert, if it is possible, became even more silent.

'If they had taken you, I would have come after you,' Wellsted assures her evenly.

The girl is as jumpy as a gazelle but still, she smiles. Wellsted knows the pang he feels is not from the purple bruise that is forming on his shoulder. When she glances at him it is as if she is casting a spell. He cannot say anything. There are too many others nearby and the words are not easy to find.

For Zena's part, she feels safe next to her master and this produces a sensation that surprises her. Unlike the thunder and lightning of his touch, for the first time ever in her life she feels an overwhelming gratitude that gives her butterflies in her stomach and a glow that a wiser, older woman would describe as affection, even love. He fetches a blanket and sits next to her, only inches away and if the rest of the caravan were not so busy checking the dunes, moving as close together as possible, looking always outwards, it would surely be noted that the black girl and the white man have a strange stillness about them, as if the world's lens is focussing solely on the two of them. As it is, a guard is mounted and the camp settles slowly without noticing what has happened.

I will never sleep, she thinks. Out here, if she is stolen she knows that most likely she'll never leave the wide, sandy expanse again. Zena does not want to spend the rest of her life milking camels and pitching tents, traded between dirty, ragged settlements at the whim of one man or another. Strangely, though, calmed by Wellsted's presence and as all falls to stillness once more, she drifts off as she hears him breathing smoothly beside her, and in the morning, just as dawn is breaking, when they wake, their fingers are entwined.

'*Ana mut asif*, I'm sorry,' she says, rather formal in tone, as she pulls her hand back towards her body quickly. It is as if his touch burns her. He cannot see her cheeks colour, but she feels mortified, far beyond the level of the offence. Instead of awkwardness, he smiles openly. He thinks he will apologise but then there is no time, for Ibn Mohammed and Kasim are kicking towards him across the sand, their eyes sharp in the morning light, and Zena withdraws towards the fire to help brew the coffee.

'The attacker left tracks.' Ibn Mohammed points over to the west.

'Shall we hunt him?' Kasim asks eagerly.

Ibn Mohammed shakes his head. 'We will not turn back where we came from,' he says, for there is no measure in that.

The man is lucky in that, at least. Had he blundered off to the north or east he would be dead before midday, they would have seen to it.

'Come, my friend,' Ibn Mohammed, gestures at Wellsted's prayer mat, which is poking clear from his saddle. 'It is better to pray than sleep. And then we shall break our fast.'

On Ibn Mohammed's orders, as the men rise sleepily into the dawn and the rite of the prayers are undergone, the bodies of the *Wahabi* assassins are left where they fell, as carrion for the vultures. Such men do not merit any honour. Their weapons are taken and the bodies searched. They must have left their booty stowed in the saddlebags in their own camp for they are holding not a single dollar anywhere on their persons. Ibn Mohammed spits on the corpses and motions the party onwards.

The birds are already circling the fresh flesh as

the camp is taken down, the fire is extinguished and the last camel leaves the high, golden dune. Zena follows Wellsted so closely that she could be his shadow. It feels to her as if she is tethered to him willingly now. Something has changed. When Wellsted disappears at one stage across the top of the high ground, to Zena it is as if the whole desert is on tiptoes to try to see where he has gone and the sky and sand are all the emptier for his absence.

★   ★   ★

In future when they meet the *Wahabi*, the slavers fall into the pattern of keeping Wellsted to the rear with the servants. The sight of a Turkish free man is clearly too much for the xenophobic ire of the northern tribes. Ten years ago, Kasim says, it would have been different, five years ago perhaps, but in the turbulent times that have come to pass the *Wahabi* grow wilder eyed and more vengeful by the month.

'We will say you are a *huss*,' Ibn Mohammed spits contemptuously, though it is easy to see that it amuses him. 'And in my employ.'

It seems a Turkish camel man is acceptable. A business associate is not. So in company now Wellsted tends a camel and eats second in turn, taking orders from Kasim, whose eyes burn brightly with silent laughter as he tells the lieutenant what to do. Though he must admit, the white man plays the part they have given him well.

As they continue northwards. The news is not good.

'A long time,' Kasim grits his teeth when they receive news that the camp might have moved beyond Riyadh, perhaps as much as a day.

Wellsted knows that to complain is simply not on. It is something the British have in common with their Arab counterparts and he understands the notion instinctively. He worries though that the longer it takes, the less chance they have of freeing Jessop and Jones.

'It's given me a chance to grow my beard,' he says lightly and passes a hand over his chin. The beard, now fully grown, has completed his disguise. 'I can't complain, old man. After all, I have learnt a very great deal about the needs of the camel.'

'Ten days,' Ibn Mohammed growls, ever short of temper, but Kasim laughs.

The *effendi* is turning out to be better sport than he expected. The white man would never survive alone, of course, but for a *Nazarene* the lieutenant is acquitting himself admirably.

30

Because he only sees the camp on the occasions when the emir decides to have the tents taken down, loaded and transported to a new location, Jessop has become attuned to the noises that surround such an operation. The dismantling itself is all but silent, more distinctive is the hubbub of men and women performing strenuous work in the heat (even though the removals do not take place over the hottest six hours of the day). Jones has not spoken for a long time, the doctor notes. He considers saying something, for the camp is definitely coming down and he knows that they will be fetched and herded like livestock, in fact, alongside the goats, to whichever new location the emir has chosen. He lifts his hand, which moves Jones' wrist and disturbs him, so that the lieutenant grunts and snores. *Ah*, the doctor thinks, *he is deep asleep. I shall leave him.*

Jessop smiles as it passes across his mind that the details of tribal life in the interior is exactly why the two of them were sent here and there is some irony in that now he is something of an expert. He knows the tasks the women perform and what is the men's responsibility. He has a good idea of the spiritual considerations that are taken into account when the *Bedu* make decisions, and he has a particularly sharp understanding of the importance of water. Water

shapes this culture, water drives it. There is little
for the British to trade here. The country lacks
any kind of effective infrastructure and Jessop
cannot imagine a demand for either British
textiles or even opium. The Arabs are puritan in
their tastes and Allah, he is sure, would not
approve of the poppy. He imagines a railway
built through the desert and then laughs out
loud. It is an outrageous and ridiculous notion.
The doctor is no engineer but he is sure it would
be impossible, for large stretches of *Rubh Al
Khali* is made up of shifting dunes. However, he
allows himself the luxury of considering a few
station names. The doctor favours the romantic
and picks out *Oasis of Stars*, painted with white
enamel on a burgundy plaque. He imagines
purchasing a ticket from the Oasis of Stars all
the way to the station at Euston, which he has
read is under construction.

'If I start now, I might even get there in time
for the Grand Opening,' he smirks.

The tent flap is pulled back and a tribesman
Jessop hasn't seen before enters. He is taller than
the usual jailer and, surprisingly, he smiles
broadly when he catches the doctor's eye. It is as
if he has blundered into the tent in the confusion
of the whole camp packing up.

'*Salaam aleikhum*,' he bows.

The doctor is not quite sure how to respond.
He's been treated like an animal for so many
weeks now that such courtesy is strange. He
smiles cautiously and flicks his wrist several
times to wake Jones, who jerks into consciousness with a squeal.

'We're moving, Jones,' the doctor apprises his lieutenant.

The man leans down and loosens the bonds so the prisoners can use their hands. Then he leaves the tent and returns a few seconds later in a waft of fresh air. He pauses beside the infidels. In one hand he has a goatskin flask and in the other a huge flatbread. Jessop tries not to breathe in the smell in too obvious a fashion, but there is no question that the flatbread is filled with meat and garlic. It is fresh. In fact, if the doctor is not mistaken, it is still hot.

'Here,' the man lays the flask and the bread on the ground. 'We have far to walk.'

Both Jones and Jessop are so stunned by this unexpected generosity that they freeze momentarily. They cannot help wondering if this is some kind of trick. Over the weeks of privation they have worn down to all but skin and bones and the doctor doubts that the two of them together weigh as much as he did alone when he left the *Palinurus*. After an initial pause, both men fall on the food with vigour, stuffing in strips of fluffy bread, sucking the meat of its gravy and licking their chins of the grease. The water is quite fresh and the two of them finish the whole goatskin in what seems less than a minute.

Jones puts a hand on his stomach. He can feel the food and water inside. It is a comforting, pleasant sensation. 'Now that's what I call a decent breakfast,' he grins.

The man looks shocked at the feeding frenzy. Not all the tribesmen, it would seem, are aware of the way the prisoners have been treated. He shrugs, deciding it is none of his business, and then beckons them to their feet, rebinding their hands and leading the men out of the tent. Outside, the afternoon sun is astonishingly bright and the white men squint towards it. The camp is already loaded onto the camels and the children run around in excitement, charged with ensuring the goats do not wander. Women carry pots on their heads and some even have babies swaddled across their *burquahs*. The man who fetched them is having a heated exchange with the jailer, who is crossing the sand with a plate of scraps.

'You fed them?'

'Yes. There was bread left.'

'You let them have bread?'

'And some water. We will walk all night.'

The jailer blusters furiously. 'I saved this,' he spits.

The scraps are rotten. Jessop can smell them from where he stands. But he'd eat them. Of course he would.

The jailer pours the contents of the dish onto the ground and kicks sand over them. 'I waste my time!' he exclaims. 'The goats have eaten too.'

'But I was trying to help,' the other man defends himself.

'I think we were rather lucky there, old man,' Jones points out.

The doctor nods. He hopes that the jailer doesn't take it out on them later. Still, for fresh food and a decent drink of almost fresh water, he'd happily endure some abuse. 'I wonder where we're heading?' he ponders.

'Near Riyadh,' Jones says nonchalantly. 'I heard one of them say the other day, that the camp was moving to somewhere beyond Riyadh. Some oasis. Middle of nowhere, I expect.'

The men begin to move forward and fall in with the caravan that is forming. At moments like this it always puzzles the doctor how, without any overt leadership, the tribe decides to move out all together. You'd never wrangle sailors this way. It is late afternoon, he calculates by the sun, and they are heading east. He heaves a sigh for he is exhausted already. It is going to be a long night.

31

Four days off Riyadh and the last day of October 1833, Kasim captures a hawk. They hit a patch of rocky, arid land in the run-up to the settlement. It is still desert but there are no dunes. The going is easier and there is sparse grazing for the camels — sticks of grass, thorny acacia and a scattering of rigid bushes with tiny, grey leaves. Kasim checks under the bird's wings but the feathers are not fully developed and it is too young to fly, though its talons are sharp enough.

'The chick must have got separated from its parents too early,' Kasim explains as he covers the bird with a light rug so it stops flapping. He feeds it a little meat and tethers the creature to his saddle. At night he fashions a hood and begins to train it. Over the next three days the bird becomes as devoted to him as a wild creature can be. It sits majestically to the rear of his camel, perched on the saddle like a mascot. When he sets it free it wheels high above the burning oven that radiates from ground level and soars to the cooler air so that it is visible only as a tiny dot. Still, it returns to Kasim's arm immediately at the whistle. As they finally come into Riyadh a group of *Bedu* ask to buy it and offer a price that is more than fair, but Kasim shakes his head. He is, Wellsted thinks, a strange fellow. Cold to a *habshi* and kind to a hawk. A slaver who turns his back on coins of profit, freely offered, when the bird cost him nothing but his occupation in training it.

After the desolation of the desert, the sight of Riyadh on a Friday afternoon is a shock. The slash of green that rises out of the sands is startling and complex. The orchards waft fresh scent through the thin streets and the straggle of white houses on the outskirts dazzle like gemstones on a green, velvet throw. The town is a place of tremendous fecundity. As they move towards the centre of the settlement, the whole party is diverted by the sudden sight of so much life. The *jumaah*, Friday prayers, are over and the dusty alleyways echo with music and laughter — there are people everywhere outside their houses and shops. It has been a long time since the caravan has been anywhere even remotely urban. Baskets overflow with food, the wells give clear water and the air feels succulent as if it has been freshened ready for their arrival with bergamot, mint and coriander. There is so much to do that everyone forgets the heat and simply surrenders to the spectacle of what is going on around them.

In the marketplace, the party dismounts, the slaves queue to refill the water skins and refresh the animals. The free men resupply with dates and ask for news of the emir. Wellsted finds himself distracted by the constant movement of the crowd. The children's outfits shock him with their exotic flashes of colour as they tarry looking at the collection of dusty strangers hanging

271

around the fringes of the bazaar. Two men sit in the shade of a lush tree with boughs of trailing leaves that Wellsted cannot identify. He notices one of them, lazy-eyed, cannot rip his gaze from Zena, who is holding her camel's bridle as she leads the animal back from its long, thirsty drink. Wellsted buys mint tea from a street hawker. He hands a cup to Zena and stations himself, like a guard, beside her in the shade of a huge palm.

'Thank you,' she smiles.

She tethers the beast so she can sip silently. Prettily, if it comes to that. Wellsted wishes he could get her out of sight off the street, but he cannot see how.

Kasim, a poke of honeyed nuts in his hand, strolls over. 'We will stay here tonight and tomorrow we will make for the emir's settlement. It is not so far — a few hours. The move we heard of has taken the camp further south but no further from Riyadh. We will be there before sunset tomorrow.'

Wellsted grins openly at this stroke of luck. 'We have made it!' he says. 'Is there any news of the men?'

Kasim shakes his head. 'Not yet,' he says. 'But tomorrow we will know.'

'And we are safe here overnight?' Since the *Wahabi* attack, Wellsted is suspicious of all strangers, even the open-faced *Bedu*. 'They are watching Zena.'

'You are right,' Kasim acknowledges. 'She is worth a fortune this far north. This is where Al Mudar said you would sell her, is it not?' He

272

nods towards the group of men loitering around the stalls.

'I won't sell her. Not for any price,' Wellsted maintains steadily. The thought makes him angry. 'She is to be free.'

Kasim shrugs his shoulders. 'She is very beautiful,' he says. 'We will have to be watchful. Stay close.'

When, after a few minutes, one of the *Wahabi* approaches and asks tentatively if Zena is for sale, Wellsted almost spits his reply. The man backs off as if the Turk is a dangerous fool — Riyadh's newest, crazy *majnoon*. He only asked a question.

The party settles in the shade, a couple of the servants head into the bazaar to barter for indulgences. Wellsted brings out his notebook.

'I like that picture,' Zena says, shyly, peering at the paper. 'That is my camel, isn't it?'

He has drawn the caravan across the top of the page, and it is true, you can pick out her camel. Wellsted turns over, where he has jotted some maps.

'The scale is wrong, I expect,' he says. 'But it is as close as I could get it.'

'We have come all this way?' Zena asks.

'Yes. Over 800 miles as I reckon it.'

Zena takes in the information. Wellsted has been mapping their journey with impressive accuracy. 'And on this map, where is Africa?' she asks.

Wellsted turns a fresh leaf. He draws the relative positions of the continents and shows the route of their journey north from Muscat. Zena thinks a moment. She measures with her fingers the distance of the journey from her home. It is twice as far as they have just travelled.

'Do you miss it?' he asks gently.

Zena hesitates. 'I am glad I met you,' she says.

One of the other slaves turns, listening idly to their conversation. Wellsted wants to say that he is glad he has met her too. He wants to suggest that she comes back to London with him, but then he catches himself, for that will never be possible. When you are in Arabia and the colour of a person's skin is of little consequence to their social status, it is easy to forget that in England Wellsted's feelings for Zena would be a scandal. In England, the girl has almost no value at all.

'England,' he continues unsteadily, making a mark to the north, 'is up here.'

'And the friends you hope to free — they are from England too?'

'Yes.'

'You will see them tomorrow.'

'I hope so.'

It occurs to the lieutenant that few English women would have managed the journeys that Zena has endured, both in the desert and before. He is struck by her calmness and admires her grace. A duchess could do no better. Still, he senses in her a steely edge and he likes it. He has seen her make up her own mind in small things when others would simply do as they are told. He's seen her looking at Ibn Mohammed as if she'd like to stab him in the heart.

'Come on,' he says, 'that's tomorrow. Let us enjoy Riyadh this afternoon.'

As the heat fades and the sun sinks, the town comes to life. The sound of the *doumbek* drums wafts from the marketplace nearby and someone is pounding a tambourine in time. Occasionally, there is singing and even if a man cannot sing or play an instrument, he still claps enthusiastically to the beat. One or two dance, fired up by the smoking of *shisha* pipes and the excitement of new company. A fellow with a basket of snakes joins the party and is welcomed enthusiastically. He soon has the servants and slaves captivated with stories of the reptiles.

'I have one that can dance,' he says, winding his arm high in the air to show what the snake can do.

But he will not charm it without a silver coin and the free men are not interested. No amount of coffee or dates (the only material goods the others have to hand) will convince him to bring the snake from its basket.

As the sky moves from evening to night, the streets of the little town are positively balmy. The men have eaten and drunk their fill and spirits are high. One entertainer, an acrobat, tumbles like a waterfall. Then, down an alleyway, three *Wahabi* approach with torches and Ibn Moham-med jumps to his feet in readiness with Kasim and Wellsted close behind, but in the event there is no trouble. The men are smiling and one in particular is finely dressed. Riyadh it seems, is in an unrelentingly good humour.

'*Salaam aleikhum.*' The *Wahabi* greet the

slavers and one offers them the use of an empty house in a nearby street overlooking the bazaar. It belongs to his brother who has gone to trade salt in the north. 'It is a humble dwelling, but it will accommodate you. My family will be honoured. I am sure your home in Muscat is far finer.'

The man is in awe of the slavers — their reputation has reached even this far. Ibn Mohammed with his cold politeness says there is no need. 'We have been sleeping in the open for weeks now,' he says. 'Though it is very kind.'

Kasim bows. When you are offered hospitality the custom is always to take it and both he and Ibn Mohammed demur only very slightly before, with Wellsted in their wake, they are shown the door of the vacant property — a square, pale box that runs over two storeys. It is not locked, for in a small town like this there is no need for such precautions. Friends and brothers are everywhere and while the community might steal from a stranger or hike prices for those coming off the sands and eager to procure the luxuries Riyadh can afford them, it protects its own.

Inside, the man lights a *naft* lamp and reveals that the place is all but unadorned — a few rugs on the floor and some cushions for sitting or sleeping. There are clay water jars, dry as bone now, and a few utensils for cooking, clearly deemed too luxurious to be taken onto the sands. To be inside, within four walls, feels strange beyond measure though the house is pleasantly cooler by several degrees than the air outside.

'Go!' the man ushers one of his slaves. 'Fetch water!'

Barefoot, the man disappears, carrying the pitcher on his shoulder into the night.

'And brothers, will you tell me of your travels?' the *Wahabi* asks. He is young and has not ventured far. 'Did you come from Muscat? Truly?'

The slavers nod. 'Come.'

Kasim and Ibn Mohammed lead the man back to the group outside and drink coffee with him. The slaves are sent to buy whatever pastries are left on the market stalls. He may be a *Wahabi* but he is more relaxed than most of his tribe and soon they are talking animatedly about something — a story told so fast that Wellsted cannot follow it. Besides, Kasim waves him off quickly, for as a mere servant the lieutenant should not linger with the free men without an invitation, and they see no reason to proffer one.

Later, the *Wahabi* takes his leave, the last of the market stalls closes and the streets of the little town are all but empty. Ibn Mohammed and Kasim call Wellsted to walk with them into the safety of the darkness, a little way off from where the servants and slaves have congregated around the fire and are, in dribs and drabs now surrounding Zena and settling to sleep.

'Tomorrow, when we reach the emir's camp, you must stay with the girl and watch her. Between her value and the hatred of the Turks, it is best you stay out of the way. I know you want to see your friends, but you must let us undertake the negotiations.'

Wellsted hesitates. There is a lot at stake here. Over the months he has come, more or less, to trust these men, but a knot tightens in his stomach, for in truth, how can he not take responsibility? This will be the most important day of the whole trip and he cares about the captured men far more than the slavers care for anyone. They are so close now.

Kasim sees Wellsted's dilemma immediately. 'We are at the *soultan's* service,' he says. 'I could have stuck you like a goat if I'd wanted to, long since. Any day on the sands I could have. And truly, my friend, this is for the best. All the men here ask about you — there have been very few Turks through Riyadh since the Circassians were routed. Your very presence renders them uneasy. The emir is best dealt with by his fellow Arabs. It is best for all of us — the men we have come for most of all.'

'Jessop and Jones are my friends and brother officers,' Wellsted whispers. 'Whatever offence they have given they are my fellows. Will you promise me to do your best for them?'

Kasim and Ibn Mohammed are surprised by the white man's dignity. Infidels are not famed for their humility.

'I give my word,' Ibn Mohammed finds himself saying and he does not even say it with his hand on his heart, the usual position he adopts when he has to lie.

Kasim shakes Wellsted's hand. 'This is how you do it, is it not?' he says. 'You have my word also.' Then he takes a breath for he is about to say something that is out of character but the lieutenant has acquitted himself admirably. 'We have travelled together. I have fought alongside you. I swear my loyalty. Have no fear.'

The lieutenant is not sure what to reply and he pauses a moment. Kasim has taken him by surprise. 'Thank you,' he says finally.

Kasim puts his arms around the lieutenant and hugs him, clapping him on the back. Ibn Mohammed follows suit. Wellsted realises there is something about the desert, about fighting off the *Wahabi* raid, about the shared intrigue of cloak-and-dagger disguise that has instigated this loyalty by stealth. He laughs. He is unsure what they would make of this sentimentality in London. *I will have to edit it out of my account*, he thinks.

'We are like old women,' Ibn Mohammed spits with a note of disgust in his voice.

'We must sleep,' says Kasim. 'In the house. Bring the girl. It is safer. And tomorrow we will fulfil the *soultan's* orders.'

Wellsted returns to the campfire and lingers for a minute or two before he silently motions Zena to follow him. 'It's best not to leave you here,' he whispers, and they sneak through the front door of the dwelling.

Inside, Zena shivers. She has become used to the balmy, open-air nights and is sensitive now to anything colder. Kasim lies downstairs, already breathing deeply with the only lamp doused beside him. Wellsted motions the girl towards the stairs and they climb upwards into the darkness of the upper floor. A tiny window, a mere slit in the thick, cool wall, casts a sliver of shady,

279

night-time light and Wellsted can see a further run of thin, wooden stairs against the whitewash. He motions to Zena and they climb upwards again, towards a door so small he has to stoop very low to get through. Outside, there is a flat roof and the usual startling canopy of stars. The huge, bright slice of the moon is a little way off tonight rather than suspended above the highest nearby dune. Zena walks to the edge of the rooftop, which is delineated only by a line of single bricks. She peers cautiously across it and then crouches, watching the other servants and slaves by the fire. Most are asleep but two men sit, still talking quietly about the dancing snake.

Then there is a movement. Up the street, his black *jubbah* and *kaffiya* making his very person seem like a black hole in the landscape of the little town, Ibn Mohammed walks silently towards the house. Ready to sleep, he disappears through the front door and they hear him climb the stairway. There is a snort or two and then he settles in the room beneath their feet.

'Shhhh,' Wellsted hisses.

They wait. Zena turns away from the view over the simple parapet. She smiles and then raises her arms to stretch like a lazy cat. There are no strangers to stare at her here — she is alone with Wellsted for the first time. She thinks back carefully. Yes, she has never been alone with her master before in all the weeks on the sands. Caravans simply don't travel that way. Wellsted grins back. He has realised it too.

'Remove your veil,' he whispers, 'I want to see your hair.'

Zena unwinds the fabric carefully and puts up her hand to feel the plaits. She thinks that she must look ridiculous, but the master peers from side to side, inspecting her carefully. He gives an approving nod.

Riyadh turns in its sleep. The swaying of the palms, the click of doors and the occasional sound of laughter cut through the darkness. The camels grunt and the goats bleat. The town feels like a metropolis after living with the same people for weeks — the noises in the night are usually so familiar that you can tell which camel will not settle. It seems impossible that the mass of people here will do anything at the same time, let alone sleep. There are one or two solitary lights dotted from house to house. An old man who is restless stays up reading. A slave cleans a pan in the kitchen. From the vantage point they peer down onto the maze.

'Let's not disturb them downstairs,' Wellsted whispers. 'Let's stay here. It will take some getting used to — walls and stairs and ceilings. It feels like a box, doesn't it?'

Zena curls up obediently. She puts her hands behind her head and stares at the stars. Wellsted crouches next to her. It occurs to him that all his life people have wanted things of him. Old Thomas wanted his name in perpetuity and his father wanted the same. The friendship between officers is tarnished by the need for one or another to be promoted. The kindness of a captain is predicated on the obedience and efficiency of his underlings. Everyone has always judged him on whether he might or might not produce any significant action on behalf of a ship, a family or a country. Yet Zena, it strikes Wellsted, seems perfectly content simply to be with him. She is happy to belong to him and appears to enjoy his company only for himself. He need not speak. No proof is required of his worthiness to hold the rank of lieutenant or his undying devotion to the Wellsted name. All he offers is normal, human kindness and she likes him for it. This out-and-out acceptance is an intoxication that makes the lieutenant happy.

'I have something for you,' he says.

Since her kidnap, the girl has received nothing that could be deemed a present. She feels wary. The master laughs. He'd love to see her festooned in silk, lace and diamonds, he thinks, but this gift is only a small thing.

'It's nothing dramatic,' he says. 'Here.' He hands her a thin, cloth bag. 'Only a sweet. I bought it from one of the stalls this evening.'

Zena sits up eagerly. She slips the plump jelly into her mouth and the taste of rose-water explodes. After weeks of unseasoned couscous, rice and bread interspersed with coffee and an occasional piece of meat, it feels almost magical to have this intensely sweet and delicate flavour. She makes an appreciative noise as it slips down her throat. Then she remembers she is supposed to be quiet and she giggles.

'You seem happy.'

She nods. 'I am.' The admission surprises her. 'Though I like Muscat better than Riyadh, the little of it I've seen, anyway.'

'It is,' the lieutenant comments, 'a far more cosmopolitan place. I would expect nothing less from my Ethiopian princess.'

Zena starts. 'I am your slave, sir,' she points out. 'I am not a princess.'

'I will free you. I promise. Sometimes men call their girls 'princess' where I come from, not as a title, you understand, but simply as a term of affection. Please, don't worry. You must not like being owned, being a slave. Did you never want to run?'

'They behead you if you run,' she says simply. 'An old *sidi* in Muscat told me so. Sometimes they cut off your legs.'

'Not if you get away.'

'I thought of it,' she admits. 'I thought of it many times. But I was too afraid.'

Wellsted nods. 'I would run in your position. I think, if I got the chance, it would be the right thing to do.'

'White men,' Zena says, as everyone is always pointing out, 'do not make good slaves.'

'Well,' he smiles, 'perhaps that is why.'

There is a pause and they settle comfortably into the silence and watch the stars. Zena has never felt so close to anyone. Not even her grandmother. *Yes*, she thinks, *loving the old lady felt different from this*. His elbow brushes her shoulder as he moves and she feels the now familiar tingle rush through her body. But he does not do any more than that.

'Master,' Zena asks, for she is curious, 'do you prefer men?'

Wellsted baulks. A lock of his hair escapes the

kaffiya and flops over his eyes. 'You mean, am I . . . ?'

Zena's eyes widen. The answer is clearly no. It is, all things given, to her mind a fair question. Still, the master seems shocked.

'No, I don't. I prefer women,' he splutters.

His hand, gesticulating, lands on the crown of her head and he does not remove it. Wellsted is flustered and the girl seems so sure of herself — so cool about it. The truth is that for all the years he has on her, he has little practical experience in this kind of matter. In Bombay there are brothels aplenty. Many of the officers frequent them and enjoy an array of smooth, brown beauties for a shilling the night. For men who require the devotion of one woman the *bibis* are so plentiful that you can scoop them up like mackerel and install them in perfectly nice apartments where they wait, well-fed and patient upon your attention. Officers (mostly titled, with private monies and certainly intending to wed a respectable — and, most importantly, pale — society beauty back in London) have been known to indulge in a *bibi* or two, housed in separate quarters and still frequent the better bawdy houses. It has been remarked that the heat often brings on that sort of thing. To Wellsted this seemed always a waste of money and of time. Until now. How on earth could she ask him that question?

Zena does not pull away from her master's touch. Instead, her body moves smoothly, like a fish in the water, closer to him. She rolls over and stares without flinching. Wellsted finds himself, without thinking, laying his hand on her belly, stroking her smooth skin, leaning in and touching her lips lightly with his own. Her mouth tastes sweet. His heart is pounding and when he kisses her it is as if the whole of Riyadh disappears — the wide sky, the hard surface of the roof, the date palms and the water wells. He cannot think. He can scarcely breathe. But he has no desire to either, he simply wants to keep kissing her.

Though she is trembling, Zena finds her rhythm. Her heart is pounding. She thinks, fleetingly, that this is nothing like kissing her master in Muscat. This is more like a dream where she is flying. She cannot stop any more than he can. She does not want to.

He puts his hand onto her thigh. Her skin is like silk. 'Zena,' he murmurs.

She answers by gently biting his shoulder. Her breathing is fast and she is murmuring — not real words, only noises.

'Shhh, my dear,' he coaxes her. 'Do you know how? Have you ever?'

She kisses his cheek again and pulls the *burquah* over her head. Her body is beautiful. 'Only with you,' she assures him. 'I want to only with you.'

Wellsted buries his face in her breasts before he moves his pale body on top of her dark one. Zena feels herself opening. She pushes against him and he swears he can feel the blood pulsing through her body as he slips inside her. God, it is heavenly. In English, he tells her he loves her. He's known it for weeks, and uncomprehending,

285

she wraps herself around him, a jumble of encompassing arms and legs. *Who would have thought, it crosses her mind, that moving together, just moving together could be such a joy? No wonder women marry. No wonder men want to. No wonder. Wonder. Wonder.*

'You are everything,' she breathes.

★ ★ ★

It is not until afterwards, when they both are sated, that he worries he might have done something awful, something damning and unkind. Zena is asleep now, her hand still cupping him beneath his *jubbah*. Senior officers in the mess bluster about their fellows who have gone jungly, as if it is the worst thing they can imagine. And yet it feels entirely natural. He'd be happy to stay here forever now. Perhaps, he thinks, he can arrange a suite of rooms for her wherever he is posted. He wants to look after this woman. He wants to be with her all the time. He reaches out and strokes the curly jumble of Zena's hair and she murmurs, her voice heavy with sleep.

'Master,' she sighs.

And immediately he realises, with a sinking stomach, she does not even know his first name. The girl is still his property. The thought makes his gut turn. She could, in such circumstances, hardly turn him down. Does that make what they have just done, rape? No. No. She enjoyed him, he's sure. But still, his conscience smarts. *If she was free, he wonders, would she even want me? Did she consider this the payment she must make for his offer of freedom?* He thinks, in panic, *I have just taken a terrible liberty, a dreadful advantage like some old goat of a colonel grabbing a maidservant onto his knee.* The idea rattles around his mind and it is very late when he falls finally into a fitful sleep.

In the morning when Wellsted wakes, she is already gone and the pang of loss that stings him is laced with confusion about what was right and what was wrong. He peers over the edge of the parapet and sees her at the fire, brewing coffee, her wrists held elegantly aloft as she pours. She is surrounded by the others and there will be no chance to talk at least until night falls again. Besides, he remembers, today is the day they have been moving towards for weeks. It's the most important day of the whole trip. Today is the day they will liberate Jessop and Jones.

'I must think on that,' Wellsted tells himself. Surely nothing is more important.

32

Having endured four months of captivity, Dr Jessop has been trying to sleep during the day. He thought it was better to absent himself, or at least his consciousness, from the stifling goats' wool tent when the sun was at its height. At the beginning, it is a fitful business, but after a few days he discovers his body easily becomes accustomed to the nocturnal habit. In fact, his body almost shuts down and he starts to sleep not only during the day, but for much of the night as well. Twice he almost dozes through the dispersal of food and water. He is kicked awake roughly and the goatskin put to his lips before he has raised himself fully so that more of the foul water than usual slips down his chin and he does not have time for his stomach to turn before the rancid leftover scraps the man proffers are halfway down his throat.

Perhaps I am delirious, he thinks hopefully, though he knows the very fact he has thought it makes the diagnosis unlikely. Whatever is happening to his body, however, he is grateful for it. He is hopeful that it is a prelude, a steady step closer to the blessed relief of death. Perhaps he will pass in his sleep. He hopes it will be soon.

It is with surprise, then, that he is started awake by a rousing recitation of *Joy to the World* by Lieutenant Jones. Jones has taken to singing. It is, as far as Jessop can tell, some kind of escape for the poor soul and he chooses alternately, navy drinking songs (some with lyrics so lewd that the doctor, who received a first in anatomy, is unsure exactly to which part of the ladies' body they refer, though obviously he understands the general gist) and the highlights of the Church of England hymnal. Sitting ramrod straight, Jones has gone for the godly choice today and is belting out the tune with his eyes bright, the tatters of his *jubbah* and the long locks of his filthy blonde hair swaying to the rhythm as he sings like a zealot on Christmas Day.

He is projecting his voice particularly well this morning, Jessop thinks, *though he does smell worse than usual.* Such niceties are not to be quibbled over, and at the least, the lieutenant's recitation is diverting. After a minute or two, the tent flap is pulled aside and the curious face of a small boy appears as Jones embarks on the third verse.

> *No more let sins and sorrows grow,*
> *Nor thorns infest the ground;*
> *He comes to make His blessings flow*
> *Far as the curse is found,*
> *Far as the curse is found,*
> *Far as, far as, the curse is found.*
> *Joy to the world, our Saviour's come.*

The boy starts to laugh and Jessop finds himself laughing too. It is, of course, damn ridiculous. It's nowhere near Christmas, he's sure of it. And then, in the full flow of the chorus, Jones stops very suddenly. His entire body tenses for a moment as if in spasm and then he slumps in an unnatural fashion, his whole weight on the rope bound at his wrist. Jessop knows it is a painful position to hold, even for a moment.

'God damn it,' the doctor strains at his bonds to try to reach out and check Jones' pulse. But he knows already. The lieutenant has died. There is no logic in it. Jones has retained far more of his body weight, he has even been allowed out of the tent on a regular basis, he has undoubtedly been better fed and he is younger by five years, but there it is. Jessop curses once more and then lets out a moan. '*I* want to die,' he spits furiously. 'It's not fair. I want to die.' He makes a strangled sound as his voice breaks in sorrow, but he cannot cry, for he is far too dehydrated to be able to waste tears. If only he could do so, he thinks, it might tip him over the edge. Instead, incandescent at the injustice of what has happened, he rages. 'Why?' he shouts, jerking like a thin goat tethered by his master and trying to get away. 'Why?'

It makes no sense.

The boy watches the doctor's tantrum silently from a distance. He scratches his chin. Then he edges further into the tent and keeping well clear of Jessop's frame he pokes the prone body of Lieutenant Jones.

'He's dead, you fool,' Jessop rounds on the child. 'Dead. *Mat*,' he intones, surprised at how easily the Arabic comes to him.

A grin spreads across the boy's face as he understands and then he pokes Jones' corpse once more. Then, emboldened by curiosity, he pulls the lieutenant's head back by its filthy, ragged mat of blonde hair. An expression of absolute peace is evident on Jones' face. He looks beatific. Jessop screams with frustration and this last, desperate sound is clearly heard elsewhere in the camp. In a rush, the entrance flap is pulled back and one of the guards enters the tent. With one hand he grabs hold of the boy, clearly afraid that despite their enfeebled state and the fact they are tied to the stake, the white men have put the child in danger. With his free hand, the man strikes Dr Jessop hard across the face. Then his eyes fall on Jones' corpse and, unaccountably, given that he has systematically been doling out starvation rations for weeks, he looks perturbed that the lieutenant has finally succumbed to the harsh treatment. There is a pause that hangs heavily on the still air.

'Your friends are here,' the boy says quietly from the other side of the tent.

It is almost a whisper. Jessop is not sure that he has heard correctly but nonetheless, his mind races. He strains at his bonds. 'What do you mean?' he asks, frantically. 'My friends? What did you say? What do you mean? Tell me.'

But the boy is ushered out quickly before he can say any more. The guard stares at Jones' body for a moment and then decides that removal of this corpse is not a priority. He doesn't even untie the ropes before he dashes from the tent without so much as wasting his time looking at the doctor.

Jessop considers a moment. He listens

carefully but he cannot tell what is going on. Still, he is sure what the boy said. *It is a damn shame about Jones*, he thinks. To have come so far and peg out just as something interesting seems about to happen is very bad luck, especially since all along it was Jones who expected a rescue party. He was the one who had had the faith. As the doctor strains with all his might against the bonds, he finds that, after all, his long-banished hope is easy enough to rekindle and he has the energy to rally. He has no idea of the identity of the friends to whom the boy referred but he cannot imagine them to be worse than his enemies, or for that matter, any circumstance in which his situation could appreciably worsen. So, as excitement flares in his empty stomach, he takes a deep breath and makes himself known.

'Help! In here! In here!' he shouts loudly, the rope already cutting into his thin wrists. It is the first struggle he has put up in weeks.

At this moment he considers the pain to be edifying. If anything, it makes him feel more alive. As he pauses for breath, he is more than somewhat surprised that he doesn't want to die after all. He'll take any chance of help. He'll grasp at the very thread of life if it's offered. How wonderful.

'I am Dr Jessop of the ship *Palinurus*! I am a subject of His Majesty and I require assistance. Help me! For God's sake! Help!'

The good doctor does not stop shouting when the guard returns.

'I'm here!' he screams, ignoring the man. The

292

jailor eyes him as if the *Nazarene* is a recalcitrant camel and then he hits the prisoner on the jaw with such force that the doctor passes out immediately, slumped beside his fellow officer's corpse.

'They will not hear you,' the man snarls, the hatred oozing from his voice, and he rubs his hand.

It hurt to administer the blow, but he could not have the prisoner shouting like that. The emir would be furious. The ruler has become more tetchy than usual the last day or two — ever since he heard the slavers' caravan was almost at Riyadh. The guard walks back into the blazing sunshine and wonders what will happen today, for never before have they received visitors of such renown as the two famous slavers. Now the caravan has arrived, the camp is buzzing with rumours of people who are both whiter and blacker than usual and all the news they can wring from the visitors (albeit three months out of date) from Muscat.

33

As the slavers' party approaches the emir's encampment, the scattered tents are coming to life. When there is shelter, it is the custom to rest in the middle of the day though that time is now passing and shortly the whole camp will emerge to drink coffee, play games, talk and, of course, inspect the visitors more thoroughly. Emerging from the tent flaps new faces eagerly search the caravan for points of interest and land on the inevitable — Wellsted's blue eyes, the famous slavers and Zena's dark skin evidenced only by what is visible around her eyes, hands and feet. A child points.

Zena turns inwards, towards the camel. 'They can hardly see any of me,' she murmurs, expecting that the creature will understand better than anyone. For a moment she thinks of her nakedness on the roof the night before. 'Perhaps,' she mouths, 'we will have to fly.'

There is certainly a sense among the men that this is the most dangerous part of the mission. Kasim came up to her that morning and, out of the blue, assigned her a *khandjar*. He has scarcely spoken to her the whole journey and all the way she has masked her loathing successfully.

'We may need you to use this,' he says.

She nods silently and stows the knife in the sleeve of her *burquah*. It is completely plain, unlike the heavily adorned weapons that Kasim and Ibn Mohammed holster at their waists, or even Wellsted's middle-of-the-road specimen. Zena does not care about the fripperies of her knife's decoration, for, she tells herself, if necessary it will do the job just as well as if it was encrusted in emeralds. Now her fingers find it and she holds the horned handle for comfort. Though she has never before been armed, she has watched Wellsted sparring with Kasim for practice all the way from the south, and she is sure she has some idea of what to do with the blade, should the need arise. It is a good feeling. *Yesterday,* she thinks, *was an amazing day and full of surprises.* She chooses the word for how she feels carefully: she is transformed. She cannot stop thinking about what happened on the roof. *It is madness,* she thinks. *A wonderful madness.*

Since they rode out that morning, Wellsted has caught her eye several times. On such occasions she smiles spontaneously and he grins back. Nothing has changed, of course. The white man owns her — he can do as he pleases and if it pleases Zena too, so much the better. She is pragmatic. She feels strangely whole though and also powerful. Yes, *powerful* — that's the word. She is glad that she waited so long to do that midnight dance. She is glad her first master did not demand it of her in Muscat and now she thinks on it, she is even glad that the slavers came to her village when they did. Any longer and her father almost certainly would have married her off. A girl of fourteen or fifteen is considered a spinster, never mind one who has seen a full seventeen summers. But to wait for Wellsted was right. She likes him. Like seems too small a word for it. Enjoy is perhaps better. Love. Love is best of all. It is the first time in a long while that her daydreams have not included the fantasy of managing to get away. She is simply too busy thinking of what they did the night before and letting it take her over completely. She feels that she is on the cusp of something truly liberating. Under the circumstances, it is an odd sensation.

Zena holds the camel's bridle and waits for orders. The agreement is that they must not unload. Ibn Mohammed and Kasim are unsure of the welcome the party will receive and it was decided at daybreak in Riyadh that the beasts will only be unburdened on a signal from Ibn Mohammed once he is sure they will not need to flee. The whole train has been primed to this fact and there is palpable tension among them as a result, though in truth the settlement looks like any other encampment they have come across.

Ibn Mohammed dismounts. He does not make any gesture. He and Kasim are greeted and disappear inside the emir's tent to tend at last to the business they have travelled so far to pursue. Still, Zena does not see why she cannot at least tend her camel — she has become very fond of the animal. It is a good deal more reliable and genuine than any of the male servants or slaves of the party. She continues to talk to it — quietly, for they will treat her like a halfwit if she is caught confiding in a camel. And there is little in the whole of Arabia that receives poorer treatment than a halfwitted woman.

As the caravan dismounts, she moves off to tend to the animal's needs. Some of the slaves clearly feel likewise and the men of the emir's entourage motion them towards the well and bow, mouthing words of welcome while they eye the Turk carefully. The slaves draw water for the animals. Zena cannot keep her fingers from returning to the bone handle of the *khandjar*. The weapon emboldens her and she indulges a fantasy of revenge. As she waters the camel, she imagines drawing the knife and stabbing Kasim. Of all the hostile men around her (and over the weeks she has certainly felt hostility), he is the one upon whom she would most like to wreak some vengeance. As it rises, her anger surprises her though, in truth, she has no real intention of committing a murder. Still, she cannot help envision the look on Kasim's face. She has yet to see either of the slavers look taken aback by anything.

'Imagine if I were to raise their eyebrows,' she whispers in the camel's ear, and turns to rejoin the others. It would be nice to surprise them.

★ ★ ★

With the dignitaries out of the way, the camp sets to brewing the coffee and swapping news. Two of the party start playing a game of what looks like draughts, making a board from marks on the sand, and counters from small sticks and dry, hard camel dung. The men gather. Apart from the fact that the camels are ready to bolt if need be, they could be in any settlement they have come to since they crossed the *jabel*.

Wellsted smiles openly at the girl as she takes a cup of coffee and settles close to the others. 'Nearly there,' he whispers, though he sounds strained and his eyes are, she knows, taking in every movement around them.

'Your friends are here?' she keeps her voice very low.

The lieutenant shrugs. 'I hope so. We'll see. Very soon.'

He feels relieved that Zena shows no sign of awkwardness at what happened the night before. He wants to talk to her about it, but now they are here his attention is focussed on what will happen to Jessop and Jones, and besides, they are in company. Still, he lets his arm touch hers and he is glad that she does not pull away. Zena puts the master's disquiet down to the proximity of the completion of his mission. She does not imagine that he is troubled in any way by what has passed between them. Sitting by the campfire, she simply wonders what they will eat when the sun sets, for she already has an appetite, and assumes that perhaps that night, once it is dark, they might find a way to do it again. Or at least she hopes so.

Wellsted cannot take his eyes from the tent. He is willing the negotiations to go well. Zena pours her master another coffee. There is nothing for it but to wait and hope the slavers manage what the entire party have travelled all this way to achieve.

34

The emir receives Ibn Mohammed and Kasim warmly. He has known for over a week that the party is on its way, but still he feels a rush of awe and also honour when they arrive. He meets very few on his travels whom he considers men of his own quality and then, of course, they have been sent by the *soultan* too. The emir imagines that his status has risen and does not even acknowledge to himself that the slavers are here only because of the white men. A few animals have been slaughtered in readiness, the strongest of his henchmen are arrayed as well as possible and the interior of the tent is modified slightly with the use of every rug in the settlement. The emir is arrayed in his newest, finest *jubbah* and sits resplendent on a large cushion when the visitors enter. Of course, these things scarcely matter — men arriving off the desert are generally grateful for shade and a few mouthfuls of water. The Empty Quarter is not a place of material goods and a man is judged on his grit far more than his possessions. Still, there is no harm in presenting his camp at its most luxurious.

As they enter the confines out of the searing heat, the emir is not disappointed when the slavers make their *salaams*. The cloth from which they are cut is clear from the start. They have survived, after all, several weeks in the hottest part of the year and they look immaculate as they shake scented water over their hands and greet him. Their manners are perfect and the air around them is strung with a sense of purpose. They are the very epitome of what an Arab aspires to be. The servants loiter with refreshments but the emir does not motion them forwards. He is aware that something important is missing.

'You had a white man with you, I understand,' the emir points out. 'Dressed as a Turk.'

The wily old fox of course misses nothing. Ibn Mohammed does not move an inch. He stands square. 'He is tending the camels,' he says.

'He is your slave then?'

Ibn Mohammed, with the merest jerk of his jaw, makes it clear this is not the case. He does not elaborate.

Kasim leans forward with a confidential air. 'He is not so much white now, in any case. More pink. We are browning him.'

The emir laughs. The journey from Muscat is a long one and now they have got here their spirits are clearly high. He gestures and the men sit down.

'These white men are all over our land,' he says. 'Like vermin. The infidel. The Turks. They are a pestilence. And your *soultan* welcomes them,' the emir spits. 'For trade! I would not think of it. Such creatures are not even worthy of my notice. *Nazarene.*'

'You know why we have been sent?' Ibn Mohammed cuts to the nub, as ever.

The emir nods. 'And he will pay?'

'Many camels, my friend,' Ibn Mohammed assures him. 'You are kind enough to let us buy their freedom, sir?' he checks.

The emir's expression hardens and Ibn Mohammed knows he has spoken too directly.

'No, I will not let the *Nazarene* go so easily,' the emir says with finality. Then he has an idea. 'I have been waiting to kill them. I will kill them now because you are here. I will execute them in celebration. And you may execute yours as well, if you wish.'

★　★　★

The slavers do not flinch. They have no intention of killing Wellsted. Quite apart from the fact they have sworn allegiance to him, if the *soultan* comes to hear of such a bargain (which of course he will, for it is noteworthy), he will be furious. To lose a travelling companion in a battle with *Wahabi* raiders is hardly the fault of his fellows. However, to disembowel him for the amusement of the emir is entirely unacceptable. Intention is everything and Lord knows which of their body parts the *soultan* will order removed if they disobey him by falling in with such a plan. They have not come all this way to instigate a *Nazarene* bloodbath.

'Please,' Ibn Mohammed offers, all generosity, 'let me give you some slaves to execute instead. The *soultan* has taken an interest in the white men and he wishes to offer them protection. He humbly entreats you to send them safely back to Muscat.'

'Your slaves have done nothing wrong to be deprived of their blood,' the emir points out.

This is uncharacteristic liberalism on the ruler's behalf and has not in the past prevented him from beheading and disembowelling those unfortunate enough to get in his way. After all, this is a man who only a few weeks before lopped out the tongue of one of his servants because the fool spoke harshly to the emir's favourite and only black camel from which he has been trying unsuccessfully to breed a herd.

Ibn Mohammed shrugs. The rights and the wrongs of it are nothing to him, as long as he gets what he wants. 'If you prefer, you may simply keep the slaves. Do with them what you will. How many would you like?'

The emir smiles. 'But where are my manners?' he says. 'I have not even offered you coffee.'

The servants hover nearby, carrying carved, cedarwood trays that are ready with cups and a brass brewing pot, an enticing aroma emanating from its spout. He motions them forward.

'*Shukran*,' the slavers intone.

The emir seems happy to do business. So far, it is going quite well.

★   ★   ★

Outside, sheltered in the shade of a palm tree, Wellsted keeps his face covered and sits silently beside Zena at the very edge of the group. A few of the emir's men have peeled off and are engaging in lively conversation. The slaves fetch a bough of dates from the litter of provisions, sharing the caravan's bounty. However, the people of the settlement are suspicious of anything unusual and they will not speak to the Turk or the black girl, though they are not shy of staring at them. This, the lieutenant thinks, is fine by him. It allows him plenty of time to look around, get his bearings and observe. For a start, the camp is smaller than he imagined and, for the most part, the place is about its daily business despite the visitors. Some women are altering tent ropes, some are herding the goats, the camels and horses are brought to the well to drink in turn. In all there can be only a dozen tents here — fifteen at most, he counts. The children play near one in particular — it must contain the family quarters, Wellsted reckons. Between times, the *Bedu* eye the visitors, taking in the details of their clothes, the elegance of the long-legged camels and the skin of the female, which is dark as treacle, blacker than any of them has ever seen before. Wellsted sends a silent prayer that Jessop and Jones are here and alive, though there is no obvious sign that this place harbours a prize so unusual and precious.

As he watches, a rough-looking fellow enters the emir's tent and the lieutenant finds himself concerned that the slavers are safe. His fingers fly to the handle of his knife for a moment before he realises that Ibn Mohammed and Kasim would relish such a challenge and are more than capable of defending themselves. When the man comes out again a few moments later, he stares at the caravan, thinking for a moment, and then disappears to a small, grey tent pitched in the sunshine a little way off. It is strange, Wellsted thinks, for the rest of the camp has been made in the shade but that tent is nowhere near any shelter. It's almost as if they have set it up to capture the heat. He chews on a stick of *araq* and contemplates. Then he decides to investigate.

'Stay here,' he whispers to Zena.

With the coffee cup still in his hand, he takes a circuitous route. First, he inspects the grazing to the south, then he stares for a few minutes into the fire that has been set, ready for lighting. He refills his drink, jokes with one of the slaves, overlooks the board game that is being played on the sand, and finally heads towards the tent in full view of everyone. The ruse works. No one is staring at him. The conversations around the coffee pot continue, the children are engaged in an endeavour that employs a ball and some kind of throwing device, like a slingshot. He makes it almost all the way across the camp before the rough fellow emerges from the grey tent. Smoothly, the man makes his *salaams*, puts his arm around Wellsted's shoulder conspiratorially but firmly and walks him back to where he started.

'You have come a long way? From Muscat?' he enquires politely.

Wellsted nods. 'The desert is harsh but beautiful,' he says. 'The sultan has sent us for the Nazarene.'

The man does not let slip even the smallest hint of what he might know. 'The emir is talking to your master,' he points out.

'Do you think he will let the white men go?'

'The emir will do what is right.'

It is agonising. Wellsted crouches a moment. The children abandon their game and edge towards the strangers, still throwing the ball half-heartedly between them. One of the little girls is pulled back by her mother but mostly they simply stand with wide eyes.

'Did Allah punish this woman?' a boy asks, staring at Zena.

The men laugh at such a provincial view, though the child bears burn marks of darker skin on his own legs so it is easy to see where he might have got the idea.

After an hour or so prayers are called and the sun sets, disappearing below the low line of the horizon as swift as a stone dropping through syrup. It sends waves of orange across the landscape. Kasim and Ibn Mohammed have yet to emerge from the emir's tent. From time to time there is a burst of laughter from inside that lets the caravan know all is well. The animals are settled for the night and Kasim's hawk, tethered to the litter, attracts the attention of the children and some of the men when it starts to flap. Wellsted gives the bird some water and a sliver or two of dried meat. The women start to cook dinner on a fire that is lit near the family tent, and the air fills with wafting garlic and meat cooked on thin sticks. The men wait for their food, talking and drinking coffee. There is a relaxed atmosphere. The *Bedu* are more comfortable to get along with than the *Wahabi* and it feels easy enough to settle. The discussion is of the long journey and the sandstorm once more. Only one of the emir's men, a lone *Tuereg* slave, keeps his distance.

As he stares into the ebony pitch, Wellsted notices there is no light in the tent that is set on its own. He wonders if it is used for supplies, though he reasons that during the time they've been there none of the women have entered it to fetch flour for the bread or spices for the meat. If it contains something of value, he thinks, and he is caught investigating it, they will assume he is stealing. *So I must not be caught*, he decides, taking one last glance at the emir's tent for signs of progress.

He whispers to Zena to stay put. 'This is the most important thing — getting these men out of here,' he hisses. 'Nothing must come in the way of it.'

She nods in understanding and the master sets off once more. This time he saunters in a leisurely fashion in the direction of the darkness outside the camp where the men relieve themselves. He has been drinking coffee all afternoon and he has not visited the latrine area yet. It seems the logical way to leave the group.

Under cover of night, he skirts the outside of the honey-coloured campfire that flickers into the blackness. On one side there is the crackle of the flames, the sound of the laughter, a burst of singing. On the other he catches the occasional lowing of the animals — the camels asleep on their knees, they are not silent, especially when they have eaten well. It has been a day of unaccustomed plenty and now they are ruminating in

306

safety, grumbling and calling out from time to time.

Wellsted walks quickly. He moves around the settlement perimeter and, on his belly, crawls the last few yards towards the tent. There is no sound from inside. He checks behind him but he is unnoticed so, tentatively, he lifts the tent flap. The air inside hits him like a wall. It is rancid — a solid, filthy, animal smell. He coughs involuntarily and squints into the gloom but can discern nothing.

'Pssst,' he almost whistles, for he thinks there may be an animal inside.

In answer there is a low, slow moan.

'Hello,' Wellsted tries. '*Salaam.*'

A pause. Then a voice like cut crystal. A voice that would not be out of place in the mansions of Richmond or even at King William's court. 'Who's there?'

A fumbling sound. A thump, as if a man has tumbled over.

'Is that you, Jessop? Doctor Jessop?'

A gulp. A sob. 'Yes. Thank God! Who are you?'

'It's me. Lieutenant James Wellsted, sir. Have you Jones with you?'

'He died, James. He died today. Thank God you are here. Will the emir release me now?'

'We are trying. The Sultan of Muscat sent a deputation and I'm part of it. They have been in the emir's tent all afternoon.'

There is the sound of movement. Wellsted reaches inside and feels a stiff limb, as thin and hard as a tree branch. The skin is waxy with death.

'Jesus,' he says, withdrawing his hand. 'Is that Jones? Is he still in there?'

'Where are you, James?'

The voice comes from further in, he realises. Wellsted steels himself to push past the corpse. He touches an arm. It is lamentably thin, but this time it is alive. The fingers grasp at him, winding into the folds of his *jubbah*.

'You smell like the wind,' Jessop sniffs.

Wellsted wraps his arms around the doctor. He was a sturdy man, from Northumberland if the lieutenant remembers rightly. Now the bones are sticking out all over his body and he is as slight as a girl. His breath stinks of rotten meat — the smell of his own body ingesting itself for survival. Wellsted feels in his pouch and pulls out some dates and the last of the dried meat that he had meant for the hawk. He presses them into the doctor's hand.

'Did Haines send you?'

Wellsted shakes his head but the men are so close the doctor understands the action.

'I couldn't wait to get away from you and Haines you know, and that stupid damned fight about that manuscript of yours. Bloody Socotra and who discovered which damn shrub.'

The doctor's laugh is a dry, derisory bark.

'He's still fearsome about that affair. He banned me from his table the last several weeks before I left. I was glad to get off the *Palinurus* myself,' Wellsted admits with a smile. 'We'll have you out of here in a jiffy, Jessop. Don't worry.'

The doctor puts a date in his mouth and lets its sweetness dissolve. It is, he has to admit, heavenly. 'Have you got any water?'

Wellsted pulls the goatskin from his belt. 'Of course. Stupid of me. Sorry.'

He opens the cap and helps the doctor drink. The sound of gulping is desperate at first but slows to a gentle sip.

'Thank you.'

'We're a week from the coast and then we will sail back to Muscat,' the lieutenant says, planning ahead. His mind is racing. There will be boats for hire, surely, that can take them south. Arab vessels are sewn with coconut or date palm fibre, hardly the cut of His Majesty's finest, but they will do the job. In Muscat they'll pick up the first navy ship that docks. Wellsted only hopes that the doctor will survive. He doesn't have to see him to realise how frail Jessop has become physically, even if he still has the spirit to rag him about Haines and that stupid fight over the manuscript. Yes, that's a good sign, of course. Jessop is humming as he sucks the date.

'Wellsted, is it Christmas yet?' he asks.

'Not quite, old man. By my reckoning we're just about into November though.'

The doctor's mind has clearly been affected, but some decent food and care and Jessop will dine in Bombay yet.

'I must go now,' Wellsted whispers. 'They mustn't find me with you. I only wanted to know you were here. I'll be back as soon as I can.'

He pulls away, but Jessop finds he cannot let go his grip. His fingers form an iron vice around the lieutenant's forearm.

'Promise,' he says. 'Swear it.'

'I swear,' Wellsted tells him solemnly. 'We'll sail into Muscat inside of a fortnight, three weeks at most. Whatever it takes. We'll have a Christmas dinner, if you like. Early. Goose and a plum pudding. I promise. Once we've made passage and we know we're safe.'

Despite being a naval man, Wellsted has always considered the sea a barrier. In fact, he has come to think of it as the barrier between him and his desires — the thing that must be overcome. Now he knows it is the unrelenting ocean of sand that is the true barrier and that crossing a league of saltwater, even in choppy weather, is far less of a challenge than any measure of these desolate sands.

'A ship.' Jessop is smiling, Wellsted can hear it in his voice. The doctor lets go. 'I wish you could take Jones and bury him.'

'I know, old man. I know.' Wellsted reaches out and squeezes the doctor's shoulder. It isn't pleasant — none of it.

Slowly, he backs out of the tent into the clean air of the evening and is gone.

Rolling back down the sandbank in the dark, his heart thumping with excitement, a grin spreads over Wellsted's face. This is his adventure. Since he was a child he has been pushed and prodded to achieve something of significance, to rise. He is almost there. It is a shame about Jones, of course, but if he can bring Jessop home, he'll be the toast of Bombay, if not London. He'll be a hero who can lecture at the Royal Society and he'll be promoted, certainly — all the things he's dreamed of are tantalisingly close. He imagines returning to Molyneux Street an officer and a gentleman, and proudly shaking his father's hand, the old man's eyes shining at the beauty of a plan that has come off. After all the years, this is it! He's here. By hook or by crook, just like old Thomas predicted.

As he rounds the clump of palms he takes his eyes off the starry sky and he stops a moment for he can see some movement near the emir's tent. There is music — a drum — and the sound of men clapping. A whistle of excitement from one of the lower bred slaves and three children running in circles like dogs who have gone mad in the sun.

That will give me cover, he thinks happily, and cherishes the thought that though Jones is lost, at least the doctor is in good spirits, all told. The man will recover well, Wellsted is sure of it.

Wellsted traces his route through the darkness and decides to re-emerge into the light of the campfire and the *naft* lamps on the other side of whatever is going on. The music, he thinks vaguely, must be a celebration of the deal the slavers have done on Jessop's behalf. Yes, that will certainly be it — the whole affair is almost over. He hauls himself up, brushes the sand off his *jubbah* and makes to saunter through the blackness and stroll unnoticed into the throng. But as he approaches, his blood suddenly runs cold, for he can see that the drum is beating for a purpose and Zena, divested of her *burquah*, is dressed again in the wisp she was wearing when Mickey gave her away, all those weeks ago.

The girl is the focus of everyone's attention:

lithe, barefoot and dancing fluidly around the fire. Her body quivers like a leaf on a tree that is swaying in the breeze. She has a haughty expression on her face, or perhaps she is only lost in the rhythm, for she is moving like a dervish, her hands high above her head and her pace somehow both frantic and elegant at once as the cobweb of an outfit floats like smoke around her. An older man, the emir, he supposes, has come out of the tent with the slavers to watch. He is richly dressed and from the expression on his face, it is evident that he is entranced. Hell, every man in the settlement is practically salivating. Bar Ibn Mohammed and Kasim, of course, whose faces bear the stony expressions of slight amusement that has been contained as Zena demonstrates her body's flexibility by bending over backwards and flipping head over heels. When she recovers her balance she moves hypnotically once more in time to the beat of the drum, kicking up her heels and stamping. He can just make out the defiant flash of her eyes. She is not happy to be dancing for the emir's pleasure, he has no doubt of that.

'Damn it,' Wellsted swears under his breath, his pulse quickening in anger as he heads towards the light. 'What are they doing?'

After everything they have done to keep her hidden, it makes no sense. After all, Kasim ordered him to keep the girl out of harm's way. The sand is soft and difficult to run through and the lieutenant almost trips in his haste to get down into the settlement, cover her up and sort it out, but just as he breaks into the crowd, the music ends and there is a flurry of clapping and ululation from the women, cheers and jeers from the men. Zena is motioned towards the emir, who lays his hand on the girl's head while he talks to Kasim and Ibn Mohammed. There is no chance of hearing a word of what is said and Wellsted only sees the men nodding as they take Zena back into the tent. Slaves rush here and there fetching hot water for coffee and the men of the camp squat once more around the fire, leaving the lieutenant standing alone, staring furiously at the tent flap that has closed in his face with his heart pounding.

35

Robert Townsend Farquhar finds that he is settling in. It has taken some time but becoming a Member of Parliament has kept him well occupied and he likes the little constituency of Hythe in Kent that he has taken on. That and his directorship of the East India Company mean that he is never bored. Of an evening, Townsend, for he has dropped his real surname from common usage and instead assigned it to the baronetship he was honoured with in 1821, likes to walk from his mansion in the city down to the line of the river as far as Westminster Bridge. It pleases him to see the old Palace of Westminster — the very symbol, he thinks, of immoveable power. There is something quintessentially English about strolling through Whitehall at sunset, muffled against the cold; the view of the river at dusk sums up everything about England Townsend enjoys and after years in the tropics — Madras and Madagascar, Reunion and Muscat — he has come to love London and its reliable coolness in all things. The hub of the whole operation, he calls it. His erstwhile appointments in the colonies seem like paddling in the backwaters when here, not a mile from where he is standing, for that matter, not a mile from where he started at school in Westminster, he can dine with the Prime Minister of England and attend the opera where from his box he is habitually greeted by the King.

Townsend does not know it, but he has only a few weeks to live — he will keel over in his bedroom three Thursdays from this very day. If he was privy to this knowledge, it is uncertain if he would be quite so interested in the survey of the Arabian Peninsula that is currently being undertaken by the officers of the Indian Navy. He might, for example, choose to spend his last days with his wife, Maria, an heiress from Madras who he married for her money then found he loved to distraction despite it. Or his son, Walter, who, with a genuine regret that cannot be credited to every premature heir, will inherit the title of baronet in a mere twenty-four days. However, like all of us, Townsend has no idea what the future holds three weeks on Thursday and when he bumps into his friend and fellow company director, William Thornton Astell, who is in town from the far-flung Surrey village of Clapham, the conversation turns to business. Once, that is, they have had the inevitable discussion everyone has with their acquaintances the first time they meet them after the nation's bereavement for Wilberforce's death has cast a shadow that will keep London consoling itself for months on end.

'Damn shame about Wilberforce,' Townsend nods.

Astell knew Wilberforce most of his adult life and shared the great man's views on abolition from the very early days when many considered the ardent campaigner's liberal open-mindedness the dangerous ravings of a radical and the men were accused of threatening the social order put in place by God Almighty Himself. For a while, Wilberforce and his associates were even nicknamed the Clapham Sect, though the maligning of The Cause has diminished over the passing years — in fact, their views are now considered thoroughly respectable and generally *right*. Astell has found it difficult to sleep in the months since the funeral, for Wilberforce's death, a loss as it is, has served to remind him of his own mortality. The two men were as close in age as they were political outlook.

'He was a wonderful man,' he says simply, keeping his upper lip as stiff as possible.

To preserve Astell's dignity, Townsend takes a sudden interest in a Thames skiff piloted by a fisherman who is most definitely the worse for wear. The little boat is dodging its way to the east and the man is alternately swigging from a pottery bottle and singing a lewd song, the lyrics of which, in Townsend's opinion, should not be heard in public. There could, at any time, be a lady nearby. The skiff skites off towards the bridge and narrowly escapes crashing into one of the stone archways and then into a larger brig coming in the opposite direction.

'Damn fellow,' he says.

Astell recovers himself. 'Where are you off to?' he enquires.

'Oh, just taking a stroll, you know. Thinking about this business with the French.'

'In Egypt?'

'Well, if they get antsy again it might not be so

easy next time. Touch and go, one of our officers called it. This survey of ours is taking a long time. Tricky coastline of course, but still. It's an investment really. We lost too many for lack of a chart. In this day and age too. The Prime Minister thinks that the bally Frogs are still trading slaves despite the embargo, under their own damn flag too. He's got some evidence now. A ship that was caught on the hop — wrong place, wrong time and definitely wrong cargo. They are an immoral bunch. So the chart, well, it's vital to our interests. 'Best get on with it,' he said to me, and when Charles Grey has spoken, we must all jump to action, what? Next thing we know they'll have their beady eye on India. Besides, if they are still slaving, well that just isn't on, is it? Never mind simply protecting ourselves from the beasts.'

Astell nods in agreement. The slaving is an abomination. The French are ingrates to continue. His wife, an ardent abolitionist since the early days, idolises her husband for his part in the political and moral sea change and Astell takes the French ignoring the embargo as personally as if they had propositioned an indecency with his good lady, for if she hears of it she will be just as distraught. However, there are more important matters than even that. An experienced politician, he is well aware that a very great deal comes down to the pounds, the shilling and the pence, and having abolished the slave trade, British ingenuity must make up the financial deficit left in its wake.

'It's vital work, I agree, Townsend. Besides, if

we can find a direct passage, well, it's worth a fortune to us,' he says.

Though Astell is a man of the world in many senses, he has never been further than Brighton. He is, however, both astute and curious about what goes on beyond the English Channel and he keeps himself well informed.

'Damn tricky, the Arabs anyway, are they not? Law of the jungle.'

Townsend ignores the fact that there is no jungle on the Peninsula and simply nods. He enjoyed Muscat when he was stationed there, but the situation was inflammatory. The children of Islam are not the easiest natives he's ever had to deal with and they are proving unbiddable. The Arab temperament, he is often heard to remark, is painted in black and white. There are no shades of grey.

'I'm not sure that people here really understand the difficulties. Our fellow members often think that if we've won once, then it will naturally be that way again. It was touch and go, Astell, I don't mind telling you.'

The older man considers a moment. 'Wilberforce always said in these matters it is knowledge that counts. When people know the situation they will make the right decision. Back the right horse, as it were. That's why he brought former slaves to London. Horse's mouth and all that. It certainly worked. No question of it.'

Townsend pauses for a moment. 'Well, I can say it till I am blue in the face,' he observes, 'but perhaps it will take more than just me.'

'One of the chaps in the field, you think?'

Townsend smiles, the idea forming. 'Yes indeed. That might be the thing. A promising officer. Brave. Bold. British.'

'I might know just the chap.' Astell is excited at the prospect — for if he can contribute here to stopping the slave traffic upon which the French are so abominably engaged, it will be most gratifying — a fitting memorial for dear Wilberforce. Astell is always delighted when he can help. He wishes his contribution had been more all along. 'I had dinner with that publisher fellow, Murray, the other evening and he was talking about some chap — one of ours. Been to an island. Written a book that Murray is going to publish. Now, he'd fit your bill. Surveyor to trade I understand. We need to get someone like that back and put him in committee in the Palace of Westminster. Royal Society too perhaps. Let the doubters ask him whatever they want. He'll know the Peninsula, and damn sure he will have been on ships that are taking part in the embargo. He can testify to all of it. Murray will be delighted, I'm sure. All to the good of England. Apparently the book is quite excellent. Exceptional plan all round, don't you think?'

'Capital. Yes. You're right. Quite right. Leave it with me.' Townsend shakes Astell's hand. 'I'll see what I can do. Eyewitnesses, nothing like them, and if we can bring your young buck home on a tour of leave, well it will focus the mind. He's going to be published, is he — one of Murray's? A surveyor too? That adds a certain gravitas.'

That evening Townsend writes to Murray, Sir Charles Malcolm and the chairman of the Geographical Society. *We need a Champion.* He underlines the word. *Could this Wellsted fellow be our man?*

36

The emir sits on the cushions and motions for the slavers to join him. Zena stands frozen, just inside the tent flap. Her face is expressionless and she casts her eyes down over the jumble of worn rugs that cover the sand beneath her dusty feet. The tent is lit by *naft* lamps and the emir motions the girl into the pool of light before him. As she moves towards him he sighs.

'A treasure,' he says.

Zena wants to curl up on the ground so he cannot look at her with such lazy desire but she forces herself to stand still. Ibn Mohammed and Kasim stay silent. They know the sight of Zena is more compelling than any words they may care to hazard.

'You are right,' the emir comments squarely, stroking his beard in contemplation of her beauty. 'She brings the night to life.'

Ibn Mohammed licks his lips and lets Kasim seal the deal. The men have already discussed a price with the emir for the release of Jessop and Jones, and the figure they have come to is surprisingly low. The emir has not let the slavers inspect the white men. 'We have held them for months now,' he admits frankly, 'and they smell like the dogs they are. It will put you off your dinner.'

This in itself is not unexpected. The white men must be in a terrible state and a good salesman will not let the customer have sight of shoddy goods. However, each time it has come to shaking hands, the emir has evaded concluding matters. Twice now the slavers have tentatively offered more money (for the deal they have done comes in well below the *soultan's* budget) and twice the price has increased, but each time when it comes to the moment, the emir will not give his word. There is something holding him back and since more money does not seem to bring matters to agreement, Ibn Mohammed instinctively came up with something to help seal the deal.

'We keep a dancer with us,' he said. 'The desert nights are very long. Why don't we have some entertainment?'

The slavers generally enjoy the challenge of long negotiations. Even in the *souk* over a parcel of goods worth less than a *taler* it is the custom to haggle for an hour. Every trade is a discussion in Arabia. Now with the girl at his feet they capitalise on it.

Kasim coughs. It is time to decide. 'My friend,' Kasim says, as if it is a peccadillo — a small consideration — the nothing he considers Zena to be, 'when we leave tomorrow with the white men you can have this girl. A parting gift.'

The emir's eyes gleam. There is a lascivious pause during which, there is no doubt, he is considering what he would do with this woman if he were to own her. A bead of sweat appears under his nose. Zena's stomach turns. Her fingers feel suddenly clammy as if they are soiled. There is nothing she can say or do to stop

322

this and she knows Ibn Mohammed will kill her outright if she runs from the tent. She is frozen with terror and humiliation, her mind racing. The idea of doing what she did only the night before with her master with this old goat is unthinkable. It is not only her body that is possessed by her master it is her spirit too. A mere day ago she had no idea — she might have tried — but now, it is simply impossible. She holds her breath. Where is Wellsted? Where is he?

The emir smiles. He inclines his head and touches his heart. 'Yes. It is all settled, my friends. And with honour. You may have your *Nazarene*.'

The atmosphere in the tent explodes into conviviality around the still figure of the dancing girl as the men celebrate the agreement. They clap each other on the back in congratulations.

'Dinner! Dinner!' the old man orders.

The very idea of Zena knocks ten years off him. He grins enthusiastically and quaffs a glass of coffee that has appeared at his elbow. As the emir's men enter the tent and the food arrives on large ashettes, the girl is pushed to one side. She wants to scream. She curses that the *khandjar* knife is outside with the rest of her clothes. She'd hack them to pieces if she could, or die trying.

'Wait outside,' Ibn Mohammed waves a languid palm and the men settle to their meal completely unware of the girl's fury.

★ ★ ★

As Zena emerges into the fireside, the music has started again and there is a babble of excitement.

The children are screaming. Dinner is ready and piles of bread are being passed from one to another as the people of the emir's encampment and the slavers' party mill about finding their places.

'Dance again! Dance again!'

The men poke at her. The women merely stare. Some of these women, she thinks, must be the emir's existing wives. One leans over gracefully and whispers in another's ear, bringing up her henna-painted hand elegantly to cup the words towards her sister. A movement of the veil (perhaps laughter?) and then they all stare again. From the recesses of the family tents two heavily pregnant women emerge, their curiosity so piqued that they will risk being seen by strangers. Zena declines the order to continue dancing. Still, in the rush, the music plays and some of the men strut to the beat while the first of the food is served.

Then out of the chaos, Wellsted appears. She is as glad to see him as she has ever been to see anyone in her life. He herds Zena away, hands over her *burquah* and secures a tent in which to change.

'Have they freed Jessop?' he asks, his eyes blazing. 'What happened?'

Zena stares at him blankly. Of course, his friends are his first concern. The master said, after all, less than an hour ago, that the only thing that mattered was their freedom. She is sure that to babble her distress will not help. To scream her intention of hacking out Kasim's heart and removing Ibn Mohammed's eyes will not bring the master over to her side. In fact, it occurs to her slowly, the master might not be on her side. *If he is forced to choose,* she wonders, *where will his allegiance really lie?* Slowly, she bites her lip and shakes her head.

'What happened?' he insists.

Zena is shaking now; she does not want to cry in front of him, but her mind is made up. Somewhere in the jumble of thoughts she realises that she cannot trust Wellsted to help her. He has other concerns. Everything she had hoped for is dashed yet her resolve is steely. She has had enough. They have stolen her, sold her, gambled her and profited by it. Whatever it costs her this time she will not comply.

'I need to get dressed.' The girl grabs her clothes and covers herself gratefully in the *burquah*.

'Zena,' Wellsted entreats, as if she is being unreasonable. 'Tell me! Why did they make you dance? Are they freeing Jessop? What is going on?'

'I think they have arranged to free him,' she replies carefully.

In the sleeve of her *burquah* she finds the *khandjar* knife in its place and she holds onto it tightly. Her mind is running through her options. Her eyes jerk to one side, in the direction of Jessop's tent to ask him what he has found. It will give her time to think it through.

Wellsted smiles. 'Yes. They are there. Well, one of them. You should see him, Zena, he is a skeleton. Thank God we arrived in time.'

She flinches. Wellsted puts his hands on her shoulders. He moves the veil to one side.

'You're safe now,' he tries to comfort her. 'I'm here.'

Zena masks the rush of fury that is taking her over and calls every fibre of her being into check. She runs through everything Wellsted has ever said to her. *If I tell him*, she thinks, *he'll watch me like a hawk. If I tell him, I won't be able to do anything for myself. I'm sick of being at the beck and call of others.*

Wellsted knows something is wrong. The girl is distracted and he can't get a proper answer to any of his questions. 'Zena!' he raises his voice, and lays a hand on her arm, to shake a response out of her. 'Don't ignore me!'

Zena steels herself. She will keep her own counsel. It is the best chance she has of making up her own mind about what to do. She pauses a moment, her hand on the blade of the knife. An idea is forming. It is the biggest decision of her life.

'Sorry,' she says. 'Everyone was staring at me. Let's go back to the fireside.'

Wellsted's blue eyes are alight. 'Thank God,' he grins. 'For a moment, you had me worried.'

As they emerge back into the company, Zena remains the focus of the party's attention. The questioning of the children continues, as the emir's men eye her with sullen interest. She sits it out until the camp falls to rest with Wellsted like a faithful dog by her. He fetches food, but she cannot eat it. As the evening winds down, she forms her plan until one by one, everyone settles to sleep. The silence and the darkness feel like a relief.

37

The emir lightly dusts Ibn Mohammed and Kasim with rosewater from an etched, silver shaker and motions forward one of his slaves to waft the burning frankincense. Ibn Mohammed cups his hand as if he is swimming in the trail of smoke and Kasim simply lets the musky fragrance rise through his clothes. It is late and outside in the camp there are only a few stragglers left by the fire.

The emir rises, for no one shall sit after the incense is lit — that is the custom. He breathes in deeply and pats his belly, still sated after the fulsome feast. His wife prepared his favourite Moroccan recipe that came from her mother as part of her dowry along with some livestock, a set of *Tuereg* jewellery and the slave that went with it. The emir thinks that he will visit this lady to round off his evening. Zena has put him in the mood for some activity in the marital line and she will not be his until tomorrow.

Still, it has been a most gratifying day. The emir has enjoyed the slavers' company. Perhaps, he thinks, it is time that he set out again for the fellowship of the city, where there are men such as these with whom to dine. His father was from the ancient capital of Nizwa. He will return there. He smiles as the thought comes to him. Yes he will return, for a time, at least. There is a camel market and copious water supplied by the *falaj daris* — one of the most ancient waterways on the Peninsula. This business of Jessop's release will soon be done. In the morning he will tell the slavers that Jones is dead. He will tell them that the infidel simply passed away unexpectedly in the night. Such an event is surely the will of Allah. They will shake hands again, perhaps make a small renegotiation and the slavers will be waved off for Muscat. Then it will be easy to pack up the camp and set out for the dusty, palm tree-strewn streets he remembers as a child. He is in the mood to make the journey south as soon as possible.

'Thank you for your hospitality, brother.' Kasim and Ibn Mohammed bow. 'The *soultan* will be pleased. He will extend you a thousand thanks more,' they swear as the tent flap drops into place behind them.

Outside, the fires are dimming and the moon is a mere sliver in the dark, velvet sky. A child coughs and one of the horses whinnies and pulls at its traces. The slavers walk in a cloud of scent, among the sleeping bodies. It takes only a second to spot Wellsted, who is lying awake with Zena next to him, huddled silently in her *burquah*. He jumps to his feet.

'What happened?' he asks. 'What took so long?'

Ibn Mohammed motions towards the darkness beyond the confines of the camp. They will only talk once they are out of earshot. Zena turns on her side so she cannot watch their figures disappear into the blackness. She does not want the slavers to see the fire in her eyes, but she need not worry for, delighted with their efforts, they are focussed on giving the good news to Wellsted that the deal is concluded and the next day they can start the long journey back to Muscat.

Out of sight on the dunes, the men huddle together so no one will hear.

'Good tidings, my friend. He will release the men.' Kasim puts his arm around Wellsted's shoulder. He announces his success in a jubilant whisper. 'We leave at dawn.'

Wellsted corrects Kasim. 'He will release the man, you mean. There are no longer two of them.'

Kasim's eyes open wide. 'What do you mean?'

'Jones is dead. I saw his corpse myself. They are held in a tent on the other side of the camp. I spoke to Jessop not two hours since and he is frail, I'd say, but alive and in good spirits. Still, there is now only one of them.'

Kasim freezes. Ibn Mohammed's hand moves to his knife. 'You are sure the other one does not live?'

'I am. Jones died today — more or less as we arrived. The doctor told me. I felt his body myself for they have left them bound together. To my knowledge, the man's corpse is still there. I have not seen anyone go to fetch it. What happened in the tent?' he repeats. 'Zena seems . . . ' he is not sure how to put it, ' . . . perturbed.'

There is a short silence. Ibn Mohammed works through what has happened, and recognises that the deal they have done now makes

329

more sense to him. It seemed all along that the price was too low. If the emir has lost one of his prisoners, the truth is that he could not in good faith, hold out for more money.

'Well,' Ibn Mohammed shrugs his shoulders, 'the emir will surely give us the body. He did not mention the death, but it is no matter now. We have one alive and he will be freed, my friend. We have completed the mission.'

'It matters to Jones, I'm sure,' Wellsted insists. Even in the darkness he can tell that a shadow has crossed the slavers' faces.

'You do not wish to have your friend's body. To bury him with respect?' Kasim asks, solemnly.

Wellsted drops his head. 'Sorry. I did not mean that. I want to bury him. Of course. Only he did not tell you, did he? The emir held it back. Don't you find that suspicious?'

'How did the man die?' he asks.

'Starvation, I expect. The doctor is very thin. I fed him a little.'

'So they did not kill him in violence?'

'No. No, I expect not. I felt no blood and there was none on my clothes when I came out of the tent. Jessop would have told me, I'm sure. I think the poor fellow simply could not last the conditions.'

Ibn Mohammed shrugs. The white men never understand how to haggle or the process of making a deal. They have no concept of how his people view their honour and what is shameful to admit to and what is easy. He is unsure how to convey to Wellsted that it is a tricky situation for the emir to explain to two esteemed guests who have travelled so many miles on account of the prisoners that one of the men is dead. Especially when they didn't kill him, as such, he simply died. It strikes him that the deal they have struck makes better sense now — if anything, Jones' demise illuminates the situation. Still, how to frame that to the lieutenant is a mystery and even if he does, he can see Wellsted taking a damn note in his damn book about it. The infidel never will understand.

There is a pause, the silence broken only by a tinkle of goats' bells in the distance. Wellsted sits down on the dune. He wants to know why Zena is so upset. He wishes he could see her from here. 'What is the price?' he asks.

'A thousand *taler* dollars and a slave,' Kasim gestures, clearly delighted. 'Less than we had anticipated. The *soultan* said we could go to five times that. To secure them we would have gone higher still out of our own pockets. For the *soultan's* pleasure, of course.'

The penny drops. Wellsted's stomach lurches as a wave of nausea rises in his gullet. 'It is the girl, isn't it? The slave? It's Zena.'

Kasim feels himself growing angry. They have done an admirable job in only a few hours. For a start, no one has been killed and that is a feat in itself. Yet Wellsted has not congratulated them and does not seem even mildly pleased by their achievements. The emir told them that his daughter is dead and he is letting go the man responsible and for a sum far less than they were prepared to pay. This is possibly on account of

331

the second man dying and the embarrassment it has caused him. Still, what more could Wellsted possibly wish for? What is he thinking?

'Of course it's the girl,' Kasim spits. 'It was the least we could get away with. But now you and your friend will be free to return to Muscat and dine with the *soultan*. Do you think that Ibn Mudar gave the girl to you for any other reason?'

Wellsted's hand shakes. It's only a slight tremor but he can feel it reverberate through his entire body. He feels suddenly rather hot and thinks he might be sick. He knows his duty and it is as hateful as it is unthinkable. Despite the baking heat, the ire of his companions, the *Wahabi* attack, it has been, if not exactly easy, certainly too simple up till this point. Adventures are not as they are portrayed in stories around the captain's table or late at night in the mess. They are fearsome, sickly, wicked things and heroes are brave men for a host of reasons for which, no doubt, they should rightly be ashamed. His head has been on the matter of maps and glory, he realises, and now his stomach flips at the mistake he's made.

'She was not yours to bargain with. You should have given him two thousand dollars. Three thousand. All five. But not — '

Kasim strikes the lieutenant hard across the face. 'He didn't want more money. He wanted the girl,' he says simply, jabbing his finger at Wellsted's chest to make the point.

Ibn Mohammed looks back towards the camp. He cannot bear to look the lieutenant in the eye. He is tired and the man is a fool. They will not sleep tonight, for they will have to watch over him. Who knows what the white man might do with the darkness for cover if he cannot even hide his emotions from those to whom he should be grateful and respect as friends? Despite all his promises, the slaver wonders fleetingly if he should slit the lieutenant's throat. It would be easier and his commission, after all, is to return with the hostages. As long as he does that, will the *soultan* really blame him if the blue-eyed one falls by the wayside? Kasim will cover for him — some story about a brawl, perhaps. He considers it.

Wellsted rises to his feet before Ibn Mohammed can make a decision. He looks up at the stars and pushes down the instinct to scream loudly. 'Damn,' he says. 'I should thank you. I know. I am sorry. The girl has gone to my head. How can I blame the emir for desiring her?'

He does not mean a word of it, but he knows he must play for time. He glances towards the caravan, trying to catch sight of Zena. No wonder she wouldn't speak. *If I leave her and get Jessop to port I can come back and rescue her, buy her back, surely. Jessop will not survive much longer and has to be freed*, he thinks. His head is swimming with possibilities, but it is an impossible situation. All he wants is to hold her. He has the whole night to come up with something. Anything. Did Mickey know that this would be part of the deal? Can it be reneged upon?

'We should sleep,' he says.

Uneasily, the men tramp back in silence to

Wellsted's place by the fire. On the ground there is an empty indent where Zena lay and a mess of felt blankets, hastily put aside. As one, they look to the fire, for she often cannot sleep and stokes the flames in the night, but there is no figure in a *burquah* crouching among the ashes. The camp is absolutely silent. Kasim gestures vaguely towards the latrine quarter but Ibn Mohammed lifts the blankets. It is he who first understands.

'Where is her bag?' he spits angrily.

The men sleep with their saddlebags at the head, like a pillow. If Zena has taken hers it is proof that she has flown. Runaway slaves always provoke irrepressible anger in Ibn Mohammed. He cannot bear insubordination. The enslavement of his prey is inevitable and runaways are simply fighting nature. They are an abomination and one that he takes personally. He peers into the darkness.

'She has gone,' he says as if the realisation is a decision. 'Did you do this, Wellsted?'

There is a fearsome edge in his voice and he looks taut, as if he will lash out at any moment.

'No,' Wellsted replies honestly. 'She didn't even tell me what happened.'

From the edge in Wellsted's voice, though, it is clear he is glad she has made an escape. There is no time to deal with that now. The slavers must find the girl.

'Check the camels,' Ibn Mohammed hisses. 'She cannot have got far.'

They head first for the tethered animals. With the emir's livestock jumbled with their own in the darkness, it is impossible to tell if one is gone. The supplies, however, are easier to trace. Two goatskins of water and a bag of flour and fat have disappeared.

'How dare she?' Ibn Mohammed radiates fury, his words dripping venom. 'The stupid, ungrateful . . . ' He has been known to behead runaway slaves for his own amusement. Once, he buried two women up to their necks in sand and left them to die slowly in the searing heat. In this case, neither of these solutions is in any way helpful (however satisfying) and Kasim is more pragmatic. He has no feelings to speak of, only strategy.

'Dawn is four or five hours away,' he thinks out loud. 'Can she navigate?'

The lieutenant shrugs his shoulders. He does not want to catch her. *Good girl*, he thinks, *good girl*. Zena constantly surprises him. He feels a flood of hope, of love even. He would not have suggested she run, but now she has he is delighted. He only wants to help in any way he can.

'I should kill you now,' Ibn Mohammed spits for he is sure that Wellsted must have known of this mutiny. The man is not the least distressed.

Kasim lays a hand on his friend's arm. 'Holster your blade,' he counsels. 'We might need him.'

Kasim stares at the ground. The situation is impossible. Damn the girl. Damn her. Kasim struggles to think of an honourable way out or at least a way to salvage the situation. He makes a quick calculation. If they fly in the night, they can at least make good the *soultan's* wishes, he decides. They must take action.

'Where are they holding your friend?'

Wellsted points in the direction of the tent.

'And you think he can travel? We have no litter — can he ride a camel?'

Wellsted nods. 'With some help,' he admits.

Kasim motions the others towards him. 'Look,' he says, 'we can't find the girl in the dark. She has shamed us all in this for we have given our word to hand her over. In the morning, the emir will be furious. He may allow us to track her and bring her back. He may agree to that, but we have no certainty that we will find her before she dies and, in truth, we do not know what he may decide to do in anger. He has the reputation of a man who might take drastic action. In any case, with the girl gone and the deal broken, he has every right to kill your Jessop if he wants to. We'll be most fortunate if that is all he does. We cannot run tonight with our whole party. That would raise the whole camp and even if we succeed in sneaking all our men and camels away, he will have the right to pursue us. We have made a deal with him and reneged on it. In daylight, his men know this terrain well and they have horses rather than camels. We will stand little chance. If we could get away, I'd say to do that. If I knew we could find her, I surely would. But there are no certainties, so here is what I propose.'

Ibn Mohammed and Wellsted lean in.

'We must take only those we need. Leave the slaves and take half a dozen of the servants — those best camel men. Ibrahim, Jasouf,

Hamza and Hassan. Perhaps Tarif and Sudar. No more than that. They are the best. We will steal your doctor, Lieutenant, for the sake of the *soultan*. And in return, in the hope it will appease him, the emir can have our slaves, the rest of the camels and supplies and we will leave him two thousand *talers* — the thousand we agreed and another thousand in compensation. It is more than the girl is worth. He will be angry, for it is hardly honourable. He will probably kill our men. But if we leave enough by way of compensation, he might not follow us. In fact, it will save him face, for he will not have to come clean about your Jones being dead. Besides, if he does not slaughter those we leave, he will have at least another six hundred *taler* worth in the livestock and slaves — maybe more. With a small party and travelling at night, we can make for the coast. We will not complete Said Ibn Sultan's bidding with honour, but it will cost him less than his five thousand *talers*, he will have the doctor and as far as I can see, it is the best we can get away with.'

'If we find the girl, I will kill her,' Ibn Mohammed sneers, though he nods in agreement.

Kasim says nothing about Ibn Mohammed's threat. The slaver has every right to punish a runaway as he pleases, and in terms of the mission it will not matter by the time they find her whether the girl lives or not, though it is a waste of a few hundred silver coins in his opinion. Ibn Mohammed, however, has enough money to waste should he wish to and Kasim

337

harbours neither love nor hate for the girl. He only wants to complete what he came to do and be free to pursue his *Zigua* once more.

Wellsted stares into the blackness. He hopes Zena will make for Muscat. She has a camel and supplies, and though he has not said so, he knows she also has a small goatskin pouch of silver coins. He smiles, for he has just realised that it is missing from his belt. *She is most impressive*, he thinks with pride. If they catch her and Ibn Mohammed wants to kill her, he will simply have to strike first. At the first sign, he'll slit the slaver's throat. Meantime, they must rescue the doctor.

'All right,' he says. 'If you raise the men, I'll fetch Jessop.'

'I will come. You may need help,' Kasim smiles. He may not want to kill Wellsted, but he no longer trusts him.

Ibn Mohammed nods towards the camp. 'I will fetch the men,' he whispers. 'It will take five minutes.' Silently he congratulates himself they never took the saddles and packs from the camel's backs and notes that it always pays to be circumspect. 'We will meet at the camels,' he orders.

* * *

Wellsted and Kasim move around the perimeter of the settlement without a word. Wellsted motions towards the tent and they make their way down the incline of soft sand with a balletic roll. Behind them Ibn Mohammed is moving like

338

a shadow among the sleepers, raising the men chosen to travel into the night.

'Jessop,' Wellsted hisses.

'I am here, James,' the reply comes.

They enter the tent.

'We have to take off,' Wellsted explains. 'This is Kasim,' he motions towards his companion.

The slaver makes a sound, not quite a grunt, but no *salaam*.

'I am tied,' the doctor explains.

Kasim feels for the rope. He draws his *khandjar* and slits the bond easily. There is a noise as Jones' corpse, now stiff, is felled to one side. The men ignore it. They have no time to tend to the dead, and Kasim thinks that in leaving the body they are underlining to the emir that he also has reneged on the deal by omission. Wellsted leans towards the doctor.

'Can you walk, Jessop?'

There is a good-humoured snigger. 'It's been a while. I'll try.' Then a soft thump. Kasim moves forward but Wellsted motions him away and envelopes the doctor's thin frame as it lies slumped on the sandy floor of the tent. It will not take two of them to carry him.

'He would not trade us, then?'

'Long story, old man.'

As he touches the doctor's body, the lieutenant feels a sense of revulsion at how fragile Jessop has become and of course, there is the smell. He steels himself.

'Upsadaisy,' he whispers as he lifts him. 'Just keep very quiet and your fingers crossed, if you can.'

They sneak back into the darkness towards the camels. Ibn Mohammed is already directing which animals they will take. There are ten thoroughbreds, the rest will be forfeit, along with the slaves. It is not a high price to keep the emir from pursuing them. Ibn Mohammed orders a large casket of *taler* coins to be placed in open view. As the servants carry it over and place it on the ground, Wellsted stops and draws breath. By the moonlight he can see his friend properly for the first time. He tries not to show his concern. Jessop is all skeleton. His *jubbah* is a filthy, stinking rag and it is stuck to his skin where he has defecated. The doctor's hair is patchy and in knots and his unkempt beard is wispy. All over his body the skin is badly marked and so terribly pale that in the moonlight he looks luminous. He is a pitiful straggle of a fellow and he has the air of a pauper, if not a lunatic. However his eyes are still bright. The lieutenant does his best not to stare in outright horror at what happens to an educated, country gentlemen when he is not fed.

'The stars,' the doctor motions into the distance.

They are beautiful, of course. The same twinkling panorama that adorns the desert sky every night. Wellsted swallows his pity and tries to remain pragmatic.

'We're lucky the moon is so slight. I'll get you something to eat,' he promises, below his breath.

A smile breaks the doctor's face. He is so thin that his teeth look eerie — they are the only part of him that has not shrunk away.

'I have to take it easy, James, with the food.

340

Ease myself in. A decent meal would do for me now — I probably couldn't take it, but if you gave me food I'd eat it. I wouldn't be able to stop myself.'

'A decent meal we'll keep for Bombay then. But perhaps you could manage some camel's milk?'

The doctor nods. 'A little,' he agrees. 'A little every couple of hours — like a babe.'

'As soon as I can. And I'll ride with you.'

The man can't stand, Wellsted thinks. If he gets on a camel there is a good chance he'll simply slip down the flank onto the sand. It would be an easy thing to lose him in the darkness. If he fell it would be close to silent — there is no weight to him at all. Wellsted realises that they have arrived in the nick of time. Not much longer and Jessop would have gone the way of Jones. It is best this way. *Zena*, he thinks, *will have to fend for herself for a while*. She has proved, so far, surprisingly capable.

All of a sudden, Ibn Mohammed motions the men to be still and, alert, all fall to their haunches. There is some movement between the tents behind them. A woman walks out to relieve herself and is followed by a whining child. The men hold their breath and stand stock-still while she moves across the camp with the child in her wake like a familiar. She has not noticed the missing bodies — why should she? Still, if they move the camels she will certainly be able to see them.

Everything stops and the night is once more as silent as it should be. One of the slaves stirs in his sleep and turns over. A donkey brays.

Then, perhaps two minutes later, the woman returns, carrying the child and humming a lullaby below her breath. She disappears back into the family tent. Ibn Mohammed motions everyone to stay in place another minute. The time passes painfully slowly. They can hear their own breathing and the pounding of their hearts. Then, like a conductor in concert, he bids the men rise and lead their camels into the night. They will mount the saddles when they are further off.

Wellsted cradles the doctor, who still has not taken his eyes from his rescuer. The stench of him comes in waves and Wellsted averts his face, pretending he is checking the sand beneath his feet for rocks. The doctor says nothing. Beyond the camp they climb up and Wellsted ties Jessop into place on the saddle. It is like riding with a child who cannot hold their seat yet.

'All right?' the lieutenant checks.

The doctor turns away. 'I am alive,' he whispers.

Wellsted suspects he is crying. He puts his hand on Jessop's and gives it a squeeze.

No one can see. The Arabs wait for him to nod that the doctor is secure and to mount the camel himself, then Ibn Mohammed points the way and the caravan rides quickly eastwards. They have four hours until the sun rises. It is not much of a head start.

PART THREE

'Do not lose hold of your dreams or aspirations. For if you do, you may still exist but you have ceased to live.'

Henry David Thoreau 1817–1862
Poet, naturalist and historian

38

Once she can no longer see the camp in the distance and the light of the fire has disappeared into a pinprick, Zena vomits onto the sand in terror and tries to bring her racing mind into check. Slowly, she calls herself to order and through force of will she makes herself think clearly. She pulls a pale blue *dishdash* and orange *hauza* from her bags. She stole these tatty clothes from a tent in the encampment and now switches her *burquah* for the man's garb, carefully binding up her hair in the orange turban so that from a distance she will look like a poor *Bedu*. Then she straps on her *khandjar* as she has seen the men do and hides the small purse of coins. The disguise, she knows, will not fool any of the slavers' party who come to find her, for even from a distance they will recognise the camel, but perhaps anyone else she comes across will leave her alone. To travel openly as a woman is unthinkable. Next, she turns her mind to navigation. She knows the direction she has come from and remembers where the sun set, so it is not difficult to find her bearings. She considers this and then steers the camel to the east. Returning to Riyadh is out of the question — it is the emir's closest settlement and news will reach there of what she has done with the lightning speed that gossip travels across the sand. To the west and south there is little but open country for hundreds of miles, but to the east there is an ocean. The Giant Blue. She has seen it on the map the master drew. She is sure of it.

Zena does not really expect to live for long enough to see the sea, but what she knows is that if she does not go now, she will never have a better chance to get away and she is determined that she will not be trapped in the service of the emir. Finally, she has found the courage to make a choice. It is just as the master said — he'd run himself if he was faced with the prospect of slavery in the desert. You have to run for yourself, she realises, no one else can do it for you. At first she thought her only option was to slit her own throat with the *khandjar* rather than be left in the encampment. But the more she thought about it, the more it seemed a foolishly dramatic gesture and she would far rather live if she can. The thought of what killing herself in front of him would do to the master horrifies her almost as much as the deed itself. As she mounts the saddle she feels surprisingly calm. She thinks of the boy who ran into the sea that first day on the coast when she was captured all those months before. She remembers Kasim and Ibn Mohammed sneering at his chances of survival. They were right, of course, for the boy was dead within two days of boarding the *mashua* and, in truth, she knows her odds are probably even less than his.

But I will try, she thinks and a shimmer of a smile plays on her lips and it feels like magic. After all, on every trip there is a boy who runs into the sea, but a slave girl who steals her favourite camel and makes off into the night surely is a rarer creature. They can have no template for that. She wishes she could see their faces. And at this moment, it feels exciting, almost fun to be — she pauses a moment — free. Free. Yes. It has been a long time.

The camel moves smoothly and she makes sure it keeps its pace, peering over her shoulder into the darkness. She has a good idea of everything she needs to know. For a start, she is aware that they will not willingly let her go and that they are skilled at moving silently at night, but if they could not track the escaped *Wahabi* till dawn then they will not be able to track her either. The night gives her respite and for now, at least, the going is easy. She will make good way before the sun rises. Zena's mouth is dry, more from the excitement than anything else, but she does not tap her goatskin. Instead, she sings a lullaby — not in Arabic, but in her own language. It sounds as comforting as a flowing stream as it bubbles up from inside her. The camel likes it, she can tell, and Zena picks up the pace to encourage the animal to push on faster. At first she sings it very low, but as the miles roll out she is emboldened and sings freely.

After several hours, just when exhaustion begins to overtake her, there is a sliver of sunshine on the horizon and then, as if there is a box of light hidden behind the dune, the dawn bursts upwards. It stops Zena in her tracks. The stillness is incredible — the silence of being alone. She looks all around, but there is nothing.

Where are they all? It is almost too much to wish for. Zena shrugs her shoulders.

'*Seent*,' she calls to gee up the camel, but now it has stopped, the beast is nonchalant. '*Seent*.'

The animal moves unwillingly and sets a course slightly to the south of the sun. Zena notices the deviation, but she heard a *Bedu* once say his camel knew the desert far better than he did, and that they can find water, so she lets it be. East-southeast will be fine.

At length they come to a parched-looking oasis and Zena dismounts. The plants are mostly dead, but still she draws what little water she can from the well, unloading the skins into a shallow, rock-lined indent built for the purpose of watering camels. The liquid is brackish and clouded with mud, but she takes a long draught and then sets the animal to drink the rest, patting its long neck as much to comfort herself as anything else. After the camel is finished, she milks the beast and fills her own stomach.

I should have stolen some coffee, she thinks as she downs the thin milk, though she does not want to stop long enough to make a brew. She was right to trust the camel. Now, very aware she is one, small figure in the vast landscape, the desert seems astonishingly empty and she cannot quite believe that she has got away. The camel brays, she is as tired as her rider. They will both need to sleep soon, though Zena is sure they can make a few more miles before they have to stop and rest.

Then, as she makes to remount, her legs stiff with exhaustion, she senses a movement on the horizon behind her, somewhere in the distance. Dark eyes darting, one hand flies to her *khandjar* and she mounts quickly, ready to bolt. As the figure moves closer she can tell immediately it is not Kasim or Ibn Mohammed. Nor Wellsted either. The clothes are wrong and the camel is too short-legged. Then, behind the first rider another three appear and she realises, her stomach sinking, that they must be the emir's men. If she makes a run for it they will follow her and she is not confident she can outride them — in fact, it is an impossibility. She hesitates a moment and then slips to the ground, steeling her heavy heart. She expected, if not this, then something and whatever happens she wants to meet it with dignity. The blade of the knife will be hot, she thinks sadly, but at least it will be her own choice and the master will not have to watch her die.

As the men approach, she pictures him, his strong body, his blue eyes and his softly spoken tales of London. She cannot fight four of them but she decides she will wait until they dismount before she kills herself. She has something to say. It is odd, she knows, but she wants to tell them how she feels. She wants to tell them that she made her bid for freedom not out of disloyalty to her master but out of horror at what he would be forced to do by the slavers. She feels a rush of emotion, glad she had that night with him in Riyadh. At least she experienced that, and now death is infinitely preferable to an Abyssinian woman of noble family who has been so cruelly treated by fate that she has ended up traded as if she is nothing. Yes, she'll tell them that. Still, her heart is pounding as the first rider's roll of dust reaches her feet and the *Bedu* dismounts. Zena takes a deep breath and slides her hand onto the knife's handle, but before her final words can come the man smiles and greets her as a brother. As a man.

'*Salaam aleikhum*,' he says.

She does not recognise him. She is sure his face was not part of the jeering crowd watching her dance. The other men do not dismount and she squints slightly as her eyes flick between their faces and she sees that she does not recognise any of them. The men do not seem angry — quite the reverse.

'*Aleikhum salaam*,' she replies uncertainly.

'My family saw you from the dunes. You are alone. Do you need help, friend? Can we offer you hospitality?'

Zena's limbs relax. This party has not come from the emir's encampment at all. They have seen only what they expect — a man in a pale blue *dishdash* on a camel, travelling alone. They do not know who she is or what she has done and they have no idea about Kasim or Ibn Mohammed and the deal they made to barter her. This is a chance meeting on the sands like a hundred others. She has seen faces like these before, in practically every camel train, all the way from Muscat. These men want news and in return there may be kindness and, for that matter, coffee. She thanks her stars she stole the clothes and shifts her gait slightly to feel more masculine — more solid on the sand. Her decision is made in a flicker — no more than that. This is not dangerous. These men are doing what *Bedu* do all across the *Rubh Al Khali* and with their help surely she has a better chance at survival than if she travels alone.

'I am searching for my master,' she smiles and bows with a slight flourish as she lowers the timbre of her voice. 'I am his boy. There was an argument and he left his family. My poor master. I cannot let him go to the coast alone. He will dive for pearls he says, but who will look after him? I have been travelling for a long time. Am I headed for the sea?'

The *Bedu*'s eyes are alight. There is not a tribesman alive who could resist such a potent suggestion of family scandal, the need for instruction and a slave so devoted to duty and his master that he will risk death.

'Yes,' the man says, 'the sea.' He waves further in the direction upon which Zena is headed. 'But, please, eat with us and join our party. Like you, we are heading for the coast and it will be far better to travel in a group. It is the way of our tribe. What is your master's name?'

Zena hesitates, as if unwilling to embarrass the noble family to whom she belongs. The *Bedu* waves his hand in the air to dismiss his question. Every tribesman on the sands knows to which family she refers — the pearl-fishing teenage renegade has been the gossip of the caravans the whole way north.

She ladles it on with vigour. 'My master saved my life when the *simoom* came. I owe him everything. I cannot let him down.'

351

'Of course. Of course,' the man says, in an understanding tone. 'Come. Are you hungry? We are stopped for coffee and dates. Please, it is not far . . .'

Again she hesitates, just long enough. 'Thank you,' she says graciously. 'My name is Malik.'

She mounts fluidly, her stomach rumbling at the very idea of solid food, for she has become used to it again. She pats her camel and follows the *Bedu* to their stopping place. This is the best possible outcome. These men have supplies and they know the way. Her pursuers will be looking for a lone traveller — a woman — not a slave in a party of *Bedu* and she knows that one way or another, she will be followed. *I must play this part*, she thinks, holding herself with less grace and more solidity, like a man. She only wishes she had bound her chest. She will do so in the evening while the men are sleeping, and in the meantime she is careful to slouch. *Perhaps*, she ponders, almost incredulous that it is possible, *I will survive now.*

As the little camp comes into sight, she smiles. There are ten men of mixed ages in the group. She dismounts and greets them all, sipping the coffee proffered in her direction and sucking on a sweet, juicy date. They are driving camels to market.

'*Shukhran*,' she whispers and squats down on her haunches, ready to play the part she has cast for herself. 'Is it far to the sea?'

The *Bedu* shrug. 'Not far. Three days. A good journey. We will enjoy it.'

Better and better. Three days is surely not so

352

long that the news of her real identity need overtake them even if they are (as the *Bedu* tend to be) optimistic in their estimates. For three days or so she will be fed, at least, and if they come for her, they will have to get close before they uncover her identity.

'Tell us your story,' one of the men asks.

Zena takes her eyes from the horizon, and accepts that for the moment, she is safe. 'With pleasure, my friend,' she says, squatting to join him. 'Of course. I will tell you my whole tale.'

39

The first to see what has happened is the *Tuereg* slave. He has risen to stoke the fire only ten minutes before the rest of the men get up to pray. He stands stock-still and staring, as if the scene before him is not possible. Behind his blank gaze there is a panicked expression as he looks this way and that. He feels a rising terror — as if a deadly snake has been spotted in the camp and it is his job to find and capture it. He counts the sleeping visitors again and confirms that there are far too few of them and that the distinctive outline of the slavers is not among the prone bodies scattered around the fire. He knows that the man who brings this news to the emir's attention may, at the very least, be beaten, but with a sinking heart he wonders how the duty cannot fall to him. He will be beaten anyway if he does not stoke the fire before the men rise and make their obeisances to the east. As if to check the extent of the disaster, he trots quietly to the tent where the *Nazarene* are held and pulls back the flap. Jones' corpse lies jack-knifed on the ground, and at the sight of it the slave feels his heart turn a somersault, for he does not know that Jones died the day before. Besides that, the other infidel, the one with hair the colour of mud, is definitely missing. The slave's duty is invidious, but, cursing, he knows what he has to do.

As he turns, afraid, back towards the camp, he runs straight into one of the emir's free men, who has risen early and come to bring water to the *Nazarene* and clean them before, one dead and one alive, they will be handed over to the slavers. The man is glad to be rid of the white men, for looking after them, if you could call it that, has been an odious duty for the past months, and he walks jauntily, happy that today will be the last time he will be troubled by it.

'What are you doing here?' he grabs the *Tuereg* by the ear.

The slave's legs give way under him. 'The visitors are gone. Some of them. And one of the *Nazarene*. Gone.'

The free man turns to the camp — he had not looked closely at the figures on the ground for his eyes were still heavy with sleep and he was set on what he had to do. Now he focusses. Then he shouts a curse and runs for the emir's tent, hollering as he goes to call his brothers to arms.

At once, from all quarters, men emerge into the blue shadow of dawn, every one of them holding a drawn blade. The slaves who have been abandoned by Ibn Mohammed and Kasim spring into action too. Their first thought is that their missing companions have been stolen and slaughtered. They draw their knives and, surrounded, fall into a defensive formation — a rough circle spiked with sharp protuberances on every side. Everything happens very quickly and the shouts are such a babble that it is hard for one side to tell what the other is saying. One of the emir's men kills a slave, flat, and for a

355

moment it looks as if there will be carnage, but the emir's voice rings out and his natural authority is such that everyone freezes. In the tent flaps, women hold their children close.

The emir surveys the scene. It does not take a *fakir* to know what has happened. He roars with anger and then motions at the remaining members of Ibn Mohammed's party.

'Bring them forward!' the emir orders.

The slaves are herded together.

The emir makes a movement with his hand, and the men are willingly disarmed. They are, after all, slaves not soldiers.

'Where are your masters?' he demands.

The men are silent. They look at the ground. The emir jabs at one of them so quickly that it is difficult to see how he could have drawn his blade. Doomed by his proximity, the fellow makes a gurgling noise and falls in a sliding sheet of blood.

'Where are your masters?' the emir turns to the others.

One musters the courage to speak. 'We do not know. They were gone when we awoke.'

Then they all fall to their knees and one or two of them whimper, for now they are at the emir's mercy. Their masters are gone.

'The *Nazarene?*' the emir enquires.

The man who raised the alarm tells him the news.

'And the *habshi?*'

'She is not here.'

'Go,' the emir orders, with a flick of his chin. 'You must check the camels.'

In less than a minute two men return with the casket of *talers*. The emir throws open the lid and kicks the side of the box in temper, sending a shimmer of coins cascading onto the ground. They have left the corpse. It seems to him that it is likely they found out late at night that one of the men was dead. This box contains far more than the thousand Marie Theresa dollars agreed upon. Ibn Mohammed and Kasim have simply changed the deal with the changing circumstances. The emir eyes the slaves before him, counting their value as he enquires how many camels were left behind. It is a good enough showing for one half-dead *Nazarene*, though he wishes they had left the girl. However, to his surprise, he finds he is not as angry as he might have been. It passes across his mind that perhaps he is getting old. Or perhaps he can understand why this has happened. It will be easy to find them, if he decides to. They will have gone east, of course, and, he considers a moment, that is not the direction of Nizwa.

Ever mercurial, the emir has been considering his plans overnight. He wants to go home. He wonders how this story will play with the elders in his family's town and decides that if he portrays the events correctly, he can be a hero. The slavers, great men though they are, were so afraid of his wrath that they have run like cowards into the night. In time, he may dine with the *soultan* himself and convey an air of superiority in the matter, for the pride of Muscat have not dispatched their duty with honour. The thought pleases him. The *soultan* is one of the richest men on the Peninsula, but the emir surely has this over his reputation. Still, he'd like to be sure what happened.

'Look for signs in the sand,' he says to his eldest son.

'Let me track them, Father,' the boy pleads.

This is the chance for which the child has been waiting. If he can track down the thiefs-in-the-night and avenge the slight, his name will be made. The emir, however, looks nonchalant. The boy's need to establish a reputation is not of interest to him — he is not dead yet.

'Come back to tell me,' he says. 'I will decide when we know their direction.' At that, his son disappears.

The emir takes a deep breath. This is not how he intended to start his day.

'You,' he snaps, picking one of the slaves from the line-up — one who so far has managed not to piss himself. The man raises his eyes and it is clear that he is expecting to be killed. He steps forwards slowly with as much dignity as he can muster.

'Make coffee,' the emir orders, and with those few words the relief of the entire camp is palpable. The women disappear back into their tents and the men lower their weapons.

'And, Sharif — you must count this,' the emir tells his closest henchman.

Even without knowing their number, the generous chest of *talers* is enough bounty to boast of and, the emir considers carefully as he pictures his homecoming to Nizwa, no one ever need know what they agreed about the girl.

40

For a long while, Wellsted is unsure whether the doctor will survive the journey. They have driven the camels hard, with only the briefest respite, for five days and nights. No one has had more than three or four hours' sleep at a time. Jessop manages to digest his milk, however, and he seems to be getting stronger, despite the travelling and the unrelenting heat. The only shelter they can afford him is a ragged *hauza* draped across his forehead. He dozes, tied into his saddle with a rough string made of plaited rushes, and yesterday he pointed his thin finger with an eagerness that he had previously not been able to muster and asked for a piece of *khubz* from the fire. He ate it to no ill effect along with two dates and he has taken bread with his milk ever since. There is a slight flush today on his thin cheeks though, of course, that may simply be the searing temperature. Much of the time he sleeps or, more accurately, passes out. It is, Wellsted reassures himself, all part of the doctor's recovery.

As they crest the final hilltop they look down on what is a very welcome view: they are a couple of miles from the coast, and the party can see the bright gem of the ocean. Ibn Mohammed is, as ever, vigilant. He has sworn he will kill the girl when he finds her and he intends to make good on his promise. There is, however, still no sign of her as they take in the vista before them. Wellsted nudges the doctor and points at the expanse of water. Making it to Bombay now is surely a real possibility; the doctor beams.

'James,' he whispers. 'I want to wash properly and to shave. Whenever we can.'

Wellsted nods. He is glad Jessop is feeling strong enough to be troubled by his appearance. However hard he tries, though, he cannot stop thinking about what has happened to the girl. Given Ibn Mohammed's fury, her complete disappearance is perhaps fortuitous. Wellsted only hopes she turned in the right direction. Zena is no fool, he tells himself. When he showed her the maps he had made, she could read them.

At night he feels a strange bond with her, as if he should somehow be able to tell where she is by mere thought alone. His imaginings spiral into crazy plans of taking her to London, though he knows it would be impossible to introduce Zena into society either as his slave or as his lover. A black servant is just about acceptable, but he does not want to oblige Zena to be in service to him and the disapproval at a hint of anything more than that would make a happy life in England impossible. Wellsted lets his mind wander and toys with the most forbidden word of all: *wife*. The girl has touched him deeply. There is something in the connection between them that he cannot explain and that, alongside the fact he feels he has disgraced her, makes him dream of a legal union, something binding, something that can offer her real protection. It fires him and, almost for the first time, he finds he wants something for himself — something private, that does not pertain to his family, his father, his grandfather, society or the needs of the Bombay Marine. He wants Zena to marry him and be his alone.

Wellsted knows no white person married to a black and is well aware that such a scandalous undertaking would sully his reputation for life — he has not even heard tell of a docker who has attempted it, never mind one of His Majesty's naval officers. As an up-and-coming gentleman, such an action would be unthinkable, particularly for a man in his position with little social standing or rank. He must conform and the truth is that in London he has no stomach for taking on such a challenge. To admit to sleeping with her would be considered bad enough. However, he is coming to an accommodation in his daydreaming, for in Arabia their union would be not only accepted, but considered quite normal. What seems strange, in fact, is that at home they believe this land less civilised than England when here a slave can marry a master, a brown man can marry a white women and Zena can be his wife.

He lingers over the memory of Zena's pitch skin covered by his milky body and he feels a frisson of excitement, though the girl's spirit is as intoxicating as her beauty. He will install her either here or in Bombay and hopes that by Arabic law she can become his wife, though in polite society, or rather, amongst Europeans, they will never be able to admit it. Arabia is far more accepting in that regard than Wellsted's home can ever be. That does not matter now, however. He simply wants to cosset her. If only she has got away safely and he can make it possible. If only she will accept him for, his conscience twinges, he has let her down. He has not only presumed on the girl but then forced her on her own resources which, luckily, have proved formidable so far.

As they make for the lower ground, he affirms for the umpteenth time, *I would certainly feel it if she came to any harm*. He has, of course, no grounds for this and ignores the shame he feels at his unscientific ponderance. People are lost on the sands with regularity and he knows from the *Bedu* that in general they do not come back safely. Even though it's only a glimmer, the thought fills him with dread and he pushes it away. She is tough. She has water, food, a good camel and ample money. She knows how to travel.

'What *are* you daydreaming about?' Jessop teases him.

The doctor cannot help but notice that the lieutenant is more often than not a million miles away and several times each hour the man turns and stares at the expanse of land behind the caravan, as if he is expecting to hail a hackney. It is most disconcerting. They have stopped now and dismounted halfway to the village but Wellsted continues to check behind. The lieutenant says nothing about Zena. A man's business is his own in these matters.

'I am thinking of my duty,' he teases the doctor back, his voice serious.

It is, after all, his duty to keep his word. He made his promises willingly and so far he has failed in keeping them. He has little choice in what he can do now. He knows he cannot send Jessop back to Muscat alone, for the doctor is still far too weak, and even if he turns back to find Zena, most likely Ibn Mohammed will insist on accompanying him. No, Jessop's life is in the balance and one duty rubs uneasily against the other with the certainty of the doctor's survival and the ingrained loyalty to his family and country winning out, at least for the time being. Still, when they do return to Muscat and his charge is in safe hands, Wellsted is resolved to turn back immediately towards the desert and retrace his steps to find her.

The party makes its way down the hill in the direction of the little harbour and the shores of the Red Sea. It is a sound, well-protected spot at the base of the Gulf of Bahrain. The ocean here is the colour of sapphires and it comes as a shock after months of muddy well water and a vista composed exclusively from a limited spectrum, the colour of sand sculpted into dunes by the wind and seen in varying degrees of bright light. As in Riyadh, the houses are fashioned of a pale, baked mud and in the distance there are a variety of promising looking vessels of all sizes that are potentially for hire or even for sale.

No more than a mile off, Wellsted notices Kasim and Ibn Mohammed whispering to each other and the servants shifting as if uncomfortable. Something is amiss. The lieutenant sits up in his saddle, nervous that they have found her.

He will have to fight them both, in that case. He is ready to do so. When he sees where they are pointing, he peers again at the houses. From here it is clear the village boundary is closed. A makeshift camp has pitched on the outskirts and even from this far away they can hear the keening sound of mourning women. Wellsted feels relief. He has little confidence that he would win a knife-to-knife battle with the slavers. Still he is not prepared for the danger of what they have encountered.

'There is plague,' Ibn Mohammed pronounces. 'They have closed their gates and locked themselves in, waiting to see who Allah wills to live. See,' he points and explains for the benefit of the *Nazarene*, 'on the outskirts, their relations watch to see if there is life inside the infected houses from the smoke of cooking fires.' Here he makes a wisp-like gesture. 'Many people will die. We cannot break the boundary.'

'Can we still . . . ' Wellsted starts, but the look in Ibn Mohammed's eyes stops him from even finishing the question.

They will not be rocked to sleep on the swell aboard a ship tonight. It is far too dangerous and they will have to carry on down the coast to find passage.

*   *   *

Turning south and feeling unaccountably heavy, the caravan travels one more day and night, following the shoreline. Now there is plague in the miasma, when they see other travellers there is no question of stopping. After the elaborate hospitality of the desert, it goes against the grain to shun company, but the mounted men pass each other at a distance and at most there is a nod and a troubled smile. The sound of the waves, never far now, lulls them to sleep at night — a noise so strange after all these months that they are kept awake by its novelty.

'I wonder if it *is* plague,' the doctor muses. 'Of course, it's far more likely smallpox. People make all kinds of mistakes in diagnosis. Anything with a pustule is called plague on the Peninsula. I don't expect they have the vaccination here, though. Furthest it's come is Turkey. Have you been vaccinated, old man?' he asks.

Wellsted nods. All midshipmen are vaccinated with cowpox, they have been for many years now.

'Well, that's both of us immune. I wonder, do you suppose I might be able to examine some of the patients?'

Wellsted laughs out loud. 'Look at you. You're eight stones at the outside, you're a sleeping shadow who isn't even capable of staying awake for more than a few minutes at a stretch and you can't eat meat because your stomach is too weak. I'm not sure you'd survive the examination of an Arab with plague, old man. Even the strong die of it, don't they? What if it isn't smallpox and you aren't as immune as you think?'

Jessop grins his eerie smile into the darkness. 'Oh, if you think I got through the ministerings of that emir bastard only to catch a bubo or two, you are very much mistaken. I never catch anything, James. Never have. It was one of the reasons my father thought I should study medicine. And besides, if I am going to die of anything, I wouldn't choose plague. I'd go for tuberculosis. Highly fashionable — artists and poets die of tuberculosis, think of Keats and Henry Purcell — John Calvin, for heaven's sake — with all the romance of a direct line to God. No one dies of the plague these days. Really. I'm invincible. I'm sure of it.'

Wellsted laughs. Jessop's spirit is admirable and he can't refuse him. But the doctor's arms are still stick thin and he wheezes sometimes when he moves too quickly.

'I'll try to keep you fashionable, Doctor, don't you worry.'

* * *

In the morning, they arrive at the next town down the coast. Here, too, the gates are closed. This time, however, the purpose of the quarantine is not to contain the infection but to keep out all visitors who might carry it. Standing on the high walls, two guards agleam with weaponry bear over the party with menace. They are so comprehensively swathed in dusty fabric that their eyes are not clearly visible.

'Go away!' they call, waving the visitors off with drawn blades. *Imshi. Imshi.* 'None can enter here.'

Kasim shouts back, trumpeting their names, their mission for the *soultan* and explaining that they avoided the plague town — they did not go

366

within half a mile of it, he enunciates with precision. Every one of them is healthy (here he swears an oath) and all they seek is to do business — hire a *dhow* and buy some slaves, if the citizens have any to spare. The guards stop shouting. They confer a moment and then disappear from sight without a word. It is a promising sign.

Wearily, the servants dismount into the shade of the town walls. They brew coffee over a tiny fire while the caravan waits for the pronouncement. Such decisions are the province of headmen and councillors. It takes twenty minutes or so before an old man appears on the battlements.

'Your name?' he shouts down.

Ibn Mohammed obliges and trumpets his mission for the *soultan*. 'He will send you a thousand thanks for any help you can give us. We seek only to trade. We have coin.'

The old man, an *imam*, peers. 'You have not visited the plague town?'

'I swear it, brother.' Ibn Mohammed touches his heart. 'We came from the sands.'

The *imam* considers this a moment. 'I met the *soultan* once,' he replies.

A minute later, the studded, wooden gates creak open to reveal the dusty, barefooted swordsmen. Behind them, an array of stony-faced citizens emerge from their houses to see the visitors, for these are the first men to enter the town in a month. There is a subdued atmosphere as the guards lead the caravan to the headman's house — he is older than he appeared at a distance and is sporting the longest beard Wellsted has ever seen. The *imam's* black eyes gleam like polished jet, embedded in a swathe of brown wrinkles.

The elder motions in greeting, his dry palms outstretched and his simple bright, white *dishdash* dazzling. The travellers do not know it, but this impression of spotlessness is illusory. The *imam* is a wily impresario who wrings the best from every situation. After the *simoom* he appropriated fifty camels and over a hundred goats that belonged to the dead. His men scavenged in a radius of forty miles and, with the old man's guidance, the little town worked away quietly and swelled its coffers while the survivors of the storm wandered half-blind and half-mad. The *imam* lives in a modest house and does not trumpet his money. He despises the *soultans* and emirs who keep vast *harims* of women and decorate their homes with unnecessary ornament. He is, in Western terms, a dangerous kind of monk, some kind of Jesus. Now he greets the visitors solemnly.

'We have only fish,' he says, humble in tone. 'But you are very welcome.'

Supplies in the town are running low, or so it would seem. The animals are herded to the south, well out of the way. The villagers fortify what they have by casting their nets a few hundred yards out on the water, for in time of plague no man will go further. The *imam* explains that the day's catch is shared between everyone but with supply lines cut off there is little else but some flatbread, milk and, he explains as if he is embarrassed, a few eggs, which he has reserved for the pregnant women and nursing mothers, sick children and the very old. As he tells of the impending want, he eyes the slaving party, costing every piece of their clothing and appraising the camels with an expert eye. He is adept at all forms of judgement.

'Please,' he says, 'water your animals. Our well, at least, is copiously supplied by Allah.'

The old man casts his eye suspiciously over the doctor's white skin and quickly appraises Wellsted's true provenance. His voice is concerned as he asks Kasim, 'My brother, have these infidels corrupted you?'

Wellsted smiles at the very thought of either he or Jessop having any effect whatsoever on the slavers and listens as Kasim humours the elder, hiding his mirth. 'We would surely rather die, father.'

'Come, join me,' the *imam* offers. 'Sit by my side.'

Before entering the house, Kasim presents the old man with two boughs of dates — all they have left. Inside, the room is austere, furnished only with thin, goatskin cushions on the mud floor, bare apart from a single, loosely-woven, faded rug. They talk over coffee served in plain, thick, earthenware cups, discussing the villages affected by the sickness. The house smells faintly of fried fish and frankincense, though there is no incense burner on view. Elsewhere there is the sound of movement — the creeping of women, most likely. The *imam* has three wives who inhabit the upper floor of the house. They own no more than two *burquahs* each and one pair of sandals.

'This sickness is sent from Allah,' the *imam* starts.

He believes it is a punishment for those who have strayed. Perhaps, a punishment too for those whose wives wear jewellery, or those men who indulge in vanity and tile the floors of their houses or allow themselves the luxury of opulent feasting. The truth is that the villages to the north are the first a traveller will come to off the dunes and are placed in the path of the prevailing tides. As a result, they are busier, more cosmopolitan and the home of merchants who wish to display their wealth rather than holy men who wish to conceal it. The wrath of Allah strikes, the *imam* swears, very quickly — a fever and delirium and then swift death in most cases. For those few who survive, the sickness leaves horrible marks on the skin. One woman who received Allah's grace and was cured, flung herself from a high wall into the ocean when she saw her beauty so destroyed. This lady was famed for her appearance and thought her husband would not desire her anymore. In another case, two nephews killed themselves at the news of the death of a favourite aunt who had been stranded in the town when they were delayed in accompanying her to the family home, some way to the north.

Ibn Mohammed and Kasim listen with seriousness to these tragic stories.

'Please, sir,' Jessop interrupts, 'where on the

body do the pustules grow?'

The *imam* hesitates then motions airily to show that they are all over. He does not want to speak directly to the *Nazarene*.

'Everywhere?'

He nods again.

'And they rise with a fever?'

Another nod.

Jessop falls silent but at the next opportunity he mouths, 'Smallpox,' to his friend.

'By Allah's bounty we are spared here,' the *imam* finishes.

Ibn Mohammed, of course, has no interest in the misery the sickness has brought nor, indeed, in diagnosing what it is. The polite formalities over, he gets down to business. He offers the camels in return for the *imam*'s permission to allay the embargo and allow them to take a boat and set sail for Muscat. Ten thoroughbred camels will feed the town for at least four days, and if the meat is rationed it will last twice that. The *imam* considers this carefully, as if such a small offering might tempt him. His air of humility has proved over the years a most effective trap. Indeed, he is so good at affecting the emotion that he quite believes it himself.

'It would be most kind, most kind indeed, for you to leave the creatures behind. And you are right, of course — they do not travel well on the water, and in any case you may find it difficult to house eight — or is it nine? — animals on a vessel.' He underestimates the number deliberately. He wants them to think of him as naïve and trusting — a bumbling *fakir* with a poor grasp of worldly matters.

Ibn Mohammed bows. The old man has him there. What was he intending to do — load the animals up and ship them south on what may be little more than a raft, for all he knows? There is no way to tell what kind of boat may be available.

'Of course, we are interested also in hiring a boat for which we are happy to pay very generously. In addition.'

The *imam* looks around as if he is surprised. 'I cannot allow any of my men to sail a boat south,' he says sadly.

The implication is that it is too dangerous. Who knows what they may carry by way of infection and, in such time of danger, all men want to stay close to their families. It is an indecent suggestion and one that Ibn Mohammed is quick to amend.

'Then we will buy a boat, if that is permissible?'

The *imam* pauses as if the idea has only just occurred to him. He has, in fact, three vessels at harbour that belong to men who are currently in the north with their families, trapped in the very town where the plague has hit. There has been no news of their welfare. Still, the old man is silently hoping and, indeed, expects that none of them will survive. The plague kills well over half of its victims, so he is likely right. Even if he is not, he can always hand over the money when the men get home — or at least part of it — and still play the honourable retainer who has generously looked after their business while they were away. He knows these Muscat wideboys will pay anything he asks. The *imam* thinks he will sell them an Indian-built *dhangi* that belongs to the youngest of the traders. The old man prefers Arab-built ships in any case and will be glad to have the vessel's distinctive outline out of his harbour. Anything foreign in origin causes his flesh to creep. The boat is almost a hundred tonnes and well beyond what is needed to transport ten men down the coast to the Omani capital.

However, when he finally speaks he says only, 'When I make any decision, I have to consider everyone who lives in this town, my brothers.'

The old man settles onto his goatskin cushion to let the slavers wait. This kind of negotiation can take a while; indeed, his experience is that he comes off better the longer he can spin things out. The *imam* sighs heavily, as if weighing up his civic duty is a serious and odious business.

'I think some mint tea,' he says casually to the scrawny slave who stands by the door.

He'll wait for it to brew before he tells them how much the boat will be. They might need something to refresh them, for the shock.

41

Zena cannot take her eyes off the horizon and sleeps only fitfully. She constantly expects the emir's men on horseback or the familiar figure of the slavers and their camels to overtake and unmask her. Her disguise is working, but these men do not know her and have no idea there is a runaway *habshi* in the region.

It transpires that she is travelling with a party of cousins. Against the sunlight, the men are so alike that Zena finds it impossible to tell one from the other. They joke constantly and laugh at practically anything. On the first evening, her heart pounds and her fingers become weak as they rag her around the campfire. But she realises quickly that these men are truly pleasant people with no scrap of harm in them — at least in the situation they believe themselves to be in. Still, she is terrified that her true identity might come to light in the scrum of horseplay after sunset and then she knows the situation would change. As a woman, this smiling family would steal her away as quickly as any on the Peninsula. On the first night, when she is pushed good-naturedly, she protects herself so fiercely that the men conclude that the black boy is slightly strange.

'Slaves can be that way,' she hears one whisper to another. 'Malik has lost his master and is travelling alone. Who knows what he has had to endure?'

This, for the *Bedu*, is enough to confirm the itinerant slave boy's oddity, and Zena is happy enough to let them believe that her lonely trip is the strangest thing about her.

She wishes she could see her reflection. It is a disconcerting feeling not to know what she looks like now she is arrayed in men's clothes. The first night she sneaks away from the sleeping figures. As quietly as she can, she rips a strip of material from the veil of the *burquah* she has packed away and tightly binds her breasts. She is lithe and long and her curves are not pronounced so can be hidden. Once the binding is in place, the outline of her body could be that of any teenage boy. Safe from that pitfall, she simply sets her mind to avoiding all the other clues to her real identity. She must not make a single slip of the tongue, she must control her expression (not easy always, for she is used to her face being obscured from show), she must pray with the cousins for her duty to Allah must be clear and she must be careful when she relieves herself. The *Bedu* pee crouching, but of necessity they lift the *jubbah* hem. It does not rise all the way, but still, if she is not careful, they might notice that she isn't what she is pretending to be.

I must be aware every moment, for the smallest thing might betray me, she thinks. Her nerves are wracked.

During the long six days of the journey (for the *Bedu*'s original estimate was, as ever, optimistic), she is always the last to sleep and the first to wake. She watches constantly for any sign that the men have noticed a detail out of place or for the familiar outline of a search party on the horizon. She ransacks her memory for every tiny movement, every word of the slaves in whose company she has travelled three long months and she emulates them on each count. She even shyly tells the men that she is in love with a servant in her master's caravan. A girl of thirteen she calls Jaminda, whom she has had to leave behind. For her feelings on this she need only think of Wellsted, and then such an air of sadness comes over her that no man would not believe that poor Malik has left behind his true love in order to fulfil his duty.

The *Bedu* already know about the sickness at the coast. They and their fellows trade with the harbour towns and news of what transpires there reaches them regularly. As a result, they direct their caravan further north than usual to avoid the affected areas. This way it is longer to Muscat, but Zena has no desire to risk infection. The trip is risky enough as it is.

★   ★   ★

When the sea comes into view, she feels like whooping for joy. 'I've made it here again,' she breathes very quietly.

She has loved the Giant Blue since she first set wide eyes upon it all those months ago, and in the repetition of the experience, her delight and excitement does not fade. She thinks of the view of the Straits of Hormuz from her Muscat master's rooms and decides that the sea here is quite as pretty. The deep blue waves are fringed with white foam and their movement is hypnotic while the scope of the horizon stimulates the imagination. Sunset, Zena ponders, is never as pretty as when the orange orb sinks into a distant line of shimmering water. After the arid sands, she feels invigorated at the sight of so much liquid, though in memory of the boy who ran down the beach in Abyssinia, she does not dismount and run towards the surf and instead hides her delight at the ocean's magic.

The party hikes along a dusty outcrop where the cliffs drop sheer onto pale rocks below. A way off there is a harbour and a scattering of houses. A flock of black-faced sheep with dirty brown coats is driven haphazardly down the slope leading to the village. The pearl divers have settlements like this all along this coast. The region is known for its exotic coral reefs that seamen consider deadly. It is a natural defence for the bounty of the pearls, which are well worth risking your life to acquire by diving through the strange fish and shards of rock and coral. Here, it is sworn, one man found a hoard of pearls — a cache of nature — eight baubles, each as big as a baby's fist and as pale and white as the cooked flesh of a fish. On such treasure a life's fortune is made and a whole family can secure its future. Grandfathers tell the tale to their youngest grandchildren; mothers whisper of it over the baby's basket, hoping their young ones will have healthy lungs to dive deeply; old men with parchment for skin reminisce that they have spent a lifetime in searching for the perfect luminescent orb and sigh with despair on their deathbeds that they never laid hands upon it. It is like a cult here. Though the people are poor, they believe that good fortune is only a dive away. Holy men in these parts compare a man's spirit to the sheen of a pearl, women string shell necklaces and wish they had somehow garnered the real thing and all words associated with the industry are lengthened into adjectives that mean good.

The cousins laugh as they make their way along the cliff path. As they come to the shoreline towards the settlement, the youngest, a boy of thirteen, jumps onto the sand and kicks in the spray while the others look on, their dark eyes identical. The camels groan, for they know sea water is not good to drink and they cannot imagine why the party is stopping when a few minutes more will have them at a well. The braying sound only makes the cousins laugh and quip about whether the men lead the beasts or vice versa. Amid this banter, three men from the village approach and tentatively ask the party's direction of travel. They will warn them off if there is any chance of infection. When they are satisfied that all is safe, they greet the cousins warmly and wave them through, breaking into a run in their wake.

At the water's edge, where the houses start, there are three short jetties where two fishing boats are unloading the day's catch onto the front. This comprises a motley-looking collection of strange sea creatures, for in this region the fish are varied in appearance. Today there is a small shark and a full basket, almost a shoal, of oval-bodied plaice with peachy skin.

'We are come to trade camels,' the *Bedu* announce. 'And we bring news. But we need your help too. This dark-skinned brother is called Malik. He seeks his master who headed this way only some weeks ago. Have you seen or heard of Ben Ibn Ahmed?'

Zena can hardly breathe. It has only just occurred to her that she does not know what she will do if the cousins succeed in finding the renegade son who is supposed to own her. Is he here? Will someone have heard of him? She keeps her silence.

The fishermen shake their heads. 'The pearl boats and the fishermen will return in a while,' an old man tells them. 'I have not heard of this son of the *Bedu*, Ibn Ahmed, but perhaps someone at sea might know him.'

They motion a little way up the hill where there is a flat marketplace with a rough stone well. If they cannot bring news of the man in question, at least they can offer refreshment for the camels and the shade of a palm tree under which coffee can be enjoyed.

Up the hill, Zena waters her camel with the others and takes a cup of mint tea. 'If my master is not here, I will head for Muscat. He has an uncle there,' she says casually.

No boats here go to Muscat, she is told. The Omani capital is over five hundred miles to the south, even as the crow flies. The journey is quickest by boat, of course, far more so than the overland route, back into the Empty Quarter and south. Still, the village is too small for regular passage to anywhere bar a couple of the local trading ports, which are visited weekly with the harvest of pearls, or at least they were until the plague broke out. Now, the villagers will hoard their treasures until the infection is declared over and it will be safe once again to travel to the trading posts.

The cousins chat to the fishermen, buying a few strips of *qat* leaves from a man who has a large supply, and then they settle, squatting in the shade to chew away what is left of the afternoon.

Zena walks barefoot to the end of the jetty. She stares across the rippling water as fish dart below the boards, attracted, she thinks, by the dapple of her shadow moving across the surface of the water. She has no idea how to handle a boat. Even the tiny fishing barks tied up here seem an incomprehensible jumble of compli-cated, knotted ropes and piles of canvas and nets. Further out, she can see a ship with a sail turning in the wind and zigzagging elegantly towards the harbour. There are string pots on the deck and three or four men working together, hanging over the side, using their weight to balance the vessel so that the sail is positioned correctly and carries them smoothly to their destination.

If I am going to Muscat across the water, she thinks, *I will need help.*

Her hand falls to the pouch she stole from Wellsted's belt. It is made of the balls of a sacrificed goat — exactly the right size for a handful of *talers*. Many of the men carry these pouches. Concealed under her *dishdash*, she has stuffed it with a strip of cloth so the coins do not make a sound as she moves. Still, offering to pay would be dangerous — no slave has his own money and the story she has constructed involves her abandoning the family and setting out to find her master without any preparation or direction from anyone else. She has no explanation for how she came by the money.

From under the palm trees the sound of hysterical laughter wafts down the hill. The cousins, their dispositions mellowed even further by the *qat*, cannot contain themselves. Zena does not want to join them. She sits on the boards and dangles her feet into the cool water as she considers what best to do next. She thinks of Wellsted every hour. Travelling with the cousins has been strange, if in nothing else, in the fact that her odd-looking, white-skinned master did not accompany her. If he survives the emir's wrath, it is to Muscat Wellsted will return and she wants to see him. In truth, she wants to touch him again. This burning feeling of being driven, of belonging with someone body and soul, is entirely new to her and, baffled by it, she does not dwell on the notion. She simply has to head south. Muscat is her only option. Zena knows Ibn Mohammed and Kasim have houses there. She knows that if she encounters the slavers a third time, she will not simply be taken and sold. She has run now and that holds its own punishment, a lifelong sentence hanging over her head. Still, Muscat it must be. Somehow. For finding Wellsted again is her way to freedom and forgiveness. And she is in love.

As the fishing boat sails towards her she can see the catch on the deck. The sailors grin and one waves. Zena shakes her head as if to clear it of the image of Wellsted's smile in the moonlight and his habit of making promises to comfort her. In his absence, she has noticed she makes the same promises to herself — that it will all be well, that she will be granted freedom and set up securely. Now she jumps up and helps dock the boat while a thin boy, a child still, secures the rope to the jetty with what looks like a complicated knot.

Salaam aleikhum. Aleikhum salaam.

Being male, she thinks, is so easy. There is brotherhood everywhere she goes. A smile, a bow and three kisses on the cheek.

★   ★   ★

That night, once the fires are dimmed and after a delicious dinner of chargrilled fish and rice, the fishermen offer to take Zena out with them the next day. On the water they often meet boats from further down the coast.

'Come with us and fish. You look as if you could dive,' a half-toothless ancient smiles revealing a scattering of what look like mismatched seed pearls protruding from his gums. 'Tomorrow we will sail out a little way only, but to the south. We will meet others on the fishing fields from villages on your way. Perhaps they will know of your master there.'

'I cannot swim,' Zena tells him, though in truth she is thinking that she cannot get wet. The thin material of the *dishdash* will easily become transparent and she is unsure how much of her true shape will show through. Still, it will be easier than making the journey overland. 'I can help though,' she offers. 'I would like to help.'

The old man nods and explains that by changing vessels bit by bit, she can leapfrog southwards, working for her keep. The boatmen are generally happy for an extra pair of hands. Then, as she makes her way south she can take passage to Muscat from one of the larger settlements — boats leave for the Omani capital with regularity from the ports of Shams or Ras Al Khaimah or Sharjah, or even from the island of Rafeen. As far as everyone knows, the plague has not reached any of those places. Still, it would be better if she could dive.

Zena shakes her head. 'I am afraid,' she admits, thinking of a lie that will be plausible. 'My father drowned and I am afraid.'

The men nod in understanding. She is good at this. The months on the sands have taught her every detail of how slaves express themselves, how to crouch in prayer, how to eat. The grudging mention now and then of long-lost family. The air of sadness.

The cousins are dozing now. They have said they will look after her camel. The family sleeps bunched together — a shamble of sleepy limbs. Zena decides that as she works her way south she will stop telling the story about her fictional master, for she might inadvertently find him. That night she sleeps propped up against the mud wall of a house and for the first time she does not wake before the rest of the group. The fishermen leave early, before the sun has risen.

'Come, come,' they say, shaking her by the shoulders.

Her eyes feel heavy, but she drags herself up into the darkness. Hurriedly, she pats the camel to say goodbye, but does not wake any of her travelling companions. As she makes for the shoreline with the others, the moon is still reflected on the choppy water. It is jumbled into uneven stripes of white light against the shifting, black surf.

'Here,' the boy who yesterday tied the rope gives her a folded net to carry aboard. 'Like this,' he shows her where to lay it and how to sit, squatting on the wooden deck until she is needed.

When they clear the harbour the men share bread, still warm. By the time the sun rises, a shimmering orb of honey light, the village is out of sight and all Zena can see are glittering waves in all directions. Aboard the *mashua*, the slaves were stowed the whole voyage. Now, she feels marooned by all the water and low set, with only a few strips of what looks like some kind of wooden frame and waxed hide bound by woven rope, she feels perilously close to the blue chasm that, though bright on the surface, is inky beneath it. Last night by the fire there were elaborate tales of sea snakes. The boy laughs at the expression on her face as she remembers this, and then they are both called to help cast the nets and it is easy to forget the grandeur of the vista or the menace of it, for, she discovers, a fisherman mostly looks down into the water no more than a few feet and does not raise his eyes more than a few feet above it.

'All life beneath the surface here,' the boy beams. 'Good fish. Good fish.' He culls a large one, thrashing about the deck. 'This one will take too long to die otherwise,' he explains. 'You now,' he offers.

Zena brandishes the cull, taking care not to get splashed too much. This feels like work. It feels good. Once the shoal is passed, the old man changes course.

'Now we will head along the coast,' he points, though the coast is out of sight. 'We will meet other boats. Perhaps one of them will take you.'

Zena coils a rope and lays it in a spiral on the deck. The boy nods in appreciation, for she has done well for a beginner.

'Never before?' he checks.

There are no other occupations here, so it is strange to him that there might be someone who was not born to a life that involves an understanding of ropes, knots, nets and culls. It seems to him that even a toddler should know about wind directions and the trim of a sail, for in his village many of the children can swim proficiently before they have fully mastered walking.

She shakes her head. 'Never. Inland always.'

'Good,' he nods as if she has told him a joke. 'Good.'

Together they sit near the prow to watch the horizon. The movement of the boat is fast compared to travelling across the sands. With nervous fingers Zena reaches into the spray and feels the passing of the water.

'No,' one of the older men stops her. 'Respect,' he says simply.

Zena apologises. Of course. The water must be treated with deference.

'Is it bottomless?' she whispers to the boy.

He giggles and shakes his head. 'Sand at the bottom. Like desert underneath,' he whispers back.

Zena decides not to think about it. She raises her eyes and feels the breeze on her skin. *I wonder*, she ponders, *what might come my way next?*

42

John Murray is settled in his plush, canary drawing room and is in the humour for a day of amusement. There is little else to do today, Friday or not, as it is November and it is raining too heavily to consider his habitual ride in Hyde Park or even an outing to the club. The park this afternoon will be nothing but a morass of mud, for the weather has been frightful for over a week now. Murray's desk is scattered with manuscripts though he has spent the last two days reading and discarding a very large pile of what has been sent to him. There seems to be rather a vogue at present for ladies writing poetry about the evils of slavery or worse — *novels*. Mr Murray, naturally, deplores the institution of slavery and is a hearty proponent of the emancipation, however, in all likelihood he deplores the poetry and novels of ladies who espouse The Cause far more. Even the measured script of their handwriting sets his teeth on edge, for manuscripts written by a man, in his opinion, have more character. After subjecting himself to over two dozen attempts at capturing the spirit of the age this morning alone, he'd be hard pressed to make a choice between banning slavery and banning well-meaning ladies with any pretensions to literary prowess.

The panes of the high sash windows rattle in the wind and Murray swears he can feel lightning in the air. The blanket of grey sky rolls very low over the whole city and Albemarle Street is so dim that people outside are carrying candle lamps in order to go about their business. He walks over to the fire and inserts the poker, stirring up the logs so that new flames lick and crackle in the elegantly fashioned grate. The prospect of clearing out more manuscripts is singularly unappealing. Surely the man will get here soon.

Directly on cue there is a brisk knock on the door and the butler enters.

'The upholsterer is here, sir,' he says the words as if they are a question.

Generally it is Mrs Murray who deals with such matters. Mr Murray has little interest in household affairs or even in his own attire. Mrs Murray, tiresome lady though her husband finds her, orders his waistcoats and has his shoes made, ensures that the trimmings of the drawing room cushions are renewed as need be and purchases household essentials from time to time at auction or, failing that, orders linen made, mattresses restuffed and curtains designed to her own specifications in a variety of workshops in the nearby streets.

'Ah!' Mr Murray says, clearly delighted. 'Yes. Good. Send the fellow in.'

Mr Wellsted drips when he enters. He has taken off his sodden greatcoat and his hat but his shoes are soaking and drops of water balance precariously at the base of his ears. His nose is a very bright pink. Murray nods and offers his hand. The man may be wet but he is clearly neither impoverished nor intimidated at being summoned to a grand house on Albemarle Street on short notice. The cane he uses to help him walk is of good quality and plain design. Murray has arranged this meeting to test the lie of the land — to find out as much about James Raymond Wellsted as he can. After all, the chap is out of contact, it would seem, and Murray might as well find out what he can. He intends also to enjoy himself doing so. He sizes up Wellsted Snr in a flash. The man is not an embarrassment. It is a promising start.

'There is some kind of an emergency, Mr Murray?' Wellsted enquires as he shakes the publisher's hand.

The question is the only dry thing about him.

'Ah. Well. Yes. There is the matter of this chaise,' Murray indicates the piece he means. It is a dalliance, nothing more. 'It requires to be recovered. In some material suitable to the room. Yellow, you see.'

James Wellsted Senior casts an eye over the piece. This constitutes, even for a man who takes his business very seriously, not much in the way of an emergency. The chair is not worn at all, not even at the edges.

'I see,' he says, his eyes are still and they do not betray his annoyance at being called out for a job worth no more than a shilling or two in profit on a day such as this. 'I can have some materials sent over for you to choose from and my man can pick up the chaise later today, if that will suit you.'

'Oh, yes. Materials. Well, no need. I think I can

trust your taste. The Marquis of Malvern tells me you have a good eye, sir.'

Wellsted does not blush at the compliment. 'Certainly. I shall see to it,' he nods and lingers only a moment before he makes a little bow and turns to take his leave.

This is not going the way Murray had expected. For no reason, he had thought the matter of real interest might simply arise. Now he forces the point before Mr Wellsted can leave the room.

'I wonder, sir,' Murray cuts in, 'you have such an unusual name. I wonder if you might . . . No, it is foolish.'

He decided when he summoned the tradesman that he would not tell the man he knows exactly his connection to his point of genuine interest. He had intended this as a game, for Murray is a gaming man. But now he is here it is proving a difficult business for the fellow is not in the least conversational.

James Wellsted Snr turns. 'From Kent, sir,' he says, to oblige the gentleman. Not all Wellsted's customers want to chat, but he is equal to the task if it is required. 'I'm from Kent. Not an uncommon name in those parts, Wellsted, you see. Though my family have resided in London for some years now.'

He stares at the piles of papers stacked all over Murray's desk. He came as soon as he was summoned on account of the address of his new client, rather than the man's name. Being illiterate, he is not aware that the fellow with whom he is talking is the nation's greatest publisher and he wonders if the gentleman is so untidy in all his business as he appears to be with his written matter. He has clearly been scribbling rather a lot if the heaped up mounds of papers are anything to judge by.

'Ah, Kent. But that is not what I mean. I'm afraid . . . ' Murray smiles. 'Thing is,' he comes clean, 'I wondered if you might be related to a Lieutenant Wellsted. James Wellsted. Of the Indian Navy?'

Wellsted Snr looks perplexed. James has been gone from London since he was a nipper — he has never come up in conversation since, or at least not outside the family.

'That gentleman is my son,' he says. 'Do you know of him, sir? We have had no news for several months now.'

'I do,' Murray beams. 'I do know of him, Mr Wellsted. Please, please won't you sit with me? You are cold, are you not? I can have someone bring tea perhaps or better still some scalded brandy. Would you like some brandy, Mr Wellsted? Or whisky, perhaps? It is a weakness of mine. I have a Scottish grandfather and my dear, late father considered himself Scottish, despite the fact that he was born here in this house, a great many miles too far to the south to justify his claims. A toddy, sir?'

The upholsterer nods his greying head. He sits warily on a chair next to the fire while Murray rings the bell and makes arrangements. It feels eerily as if he is being *received* in a house on Albemarle Street. The sensation is extraordinary.

'The thing is,' Murray says, 'that your son has

sent me a rather interesting account of his travels. I intend to publish it.'

'Publish?' Wellsted mouths.

'Why yes,' Murray continues. 'Fascinating account, you see. Of Socotra — a small island in the Indian Ocean.'

'In a book?'

Murray ignores the question. 'He is very talented your son, Mr Wellsted. Oh, I did hope there was a connection. And you see, when we can find your boy — well, I understand he is to be recalled for a while — the Geographical Society want him and there have been some enquiries from Members of the House that ministers are hoping he can help settle.'

'The house?' Wellsted repeats.

'Yes, sir. His Majesty's Parliament. The Palace of Westminster.'

The butler enters with a tray and places a fragrant toddy at Mr Wellsted's side and then serves one to Murray. He is accustomed to Mr Murray entertaining unusual visitors from time to time, but the master has never taken sustenance with a tradesman before. He wryly wonders if he will shortly be serving dinner to Ned Spencer who delivers the household fish twice a week or perhaps ordering a carriage for Molly Rankin, the wife of the chimney sweep. Mr Wellsted, however, is far too shocked to notice the man's offhand manner and for Murray, well, it only adds to his amusement.

'James is coming home — and to all that?'

'I hope so, sir. You have a very fine boy there.'

Wellsted's hands are shaking so violently that

he does not want to attempt to lift his glass, however, he is sorely in need of a drink.

'Well I never,' he says, staring longingly at the toddy, which is letting off a small cloud of steam. He breathes deeply. 'Well I never. The boy did it! He did it! Think of that!'

'Did what, sir?' Murray enquires.

Wellsted steels himself. He is not sure what to say, but he'll be damned now if James isn't eligible for at least a lord's daughter if not something slightly grander. There need be no tenuous connections for a man who will give evidence in Parliament and speak at the Geographical Society. He can surely take his pick of almost anyone.

'He did his duty,' the upholsterer grins. 'The boy did his duty!'

Murray continues, 'Well, certainly he did. They are having difficulty finding him, of course. These men of action — common problem. The high command in Bombay say he's gone into the interior. The desert. He has been given permission by the sultan — the first of our men ever to get it. It's quite an honour. I do hope he is notating everything. The admiralty will put him up when he comes home, of course. I believe there is a senior officer who has a house on the Edgware Road. You'll be glad to see the boy, I expect.'

Wellsted nods. Yes, the house on Molyneux Street is nowhere near grand enough now. James must stay elsewhere and build his reputation when he returns to London. The old man finally manages to lift the toddy to his lips.

'Cheers, sir,' he says, taking a satisfying gulp. 'This is wonderful news. Wonderful.'

'Yes,' Murray agrees. 'Well, I want to hear more about your son, Mr Wellsted. I want to know all about him. He is, you see, a veritable rising star.'

Wellsted smacks his lips. 'Always had promise. I have to say. The boy always had promise.'

It's the first time in his life, he realises, that he feels simply, utterly proud. This news is beyond all expectation. Old Thomas was right about the child. Fancy that. Wellsted can hardly stop smiling. It's been his life's work, but finally they are there. The younger children will ride on the coat-tails of this success and everyone will go up a step or two. It is a wonderful feeling. The boy has done it!

'Thank you, sir,' he mouths. 'Thank you for this welcome news.'

Murray can't help but feel a glow seeing the old man so delighted. 'Well now,' he says, 'I expect it has been a while since you have seen your son, so I am glad you mentioned that he does write from time to time. You see, I am very much looking forward to meeting James for myself, but until then, will you brief me?'

Mr Wellsted nods. 'Anything, sir. Anything you'd like to know.'

⋆ ⋆ ⋆

Later, back at his desk, Murray clears a space. It has been a most entertaining afternoon. He pens a quick note to George, addressing it to the

394

Geographical Society and also one to William Thornton Astell, who has taken up the matter in the Commons now that Townsend is dead. If Mr Wellsted Snr is anything to judge by, the family will not embarrass anyone. He rather liked the fellow, in fact. He seemed to have a sense of what was fitting. By all accounts, the boy has been dutiful in writing home. There has been no blinding flash of insight into the lieutenant's character but nothing shocking that will put paid to their plans for him either. Murray rings for service and dispatches the letters to be delivered.

'Send a boy,' he instructs, for he does not trust the postal service in this weather.

Then, lastly, he picks up his quill once more and draws a fresh sheet of paper.

Dear Lieutenant Wellsted,
I am writing once more in the hope this finds you well and that your excursions into the interior of Araby have proved fruitful. In anticipation that this has been the case, and given that we will be publishing your account of Socotra shortly, I hope you might have further tales to tell, in the same vein, about your most recent travels. There is a great appetite for travelogues as you know, particularly those that contain the kind of detail that an officer such as yourself, with surveying experience can provide. As you will no doubt be aware by the time you receive this missive, you are to be recalled to London to testify before the

House of Commons committee. I under-
stand also that the Geographical Society has
been in touch with you about taking part in
its activities. I hope, sir, that the voyage
homewards might provide an opportunity
for you to write up the notes of your most
recent travels, which I understand have
taken you into the interior of the Arabian
desert with native guides. Our readers, I am
sure, will find this fascinating and the
sooner you can provide me with something
for them, the better. I am considering the
title Journey to the City of the Caliphs.
Yours, etc.,
John Murray III

Murray folds and seals the paper carefully. He very much enjoyed the balance in Wellsted's Socotra piece between the scientific and geographical detail and his interest in local customs. The boy clearly keeps his eyes open and does not judge the natives too harshly. It's a common problem with Murray's correspondents — that they make all kinds of horrid assumptions about the indigenous population that later prove unfounded. Often though there is nothing else to go on but the account he is sent. This Wellsted fellow has a knack and Murray feels inspired by his visit to Socotra. What the fellow will make of the desert, well, he can only hope. Murray wonders what they eat in the interior of the Arabian Peninsula. Goat, he decides. Not terribly appetising, but then the reading public loves that kind of thing — the more grisly the feast the better. Eyeballs and testicles, deep-fried. Tonight, as he understands it, his wife has organised some kind of game for dinner. A brace of partridge that were sent as a present from the estate of the Earl of Salisbury. The earl, it transpires, has written a book, which he will no doubt be asked to read and subsequently publish. Still, partridge is one of Murray's favourite dishes, and he hopes Cook has had the foresight to make a Madeira gravy. He dusts the folded envelope and rings the bell.

'This one,' he says, 'can go tomorrow morning. To the Bombay Marine.'

'Yes, sir,' the butler says, grateful that the master appears to have ceased his eccentric behaviour for the time being. 'There is a fellow downstairs to pick up the chaise. Shall I send him up?'

Murray looks down into the street. There is a cart and horse parked at the doorway. The light is fading and the street lamps are being lit.

'The chaise?' Murray repeats absentmindedly. 'Oh no. Send him away. It was ruse, nothing more. The thing doesn't need doing at all.'

43

As soon as they take to the water, the balance of everything changes. While Ibn Mohammed and Kasim are born to the desert, both men have always employed crews for their ships and know little about how to navigate on the water. Ibn Mohammed normally sleeps the entire journey, dozing off in one port and rising only for meals until he reaches another. So it is Wellsted and even Jessop, with his meagre frame, who come into their own when the *imam* finally agrees an extortionate price on the *dhangi*, the only ship, it seems, he is at liberty to sell them. Kasim congratulates himself that when they fled the emir's camp he prevented Ibn Mohammed from killing the only able-bodied man on board who knows how to get them back to Muscat inside of a week.

At the dock, skilfully divested of the camels and most of their money, they start their journey with the tide. Nervous of the reefs around the shoreline, for which the area is notorious, Wellsted and Jessop decide to head further out to sea than is normal in a native vessel and navigate not by the coastline but by the stars. A course south is easy enough to follow, and at a steady pace and with good winds they reckon the journey will take a mere five days.

Jessop sits at the prow, like a figurehead, and breathes in the sea air.

'I am holding you to the goose and the pudding,' he tells Wellsted. 'If we have to scour Muscat, I insist upon it.'

'I could manage a goose,' Wellsted replies.

The *imam's* hospitality over a day and a night has stretched only as far as a broiled fish and a little rice. On board they have some baked biscuits, salted whitebait, a few fresh oranges and three unappetising barrels of souring water. Still, they are on their way.

★   ★   ★

The first to succumb is Tariq, one of the servants. On the morning of the second day at sea, his legs give way under him and with a cry of agony, as if he has been stabbed, he keels over, knocking the brewing coffee from its stand and spreading the grounds across the thick boards of the deck. When the doctor pulls back the man's *jubbah* to examine him, the first scattering of pustules are evident and a wail goes up among the others, an incitement for help from Allah. In a blind panic, Hamza jumps off the side of the *dhangi* and has to be fished out of the water. As he cowers, soaking, on the deck, Kasim strikes him hard.

'We are too far from shore to swim back,' he sneers. 'Be a man.'

The distance from shore, both naval men know, is irrelevant now. Even if they can get there, no port will take them with a contagion on board.

'We will all die,' Hamza wails.

And, as if to prove himself right, it is he and Jasouf who are next to succumb. A fierce delirium takes them during the course of the afternoon and they are quickly soaked in sweat and a mixture of other bodily fluids upon which Wellsted does not care to dwell.

'It's the fever that will kill them. A body cannot stand this heat,' Jessop says in a matter-of-fact voice as he helps to sluice the vomit and piss from the deck. 'It will be quick at least, unless the fever breaks.'

He swabs the men with sea water and tries to calm the frantic calls as they twitch and spasm. Smallpox can be agonising and, though the men are seldom conscious, their cries of pain are terrible to listen to. In his fever, Hamza recites long portions of the *Quran* but Tariq shouts, begging for death in his more lucid moments when, between the pains, he slips in and out of delirium. At length he sets up a haunting whine that prevents the other men from sleeping when darkness falls.

Jessop finds he is acutely aware now of how difficult it is for a man's dying to take a long time. He has always been kind to the sick and it is his custom to treat a cabin boy and an admiral exactly alike. However, in the past when the sick begged to die, he considered it a weakness in their character. Now he has suffered himself he has developed a sensitivity — a progression in his understanding. It isn't weakness to give up. It can happen to anyone, he realises, for it is impossible to fight all the time and pain, sickness and degradation can be overwhelming for even the bravest of men.

The devout one, Hamza, is the first to die. As the sun rises and the healthy roll out their prayer mats, they tip his body overboard. While the servants who still can, prostrate themselves in sincere mortification, Kasim appears at the doctor's side and motions him to the prow. Ibn Mohammed, who at first Kasim thought was simply sleeping, has in fact been sick half the night.

'I brought him coffee,' Kasim says, 'and then I saw. You must tell me what to do.'

After a brief inspection, the doctor directs a swab of cold sea water, the same as the others. Jessop does not believe in bleeding a sick man. It is, he always says, like taking ammunition from the arsenal when the war is in full swing. His views are revolutionary, but they are based on his observations. He only bleeds for prevention, not cure.

'There is no more we can do but try to break the fever,' he insists.

Kasim's face hardens. 'How many men will survive this?' he whispers.

Jessop shrugs. 'Half will die. At least. Contained as we are at sea, there may be more.'

'He is strong,' Kasim points out.

The doctor lays his hand on Kasim's shoulder. 'That will help,' he nods.

★ ★ ★

Jasouf dies after midday, a trickle of blood from his nose staining the top of his *jubbah* as he

401

expires without uttering a cry the entire illness. As they heave him over the side, Wellsted speaks to the doctor in English so the Arabs cannot understand.

'They will all get it, won't they?'

Jessop nods curtly. 'Most likely. Or almost all.'

'And we?'

'Are immunised. There is still a slight risk, but it is a small one.'

There is a moment's silence. Wellsted cannot bring himself to form the question, but in the event he does not need to. The doctor understands.

'I must apply, for the benefit of the sick, all measures that are required, old man,' Jessop says cheerfully, quoting his hypocratic oath. 'I cannot fly and leave these men in need of medical help.'

'I only wondered,' Wellsted says. 'We have come this far to save you, and to put yourself at risk now . . . '

'I am at less risk than any of them. They'd have killed us, wouldn't they? If it were the other way round.'

Wellsted looks at Kasim bent over Ibn Mohammed at the prow.

'Possibly,' he says. 'But they have saved my life a hundred times. They stood by me on the sands, whatever else. I'd be dead without them.'

'Of course,' Jessop understands.

★   ★   ★

The third day of the sickness is grim. The men who have not succumbed pray almost constantly,

402

their mats rolled out on deck. *Allah Akhbar.*
Allah Akhbar. All the while, Jessop and
Wellsted continue to swab and move the sick to
keep them in the shade of the huge sail. At the
prow Kasim will not let anyone tend Ibn
Mohammed but himself. He whispers in his
patient's ear, though the slaver is comatose.
Wellsted cannot hear what Kasim is saying, but
by nightfall Ibn Mohammed is the only sick
man left alive and Tariq's body has been
consigned to the deep. The doctor examines
him once more. The pustules are everywhere
and his body dotted with yellow boils as he
twists in pain and fever.

'We were boys together,' Kasim whispers to
Wellsted.

'In Muscat?'

'Yes. We learnt to ride together. We learnt to
hunt. When my father died, his father took me
in.'

★   ★   ★

Long after midnight, Wellsted wakes, propped
up against the mast. He thinks, momentarily, of
Zena and hopes that she is safe. Perhaps it
would be best if she did not go eastwards
after all. He checks on Jessop who is asleep
beside him. Then the lieutenant rises and goes
to the barrel for some water. He takes a sip —
for he must take as little as he can to conserve
the supply, restocking will be tricky now. As he
turns he sees Kasim bent low over Ibn
Mohammed's body. In the dark shadow, the

403

slaver heaves a sob. The men are talking.

'Death is not meant to be like this. A man is supposed to invoke Allah. There is supposed to be some dignity,' Kasim sniffs.

'It is what it is.' Ibn Mohammed is pragmatic as ever. 'Allah has done nothing for me. Never. You are my brother,' he gasps. 'You will be my brother, always.'

Kasim kisses Ibn Mohammed's pus-speckled cheeks. Wellsted backs away. This is too private. A minute later there is a heart-rending sob and he knows that Ibn Mohammed is gone. He lets Kasim cry in peace a while and when he has composed himself, Wellsted pretends to have just woken.

'I am so sorry,' he says, bending to check the corpse.

In the moonlight Ibn Mohammed is already pale. Kasim puts his hand to the knife at his waist. 'I'll kill you if you try to fling him over,' he swears.

Wellsted moves away. 'It is not safe . . . Doesn't the *Quran* stipulate an early burial?'

'He will be buried in Muscat, facing *qibla*,' Kasim growls.

★   ★   ★

In the morning, Kasim allows them to set the men to basting the body with saltwater, which the doctor says is better than nothing in stalling the inevitable decay. Kasim swaddles Ibn Mohammed's corpse in a black shroud made of his *jubbah* so that they do not have to look at his

404

face, and then he stows the body at the far end of the vessel, respectfully facing *qibla*, or as near as he can reckon it on a moving vessel. He mutters the words of a prayer and draws his *khandjar* to keep watch.

'You're consigning us all to further danger by keeping him here,' the doctor tries to reason, but in his grief the slaver will not listen.

'I'll not have him thrown overboard like a filthy slave,' he swears. 'He will be buried in the ground, properly. I'll kill you if you try to move him.'

★ ★ ★

Jessop retreats to sip a coffee and eat a biscuit as if he has been served it at his club. Sudar has a slight temperature but no pustules. He is refusing any help, believing that if he succumbs to care he will get sicker. The doctor tries to rest. For a while there will be no one else to nurse, but the danger is not over. Smallpox can incubate for a week or more.

'We don't want any more casualties — it's recoveries I'm looking for. I'm not much of a doctor if none of them makes it, am I?' he says.

But there is nothing for it but to wait the sickness out. The officers check the supplies. There is some food left but not nearly enough water.

'We should be quarantined at least seven days with no further casualties before we make port,' Jessop directs.

'We'll have died of thirst by then,' Wellsted

says. 'We have to dock.'

'Give it a day,' Jessop replies. 'We have enough water to keep going another day. If no one else gets sick we'll have to chance it.'

44

Ormsby is on watch on the deck of the *Psyche*. Duty through the night is the closest it is possible to get to being entirely alone on board, and with the darkness comes cooler air. In climes such as these, any breeze at all is what the midshipman's illustrious grandfather would call a heavenly blessing. In Ormsby's experience, though, the Persian Gulf is never anything less than balmy even on the darkest November night, and on the evenings there is a storm the weather remains distinctly tropical in nature even if the rain lashes onto the deck and winds howl. Tonight, though, the water is as still as the pond in St James's upon which he used to sail his toy schooner.

He draws his silver flask from his pocket and takes a swig. In Bombay he resupplied his own stores and he now has a stash of whisky among his things. These days the midshipman finds India Pale Ale on the weak side and standard-issue rum far too sweet. His taste runs to spirits and of them all whisky is proving his favourite. It seems to travel best. Last month he turned twelve. His family allowance was increased and in celebration he bought a small cask of Strathspey. He is already almost halfway through it.

The *Psyche*, he reflects, is a far more pleasant posting than the *Palinurus*. It has freed him from

Captain Haines. Though all ships work to the same strict routine, the nature of the captain affects morale. The *Psyche* is under the command of First Lieutenant Denton, who is altogether a far more cheerful fellow to work under. Denton runs a tight ship but he is both fair minded and good humoured. He has become a mentor to the midshipman. Ormsby is sure that the lieutenant will certainly be promoted soon — Captain Denton sounds very fine — and when that happens there will be a shifting throughout the service, for when a lieutenant rises so must a midshipman or two. After his actions in capturing the French schooner under Haines, Ormsby knows he is well placed, if somewhat young, for promotion and he is quietly hopeful.

The midshipman squints into the darkness. On the horizon he sees what looks like a fallen star. He reaches for the brass ocular lens and draws it to his eye. The light is white, too low to the swell to belong to a European ship, but unlikely to belong to a native vessel either, for the Arabs generally dock at night. Still, he can certainly make out movement. It is a small boat under sail, that's for sure. Suddenly, the light is extinguished. Ormsby gasps.

Better safe than sorry, he shrugs, and turns to ring the bell that will rouse the crew to action. Putting out your lights, in the midshipman's admittedly limited experience, is rarely an honourable course though, not to be outdone, and for her own protection, the *Psyche*'s own lamps, fore and aft, are doused immediately.

Denton is roused and sleepily makes for the bridge, pulling on his jacket as he goes. He orders silence, and the crew waits on deck, stock-still and listening for any sound that might prove a clue to the identity of the mystery ship. There is nothing — only the creak of the *Psyche*'s timbers as the vessel holds its position on the swell.

'You are sure it was in that direction?' Denton whispers.

Ormsby nods. 'Yes, sir,' he says.

He might be drunk but he's found that as long as he's conscious he can assess degree to within a point and can calculate without the aid of any instruments some of the easier mathematical equations required to navigate a vessel. If anything, a few shots of whisky make him sharper. This natural intelligence will mask Ormsby's alcoholism for the whole of his life and the devil-may-care attitude that goes alongside the administration of a dram every waking hour will see him gain a reputation as a spirited fighter with the kind of pluck that the Indian Navy is happy to reward in its officers. In less than ten years he'll be a captain. Denton trusts him already.

'Take a boat and half a dozen men. Arm everyone, Ormsby, but don't fire if you don't have to. Just investigate what the hell it is. We're too far out for it to be simply moored for the night. The Arabs don't do that on trading vessels and certainly not on fishing boats. Perhaps it's the French on reconnaissance. Try and hear what language they're speaking. Be as quiet as you can and, for God's sake, be careful.'

Ormsby moves into action immediately. He tags the men he wants with him as he passes along the deck, and a rowing boat is lowered silently onto the water.

'Don't show yourself unless you are in trouble. Light a lamp if you want us to come for you,' Denton promises. 'Light two and raise them if you want us to open fire.' With that, he salutes and takes his place at the helm to keep watch.

Ormsby returns the salute and drops over the side. This is just the kind of adventure a midshipman hopes for past midnight. The prospect of rowing into the blackness is thrilling and if they can capture another French vessel he will have a double dose of prize money coming his way. The men lower their oars into the water and set off.

As the weather goes, it's perfect tonight — it is extremely still and there is only a light swell so it is easy for the men to row, and so silent a whisper will carry orders easily. Ormsby steers in the direction he last saw the light and watches keenly for a shadow in the shape of a ship. His eyes are accustomed to picking out vessels in the darkness as much as he is adept at spotting the shoreline through heavy cloud. When he judges himself halfway across, there comes the sound of a whistle. It's an eerie call, but Ormsby laughs out loud. It is an English boatswain's whistle, directly ahead. A plain up-and-down note he's heard a hundred times. *Away boats! Away boats!* He stops the men rowing. It's a risk, but the sound of the whistle emboldens him. The French calls are different and the sound of the whistle is such a bizarre attempt at communication that who else can it be but one of his own?

'Ahoy there! Are you a naval vessel?' he calls blindly.

Silence.

'Are you one of His Majesty's ships?' Ormsby belts.

'Ormsby? Is that you?' comes back the cry from a couple of hundred yards.

The voice is familiar and authoritative, but the midshipman can't place it.

'It's the only bloody call I can whistle without, well, a whistle. Stay off. That's what I mean. Stay off.'

'Who is there? Identify yourself!' The oars splash in the water.

'Don't come too close, man! Stop! For God's sake. How many men have you?'

'Six, sir.'

'To which ship are you attached?'

'The *Psyche*, sir. Under Lieutenant Denton.'

'Well get back to the *Psyche*, Ormsby, and tell Denton to pass us by. We are under quarantine.'

'But,' Ormsby asks as the question pops into his head, 'why didn't you just raise the flag?'

There is a short bark of laughter.

'That, son, is a long story. We have no flags. We're on a native vessel. And we didn't know who you were, did we?'

'Permission to come aboard?'

'Not unless you want a dose of smallpox. Can you be sure everyone on the *Psyche* is immune?'

In the little rowing boat, the able seamen

squirm on the planks and the vessel rocks unsteadily in the water. Seamen are superstitious about even small things and this is a real and sizeable threat. About half of them have been immunised, of course, but far less than that number really believe the small scratch they received on their arm is any real protection. The occasional case of an immunised man who goes on to die in agony fuels rumours below decks, were any fuel required to have the men well and truly terrified. What is certain is that, when contained on a ship, diseases spread as quickly as fire through dry gorse. Ormsby casts the men a harsh look far beyond his years. He has a natural authority and the punishment for not heeding even a junior officer is severe. The men settle immediately.

'Total immunisation is unlikely, sir. We'll hold off. Can we carry any messages for you?'

'Only pray for us. We have four native allies dead already. When you get back to Bombay tell them Wellsted and Jessop are alive. We will make for Muscat when it's safe — with all who survive.'

Ormsby baulks. In the mess and at the captain's table, the officers have toasted Wellsted and drunk to the survival of Jessop and Jones several times, without once expecting to see any of them ever again. But it's the lieutenant's voice — he remembers now.

'You did it, sir! You made it, Wellsted!'

Another laugh.

'I haven't done it yet, Ormsby. And Jones died before we left the desert. You can tell them that in Bombay too. We should be fine, though, for both Jessop and I have had our immunisation and the doctor is recovering after his ordeal. But we cannot leave these men to their fate, and of course, we may still carry the infection on board if we were to jump ship to you. We will make for Muscat when it is safe — it is our nearest port for rendezvous.'

Aboard the *dhangi*, Wellsted meets Jessop's eyes in the darkness and the doctor nods. They are agreed they have to stay. In the darkness, they weren't sure if the approaching vessel was French or English. Now they are certain it is friendly, turning down passage is a different matter to the academic exercise of what they might or might not do if the opportunity arises. The *Psyche* will pick them up if they insist, of course, but there is no chance that the Arabs will be permitted on board, for that is far too risky and of no real value to His Majesty's naval concerns.

'Are you absolutely sure you want to stay?' Wellsted checks with the doctor as the sound of Ormsby's rowing boat rocks on the swell a hundred yards ahead. 'This is a way out, if you choose to take it.'

There is a pause — a mere beat. Kasim is watching from the shadows — he cannot understand a word the men say although that makes no difference to the doctor's decision.

'Yes, I'm sure.' Jessop does not flinch. 'Completely. My duty is to stay and help these men.'

The lieutenant takes a deep breath and raises

413

his voice again. 'Get back to your vessel, Ormsby! Before we change our minds! And send us some water. We need water. We cannot dock to resupply.'

On board the *Psyche*, Denton makes the decision that they must move on. He trusts both Wellsted's judgement and that of the doctor for he knows them both well. Though four years older, he was a midshipman with Wellsted when he first arrived in Bombay a pale, skinny slip of a boy. Also, he knows the doctor's family in Lancashire. He is particularly fond of Jessop's pretty sister, Sarah. She holds a tune beautifully and plays rummy like a rogue and for stakes so high that many a duchess would lose her *sang-froid* at the same table. Leaving these men in a small ship, while an infection rages is no clear-cut decision for him. Denton is a good man and he maintains a steady conscience about whatever he does. Besides, on his next home leave he will have to face Sarah, and he knows she is no shrinking violet.

'Dear heavens,' he murmurs under his breath as he scoops Ormsby and his men back on board.

As Ormsby explains the words that were lost at a distance, the lieutenant's eyes dart. Sir Charles Malcolm, he knows, would have no truck with a hypocratic oath sworn to protect desert Arabs or the loyalty Wellsted feels he owes to men the Indian Navy has bought and paid for. The Bombay Marine needs its officers and doctors to tend to its own business. He must be careful when he mentions this in dispatches and

414

be sure to make the men's decision appear solely on medical grounds. But he will honour the decision nonetheless.

'God save you!' he shouts into the blackness, and he orders the rowing boat anchored and abandoned, loaded with a bottle of rum, two barrels of water, some ship's biscuits and a side of salted beef. On top they set a lighted lamp so the men can find the supplies easily. And then the *Psyche* disappears smoothly into the night.

★   ★   ★

The food and water are very welcome. Jessop has only one sick man in his care now. Hassan, that evening, cried out and fell. He has not moved or made a sound since, but he is still breathing. Meanwhile, Ibn Mohammed's corpse, still swathed in black, is starting to smell, the pustules on the skin have whitened and are firm as stone and when his *jubbah* is raised to douse the skin in sea water, the slaver's lips are black.

Kasim has not told the white men that he can feel the illness starting inside him. There is a dull itch in his groin and on his chest and the beginning of a nagging pain in his belly. He is sure he'll survive. As the *Psyche* relights its lamps and disappears northwards, his skin is alight and his limbs are jumpy. When the ship has disappeared completely and they bring the supplies on board, the doctor notices that Kasim finds it impossible to focus either his mind or his eyes. Allah is not always kind, but Kasim hopes he is wise. Such trials make a man question everything. He retreats aft and lays down close to Ibn Mohammed's body, hoping for sleep, but instead he finds he has tears rolling down his face. He is glad that it is a dark night and no one can see.

'Here,' says Wellsted, creeping up the deck and passing a freshly filled goatskin of water to the slaver.

Kasim takes it from his hand without looking. He does not want the white man to see that his cheeks are wet. '*Shukran*,' he says.

'You know what to do in the desert. I know what to do at sea,' Wellsted smiles.

Kasim drinks.

'The doctor says you are unwell, my friend.'

Kasim sighs. 'I will not die,' he says simply. 'I will not die.' Someone has to survive it.

'We will tend you as best we can.'

Kasim holds the white man's gaze. 'Look after Ibn Mohammed and me, my friend,' he says. 'If I go with him, we must be buried. Take our bodies to Muscat. Promise me that.'

'You can trust me,' Wellsted assures him. He means it.

Sailing south provokes mixed feelings in the lieutenant. It seems to Wellsted that his blood now runs with strong coffee and his heart beats to a *doumbek* drum. The arid desert has brought him to life. He wonders where Zena is. He wills her to be all right. A new convert to the mysteries of love, it is as if this voyage is only a strange interlude. As it happens it has turned out better that she is not with him. Here she would stand a deadly chance of catching the sickness.

He will find her again, though, he is sure of it. *She is safe, somewhere,* he tells himself.

★ ★ ★

By dawn Kasim is delirious. Jessop swabs him with sea water to try to cool the skin. As they sail slowly south, the two remaining *Bedu* who have dodged the infection continue to pray more times a day than even Allah requires. They lay out their carpets on the deck and the sound of their voices provides a background mumble from the moment the sun rises until it sets. The doctor directs them to swab the deck while he tends Kasim. Wellsted positions the sails to catch the best of the wind.

'Well, we've done what we can and we can do no more.' Jessop washes his hands in a bucket of sea water as the sun sets. Wellsted settles down to eat salted meat and the last of the oranges with him.

'If we haven't got sick we won't get it now and if we're lucky neither will they,' Jessop nods at the remaining men, still making their abeisances on the deck in the dark.

This is particularly good news as the ship will be the devil's own job to sail if there are only the two white men left alive. The servants alternately sing their prayers and mumble them, jerking like Sufi mystics, who in the normal course of events they would despise on principle. The doctor takes a mouthful of meat and chews appreciatively while he gives his prognosis.

'We'll know tonight about Kasim. None of

417

them have lasted the delirium any longer. Any idea how far we are off Muscat?'

Wellsted shrugs. In the confusion he has lost his bearings, but he knows he can navigate easily — he must simply follow the coastline and head south. The skies are clear and it is easy to place themselves by the stars. The *dhangi*'s not a bad craft for its tonnage. For a naval officer, sailing her is a simple enough job. It would be pleasant were it not for the dead.

'Three days?' he guesses in Bedouin fashion, gesturing to make it clear that he is postulating.

'A good journey,' Jessop gestures back, his hand on his heart, for that is what the *Bedu* would do. 'But you better fetch the instruments from your saddlebags,' he says. 'We should check the usual way. Haines would insist.'

45

The small island of Rafeen is known as the Rose because its sandy petals of land radiate into the water in the shape of that flower. The island is connected to the mainland to the east of Manama by three causeways. This makes it easy to defend in what is often a very troubled region and the Al Khalifa family are wise to choose it as their capital and the base for all their trading operations. It has been their stronghold for twenty-five years, and as a result, the family's hold over the region will last another hundred years and more — a long time in an area of hotly contested boundaries and complex tribal allegiances.

As on any island, most men own a boat. Access to the causeways can be erratic at different times of year and impossible if ever there is a storm so although the Rose blooms close to the mainland, the islanders are all fishermen, for why would you travel by boat and not cast a net on your way? At this time of year there are no storms. The sea is a dreamy, deep blue fringed by pale shallows radiating out from the bright sand-coloured dunes that lead up to the settlement in the centre. The low, white buildings run all the way up the slight incline, bordered by palm trees. It looks, quite simply, like paradise.

The island is some way to the south of where

Zena started her journey, and she reaches it after three weeks of hopping one fishing boat to another, working her way towards Muscat in an erratic zigzag that takes her out to sea and back again, southwards down the coast. An extra pair of hands is always welcome, and the boats are only too happy to take her as far as they go and then pass her on to another crew, based closer to her destination. If Zena really was a slave boy in search of her master, she would be enjoying herself. She has received almost nothing but kindness the whole trip south, and the sailing itself is fascinating. Calculating the best angle for the canvas to catch the wind is immensely satisfying and her time on the boats has introduced her to a kind of teamwork with which she was previously unacquainted. The resulting feeling of the vessel harnessing its power is as close to flying, dancing and making love as Zena has ever known. But the danger of exposure is ever present and she checks herself constantly all day, and at night sleeps in snatches, perpetually on her guard.

There have been some close calls. Round the fire, the night after her first fishing expedition, a young boy, perhaps fourteen, flings his arms affectionately around her. He clearly does not recognise that the body he pulls towards him spontaneously is very different from his own. Zena strikes out violently, punching him squarely.

'I wish you no harm, Malik,' the boy explains, a drop of blood dripping from his nose and his brown, puppy eyes uncomprehending. Men on the Peninsula are tactile — young men more so. Zena, her heart pounding, is unsure what to say, only whispers an apology and passes him a scrap of cloth to staunch the wound. The story has followed her and now she has a reputation for being difficult, though a hard worker.

Keeping dry is her biggest problem. The fishermen tumble in and out of the water and splash each other for sport. On each boat they ask if she can dive and she declines. One man offers to teach her and she has some trouble convincing him that it is not worth the trouble. Remaining distant from the horseplay is easy enough, but hauling the nets it is impossible not to suffer a splash or two. Once she loses her balance and slips across the bow and feet first into the deep water up to her thighs, saving herself only by catching onto a carved rope hook with her fingertips. Frantically, she pulls herself up. The thin *dishdash* is sodden, her legs clearly visible. The cotton dries quickly in the sun, but shame and terror prick her long after. She dreads to think what would happen if she fell into the water all the way and her torso was exposed.

Worse, she worries constantly in case she starts her monthly bleeding, though the sheer knife edge of terror on which she is precariously balanced has held it off so far. One slip is all it would take. A mere error in grammar that exposes her as a woman, a fall that raises her *dishdash* to expose the truth, a splash of sea water misplaced and the journey will become impossible. In one village a man tries to pickpocket her. He is adept and most people would never have noticed his skilful fingers rifling their clothes but Zena is on her guard. She draws her *khandjar* and he flees.

The further she comes, the more she believes that she will make it to her destination. *I've made it as far as Rafeen*, she tells herself. *I'll see Muscat if my luck holds.*

Now, at the end of the day she eats with the other fishermen down by the dock. The stew is concocted from cheap offcuts that cannot be sold because they are too small or damaged. It is delicious nonetheless, and Zena scoops the sauce into an indent of bread and smacks her lips, relishing the taste of the tender white flesh. The months of camel's milk and coffee are still with her and each fresh meal from the ocean seems delicate and delicious. While travelling on the sands, she was only permitted to eat after everyone else because she was a slave. Most nights, by the time she made it to the feast, what remained in the pot consisted mostly of fat, bone and gristle. Here, things are more egalitarian. The fishermen eat together and she has as much chance at the prime cuts as everyone else.

Zena watches the man next to her as he sucks the backbone of a snapper till it is dry. Everyone is exhausted for they start work early, before the sun is even up. Hauling the nets is not easy. Zena has noticed her arms have become very strong over the last three or four weeks. Now she has muscles from trimming the sails, casting the nets and carrying baskets of finned and scaled creatures of one kind or another from the fishing boats to their point of sale. It has helped her appear more masculine.

As her companions finish eating, Zena watches the dock disappear into the flat expanse of sparkling water. It will not be long until sunset. She sips the last of her mint tea and rises, walking barefoot across the pebbled walkway to stare at the horizon. The man who sucked the fish bone follows her.

'Malik, you want to go in the direction of Muscat?' he asks.

She has been here for four days, and enquires at every opportunity if there might be a passage to the capital. Zena nods. She cannot remember this man's name, for they all call each other 'my brother' and 'my friend'. When she is only in one place a day or two it seems foolish even to ask. After a day on the water it seems rude not to somehow know their names already. The man smiles, revealing gaps in the run of his teeth.

'I might be able to help you,' he says. 'My cousin is going there. He leaves in two days. You can fish with us till then.'

The trip down the coastline has been peppered with such kindnesses from unnamed brethren. It seems all she needs to supply in return is her labour, a prayer at the relevant moment and the ability to brew mint tea.

'Thanks, my friend. Can I meet your cousin? What is his business in Muscat?'

The man moves his shoulders in a noncommittal fashion. 'I will take you to his house,' he says. 'Come.'

At the bottom of the hill there are stalls and small shops where trade takes place under a ramshackle array of what were once different-coloured canopies, now faded to a uniform dun by the burning sun. A sprinkling of single-storey houses take advantage of the shade under the trees. Goats are tethered by the side gates. A solitary camel sits and ruminates next to a mule with a patchy hide. Zena and her companion stroll easily into the half-darkness. As they go higher, the buildings become larger, at first two storeys and then near the top there are houses built around a series of courtyards.

'My cousin works here,' the fisherman says proudly. 'He works for Al Khalifa himself.'

They enter a courtyard through a gate with chickens scattering in their wake. Then he leads her through a back door that is wide open and into a small kitchen where a *sidi* slave stirs a pot that sends steam up to the ceiling in thick clouds. The rooms seem darker than the twilight and the air smells of chilli.

'My cousin will go to Muscat for his master,' the man confides. 'You can fish and fold a sail so he will take you, I am sure of it.' He nods at the cook and then moves on. 'Come. Come,' he beckons.

Zena follows him along a passageway and they stop before a thick, wooden door. The man pauses and then knocks before he is bid to enter. Inside, a fat man who bears no resemblance to his fit fisherman cousin, sits surrounded by closed-topped pottery jars, piles of scrolls and a mess of feather quills, ink-stones, bent brass ornaments and thick piles of cloth. Three lamps burn, placed at intervals around the walls and the room smells of stale coffee.

'Ah, my cousin,' the fat man jumps to his feet with unexpected agility and launches himself at the fisherman, kissing him enthusiastically three times on alternate cheeks. The men clap each other heartily on the back.

'This is Malik,' the man says proudly. 'He's a good hand. He has been working with us for the last few days as he makes his way down the coast. He seeks to go to Muscat.'

'Ah. Good,' the cousin plops himself down again on his leather seat and eyes Zena. The man is amazingly clean. It has been a while since Zena has met anyone other than fishermen who, on account of their profession are wiry, but often dishevelled, and even cleaned in the sea water, still smell faintly of their catch. This man is a different class. His *jubbah* is crisp and his nails are carefully manicured. His hair is combed and set in little curls that are pomaded with sweet-smelling oil that wafts towards her over the top of the desk.

'Can you sail?' he asks.

'Yes, sir. A little.'

'And you are from . . . ?'

'My master has family in Muscat,' she says. 'I am from his house.'

'Are you a good Muslim?'

'Yes, sir.'

She has prayed with the other fishermen every day since she got here.

'Good,' he smiles. 'We leave in two days at break of dawn on *yom al-ahad*.'

Sunday. Zena's face cracks in a grin.

'Your business in Muscat?' he enquires.

'I am seeking my master. We were separated in the desert — lost to each other.'

* * *

Little by little, Zena has amended her story. She did not want to keep looking for her *Bedu* renegade master, as working her way down the coast there was every chance she might find him. Now what she says is no longer a lie. She tells them that he is in Muscat and she got separated from him on the sands. She wants to touch Wellsted again, and to kiss him too. She is not a runaway slave, she is a slave running towards her master, very definitely. In the few, quiet moments of each day, she imagines what it will be like to find him. She thinks that she will somehow feel safe again despite the proximity of the slavers. She'll risk it. She has, she thinks, nowhere else to go. And without his fellow officer to think of, Wellsted will protect her. She knows it. Zena likes Muscat — she is a city girl by nature — and sometimes it is better to hide in a crowded place, she reasons, rather than in the open.

The man behind the desk knows nothing of all this. He accepts what she has told him. 'Such devotion to a master is commendable. Come to the ship before dawn on Sunday. My cousin here will show you where it is anchored. We can use an extra pair of hands and you seem strong enough for your age.'

Zena bows low, falling onto her knees. She thanks the man profusely.

With business concluded, Zena and the fisherman walk back down the hill towards the
harbour. There are flames clearly visible along
the bay as householders light their lamps and
one or two of the crews set up braziers as much
as a place to congregate as to provide warmth.
There is a pleasant breeze off the ocean, and the
settlement is bustling as the business of the
evening gets underway — the visiting of friends
and family and the jostling through the thin
street of stalls, which remain open until late. In
anticipation of a pleasant night ahead and an
early departure to earn her keep, Zena walks
with a spring in her step. It will not be long now
until she sees the sparkling Strait of Hormuz
again and the huge, white palaces of Muscat
town. It is tremendous good fortune that the
ship is going as far as the capital.

'See,' the man says, 'no problem. And now
your eyes are bright. You love your master?'

'Yes.' Zena does not shrug off the man's arm
when he lays it across her shoulders. After her
experience with the boy she has realised that
reacting too strongly is potentially dangerous
and she must try to appear normal. In her
evenings in sundry harbour villages, she has seen
men of all stripes wandering like this in the
balmy, evening air together. With women
relegated to the shadows and no friendships with
members of the opposite sex permitted, the men
behave like schoolboys, wrapped around each
other with genuine affection until it is time to go

home to their sisters, wives and mothers to whom attention can only be paid in private. It makes her nervous, but she controls herself.

The fisherman is all smiles. 'Good. Your master will be pleased,' he giggles.

The sound is strange in the twilight and Zena squints to make out the man's face. There are few lamps lit this far up the hill, or at least few that lend light onto the street.

'I am sure he has missed you. How long have you been separated?'

'Many weeks.'

'Ah, he will certainly be missing you then.'

As he says these words, the man slides his palm very deliberately over the fabric of Zena's *dishdash* and down her back. Her heart freezes. This kind of touch is not appropriate between friends and brothers. The movement is as salacious as it is intrusive. Her heart almost stops beating and it is as if her blood is running cold. In a rush, she scans her memory to see if there is any chance this might be normal. As if to confirm his intentions, the man strokes the curve of her bottom through the thin cotton and gives it a little pinch.

'Hey,' she shrugs him off sharply and steps to one side without breaking her stride. Her instinct is to keep her eyes to the ground, but when she looks up, tentatively, the man's face betrays nothing. She can see his teeth most clearly of all in the gloom — he continues to grin broadly as he walks alongside her. Then he nods as if she has asked him a question and he is agreeing.

'Yes, yes,' he says, his voice all comfort and his

movements smooth. 'It is fine, Malik, my friend,' but even as he utters the words he lays his palm, taut, on the shoulder nearest to him and firmly steers her away from the run of houses, off to the side, where the street tapers away. The sand is peppered with sharp shards of shell and dusty pebbles and there is only the light of the moon, which tonight is partly clouded over.

'What are you doing?' she starts and pulls back, but he is bulky and very strong. She hesitates a moment. His smile is unnerving. Zena is unsure if she has missed something.

'Yes, yes, yes,' the fisherman's tone remains reassuring as he guides her where he wants her to go. 'My cousin will take you to your master. He will take you. Good. Good.'

Now out of sight of the houses, he pins her roughly against a large rock. With a sinking heart she understands that she has been too slow. She can smell the fish on his breath, the salt on his skin.

'I have done all this for you,' he smiles ominously, running his hand once more down the side of her body, 'but it is not for nothing. I have been your friend and now, Malik, I want something in return.'

Zena gulps. She cannot reach her knife. She can feel his erection stiffening against her through the thin material of the *dishdash*. Her every instinct is to scream but she swallows it, for if she calls for help it is this man's friends, neighbours and family who will come running. He can tell them anything and will most likely be believed against the word of a black stranger they have known only a few days. Even if they know what he is like, who knows what the punishment is for even getting into this situation? The stakes are high for both of them if she screams. It is not the way out of this. Still, her mind is racing trying to think of something that will get him off her, something that will mean he does not lose his honour and neither does she. She manages to move her face away from his lips, which are searching out her mouth.

'Allah sees all,' she stammers. 'Allah will judge you. Let Allah judge you now, brother.'

The man laughs but she can feel he is uneasy. His grip tightens and she wishes she could reach the *khandjar*.

'*Allah Akhbar*,' she intones.

She'd drop to her knees if she could, but he still has her wedged up against the boulder. With a strong hand he pulls her face towards him.

'*Allah Akhbar*,' she repeats. 'Please.'

'Relax,' he says, his voice syrupy as if he is comforting a child who has been foolish. 'Yes. Yes.'

His hand slides down towards her crotch. There is a pause. He scrabbles and feels left and right, for he does not find what he is expecting. Then he raises his palm to her breast. As the realisation dawns that Malik is not quite the man the fisherman was hoping for, he stares at Zena in horror and pulls back. For a moment they are both frozen and absolutely silent. Then the man makes a sound like a frightened animal and turns to look back in the direction of the harbour. It is as if he is considering the other

430

men a moment — their reaction, perhaps — and then he jerks as if he might run. But before he can move, Zena is so terrified at what will happen if he delivers her secret into the keeping of their companions that in desperation she punches him right in the face. It is a fierce right hook undercut that she delivers with her eyes blazing. A blow from the blackness.

The weeks of hauling nets have paid dividends and the man falls backwards onto the stony ground. But Zena knows that she has only bought herself a few moments. She is panting and her mind is racing. She checks the tightly stuffed goatskin pouch is still in place, tied around her waist with a rough piece of cord. If only she'd holstered it lower, she thinks, and then laughs darkly at the ridiculousness of the situation. The man groans and turns, coming round slowly, a bruise swelling already on his skin in the dim light. She towers over him and draws her *khandjar* now she can reach it.

'If you tell them,' she hisses as he opens his eyes, 'you'll have to explain what you were doing groping Malik the fisherman, won't you?'

The man won't meet her gaze. He stares solidly at her feet instead.

'Don't you like women?' she asks him.

It is a question that seems to be coming up a lot over the course of her time on the Peninsula. It is strange to think that only a few months before she had little idea what some men liked to get up to in the night, with companions of either gender.

'Of course I like women,' he spits back at her.

'I am no *khawal*. I have a wife. She lives with my family, on the mainland. But you . . . it is an abomination. You have prayed with us. You have, you have . . . ' he searches for other instances of what Zena has done to breach the law of man and of Allah, but his head is aching and he gives up.

'You seem very like a *khawal* to me, my friend. And if they find out they will punish you. I must find my master,' she says, 'and a woman cannot travel alone. If you keep my secret and let me go with your cousin, I will keep yours, I will not cut you now and I will give you five dollars,' she promises.

It is a large sum for a fisherman from a small island though she is acutely aware that if he unmasks and sells her he will make far more. A lot, she realises, depends on the extent of the man's shame and his fear of being unmasked.

'Don't forget, I can tell them what you tried to do with me. Everyone will know what you did. Everyone.'

The man rubs his head. From the tilt of it, she can see that the threat has hit home. For a fisherman from such a small village to lose his reputation is a serious matter and were Zena to make the shameful allegation the mud might stick. She knows that men can be stoned for such behaviour. In some areas, where *sharia* law prevails, there are those who have been beheaded.

'All right,' he nods slowly. 'I want more than five dollars, though,' he says, shakily rising to his feet.

Zena relaxes a little and slowly reholsters the

knife. 'That is all I have,' she says. It is a lie, but five dollars is enough. 'I will give it to you the morning I leave.'

But she has hardly finished the sentence and turned away before the man has moved, quick as a hawk, and is pressed up against her once more. First, he takes the knife from her belt and throws it into the blackness. Zena lets out a low shriek of frustration.

'Hit me, would you?' he mumbles. 'You say you have five dollars. Well, my fine friend, no woman should own her own money. Where are you keeping it?'

If he takes the coins Zena knows she is done for. She jerks furiously, kicking out. He contains her a moment or two before she manages to catch him a heavy blow to his crotch with her knee. The man doubles over and Zena jumps to the side. But as she does so she sees that he has the goatskin pouch in his hand. She cannot leave it behind. She falls on him and wrestles the purse from his grasp, then kicks him twice, hard in the head. There is no point in trying to reason with him. There is no deal to be done here. She rains blows with her clenched fist and furiously finds that she can hardly stop herself from continuing, even though the man is now lying still. In the end, her attention is only diverted by the possibility of regaining her weapon.

She leaves him where he lies, scrambles in the darkness to find the *khandjar* and slides it back into her belt. Then she thinks a moment. For a mere second she wonders if the man is dead, and her stomach shifts, unsure whether she hopes he is or not. The anger still has a grip of her, but when she leans over him there is the sigh of a deep breath. She pokes him, but he is still out cold. Perhaps it is for the best. A murder would provoke a manhunt. Things had been going so well.

'No!' she says out loud. 'Damn it.'

She searches for an alternative course of action, but all Zena knows is that now she can take no risks and she has very few options. The ship for Muscat doesn't leave for days and she has to get away from here now.

Using the sailor's knots she has learned, she ties the man's arms and legs together with a strip of cloth so he cannot follow her. She walks smartly back down the road that leads to the harbour without greeting anyone on her way. Back at the dock, she calls one of the men to the side. He is a fisherman like the rest of them and a friend of the man she has left up on the hill. She cannot accuse the man directly of attacking her, but it is entirely possible that those closest to him have some idea of his preferences and might suspect the truth if he left the campfire with a pretty young boy and headed off into the darkness.

'Your friend,' her voice is croaky, 'took me to his cousin. I was offered a passage to Muscat but the price was too high,' she looks the man directly in the eye. 'I knocked him out and left him by the boulders. Up the hill in that direction. Over there. I am sorry. I should go now. He was raving. He said crazy things. But he is all right. I just had to get away.'

434

'What do you mean?' The man puts a hand on her shoulder kindly, but after what happened Zena can't help but pull back.

'Malik . . . ' the man starts as if he is about to apologise, but she waves off his attempts to finish the sentence.

'It is all right,' she says. 'Will you fetch him? He is fine, but I tied him up so he could not follow me. I must go.'

As she turns to leave, the fisherman calls out and runs after her. 'Here,' he offers her a calabash of water. 'Take this.'

So, she thinks, *he knows*. She holsters the flask on her belt and walks into the darkness towards the causeway that leads to the mainland. There are other villages and other boats. If she follows the coastline, soon enough there will be a peppering of lamps by the water. This man will look after his friend, and she hopes his shame will see to it that she isn't followed. Besides, they cannot know which causeway she chose or in which direction she will walk. In Arabia, she has come to realise, if a slight can be forgotten or waved away, it is best for everyone. She casts her eyes to the sky to guess her best direction and then she looks back only once at the island, her first chance at a direct passage to Muscat.

Oh well, she comforts herself, *it could have been far, far worse*, and rubbing her arms which suddenly feel very stiff and bruised where the man laid his hands on either side of her, she sets off to the south again to walk through the night, for as long as it takes, with the Pole Star twinkling at her back.

46

The officers of the Bombay Marine, and Sir Charles himself for that matter, are nursing a collective hangover this morning the like of which has not been seen since the day after the Ball in Support of the Emancipation of Chattel Slavery, organised by Lady Malcolm some eighteen months before. So wholeheartedly enthused was the English community by this event (at the time, the first proper dance in Bombay in almost a year) that erstwhile reserved ladies quaffed large quantities of champagne cocktails in support of The Cause, a duel was fought and the evening resulted in not one, but two engagements, both of which have since been solemnised by the vows of matrimony. Today, however, it is only the officers and some of the men who are finding their duties particularly challenging, and not one single marriage has been announced. Instead, an unaccustomed hush has fallen over the officers' mess and naval officers and the gentlemen are, according to their prediliction, either particularly short-tempered or completely unresponsive to all around them. All this over the news relayed via His Majesty's ship *Psyche* and subsequently picked up by the *Nancowry* as it returned to the capital, that Wellsted and Jessop have been spotted on the water and, in charge of an Arab vessel and, resupplied, are heading for safety. The pluck of their endeavours is the subject of much speculation (as well as several well-supported toasts) and proof, were proof required, that the British can do anything. It's all a matter of pluck.

Sir Charles views with disdain the cup of weak Chinese tea that has been placed on his desk. In the normal run of things he is a man who has several difficult decisions to take in the course of a working day, but this morning even deciding whether to add sugar or not seems well nigh impossible. Now he searches for the words to communicate his desires.

'Take it away,' he snaps eventually and motions for the cup to be removed.

The smell of the aromatic brew is making him feel quite nauseous. Slowly, he pulls a sheet of paper towards him across the desktop, and dips his nib in the silver-bound pot of India ink.

To be held at Muscat for Lieutenant James Raymond Wellsted, he starts, and then finds himself quite mesmerised by the shape of the double '1'.

Sir, he continues, *we were delighted to receive news of Doctor Jessop's rescue. Many congratulations are due to you, and commiserations also upon the reported loss of Lieutenant Jones, a dutiful officer who will be sadly missed by his comrades and friends. Doctor Jessop must return to Bombay upon the next available passage. Please forward with him your sealed account of what transpired in which I beg you to be frank. Meanwhile, you sir, are charged to take the next ship to London and report for duty there, as soon as possible, to the residence of*

437

Admiral Rose, at 43 Edgware Road. The admiral is expecting you, we hope within the next six weeks as time is of the essence. The admiral will brief you upon arrival. Do not delay. I am told they have sold out the first run of your account of Socotra which has been recently published and there is a great appetite for more. Congratulations.

Charles Malcolm

The signature trails off the end of the paper and Sir Charles thinks that the effort of writing might make him quite sick. He falls back into his chair from where he has an excellent view of his well-stocked tantalus.

'Fetch,' he motions to the boy attending him. 'Brandy.'

The boy jumps into action. He pours the drink into a crystal balloon and brings it to Malcolm's desk on a small, silver tray. Malcolm downs it in one.

'That's better,' he gasps. 'Now. Here.' Sir Charles seals the paper with wax, as if in slow motion. He proffers the missive to the boy. 'Find my secretary,' he mouths.

Whitelock has not appeared for duty this morning. If Malcolm recalls correctly, the lieutenant made a wager with one of the other officers, though he'll be damned if he can recall the terms of the thing. Lately Sir Charles finds himself bored by the shenanigans of highly spirited young men. Their concerns reside somewhere between balder and dash and many of the youngsters simply cannot hold their liquor. *It won't do*, he thinks vaguely as he

438

pushes the boy by the arm, launching him into action.

'Find Whitelock and have him dispatch that to our agent in Muscat straight away,' he says.

Sir Charles has a busy day ahead and he already feels entirely exhausted. It crosses his mind that the broad spectrum of young officers may be full of nonsense but they are, to a man, extraordinarily brave. He heaves himself fully upright at the thought and tries to forgive Whitelock's absence. After all, both Sir Charles himself and his brother, Pultney, were no doubt, high spirited as youngsters. His head begins to thump and he stares longingly at the tantalus, but cannot rouse himself to cross the room. A boy, no doubt, will be along shortly.

'Damn weather,' he mumbles under his breath, and pulls another sheet of paper from the escritoire. His Majesty's business is neverending, and Malcolm knows it.

'Still, best get on . . . ' he admonishes himself, and thinks for a moment before he addresses the difficulty of obtaining timber around the Red Sea and how Britain may be able to provide a consistent supply for her own use or, indeed, such a sufficiency that the Company can profit from the needs of the local market. With a little planning it's not impossible, he ponders, it's just that the natives don't think that way.

47

Zena is limping. The desert by the coast is rocky and in the darkness she tumbled. It has been several days and her ankle has not yet recovered though she has kept it bound. The injury aches with dull intensity and it slows her down. Given this, it takes her longer than she anticipated to reach the town of Al Qir, which it transpires is a busy port well supplied with willing and experienced fishermen — too many for an unknown, injured black boy to take his chance. Besides, when she walks she winces and it is obvious she cannot undertake even half the duties expected of a boy on board.

In the event, she sees no reason to wait until she gets taken onto one crew or another when there are coins languishing in her purse and (at last) a direct passage, by sea less than a week's journey. She can tell a new story here. No one knows her. She nervously pulls herself up and decides she will simply offer to pay. This is tricky, of course. No one must know how much she has or where she keeps it. Still, there are no other options. Zena takes a deep breath and thinks that she is, at least, getting closer.

'That ship there,' she is told when she enquires which vessel is sailing to Muscat on the next tide.

It is large enough and the captain comes to the plank to see the dark slave boy who is offering coin. The man is surly. He regards her suspiciously and his manner of business is not like the stallholders who serve coffee and flatter, drawing their customers inexorably towards a purchase. He clearly finds Zena's request strange and is standoffish. Still, she is offering him money.

'You are injured,' he points out.

She ignores this opening gambit. She might be injured but she can stand and fight.

'I am on my master's business,' she says. 'He has given me money for my passage to Muscat. How much is it?'

The captain considers a moment. He stares at the stalls nearby and does not meet her eye. 'Five dollars,' he says. 'You will sleep on the deck and bring your own food.'

Zena is not so foolish as to accept anyone's first offer, particularly one so inflated in price. She laughs as if he has made a joke. 'That is worth only one dollar,' she states baldly. 'You will be transporting me like a goat.'

'One dollar!' the captain rebounds. He feigns shock as if she is crazy. 'One dollar?'

In time, they settle on two dollars and then Zena suggests tentatively that if he includes food and lets her sleep in a cabin below the deck, away from the other men she will pay a total of three dollars. She considers the additional coin a good investment. She needs to sleep and wants to rest her ankle. It will not get better till she does.

The captain agrees with a curt nod, slightly surprised that such a ragged-looking creature can pay. The boy's master must be wealthy to squander that kind of money on a slave.

'You eat with the crew,' he says. 'Fish.'

Zena expected nothing more and limps aboard with as much grace as she can muster.

* * *

When they set off, the captain remains brusque. Zena is not paying for his company though and she keeps to herself. On deck he makes a little conversation, trying to place her.

'Your master is in Muscat?' the question comes in a low growl.

She nods. 'I bring news for him.'

The captain eyes her dolefully. He does not believe a word of it. But he has his three dollars. Still, she feels uneasy.

'You bring news? You can read?'

It is the only reason he can think of to value a slave enough to pay for this kind of journey.

Zena nods. 'He is a powerful man,' she explains.

The captain stops a moment and then beckons her to one side. Zena looks round nervously. The crew are about their business. No one is paying attention.

'I will not go with you,' she says.

He moves from foot to foot in uneasy embarrassment.

'I am not going to hurt you, boy. I swear. By Allah. Please.'

She hesitates. After the reassuring tone of the man who tried to rape her, she sees no reason to

442

trust anyone. The captain removes his knife. He places it on a bale that is piled on the deck.

'See,' he insists. 'I am unarmed and you can keep your knife. Draw it if you want to.'

With caution, she follows him to the prow. The man seems furtive and she keeps her hand ready to unsheath her weapon. The captain, however, eagerly pulls a box from a small compartment and shows her a document that is folded carefully inside. 'Can you read this?' he asks.

Zena nods. 'Slowly,' she admits.

With difficulty, she sounds out the words. It is a contract with the owner of the vessel. The captain listens and rubs his chin. He has been wondering what it says. He takes notes of a point or two to take up when he returns to Al Qir. When Zena has finished he thanks her. *Shukran*.

She bows reverently and senses a change in him. He has no reason now to doubt the purpose of her passage or the question why she is carrying a small purse of *talers*. It is strange, she thinks, how perceptions change — so much is predicated on a sham, a show. On deck the men, she notices, work round her, treating her with a respect to which she is not accustomed. If any of them knew, there would be an outcry.

At night, she blockades the door of the little cabin. Once she has done so she enjoys the best sleep since she left her master's desert caravan and the security of Wellsted by her side. She hopes she will see him soon. The possibility makes her belly flutter and all the hardships seem worthwhile. As the boat heads south she thinks of her pale master all the time and she longs for him to touch her. It seems simultaneously as if it has been a year since he laid his hands on her skin and also as if what occurred on the rooftop in Riyadh was only last night. Zena has ceased to try to make sense of her feelings and instead stands on the prow and luxuriates in her excitement. Muscat is close. He might already be there. On the dockside. Waiting. His skin pale as a lily and his strong touch gentle as silk. She hopes his companions are not by his side and pushes all thought of Kasim and Ibn Mohammed to the back of her mind.

It is an odd sensation to have nothing to do on board, only to sit and wait, day on day, with an eye to the horizon. No one speaks to her except to offer food. Once the captain, still curious about her mission, asks what is in her bag, but she does not reply, only grasps her knife. Just in case. After that he leaves her alone completely.

★   ★   ★

On the fifth day, there is a shout on deck. One of the men has first sight of the city. The captain draws his eyeglass, confirms it and barks some orders. Zena feels her fingers tingle. She finds it impossible to take her eyes off the vista as, from a single shining speck in the distance, the dazzling white houses of Muscat glide into view. She has waited a long time for this. It has been over a thousand miles. Last time she arrived at this harbour she was filled with trepidation. Now she tries to hide the full extent of her excitement as she cranes to see and the boat moves across the last, short stretch of water between her and the Omani capital. It is as if her eyes are drinking in the sights of the city.

In twenty minutes she is close enough to make out the merchants brewing mint tea and shooing off the beggars — the same men she saw through the slats of the warehouse on her very first day. She strains to pick out Ibn Mohammed's compound, but has no way to tell if either of her captors are in residence. Her fingers tremble at the thought. There are, she can make out easily now, no European ships at anchor. But that does not mean that her master is not there. In her excitement, having made it so far, she half expects to catch sight of him immediately. After all, he is what she has come to Muscat for.

As they slow and find a place to tie up, Zena can hardly wait for the men to see to the ropes before she shoulders her bag and disembarks instantly.

'Malik,' the captain shouts, as though they have been friends. 'Goodbye.'

But Zena is gone. She comforts herself that in the big city it is easy to disappear. She notices immediately that there are other Abyssinians, in fact in some numbers so, for the first time since she left, her dark skin is not an immediate point of interest to those around her. To fit in like this once more is marvellous, and to be again at the hub of the Peninsula's cultural and trading life is a pure joy. She never wants to have to talk to men like the captain again, grasping and suspicious men who might try to do her harm.

As soon as I can, I will change back into my burquah, she decides. The strip she has taken from the veil will not stop it covering her face. Torn clothes might mark her out as a poor woman but not as a runaway slave. It is her best option. Muscat is not as harem-skarem as the hinterland and a lone woman in a *burquah* will excite little interest. It will be good to put the orange *hauza* and tatty *dishdash* behind her, for then she could be any woman. *Yes*, she thinks, *if I see him with the slavers, I will simply cover my face completely.* Not even the prospect of Ibn Mohammed and Kasim can take away the joy of seeing Muscat again and the prospect of a reunion with her master.

Zena disappears joyfully into the crowd. What she seeks is James Raymond Wellsted, but she suddenly realises, as she comes out of the dock into the bazaar, she is not sure exactly how to find him. The truth is she has not thought that far ahead.

48

Zena is not the only woman excited at the sight of the streets of Muscat on that sunny December day, or indeed, the only lady with an interest in the lieutenant. For it is the 12th of the month — St Ammonaria's Day — and Farida is particularly fond of female saints. It is not that Mickey Ibn Mudar's wife is devout in any way, but she does love a good story and the tale of the Catholic martyr Ammonaria refers not to one girl killed for her faith, but two. In addition, St Anthony had the devil of a time resisting his desire for a woman named Ammonaria — a friend of his sister with whom he was clearly if not in love, then very deeply in lust. Farida marks her time often with such stories — a day in remembrance of a saint or a mythological figure whose tale captures the spirit of a change in season or calls to mind a particular time of life. Farida does not know the date of her own birthday, for her family did not mark such fripperies, but, as a child, saints' days were hallowed and the life of the whole estate was built around them. In celebration of Ammonaria's martyrdom and, indeed, the love of St Anthony, Farida has donned her *burquah*, slipped down the back stairs and emerged furtively onto the dusty street. It is the first time she has been outside since the summer afternoon when she saw Wellsted sitting smoking a pipe with the rug merchant.

She heads with purpose, first of all towards the *souk*, slipping a pastry to the beggar on the corner as she passes. The weather is pleasant — sunny but not too hot — and Farida decides that once she has seen the horses she will stroll past Mickey's office (for the sheer thrill of it) and then progress towards the dock. The idea of sending a letter home in the safekeeping of someone she feels she can trust has taken hold of Farida's not inconsiderable imagination.

The news of Wellsted's survival has not yet reached Muscat and Farida is hedging her bets. If he does not return she hopes she might find someone else with whom she can send such a missive. It has been too long, she keeps telling herself, and there is a tinge of guilt in that realisation for when Farida headed up the Dublin Road she rashly promised to write and tell them when she was settled. All these years later, she is not sure what message it would be best to send or whether to let Mickey in on the idea, but she is considering her options and hopes that Wellsted will return soon so she can decide on a plan. Still, she must be flexible and entertain the possibility of another officer. It is in this spirit that the city has called to her this afternoon.

Passing the bakers, the smell of fresh bread assails the warm air and Farida breathes in deeply and smiles. She has not had to cook for herself for years now, but making bread was the one piece of housework she did enjoy. Leaving the dough to rise. Waiting for it. Adding some rye flour occasionally or a spot of buckwheat for variety. Being, sometimes, able to afford to bake white, fluffy rolls that she'd eat from the oven with globs of melting, golden butter. If there is a food Farida misses it is good, Irish butter, patted into squares with a little salt. Arab butter tastes goaty, there is no getting away from it.

She proceeds past Mickey's office and pauses in the street opposite the doorway. As always, she listens carefully, just in case his voice might carry down from the room upstairs. It would be an enormous thrill simply to hear her husband ordering silks or complaining of the range of available dyes or trimmings. It would feel, she is sure, as if she could possess a tiny piece of his day-to-day life — a chink through the slatted shutters of the *harim*. She wills the door to open and Rashid to pass her by on his way to carry out Mickey's orders, but the house is impassive and shows no sign of the men within it. With a little shrug she abandons her eavesdropping, for today she has other fish to fry. Her *burquah* swishes at her ankles as she strides through Muttrah and its mass of overstocked market stalls and beggars, its livestock corrals (today there are goats, sheep and mules, but a marked paucity of beautiful horses) and finally makes her way to the waterside. She has picked out not one European in the crowd all this time. The boats at the dock are *dhows* in the main and a few, larger, Indian trading vessels. Nothing European. Farida sighs.

'Ah well, Ammonaria, you haven't been lucky for me, my girl,' she whispers.

It is odd — her instincts are usually well honed and when she feels called out of her quarters she invariably finds there is some adventure waiting for her. On the dock today, however, there is only a rather large consignment of cloves being loaded, which, even tightly packed, scents the warm air with its spice and covers the stink of the harbour water. Farida gazes out over the strait, notes its prettiness, and thinks she ought to be getting back. She feels suddenly unaccountably hungry and decides to avail herself of the lush bowl of fruits supplied for her chamber and perhaps call for coffee to be served.

As she turns back up the hill, Farida hears a snatch of conversation, a tiny phrase, which stops her cold and makes sense suddenly of her desire to come into town. The voice emanates from behind her.

'Have you seen a white man? His name is Wellsted, but he travels disguised as a Turk called Aga Khalil Effendi. Has this man come to Muscat? I have important business with him.'

Farida turns slowly and steps back into the shadow cast by the plain, whitewashed, two-storey customs building behind her. She peers at the boy making the enquiry. He is a poor soul, wearing a faded *dishdash* and a poorly tied turban. He is in his teens and his skin is the blackest Farida has ever seen. Over one shoulder he is carrying a goatskin bag and he has a slight limp as he moves, following the sailors who will not break their business to talk to him. They fob off his enquiry, motioning the child away, but he persists.

'Please, brother, I must find this man. He is English. Have you heard his name?'

One Indian sailor almost spits at the kid. Still another says, 'Go to Ibn Mudar. He sees to the white man's business. Ibn Mudar will know.'

The boy hesitates. It is a tiny pause, but Farida sees through it. He cannot go to Ibn Mudar for some reason. He knows the name.

'Where is this Ibn Mudar?' he asks, but the tone is unconvincing.

If the sailors notice they do not show it. 'Up the hill,' one points. 'Go to the stall of the scribe with the green turban. Ask there. At the street with the blind beggar. Off with you now!' *Imshi*.

The boy bows very slightly and backs away. Farida follows a few paces behind. Further along the dock he asks the men on another ship if they have seen Wellsted, but none of them recognise the name and this time they send the child in the direction of the Greek brewer.

'He knows every foreigner in Muscat,' they swear.

It is probably true, Farida thinks.

The boy does not follow the directions though. Instead, he dilly-dallies in the direction of Muttrah. Farida can see his eyes, sad and searching, trying to decide what to do. From his pouch he picks out a piece of bread and nibbles on it, to help with this rumination. Whatever business he has with Wellsted is well nigh fascinating but Farida can think of no way of extracting this information without speaking to the boy — something she has never attempted

451

on her outings into the city.

He's just a youngster, she thinks, though her heart is pounding. She knows all too well how risky it is for a woman to show herself to be in any way available — asking for directions could be enough never mind enquiring about a mutual acquaintance. The boy is black, though, and most likely a slave. If there is anyone she could talk to it would be an indentured man, someone young over whom she could easily assert her authority — it should, she reasons, be all right. There is no other course of action that will get her what she wants. Farida takes a deep breath. *Feck it*, she says to herself and approaches.

'Excuse me, you are looking for the white man, Lieutenant Wellsted. What is your business with him?'

The boy blinks. His lashes are long and the motion extraordinarily slow. It seems to take several seconds as if he is sizing the question up.

'He is my master,' he says carefully. 'We were separated.'

Farida hesitates. According to Mickey's account, Wellsted entered the desert with a black slave in tow, but of course that was a female. He was, if she remembers correctly, an abolitionist and opposed to owning even that single slave.

'Where did your master buy you?' she enquires.

A mere shimmer of uneasiness crosses the boy's face. 'Muscat,' he says. 'Here. That's why I returned. To find him.'

'And he took you with him to the desert?'

He nods.

452

'And tell me, did your master find his friends?'

'One of them.'

'And they are returning?'

'Yes.'

Farida laughs. Really, Wellsted is quite the fellow — a hero in fact. She claps her henna-stained hands in delight and as she does so a glimpse of her forearm is exposed, white as milk, before the material falls back into place.

Zena gapes. 'Your skin,' she says in shock, 'it's like his skin. Your skin is white.'

Farida draws herself up and stands square. 'I could have you whipped for that,' she spits.

She has to react strongly. Such a comment from a mere boy is sheer insolence. Men simply do not make mention of a woman's appearance, never mind the colour of her skin. If Mickey were here (quite apart from being appalled at the discovery of his wife's excursions) he'd chop off the blighter's balls for his cheek. The boy realises his mistake. He backs off a little and mumbles an apology, hoisting his bag higher on his shoulder. He seems so vulnerable and, indeed, genuinely sorry, that Farida takes pity on him. He has not meant the offence, clearly. She will, she thinks, see him off in the right direction.

'The men on the ship are correct,' she tells the child, 'you should go to Ibn Mudar. He will feed and house you until your master returns. He will be glad of your news.'

The boy nods once more, silently, but his eyes betray his discomfort at this idea. Zena feels she can trust nobody. And Ibn Mudar gave her to Wellsted in the first place. He was at Ibn

Mohammed's house, drinking coffee with the men. She cannot risk it. Farida is bemused. If he really wants to find Wellsted, then Mickey is the boy's best port of call. 'There is a reason you cannot go to Ibn Mudar?' she enquires.

Intriguingly, the child does not reply, only stands stockstill, looking helpless. Farida stares as if hypnotised by the child's eyelashes. There is something about this boy.

'I can show you where Ibn Mudar is,' she says.

The child twists awkwardly, and as he moves Farida catches a glimpse inside the goatskin bag. Folded on top there is a swathe of material. It is, if her eyes do not deceive her, a *burquah*. She looks once more at the delicate bone structure of the child's face and the elegance of his wrists. She peers as if she is looking at some strange, new creature on display at the zoo. The line of hair beneath the orange *hauza*. The delicate physique — strong but still . . . There is, of course, no reason why a boy might not be carrying a *burquah*. Farida feels as if there is an abacus in her head and the beads are flying. The lieutenant took only one slave with him into the desert.

'Are you his *habshi*?' she asks slowly. 'Are you the girl who knows how to dance?'

The child looks as if he might bolt. A sigh emanates from the lips. Then she nods. 'I have nowhere to go,' she breathes.

Farida's first reaction it is that is none of her business. Then she remembers how those women from the fancy crescents thought. The women who lived in Bath when she scammed there.

454

Their worlds were small, to match their minds. The realisation knocks her silent for a moment. She always said she'd never act that way. Her conscience twists. Now, she thinks, is her chance to prove it.

'What is your name?' she asks gently.

'I am Zena,' the girl says. Then, seeing this woman is kind, she adds in a rush, 'I am a runaway and only the *Nazarene* can forgive me. I thought he'd be here.'

Softly, the girl begins to cry. A perfectly formed tear slides down her cheekbone and falls to the ground.

Farida makes the decision in an instant. It is too intriguing. She wants to know everything — how can she leave the girl behind. Why, Mickey would never forgive her.

'Now, now,' she says. 'Ibn Mudar is a soft-hearted old fool, really,' she explains. 'I've been married to him for twenty years and I should know. You must come with me, my dear. He will want to know of your journey and then, when Wellsted returns, we shall be the first to know.'

Zena sniffs. 'Ibn Mudar is your husband?'

Farida looks round to see no one has heard. 'Shhh,' she hisses as she nods. She is not sure how she is going to explain this new acquisition in the *harim*, but she is sure it is right to bring the girl home. She lays a hand on the child's shoulder for comfort. 'And you went into the desert? You travelled with them and rescued the white men?'

Zena nods.

'How many miles?'

Zena shrugs her shoulders. 'I don't know,' she admits. 'I sailed with the fishermen to come back. It has taken a long time. I had to return to him, though, and this is the only place I could think he'd be.'

Farida's eyes sparkle. 'That shows great loyalty,' she processes the information slowly. 'What high adventure and I am a woman who likes a story or two, there is no denying it. The *harim*, my dear, well, shall we say it can be a trifle dull. Whatever are you still crying for? After all you must have faced! As a boy too. And you as black as a shadow and with news of our favourite lieutenant. You must change into your *burquah*. Come. You are very welcome. Come along.'

Farida motions the girl to fall into step and Zena hesitates only slightly. This could be an elaborate ruse, but it does not feel that way. Farida's white ankle kicks out.

'For now you will pretend to be my slave. It is for the best,' she directs. 'You can call me Farida.'

'Thank you,' Zena says, slowly.

And the women disappear up the hill towards Ibn Mudar's compound through the hubbub of the dusty Muscat streets. St Ammonaria, Farida notes to herself, was right after all. All she needs now is a miracle to explain this child away without Mickey finding out about her excursions into the city. But, she assures herself, she will cross that bridge when she comes to it.

49

Three days later, when the *dhanghi* docks, Jessop and Wellsted see off Kasim on his sober mission. Eschewing all offers of companionship or help, the slaver bids them a stern farewell and thanks each for what they have done.

'I must do this alone,' Kasim says.

'Can we not help?'

'Come to the *mosque* before sunset.' Kasim motions up the hill. He cannot bring himself to say any more about Ibn Mohammed's burial.

The white men watch as he disappears into the throng. Kasim's desert attire and determined gait stand out for a long time, until the flood of people simply becomes too detailed to be able to identify one from the other, despite the shrouded body that the slaves bear in his wake. He has an invidious duty to perform for Ibn Mohammed's father is still alive and he must be told.

★   ★   ★

Mohammed Ibn Mohammed has not left his son's house in Muscat for several years. He is an elderly gentleman with a long, white beard and lively, dark eyes. *Bedu* in origin, he did not expect to enjoy living inside four walls when his son insisted that he visit and then, eventually, that he stayed. However, such is the enormous fortune generated by Asaf Ibn Mohammed's industrious endeavours that there are a good many more walls than four in his residence and the place more closely resembles a village than a house. His father, therefore, was surprised to find that he felt quite comfortable in his son's home. In the Ibn Mohammed household, nobody travels, except Asaf, of course, but the day-to-day concerns of the place are much the same as those of a roving *Bedu* encampment. Mohammed Ibn Mohammed is glad of his son's success, but he worries for his eldest boy. Mohammed is a well-balanced, unambitious soul who enjoys nothing more than a game of *shesh besh* with his friends and the opportunity to gossip over pastries and coffee. He wishes he could see Asaf similarly content.

It has been over three years since the old man lost the use of his legs and these days he is confined to his room, visited by a dwindling set of mobile elders and his doctor, who has become fond of his wise, white-haired patient. Charmed by his open nature, the young medic generally stays far longer than is professionally required and has become a firm friend. Mohammed Ibn Mohammed is also attended by a stream of beautiful slave girls, gifted to him by his eldest son and overseen by one of the boy's wives (the old man can no longer tell apart his daughters-in-law or indeed distinguish between one woman and another — all the females he remembers as individuals are long dead and his eyesight is fading). However, he enjoys watching the girls (a sweet smelling conglomeration of sunshine and shade) as they move prettily around his chamber.

They remind him, fleetingly, of his own wives, now all gone. It has been some years since the old man has felt inclined to put his serving girls to much use in that line and they simply fetch and carry for him, scent the place and sometimes play music which these days, in truth, he strains to hear.

The old man is, by his own admission, much blessed. When he named his son Asaf, he did so to break the cycle of the generations, for he, his father and his grandfather had all been named after the Prophet and he felt that it was time for a change. Though happy and stunningly competent at desert life, the sons of Mohammed were poor. The fortunes of the entire clan have been in the ascendant ever since the old man made his break with tradition and now his male offspring are all successful in both business and combat and his daughters are long since married off to the hoi polloi of the Peninsula. The old man has something approaching eighty grandchildren, a fact of which he is inordinately proud, even though he has not met most of this youngest generation.

The first Mohammed Ibn Mohammed knows of it is the ululation. His ears are not so sharp of hearing these days, but the cries still sound loud, echoing up from the courtyard and down the hallways. He sits up slightly and sips on his cup of infused mint. The slave girls catch each other's eyes and one rises from her place to peer between the shutters.

'Well?' Ibn Mohammed asks.

'I do not know, my lord.'

He bangs his wooden walking stick on the floor, not in temper, but merely to make the point in the most effective manner. 'One of you will have to go and find out,' he explains.

It is not that the women are stupid but they do require instruction, he thinks. A flurry of chiffon veils and the clinking of decorative ankle chains fills the room as they ready themselves. They are almost set to foray into the household when there is a sharp rap at the door. Mohammed Ibn Mohammed waves his hand and the entrance is opened.

The shadow in the hallway is not immediately distinguishable. Kasim is swathed in dark fabric and cannot bring himself to catch the old man's eyes. He walks slowly into the room and it is apparent to all who have known him that the slaver is not well. He is stick thin and walks heavily. His eyes are yellow where you can make them out and if you look closely you can see his hands are shaking. Kasim falls to his knees.

'Mohammed Ibn Mohammed,' his voice is steady, 'I have come . . . ' He trails off.

'Can't hear you,' the old man shouts. 'Come closer, Kasim. Come closer.'

He bangs his cane and calls for coffee.

Kasim lifts his eyes. He can't help it. A tear escapes. The old man peers into the gloom.

'You do not look well,' he says, motioning the slaver to approach.

Kasim struggles to his feet and comes closer. Very little of his face is visible for he has wrapped his *kaffiya* tightly around it, but where it can be seen the skin is marked badly with pock-shaped scars that are still inflamed. He gives up trying to speak with the *litham* in his way and loosens the mask. Mohammed Ibn Mohammed has many years of experience and the advantage of extreme short-sightedness and he does not show his shock at the full extent of Kasim's affliction, but one or two of the women step backwards and one makes an audible gasp. The skin is red raw in places, and dotted with blood and pus. The infection is passed but it has scarred him for life. It will be weeks before the inflammation finally settles and Kasim is left merely with pitted skin.

'My boy,' the old man says, 'come and sit by your uncle. Tell me what has happened to you.'

Kasim drops obediently onto a cushion at Ibn Mohammed's side. 'Your son was not as lucky as I,' he says sadly. 'I would that Allah had chosen me to go ahead.'

The cane drops sharply as the old man understands the words. 'Who are we to judge Allah's decision?' he whispers. It is the right thing to say, but the tone of the old man's voice betrays his devastation.

'I have returned with his body so we can bury him properly,' Kasim manages to get out. 'We were on the water,' he explains, 'there was nowhere.'

Mohammed Ibn Mohammed is so shocked by the understanding that is dawning that he cannot muster his own words so he quotes the Prophet. Silence, after all, under such circumstances would be impolite.

'The eyes shed tears and the heart is grieved, but we will not say anything except which

461

pleases our Lord,' he chokes, and then the old man wraps his arms around Kasim and they both succumb to crying together. 'My son,' Ibn Mohammed weeps quietly, for even in grief he is a devout and gentle man. 'My poor boy.'

Kasim heaves an animal sound from deep inside and it seems as if the entire household mourns together — all the wives and children, all the servants and slaves. Doors bang as the news travels from one to another. A scream of shock echoes across the courtyard, the servants fall to their knees and the wives clutch their children close as grief engulfs them all for the tyrant they have lost.

As the waves of mourning spread, Mohammed's personal servants remove the body from the courtyard where Kasim left it under guard. They reverently wash the corpse, afraid of the dreadful putrefaction but more terrified still of showing their disgust. They embalm the body to dampen the dreadful smell and then the master is bound in a *kufan* and the *imam* is called. By the time the holy man arrives there is, at least, the semblance of order. The tears are as restrained as they can be (for that is what the Prophet himself preached) and Kasim has given a full account of Ibn Mohammed's death. He cannot help but lie to the old man about what happened, for his son's last words were not to devote himself to Allah, as any good Muslim father would hope. Far from it. The truth is too private a matter, and Kasim falls back on the customary phrases of a dying man and instead of admitting that he begged Ibn Mohammed not to go, he says that he quoted the *Quran*.

'Good,' the old man nods. 'That is good.'

The *imam* says a prayer and Kasim is glad that after this is over he will never have to speak about what happened again. The words are choking him. He swears silently that the next time he leaves the capital he will not return. *I will see to my business, whatever I have to. Then I will quit this place. There is nothing of value here*, he says to himself. *There is nothing worthwhile in this city at all.*

In an hour or two, he will assist Mohammed Ibn Mohammed to leave his room for the first time in three years. He will see to it that the old man is as comforted as it is possible to be when you have lost your eldest and favourite child. Together they will make the short journey to the graveyard. Kasim wishes, truly, that he had not survived.

50

With the *dhangi* tied up and Kasim gone, the white men turn to each other on the deck, their mission completed. A calm has fallen. There is not a single European ship in the harbour.

'Where are they?' Jessop makes a face. 'Lolly laggers! You'd have thought they'd have sent a clipper at least to welcome us.'

'No matter. Muscat doesn't go without a British ship for more than a week. The main thing is that we have made it in time for Christmas,' Wellsted points out. 'In fact there is more than a week to go by my reckoning. It's the 15th, I'd say. I wonder what Mickey will make of us?'

'Let's burst in on him,' the doctor considers it an excellent jape. 'We've hours — Kasim said the funeral won't be till sundown.'

'Done,' Wellsted agrees, and in high spirits, they gather up their meagre possessions and leave to buy pastries from the *souk* and quaff fresh coffee even before they head up the hill, for it has been a while since they have enjoyed properly cooked food or hot drinks. It is good to be back. The afternoon streets are invigorating and the men feel like midshipmen given shore leave for the first time. They proceed joyfully towards Mickey's office, in anticipation of English clothes, a hot meal and in the case of Dr Jessop, a return to Bombay whenever the next schooner ports. Wellsted still has not confided his true intention of returning in search of the girl.

'The sun always shines on Muscat,' the doctor says, smiling.

The fact that the sun shines perpetually on the whole Peninsula is not a matter of concern, for the English wherever they are take a delight in the weather. And besides, they had encountered a small storm two days out that required some considerable skill to navigate so it is pleasant once again to enjoy the sunshine and feel the weather settled. The approach to Muscat had been a challenge. The *dhangi* was unfamiliar to them in those handling conditions and it was only by pooling their resources and scaring the life out of the men that they managed to last it out.

'It would be a fine turn of events if we survived the desert, the starvation and the pox only to fall foul of the weather at sea. It's the one thing we're trained for,' the doctor had shouted over the wind.

Wellsted agreed. His face showed an unflinching and admirable determination as he whipped the servants into action and ensured all the ropes were properly secured. Kasim, recovered enough from his illness to stand, had a bad bout of seasickness. Even his pox scars seemed pale as he heaved over the side. Sailing the *dhangi* through the squall with only four able men was not easy, but they made it and this, Wellsted thinks, as he smiles in the sunshine, is their reward. He may not have breathed a word about Zena, but he thinks of her all the time, and once he has settled

Jessop safely with Ibn Mudar he'll head northwards again, recovering his tracks until he can find his *habshi*.

Muscat is reassuringly familiar. The door of the office is opened by the boy in the yellow robe and the same rose-strewn copper waterbowl is proffered. This time, Wellsted notices it does not seem like a quaint custom. While before the rosewater was provincial, it now makes absolute sense to him. Muscat is no longer London's poor cousin, in his estimation. It is a grand and impressive city and he appreciates its hospitality. Perhaps, he considers, they should offer rosewater in Pall Mall. The men wash their hands and then the boy leads them upstairs into Mickey's office. At the top the navy agent is breezy and unfazed by the arrival of the missing men.

'Gentlemen!' he rises to greet them with genuine enthusiasm, his hand proffered in welcome. 'Lieutenant Wellsted. Welcome! And you, sir, must be Doctor Jessop. I am so very glad to make your acquaintance.'

Jessop laughs out loud at the man's accent and heartily shakes his hand.

'We are all agog,' Mickey pronounces carefully, for he has only earlier that week learnt the word, 'at your arrival.'

'You do not seem . . . ' Wellsted wonders how to put it, 'quite as surprised as we expected. Had you news of us?'

'Ah. Yes. News. We were expecting you, of course. Please sit down.'

Coffee is served, and at Mickey's insistence

466

the officers first give an account of their adventures. At the story of Ibn Mohammed's death, the agent intones a prayer.

'And you brought the body back to Muscat?'

'Yes. Kasim is taking it to his father.'

Mickey nods and calls his boy over. 'Send news to the *soultan*,' he orders, 'and to the *mosque*. They will bury him late this afternoon, I imagine. We must all attend.'

Wellsted and Jessop agree. 'Of course,' they say. 'Kasim said before sunset.'

'I will find out,' Mickey says. 'Leave it to me.'

'When I left you didn't expect to see me again, did you? Now, admit it,' Wellsted teases the agent as he sits comfortably on his cushions.

Mickey shrugs. 'Well, no,' he starts, wondering how to bring up in conversation that in fact he did not expect to see Wellsted again until three days before, when news arrived via the stick-thin dancing girl he had expected him to sell, followed shortly by a delivery of mail and news from a clipper ship dispatched from Bombay and docking only between the tides. 'I have correspondence, though, gentlemen, orders and the like. Your triumph is the talk of the Indian Navy. By all accounts the celebrations in the mess were legendary. Titanic, even.'

Jessop lifts his coffee cup in the hope of a refill.

'A hot drop?' Mickey gestures so the boy will pour. 'We are expecting two ships today or tomorrow and there may be more news for you aboard them. Well, gentlemen, will you receive your orders?'

The officers agree and Mickey rises and makes for the burr cubbyholes where he pulls down several letters.

'This,' he says, 'is from London, Lieutenant. It came only just after your departure. This one is from Bombay, from Sir Charles Malcolm himself, if I am not mistaken. And another from London — I do not recognise the seal. Doctor, here are your orders and also some correspondence forwarded with them. I expect they were holding them at the mess and thought to send them on when they heard you were heading for Muscat.'

The thick sheaf of paper is from Jessop's family and there are so many individual missives that the mess sergeant has carefully tied them into two thick bundles with twine, which the doctor easily dispatches with his teeth. Jessop falls on the letters as if he has been ravenous. He smells the pale cream paper he knows comes from his sister's writing desk. He sorts each missive carefully by date order before breaking a single seal. Meanwhile, Wellsted rips open his first London letter and his face lights at the news from John Murray. Then, Mickey notes, the lieutenant looks bemused by the second letter, which is from Molyneux Street. Short and sweet, it simply tells him that his father is most proud of his devotion to his duty and looking forward to seeing him soon. He shrugs it off. Before he opens the orders, however, he calls Mickey to one side. Jessop, he is sure, will not surface into full consciousness for hours — he is clearly engrossed in his sister's account of market day in

468

the Northumberland town where he grew up and the news of their mutual friends and acquaintances. He has a wistful look on his face and from time to time he laughs out loud.

'That man deserves some home leave,' Wellsted says in passing before he turns to the matter in hand, for if he is to find Zena, he will need Ibn Mudar's help.

'Mickey,' Wellsted starts and then catches himself at his slip of the tongue.

'Ah, please, Lieutenant, I am well aware what they call me. Please, use whatever moniker you like. I consider it a term of affection.'

'Thank you. I am not finished my mission, sir. I must return to the north. I am obliged by both honour and duty to go back.'

Mickey's eyes twinkle. 'No. Not at all,' he says.

Wellsted's intonation becomes insistent. 'Yes. Immediately. Tomorrow. I thought I would take passage by boat to go as far north as I can. I must make Bahrain at least. I will need enough money for camels and a few men. Will you provision me, sir?'

'No. No.' Mickey continues to grin openly. 'You have no duty to the north and besides your orders countermand that.'

'The seal is unbroken. I have not read my orders,' Wellsted raises the letter. His mind is racing frantically. He has to make Mickey understand. The navy agent can save him precious time in organising the expedition and he needs funds, for he has hardly any *talers* left.

'Well, I can tell you what your orders say if you would like, Lieutenant. There is little that passes me by. But there is no need for this matter to cause difficulty. I can help, I think. It is your slave girl you refer to?'

Wellsted stops dead. 'Zena? Have you news, man?'

Mickey does not rush. He pauses only a moment. 'The girl is here, sir. In Muscat.'

Wellsted betrays his shock, but not his delight. 'Here?'

'Yes. She is here. My wife . . . ' Mickey is unsure how to explain what has happened with his wife.

He does not fully understand it himself. Prior to this incident he has never found communicating with Farida anything but easy. Her Arabic, after all, is excellent, but in this instance her extensive vocabulary appears to have failed her. He understands that somehow she came across Zena who, she says, was looking for him. What he does not understand, and he suspects that his life might be easier if he never understands it, is where the two women met, exactly, and how the subject of Lieutenant Wellsted came up. He remembers telling his wife the lieutenant's story, but still, she appears to have rather more of a grasp of the ins and outs than he can with easy conscience, attribute to the tale he told her some months before.

'She is here?' Wellsted repeats.

Mickey's shoulders drop as he realises that Wellsted has no interest in how all this came about. An Arab would smell a rat immediately and want to know the details, while the white man is simply delighted the girl is safe.

'Yes. She is in my *harim*. She danced last night for my wife. The girl is an excellent dancer.'

'Yes,' Wellsted agrees, a smile creeping across his face. 'That is wonderful,' he says, incredulous as he clicks open the seal on Sir Charles' orders and casts a vague glance over the scrawled letter.

He does not take in the details, but he needs something to do with his hands. *She's here! She's safe. Really, the girl is quite extraordinary.* Wellsted feels relief pervading his body and excitement too.

'And she's dancing, you say? Oh, she can dance all right. Mickey, will you take me to her? Can we go straight away?'

'A moment.' Mickey holds up his hand. 'Gentlemen, you must lodge at my home. I insist upon it. You are quite the celebrities, you know. But first we must attend Ibn Mohammed's funeral. We must prepare you. We will not have long. The obsequies must, you will agree, take precedence.'

'Take precedence over what?' the doctor asks, blearily, raising his eyes from the page before him.

'We will go soon.' Mickey meets Wellsted's eyes in a promise.

He calls for assistance, for this is not the time for a leisurely stroll up the hill. Rashid will be back shortly with news from the *mosque*. Now he orders a palanquin. Mickey deems this the most appropriate mode of transport, for the white men should remain hidden from view. Funerals are events of high emotion and the agent, now he has the Indian Navy's most

471

celebrated officers in his grasp intends to keep them safe. Besides, he must have them washed and dressed — as it stands they smell like fishermen and are arrayed in *jubbahs* that are, if he is feeling charitable, best described as humble. It is no way for officers of the Indian Navy to present themselves.

'Find what is taking Rashid so much time,' he snaps at the boy. 'And bring some water to wash with and British clothing from the store.' It is late in the afternoon, there is little time and much to do. 'Come along,' he urges the boy, 'you must send to the dockside. There are ships due any moment and we need to know their onward destinations. Quickly! Quickly!'

51

Wellsted has never before attended a Muslim funeral. In Muscat's hilltop graveyard, every important man in the community gathers as the corpse is laid to rest on his right side, facing eastwards like a good Muslim, towards Mecca. The news has travelled with lightning speed amongst the cognoscenti and there must be a hundred white *jubbahed* mourners, maybe more. The *imam's* voice echoes the mournful *salat* and the *soultan* himself, when he hears what has happened, sends his condolences. Besides Wellsted and Jessop's conveyance, several palanquins are pitched at the graveside.

From the shade, Wellsted thinks there is a beautiful simplicity about the ceremony. He knows that few of these men can possibly have known Ibn Mohammed well, but it is pleasant, he thinks, to see them pull together in a time of mourning.

'I could not have wished for a better son,' the old man repeats over and over.

Wellsted peers. The man is so elderly it is as if his skin is paper, though he can see a likeness across the years. Ibn Mohammed shares with his father a jawline and distinctive wide shoulders. The old man, though, has kinder eyes. *How terrible*, Wellsted thinks, *to lose a child*. He has never thought of Ibn Mohammed in the context of a family. In life, the slaver seemed hardly human, more as if he was made of rock. It is a shock that he went so quickly rather than weathering over time. Already, Asaf Ibn Mohammed's story is becoming Muscat legend for he was a warrior, he was rich beyond Croesus and he died in the service of the *soultan*. The tale has all the elements of a nursery rhyme.

Jessop pays little attention. Shrouded from the proceedings by a thin curtain, he curls in the opposite corner, still taken up entirely by one letter after the other and occasionally sharing the contents with the lieutenant. It is as if, finally, he has his life back.

'My cousin is delivered of a baby boy,' he whispers. 'Sarah swears that purple neckties are all the rage. Can you imagine?'

England is far more real to him than Muscat and he has already embarked on home leave in his mind. A mere peek through the curtain and the doctor has seen all he requires. Wellsted can hardly blame him, however, for he himself wishes he could join the men (for it is only men) as they gather to mourn around the grave. Mickey, however, has left strict instructions that the white men must stay hidden from view.

'Tell Kasim I am here,' Wellsted insists.

Mickey nods. In the event, although he does so, the navy agent is not sure if the slaver really takes in the information. He is so distant it is almost as if he is drugged. He hates society at the best of times and now on the worst of all possible occasions, he hovers like a thundercloud at the centre of the proceedings, brooding so resentfully that his appearance provokes as much concern as the corpse.

'You have been ill?' they greet him over and over. 'Praise Allah you have recovered, brother.'

Kasim knows he will never recover. He cannot bear to look as they lower Ibn Mohammed's corpse into the ground and the men pray together.

As they disperse, the gravediggers fill the hole and Wellsted from his hiding place says a silent prayer. He is glad Ibn Mohammed suffered only briefly. They were, after all, brothers on the sands. He decides he will return to the graveyard and visit when it is appropriate to do so. It is not the custom here to leave flowers but he thinks he will perhaps choose something of stone or metal as a remembrance on the grave. Kasim passes the palanquin so close that Wellsted could reach out and touch him. There is a blank expression on his face and his eyes are hard. Anyone who knows him would see that he is not a man to accept any comfort.

Ibn Mudar returns and the bearers move off. Wellsted, eager to see Zena, finds that he has butterflies in his stomach. As the sun sets, and the sound of songs of mourning float down the hillside on the air, he holds himself back from jumping out and proceeding at a run. All he cares about is that soon he will hold Zena in his arms.

52

As night falls, it is as if an additional layer of darkness draws in on Kasim and he sits with his fellows at the *mosque* and feels, despite their presence, entirely alone in his grief. The society of so many of his brothers is torturous. He can scarcely tell one face from another and all he can think over and over is that Ibn Mohammed shouldn't have died. Why did he have to go, when Kasim himself survived the sickness? Around him the doyennes of Muscat society share their memories of his friend, but such were Ibn Mohammed's protracted absences from the city that he was not widely known or at least, not known well. The old man sits in the corner and basks in remembrances of his favourite son — a slave stolen kindly to order, some money advanced to a brother in need or a gift for a valued client — while Kasim finds his voice all but useless and the witterings of those around him nothing short of inanity. He cannot say what he feels, for he has no words to describe it. He knows it is expected of him to sit here and take part. It is only one night. But the minutes are already stretching unbearably and emotions rip through him like a fury. He does not blame the doctor, who he knows tried his best. Nor does he resort to the blasphemy of blaming Allah. He desperately wishes things were another way, but there is, of course, nothing he can do. For a man like Kasim that, of itself, is worst of all.

The slaver hears of it from one of the other mourners. The poor chap is only passing the time in mentioning the news and is not expecting such a violent reaction. Still, Kasim is in mourning and despite the Prophet's admonishment of loud sobs and wails and the showy accoutrements surrounding the death of a friend, the slaver cannot help himself reacting as he does. The fellow kneeling next to him is plain enough — he is a cabinet-maker, if Kasim recalls correctly, and is known for his fine inlays of mother-of-pearl.

'I see Ibn Mudar has gone home to his new woman,' he smiles slyly. The man is only making conversation and trying, he supposes, to lift Kasim's spirits. 'One wife as white as milk and then this one. She is *habshi*. Absolutely black. Young too, I heard,' he confides, 'and only newly arrived. She is a dancer, or so one of his slaves told my man.'

Kasim feels as if his head might explode as this information sinks in and understanding dawns. 'She is a black slave? A young *habshi*? Do you know her name?' he pushes.

The cabinet-maker gives a laconic shrug. 'They say she was smuggled into the *harim* by the Pearl. Though Aziz said that Ibn Mudar bought her as a gift. Rumours fly, you know. Who can tell? Though she arrived in Muscat two days ago. On that much we all agree. Ibn Mudar has a fine collection of women. I must seek your help, Kasim. My own *harim* could use a little livening up.'

Kasim feels fury ripping through him. He cannot even manage the pleasantries that the cabinet-maker is expecting of him — the 'Of course, I will keep an eye out for a suitable prize, my friend', the pat on the back, the jolly collusion. He roars like a man who has been physically wounded, his face darkens and he rises to his feet without taking any leave. All he can think of is that Ibn Mohammed would not have died if the girl had not skipped the emir's camp. The circumstances would have been different. They might have avoided the plague, somehow. They might have taken another route or had news of it in advance. And now this girl, the very cause of all this misery, has the temerity to return to Muscat and take her place in the safety of a rich man's *harim* as if nothing has happened. Ibn Mudar sent him condolences from the white men, he seems to recall vaguely, but did not mention this — the bastard. They all know and no one said anything! Wellsted and Jessop must be laughing as they plot to steal away the very person responsible for Ibn Mohammed's death. He will not stand for something so shameful and unjust.

'That girl is a runaway!' Kasim spits. 'I demand her execution.'

The mourners dodge the slaver who takes no account of the crowding in the room as he pushes his way to the door with the cabinet-maker in his wake. The poor man is utterly taken aback at the vehemence of Kasim's outburst.

'My friend,' he tries to appease his brother, making apologies as he follows him through the room. 'What have I said?' he asks, reaching out to touch Kasim's shoulder.

The slaver pushes the man's hand away so violently that the cabinet-maker loses his balance and drops the cup of mint tea that he is holding. The shards shatter across the floor.

'She should be beheaded!' the slaver shrieks. 'I will do it myself!'

Stopping only to bow quickly before Mohammed Ibn Mohammed, he takes his leave and sets out for the compound of Ali Ibn Mudar, decided upon his purpose. His *khandjar* is not the appropriate weapon to sever her head, he thinks. It is too small a blade. He will have to stop on the way and find a more efficacious instrument.

53

Straight from the funeral, Wellsted stands in the vaulted doorway of the main reception chamber of Ali Ibn Mudar's grand home. The women have been summoned, or at least Zena has, and Farida has made it clear that she would not miss this for the world and will come down from the *harim* to welcome her husband's guest. As soon as they arrive, Dr Jessop retires to his chamber. He will sleep, he swears, for three days at a stretch at least. Jessop's good-natured, easy-going character is not, in this instance, sharp in terms of understanding and he does not see the importance of the girl with whom Wellsted is so keen to be reunited. She has, after all, not come up during the course of one single conversation over the last several weeks. All he cares about is reading his letters over and over and savouring the news from home.

'I will sleep and sleep and only rise for pastries,' the doctor forms the words with delight, the missives still bulging from his pockets. 'Or perhaps to bathe again.'

'You are welcome, my friend, and if you are in need of some entertainment . . . ' Mickey need say no more. There are plenty of girls in his household from which the doctor is welcome to take his pick.

'Ah, thank you. I am not entirely recovered,

480

however. I shall sleep first, I think, and then see how my appetite fares. And that is a doctor's opinion,' he says wryly as Aziz shows him to his room.

★ ★ ★

Wellsted waits downstairs with his host. The chamber is luxurious — the tiled floor is littered with piles of soft cushions and intricately woven carpets and the air is awash with aromatic scent. An array of fine brass lamps are lit and the coolness of the night air is refreshing. Still, the lieutenant cannot stay still — he is far too twitchy. Mickey regards his newly dapper guest with amusement. No Arab would expose his emotions over a mere woman so clearly. The boy is like a thoroughbred ready to race.

'What do you think they are doing?' he asks.

Mickey draws a small square of jellied rosewater to his lips. 'Women,' he says vaguely, though the truth is that, in general, most women be they slave girls or wives race when their husband or master calls them, and he knows he should more accurately say, 'Farida . . . ' Mickey is contented though. He likes to wait. That way when he sees her, it is all the more satisfying. He is interested to see how things will transpire tonight. Farida swears the girl is mad for the white man's love, and now, looking at the lieutenant, Mickey has no doubt those feelings are reciprocated.

★ ★ ★

Upstairs, Zena paces the floor, only a few yards over her master's head. Mickey's presumption is correct and it is Farida who is holding up proceedings. She is almost dressed now and will soon emerge from the flurry of slave girls that has assembled to assist her.

'Sit down,' she motions to the *habshi*. 'Have a pastry.'

Zena waves off the notion. 'He is *here*,' she insists.

Farida laughs. '*I pass by these walls and I kiss this wall and that wall. It's not Love of the bricks and mortar that has taken my heart, But of the One who dwells within*,' she quotes from a poem they read together the afternoon before.

Zena shrugs. 'Come on,' she says.

They have been reading poetry since she arrived, or more accurately, a few hours thereafter, when Farida, having extracted a detailed account of the girl's trip into the Empty Quarter, her escape from the emir's encampment and her feelings for her master, realised that in addition to this rush of first-hand adventure, Zena was literate. The slave girl has enjoyed leafing through the books and quoting poetry aloud. Luxurious though it was in her grandmother's house, there was nothing so grand as a library, but here Farida has a well-indexed, interesting collection including some books (with illustrations) dedicated to the arts of love. It is these in which she has taken a particular interest in the three days she has been waiting for news of her lieutenant.

'Oh that,' Farida winks, as Zena leafs through

the pages, 'there is always more to learn about that operation.'

Now, though, Zena would willingly torch the lot just to be in his arms.

Farida rises at last and flicks her hair over her shoulder. Agonisingly slowly, the maid places a sheer veil of the lush colour of grass over her head while another opens the door.

Zena tries to contain her excitement and not break into a run.

★ ★ ★

He first catches sight of her coming down the stairs. They both hesitate slightly, for the terms of this meeting are unspoken. Then, when she approaches, Wellsted reaches out and gathers her close, not even noticing Farida sweep past and station herself on the cushions next to her husband. Such a public display of affection is unheard of, but Mickey and his wife simply sit side by side like proud parents and watch while Wellsted and Zena embrace.

Wellsted touches Zena's lips with his own. Kissing her is like drinking salted water, he thinks. His thirst only increases. She pushes him away shyly and smiles.

'How did you get here?' he asks. He cannot take his eyes off her.

'Boats.'

'And you bypassed the plague towns?'

She nods.

'You are lucky. Ibn Mohammed is dead of it.'

Zena feels relief at this news, but she is much

483

more interested in how the master has fared. 'And you?' Wellsted cuts a dashing figure with his uniform reinstated but she wants to hear that he is well.

'As you see me,' he confirms. 'We bought a ship. A *dhangi*. Sailed it down the coast, though the sickness held us up a while. I'm so sorry that you had to leave alone . . . ' his voice trails. 'It was so fast and you were forced to take action without any help. It weighs on my conscience but the doctor was so ill . . . '

Zena nudges him fondly. 'You're here,' she says, 'I'm here. And it is fine.'

Mickey claps for service. The spell breaks and the lovers are re-called into the room. Small goblets of blood-red pomegranate juice are passed on a tray. They stain the lips.

'Quite the cocktail party, eh, Lieutenant?' Farida smiles.

'Madame,' he pays his respects. 'I am simply so very glad — '

'She is some chicken, your lovely girl,' Farida cuts him short. She cannot bear ceremony of any kind and prefers to be on a more informal footing. The Pearl continues, 'I admit I am fond of Zena already. She is an intelligent and plucky young woman. I cannot be doing with these females who interminably scent themselves. I cannot be doing with it.'

'I have come to see that Zena is her own person,' Wellsted replies, blushing. 'In fact, I have an oath to keep, for I swore when Mickey gifted her to me, that I would set her free when we were through the desert. Is there some legal

484

process I need to undertake?'

Mickey shakes his head. 'It is a righteous act and you can simply decide upon it, if you wish,' he says.

'Then I free you,' Wellsted says. 'I free you now.'

Farida raises her goblet. 'Well, here's to it,' she toasts.

Zena hesitates. 'But, what will I do?' she asks nervously. The hairs on the back of her neck are standing on end in excitement. This is what she has wanted but still. 'Free or not, I have nothing,' she says

Mickey smiles. 'No. I would not say that.'

'Don't worry, Zena,' Wellsted reassures her, 'we will see to things.'

He is about to embark upon an explanation or an invitation or perhaps a proposal, when he is interrupted by shouting in the courtyard. Someone is making an unholy racket. Mickey looks up, a smudge of pomegranate, red as blood, on his lips. Admirably difficult to rattle, he betrays nothing, as if it is as normal for there to be a rumpus in the evening as ordering dinner or gazing at his wife. However, when the door of the room bursts open and Kasim enters with a drawn blade in his hand, dragging Aziz by the arm, Mickey takes the precaution of rising and interposing himself between Farida and the weapon. It is a long way to cross the room, but it is enough of an insult for Kasim to burst into the presence of another man's wife, never mind brandishing a blade.

The slaver's face sets in a grimace as he takes

in the scene. This is too domestic for his taste at the best of times, but that Zena is here while Ibn Mohammed lies freshly buried under the earth is a huge injustice. It is as he suspected. Everyone else knew where the girl had run to. He roars like an injured animal and flings Aziz to the floor.

'It is true then! I claim her! I claim the girl! She is a runaway slave and subject to the laws of Muscat!' he says, his voice low with menace as he continues his advance.

Wellsted does not draw his sword but he puts his hand to the scabbard. 'Kasim,' he says, 'I have freed Zena. She is not a slave now.'

Kasim is not listening. It is no matter to him. The girl must die. He crosses the room in an instant and quickly grabs Zena, forcing her onto her knees and raising his blade to take a shot at her neck. He must pronounce sentence before severing the head from the body, as custom dictates, and in that moment Zena struggles but she cannot break free. She bites the skin of his forearm savagely but this only enrages him more. As he pushes her off, the razor-edge of his blade catches the skin of the girl's shoulder, a welt opens and blood trickles down her arm, staining the sheer material of the *jilbab*.

'I am free now,' she protests, 'he freed me and you have no right. You never did have the right. You stole me. You are nothing but a thief!'

Kasim grabs Zena's hair and pulls her onto her knees. He struggles to keep the girl in place as he lifts his blade, ready to dispense swift justice. 'In the name of Said Ibn Sultan, I sentence you to beheading.'

At once Zena kicks hard, landing a blow to Kasim's crotch. The blade falls but misses its mark, only wounding her again, at the collarbone. She shrieks in pain as Wellsted launches himself at Kasim with the full force of his body. He topples the slaver with a struggle, and the men roll across the floor. Wellsted realises that his European clothes put him at a disadvantage for it is far easier to move in a *jubbah*. Still, he knows Kasim's fighting style well. All sense of being brothers is entirely lost. Both men are livid.

'He is dead,' Kasim cries out. 'Don't you understand that he is dead because of her?'

Wellsted doesn't hesitate. He lands a punch squarely on the man's jaw and then furiously tries to wrench the blade from his grasp. He does not want to kill Kasim, but he recognises he may not have a choice but to try.

'My friend,' he says, 'we have fought on the same side. Stop this. Please.'

Kasim lands a blow to Wellsted's stomach in return and the lieutenant is winded but manages to remain on top.

'You would choose her over your brother?' the slaver squeals in disbelief. 'You swore allegiance to Ibn Mohammed, and this girl,' he can hardly bring himself to spit the words; it is disgusting, unnatural that the white man favours this woman over his duty to a fellow traveller, 'she is nothing. She is a runaway whether you freed her or not. She is only a whore. A *habshi*.'

Wellsted reaches behind him and unsheathes the *khandjar* he has stowed on his trouser belt.

He carries the weapon out of sheer custom, for it has not left his possession in months but there was nowhere else to put it in his western clothes. Now he understands that it is an advantage to be able to draw it unexpectedly from behind. He holds the short, curved blade to Kasim's throat.

'She is mine,' he sneers, 'and I will not let you kill her. He's dead, Kasim. He's gone. It's not Zena's fault. He was sick. He was too weak. She made it back to Muscat alone and I'll be damned if I'll see you harm her now.'

'Weak,' Kasim chokes. It seems a strange thing to say about Ibn Mohammed. It is certainly not a word that in normal circumstances would spring to mind. He cannot bear it. He kicks to try to free himself. 'Weak,' he repeats again in outrage.

'I don't want to kill you, but I will do it,' Wellsted threatens.

Kasim's eyes flash. He struggles but realises that the lieutenant has pinned him to the floor. In frustration he tries to land a punch. Wellsted puts his hands on the slaver's throat to restrict the man's movement. Then he slides the *khandjar* to the man's side, ready to stab if he has to. Kasim feels a sob wrench his throat. That he should lose a fight under these circumstances is an horrific loss of face. Now, when Ibn Mohammed needs him to be strong and defend his honour, he is helpless. He is trapped. This is what Kasim expects to do to others and he despises them when they succumb.

'Ibn Mohammed,' he manages through gritted teeth as he pushes against the lieutenant, but

Wellsted has the advantage.

As he comprehends that he has completely failed, Kasim feels a wave of despair descend. He only wishes he had died too. He has no desire to live with this humiliation. His life is worthless. He has proved it to himself. In desperation, he lifts himself, pushing his own skin against Wellsted's blade, so that a few tiny specks of blood well up where the knife cuts through. He pushes as hard as he can and does not even feel the pain as the blade of the *khandjar* slices the fabric of his *jubbah* and lodges deep in his side. Wellsted pulls away in shock and Kasim falls back on the tiles with a curse, blood spilling from the gash. The pain starts now and it is edifying, distracting at least from the feeling of helplessness and grief he has endured all day.

'With honour,' he says, satisfied.

Zena has pulled herself to her feet and is staunching her wounds. She stands over him. 'With honour,' she sneers at him. 'How dare you speak of honour?'

Mickey motions the girl to keep back. He is so perfectly composed that Wellsted wonders briefly what a chap would have to do to shock him.

'Lieutenant Wellsted,' he says, 'will you allow me? Aziz, fetch the doctor, and the *imam* as well. Kasim is in need of both physical and spiritual assistance this evening. And as for you, my dear,' he addresses himself to his wife, 'I think it is best if you ladies both return to the *harim*. Will you go upstairs, Zena, and the women can tend to your wounds?'

It takes a moment, but without a word they all

do exactly as Mickey directs. The atmosphere is broken. Farida helps Zena out of the room. Mickey peers at Kasim's wound. Even from here he can see that the slaver has missed all major veins, arteries and organs. The agent lays his hand on Kasim's shoulder as Wellsted reholsters his knife, his hands shaking. When Jessop enters the room, the doctor glances around blearily but asks no questions. He simply comes forward to examine the patient.

'Leave me alone,' the slaver snarls, dodging the doctor's hand. 'I am ready to die.'

'Grief,' Jessop explains, 'and illness. Sometimes the fever goes but the erratic behaviours linger. He is shocked. You might have to help me hold him down.'

Mickey nods, making it clear that he will help, Wellsted is best kept away. He takes charge, bending over the wounded man and speaking low, as if in confidence.

'It is time to be calm, my friend. No one need know of this. The girl is blameless. She ran to her master, not away from him and by all accounts, you gifted her to the emir without the lieutenant's consent. Ibn Mohammed was an exceptional man — but your duty to your friend is to live. It is always so. You must direct yourself away from this, brother. You must have a long life.'

Wellsted, brooding, stands like a menacing shadow. He will never forgive Kasim.

'Pass me a cushion, old man,' Jessop interjects.

He has bound the wound with some cloth from a side table and is now engaged in making

490

his patient comfortable. Kasim will have none of it. No words in the world can help him. No doctor can ease his pain. He is a desert creature — unforgiving of any weakness.

Wellsted turns. As he does so Kasim rises like a cobra. He has the lieutenant's knife in his hand, unsheathed before any of them realise. For an instant it hangs in the air and it is not clear what he intends to do with the blade. Wellsted draws his sword once more, but before he can use it Kasim turns the *khandjar* on himself and, above the doctor's carefully bandaged wound, without hesitation, he plunges it deep into his heart.

54

Farida bathes the cut on Zena's shoulder with saltwater and orders some yoghurt with honey to be brought from the kitchen.

'It is the most comforting food, don't you think?' she says.

Zena nods silently.

'Well,' she adds, 'some of these Arabian fellows, they are straight from the madhouse!'

Zena sniffs as Farida considers the fate of her friend, Edward, who died so long ago in Bath, fighting a pointless duel entirely of his own volition. She quickly realises it is not only Arabian fellows with hot tempers who resort to swordplay, but simply fellows in general. She does not pass on this information. As the smooth, creamy yoghurt arrives with a drizzle of amber honey on top she takes the spoon in her hand. It has been a long while since Farida has cared for anyone, except Mickey, and after all, he is her husband. Aware of Wellsted's orders and the fact that, for a while at least, the lieutenant must return to London, she has a proposal for this intriguing girl. She takes a scoop and lifts the spoon to Zena's lips.

'If you would like to stay here, my dear,' she says, 'I am very glad to have you. You can remain in this house as long as you like.'

'Thank you. I do not know what the lieutenant means by giving me my freedom,' Zena sniffs.

'There is nothing I can do with it.' Kasim's display has demonstrated that amply. She is still trembling.

'Hush. Let's not think of that now.'

When the bowl is empty, Farida settles the girl to sleep. The lamps are dimmed and she is made comfortable on the cushions. Then Farida retreats. Mickey will visit the *harim* later and it has been a troublesome day, all in all. Farida finds that she is very much looking forward to holding her husband in her arms tonight. She wants to feel the warmth of his skin.

*   *   *

When the news arrives of what has happened downstairs, Farida decides not to wake the girl. By all accounts it has been mayhem, but the child is asleep and the tidings can wait. The guard has been called and the *imam* is reciting prayers for a lost soul. Servants are sent across the city to bear the news. From her window, Farida can see them, fanning out down the streets, little lamplights, receding in the darkness. One is dispatched to Kasim's household, which he himself has not yet visited since his return, another to the *mosque* where the last of Ibn Mohammed's mourners are no doubt still straggling, still more to the *soultan's* men who must always be informed. *Kasim*, she thinks, *stole both Zena and me. He brought us both here. Perhaps we will find some comfort together for a while.*

This news means that Mickey will be late to

493

bed, no doubt, and Farida will have to care for him — rub his shoulders and soothe his mind. In the meantime she sits and stares at the huge moon low over the rooftops and thinks how lucky she has been. She had felt jealous, slightly, of Zena's adventures, but tonight has brought home to her the danger of the world outside.

'I am more one for the story, I think, than the action,' she murmurs to herself, and with that in mind she retires for the night.

55

In the hour after midnight there is a palpable sense of relief in the corridors. Everyone has gone to bed, the house is all but silent and the lieutenant can hear the slapping of his bare feet against the tiles as he creeps along the hallway in his breeches and shirt, from his quarters in the other wing. The sands, he thinks, are more forgiving to a midnight lover and it is easier to move around unseen. The guard stands to attention as he approaches the door of the women's rooms.

'Will you fetch her, please?'

The man shuffles from foot to foot. However unorthodox the goings-on in the compound this evening, he cannot enter his master's *harim*, certainly not in the middle of the night.

'Wait,' he says and disappears down the corridor, returning a moment or two later with a heavy-eyed female slave who has been sleeping in a box room within calling distance.

'*Al habshi*,' he orders the girl, who disappears through the hallowed doors. When they heave open again Zena is there. She is no longer in the bloodstained *jilbab* and is simply arrayed in white cotton. Her feet are bare.

'*Salaam*,' she says quietly.

The relief shows on Wellsted's face. 'Come,' he takes her hand. 'Follow me.'

He leads her along the hallway and into the

room he has been assigned. It is a large chamber with a seating area and he has opened the windows to allow a view of the hilltop, for this room faces away from the sea. The moon is on the ocean side of the sky, but it casts an eerie light over the trees, gardens and courtyards that stretch up the hillside without showing its face.

'We did not finish talking.'

Zena drops onto the cushions. It feels to her as if Kasim might be here somewhere, and she is uneasy. 'Is he gone?' she asks.

'They did not tell you? He died. He killed himself.'

Hard-eyed, she takes this in. 'He stole me,' she says. 'He killed my uncle.'

'I did not know that'

She nods. 'I never told you.'

'I'm sorry.'

'I had thought of killing him,' Zena admits. 'It was the first thing I thought when he gave me the *khandjar*. After today I think I would never have felt safe. I'm glad he's gone.'

'I'm glad you are safe,' Wellsted replies. Her bravery is astonishing and however much he has come to admire Kasim and Ibn Mohammed he'd have done what he had to do.

Wellsted sits next to Zena and runs his hand along her cheek and down her neck. She feels herself relax. Her skin prickles with excitement once more and it is as if she is melting. She bites her lip. When his fingertips come to the scar on her shoulder, he stops abruptly.

'Does it hurt?'

Zena nods.

'I am very sorry. Kasim's behaviour was . . . '

'Worthy of the madhouse?' Zena suggests. 'That is what Farida says.'

Wellsted laughs. 'Yes. Yes he was. Mad of grief, I think. He had no right to come like that.'

'You would have killed him?'

Wellsted pauses a moment. 'Yes. I love you,' he says steadily, without taking his eyes off her. 'I absolutely love you and I would not let him harm you, no matter what it took.'

Zena smiles. She leans over and kisses his cheek. She smoothes her skin against the stubble and breathes in deeply. In European clothes he smells different, but she likes it.

'Will you wait for me?' he whispers.

'What do you mean?'

'I am recalled to London, Zena. But I will return. Will you wait for me? I have it settled with Mickey — he will look after you here, but I thought when I return, perhaps we could find a place. In Bombay. Naval officers always return to Bombay. I think you will like it there and I will look after you.'

Zena leans forward. 'Won't you take me with you? To London? I would like to see it. The House of Commons and the Great River Thames. The costermongers and the fairgrounds.'

Wellsted shakes his head. 'No,' he says gently. 'We can't. The only use of London is that there I must make my fortune for both of us. There are things I have not told you about London. Reasons you cannot go. But I will not be long. I swear it. I will return to you. To this. Zena, will you? Do you care?'

She regards him plainly. There are no choices here, with her feelings so strong. 'I've thought of nothing else,' she says. 'I never felt like this before. Never in my life. If Kasim had hurt you, I'd have killed him too.'

Wellsted laughs. This woman is extraordinary. Nothing seems to be out of the question for her. He likes that. He leans in and kisses her steadily, his passion mounting as he pushes her onto the cushion and runs his hands under her *jilbab*. Then he sits up suddenly. Zena wraps her arms around him.

'Come on,' he says. 'Come with me.'

Back along the cool corridor he finds the stairs and takes her hand to pull her upwards. Along the upper floors there are storerooms and a large nursery. He passes these and eventually finds the second set of stairs.

'Here,' he insists, and they climb once more and emerge outside, under the stars.

'The roof! Again!' Zena laughs.

'I'd choose a roof with you over a room at the finest hotel in Paris!' He swings her around. 'Please say you will wait, Zena.'

There is not a question in her mind. 'Yes. Yes,' she promises, kissing him warmly. She has a notion to try out something she has seen in one of Farida's books. 'How long do we have?'

Wellsted gestures at the vista. 'Not long enough to both swap our news *and* enjoy each other. There is a sloop due that will take me as far as Cape Town. I am recalled at once, you see. It arrived after sunset. Mickey hopes it will sail tomorrow. I must leave early.'

'One night?' It seems ungrateful, but she can't help but want longer.

'But we won't sleep. Not a wink,' he promises. 'And I'll be back, Zena, I'll be back before you know it.'

She pulls the *jilbab* over her head and shifts a little, turning so he can see her in the darkness. 'I want to hear your adventures, of course,' she says.

Wellsted laughs. 'Me too, my girl,' he whispers as he lays her gently on the rooftop, and it does not take long until they have forgotten everything except each other, as they move together in the moonlight. Any tales of adventure will simply have to wait till he returns.

56

In London, the wives of gentlemen who are fellows of the Royal Society become accustomed to eating later than usual when there is an interesting meeting scheduled. However, the bleak February afternoon that Lieutenant James Raymond Wellsted speaks to the assembled throng, two dinner parties in the City do not commence until almost midnight and one is cancelled altogether. Admiral Rose has not attained his distinguished rank only for his formidable powers in the heat of battle. He is an accomplished lobbyist and the Society's newly gas-lit rooms are packed to capacity to hear what the serious young man, his skin still pink from the desert, has to say. When Sir Joseph Hooker presents him to the party he speaks in the most glowing terms of Wellsted's adventures and his burgeoning naval career. 'The first white man to cross the Arabian Peninsula,' he says, 'and a hero.'

The Fellows are not disappointed. Wellsted is an excellent orator and he not only provides detailed information about the geographical features of the Peninsula and the political situation with the French, but brings to life the searing heat of the dunes, the smell of mint in the *souk*, the savagery of the plague towns and the mercurial spirit of the desert tribes. One or two of the younger members find themselves so inspired they consider setting out overnight for Portsmouth and taking passage to see this magical place for themselves.

'Capital evening,' Rose congratulates Wellsted as they take the steps down to the waiting carriage with Murray.

The boy has certainly done what they wanted him to do. All society is alight with talk of abominable French slavers and the need for the British to control the waters of the Red Sea and Indian Ocean. Wellsted will meet the Prime Minister and give evidence to a Parliamentary committee the following week. He has proved entirely reliable, if slightly eccentric. Once when Admiral Rose returned home, the lieutenant was standing in the garden soaked to the skin. Apparently he was contemplating the rain.

Wellsted has never been homesick for anywhere or anyone before, but now he is so thirsty for Zena, he fears he will never be able to slake it, and despite the social attentions of several eligible girls of good family (one an heiress) his heart remains under the low, full moon on a roof either in Riyadh or Muscat.

'You not succumbing to the charms of any of those beauties whose mothers presented them so eagerly at the ball the other evening?' Murray teases him in the carriage. 'I am shocked you do not have an assignation of some kind! A single man of your age!'

There is hardly a mother in England who could want a more fashionable beau for her daughter. With one bestseller on his slate, Wellsted has completed his second manuscript.

501

Murray is confident the new book will run to several editions. The account of Socotra sells out as fast as he can print it.

Wellsted shakes his head. 'Women,' he says, as if he is exasperated.

'Passionate chap like you,' the admiral comments.

'When a chap is passionate, the readership can sense it.' Murray offers Wellsted his hipflask. 'All the better if he proves damnably readable. Shall we dine at Claridges?' he suggests. 'Or the club?'

The Royal Society's business, of course, was fascinating, but it is getting rather late and Murray hates to go to bed on an empty stomach.

Wellsted stares out of the window as the carriage rocks along the muddy streets. London has been a shock. Cool, dank and grey, he feels an indescribable loneliness and oppression here. In Mayfair, Westminster and Whitehall he will never be able to be himself. When he visited Molyneux Street, it was not as he remembered — his father was an old man who did not know him, and his brothers were strangers.

'The first white man to cross the desert.' Wellsted Senior hugged his son. 'We Wellsteds shall have cake!'

It was not unpleasant, James thinks, but so strange. He cannot tell anyone the thing that is of the most importance to him. The reason he must return.

And yet the prizes are glittering — *The Times* reported his meeting at the Geographical Society and there is a hint from Rose that a promotion is in the offing. He can't wait to get back to

Muscat. A captaincy will mean the prospect of a new life with Zena. The wages are far higher and he will be able to build her a home.

He glows at the very thought. His love for Zena has given him a life rather than what now feels like a series of achievements. He can't wait to see her. There is talk of an expedition into the interior of Persia. She will come with him, he is sure. This time they can travel as husband and wife. They will be married, he has decided. As the carriage pulls up at Claridges, Wellsted steps out onto the glossy pavement.

'What are you thinking of, old fellow?' Rose asks.

'The desert and all her charms,' Wellsted says with an engaging smile.

'Can't wait to get back, eh? Our hero is missing the intrigue, I think,' Rose comments.

Murray grins. 'Well I don't blame him,' he says. 'It sounds damn marvellous out there.' Murray has no intention of leaving London, of course. He prefers his adventures second-hand.

Wellsted heads smartly up the steps and into the foyer. He has an expression of nonchalance on his face. He is a man with a secret. A wonderful secret. A secret of the sands.

Epilogue

In the slave market, the palanquin loiters with the women inside and the bearers wait on their instruction. The attention of the crowd is focussed on the auction, which has been underway a few minutes already. Farida's light eyes miss nothing — she comments upon the fat auctioneer, the crowd of men sharing a *hookah* pipe. The 13-year-old *sidi* slave who, after all he has been through, strains to get away and is restrained with brutal force by the stocky guards.

'They seemed bigger,' Zena remembers. She is no longer afraid.

Zena pulls a *burquah* over her clothes and picks up the basket the women have brought with them. She slips out of the palanquin so slyly that the bearers do not notice her disappear in the direction of the dock. The holding warehouse is unguarded now, though the door is barred. She lifts the catch. Inside, it always shocks her. The mass of bodies and the smell. She has only a few minutes.

'Here,' she lays the basket on the ground and opens it.

The scent of fruit rises through the stench and the hands begin to grab. Zena backs away, like a spectre, leaving the door open behind her. Not one of them will leave, she knows. But still, it is good they have the option.

The *burquah* gives her anonymity and she

504

disappears easily as soon as she has rounded the corner.

'All right?' Farida checks as the girl appears back through the thin curtains.

Zena nods. She'd like to steal the cargo if she could or buy them all and set them free, but there is no measure in that — one would lead to her own execution the other only encourage the slavers. This small act of kindness is the best the women have been able to come up with. They make the journey to the dockside twice a week.

'It's like being home again,' Farida chuckles. Her brothers used to bait the landlord's agent over rent.

Zena removes the *burquah* and sits cross-legged beside her friend.

'He'll be home soon, my duck, with all his fortune.'

Zena hopes so. Farida has been teaching her English and she wants to try it out on the lieutenant. That and other things.

'And now,' Farida suggests, 'shall we trouble them a little on the way home? We can probably drive up the prices a dollar or two?'

Zena finds that today she has no stomach for it. 'Let's not stay to watch the auction,' she says.

Farida shrugs. She strikes the side of the palanquin and the litter wobbles a little as the men hoist it and move off in the heat of the afternoon. 'Stop at the horse bazaar,' she orders and settles back onto the cushions to enjoy the journey.

Historical Note

This note contains spoilers

> 'Slavish accuracy must necessarily reduce the novel to a piece of archaeological pedantry instead of a living image of the times.'
>
> Edith Wharton

I am not a scholar and, though fascinated by history, I have been engaged in a work of fiction in writing this story far more than a reconstruction of actual events. That said, I spent a good deal of time examining what archival evidence remains of the Bombay Marine's mission to the Red Sea and Arabian Peninsula. I researched life in the Wellsted household at 13 Molyneux Street and beyond. I poked and prodded at the history of events in London during 1820–1842 and gathered a whole file of information referring to the same period in what are now Ethiopia, Eritrea, Egypt, Yemen, Somalia, the United Arab Emirates and Oman. I read James Raymond Wellsted's accounts of his desert travels and pondered long and hard over the gaps he left in his story. History makes my mouth water — and that is as much because of the voids in what documentation remains as what is set in stone. I am frequently moved by the bravery of many explorers and adventurers whose only memorial

506

is an entry or two in a ship's manifest or an institutional payroll and whose death is only marked by the clerk's removal of their name when the documents have been updated.

Secret of the Sands belongs to the genre that Truman Capote named 'faction'. What I've written is largely consistent with the records that remain of James Raymond Wellsted's life — both in England and while on active duty during the survey of the Red Sea and in the Arabian Peninsula. The story is also consistent with what I perceive as the atmosphere of the times — the abolition of slavery, the French/British rivalry and the spirit of adventure that spawned the British Empire (for better or for worse). Wellsted was one of the very first Europeans to be given permission to travel inside Oman's borders. The sultan appears to have been very taken with him, and though in some places I have taken liberties with his actual itineraries or dates, he did travel widely during this period and among other adventures spent a good deal of time in the desert (though not *Rubh Al Khali*) as well as visiting plague towns on the east coast of the Peninsula.

Occasionally, where historical fact has proved a barrier to invention, I simply moved a detail a little one way or another or made up a new story to get my characters out of a fix as rambunctiously as possible (history at its best is a gritty, dirty business). As a result, I have taken particular liberties with some truths and feel I must point out one in particular. Dr Jessop Hulton existed and, indeed, died of malaria (or some other tropical fever) in the service of the Indian Navy in 1836. He wrote *The Palinurus Journals*, in which he mentions the unpleasant atmosphere aboard ship when Wellsted fell out with the captain. However, although (as today) kidnapping of Europeans was not unheard of in the region, Dr Hulton was not, in fact, kidnapped by an enraged emir and held for months in the desert. I did however base Dr Jessop in the story on the character that emerges from Jessop Hulton's own writing and on Captain Haines' touching epitaph about how popular the doctor was with his fellow officers and men. I feel now, in putting that down, like a magician who has told his audience how the trick works, but there we are.

In real life there was an East African slave girl called Zena. She was stolen from Wellsted's caravan in the desert during his travels. Though he was touched by the stories she told him of her homeland, intended to set her free once his journey was over and genuinely regretted the theft of her person, there is no record that they ever met again or that the connection between them was more personal than a gentleman might admit to in his written papers. Still, Zena and indeed, Mary Penney, the protagonist of *The Secret Mandarin*, are both inspired by the stories of real women who travelled in disguise. There is, for example, the likes of the lady who masqueraded as a male servant on Louis de Bougainville's mission. This 25-year-old called herself Mr Bare, and travelled very many months before de Bougainville unmasked her. Then there is the later, Victorian case of the famous Dr Barry, who was so determined to practise medicine that she disguised herself as a man for the whole of her career as an army doctor. The deception was only uncovered when she died. Likewise, female skeletons have been uncovered, dressed in armour, on Crusader sites. There truly were some very brave women who were determined to travel and explore, no matter what it took to do so, and many more, I suspect, whose adventures (like those of Zena and Mary) were enforced and who simply had to make the best of what was thrust upon them.

For *Secret of the Sands* I chose a particular period of a few months in Wellsted's life. But of course, from there on, his real-life story continued. James Raymond Wellsted took London by storm when he returned from his Arabian mission. Billeted in the house of a senior officer at 43 Edgware Road, he gave evidence in committee at the Houses of Parliament and attended meetings at both the Royal Geographical Society and the Royal Society. Shortly after doing so, however, Wellsted fell gravely ill with a tropical fever that he had nursed during his voyage. The disease ravaged him and in a very weakened state he was sent to Herne Bay in Kent to recuperate for several weeks. Wellsted at this time was so ill that he could not attend to his own correspondence and his carer, his young brother William, acted as his secretary. To this day, letters dictated by James to William (in William's handwriting) are contained in the John Murray Archive at the National Library of

Scotland alongside the diaries of Sir Charles Malcolm during his time in Bombay.

As soon as Wellsted was able, he returned to Bombay and intended to go back to Oman from there, but he was hit by a second bout of fever, which progressed to a delirium. One night, late, and by all accounts raving, he put a gun to his mouth and fired. The shot, amazingly, did not kill him, though as a result of this injury and the fact he simply never properly recovered from the fever, he was discharged from the service, granted a generous pension of £270 per annum (which later was reduced slightly at Captain Haines' objection to £240 per annum) and, still weak and very vulnerable, he was sent home to London. Latterly, John Murray published two of Wellsted's travel memoirs, respectively entitled *Travels in Arabia* and *Travels to the City of the Caliphs*. Both were received very well by the cognoscenti of London.

The lieutenant, however, was permanently disfigured and never recovered. He spent some years in Blacklands House in Chelsea, a madhouse for gentlemen run by a friend of the Darwin family. On 25 October 1842, after a great deal of suffering, he was brought home to his father's house at 13 Molyneux Street where he died. He was 37 years of age. There was a short obituary in *The Times* two days later and then he all but disappears from history, bar his entry in the *Dictionary of National Biography*, some details in the memoir of Dr Jessop Hulton, the angry rantings in the correspondence of Captain Haines (contained now in the archive at the Royal Geographical Society) and one mention in the letters of Charles Darwin, who took a professional interest in the account of Wellsted's Socotra trip. This, I have to say, is not what I would have written for him (we novelists believe ourselves gods). He deserved a far more glorious and illustrious fate. I admire James Raymond Wellsted. I firmly believe had he been a duke's son or an Oxford man his tremendous achievements, adventurous spirit and open mind would not have been so sidelined and easily forgotten.

Sara Sheridan
Edinburgh, 2010

We do hope that you have enjoyed reading this large print book.

Did you know that all of our titles are available for purchase?

We publish a wide range of high quality large print books including:
Romances, Mysteries, Classics
General Fiction
Non Fiction and Westerns

Special interest titles available in large print are:
The Little Oxford Dictionary
Music Book
Song Book
Hymn Book
Service Book

Also available from us courtesy of Oxford University Press:
Young Readers' Dictionary
(large print edition)
Young Readers' Thesaurus
(large print edition)

For further information or a free brochure, please contact us at:
Ulverscroft Large Print Books Ltd.,
The Green, Bradgate Road, Anstey,
Leicester, LE7 7FU, England.
Tel: (00 44) **0116 236 4325**
Fax: (00 44) **0116 234 0205**

THE UNCOUPLING

Meg Wolitzer

A strange, formidable wind blows into Stellar Plains, New Jersey, where Dory and Robby Lang teach at Eleanor Roosevelt High School. Dory, is suddenly and inexplicably repelled by her husband's touch, whilst back at school, life imitates art. The new drama teacher's end-of-term play is Arisotophanes' *Lysistrata*, in which women withhold sexual privileges from their menfolk in order to end the Peloponnesian War. And all across town, there's a quiet battle between the sexes: relationships end abruptly and marital issues erupt. Women continue to be claimed by the spell — from Bev Cutler, the overweight guidance counsellor to Leanne Bannerjee, the sexy school psychologist — even the Langs' teenage daughter, Willa, is affected — until everything comes to a climax on the first night of *Lysistrata* . . .

THE MIDWIFE OF VENICE

Roberta Rich

Hannah Levi is famed throughout Venice for her skills as a midwife, but as a Jew, the law forbids her from attending a Christian woman. However, when the Conte di Padovani appears at her door in the dead of night to demand her services, Hannah's compassion is sorely tested. And with a handsome reward for her services, she could ransom back her imprisoned husband. But if she fails in her endeavours to save mother and child, will she be able to save herself, let alone her husband?